Always Jane

ALSO BY JENN BENNETT

Alex, Approximately

Starry Eyes

Serious Moonlight

The Lady Rogue

Chasing Lucky

Always Jane

Jenn Bennett

WITHDRAWN

SIMON & SCHUSTER BFYR

New York • London • Toronto • Sydney • New Delhi

An imprint of Simon & Schuster Children's Publishing Division
1230 Avenue of the Americas, New York, New York 10020

For information about special discounts for bulk purchases, please contact
Simon & Schuster Special Sales at 1-866-506-1949 or business@simonandschuster.com.
The Simon & Schuster Speakers Bureau can bring authors to your live event.
For more information or to book an event, contact the Simon & Schuster Speakers Bureau at 1-866-248-3049 or visit our website at www.simonspeakers.com.
Interior design by Hilary Zarycky
The text for this book was set in Adobe Garamond Pro.
Manufactured in the United States of America
First Edition
2 4 6 8 10 9 7 5 3 1
CIP data for this book is available from the Library of Congress.
ISBN 9781534482326
ISBN 9781534482340 (ebook)

To all who've lost their words

Fen

Two summers ago

I was in a daze. That's the only explanation I have for why I thought Eddie and I could sneak inside the villa without anyone noticing. It was nearly one in the morning—past house curfew. Of *course* Mama was waiting in her nightgown on the bench by the staircase. I just didn't expect her to be sitting in the dark.

She turned to us like a haunted doll in a horror movie, face lit eerily by her phone's screen, and I couldn't tell if she was angry or upset. That couldn't be good.

"Don't tell Dad I let you drive his car," Eddie whispered as he closed the Mediterranean wrought iron security gate in front of the door. "I forgot the code. You re-larm it. Relarm. Ha! Rlaaarm." He snorted a laugh and finally looked across the foyer. "Oh, shiiit . . . Mama. You scared me. What's that movie where the doll is haunted? You know the one, Fen."

I didn't answer because he was obviously still drunk, and that was the main reason why tonight was such a disaster. The other being that my brother thought he was a god.

"Why haven't you answered my texts?" Mama asked me. Not Eddie. Even though he was eighteen and would start college in the fall. He was the oldest. "I've been calling like the world is coming to an end. Do you think I enjoy leaving voicemails? I do not."

"My phone isn't working. It got wet. I need to put it in rice or something. So much for that waterproof thing."

"It's only waterproof to a certain deepness, duh," Eddie said, kicking off his shoes.

"Depth," I corrected wearily. And what would he know? Nothing, that's what.

Mama hurried across the dark foyer, nightgown swishing, and stopped in a slant of moonlight that streamed through the door gate. As she pushed dark curls away from her face, her gaze jumped from Eddie (disgust—she knew he was drunk) to my face (angry that I was involved) to the watery footprints on the terra-cotta tile around my sneakers. "What is this? You're soaked? What happened? Are you okay? Fennec? Why won't you answer me?"

When Jasmine Sarafian asks Too Many Questions, it's only a matter of time. She fires them like a volley of arrows, knowing one will hit its mark and kill you.

"He jumped in the dam. *Kapoosh!*" Eddie said. "And saved a girl who was drowning when we were checking out a band at Betty's."

You freakin' peanut brain. I swear. . . . How could I help him when he was *trying* to get us caught? I mean, that's what it felt like.

Mama went very still. "You were out at the dam?"

"Sorry," Eddie said, shrugging. "Some friends talked us into it. You know how it is."

"Us? You took Fen? I know what kids do out there, Eddie. They drink and get high. Your brother just turned sixteen!"

"Never too young to be a hero," Eddie said, golden face dimpling as he flashed her a drunken smile. "Be proud, Mama."

Oh, how I was hoping to avoid this conversation. If Eddie had been smarter—and trust me, he was not—he would've lied. Because listening to a band that was playing at Betty's on the Pier was exactly where we were not supposed to be. Betty's was a bar with a pavilioned stage at the end of its pier. If you were old enough to pay the cover charge, you got to watch the show under its outdoor pavilion. If you weren't? Well . . . you caught shows from boats around the pier—or a little way off, where Blue Snake River met the lake, up on the Condor Dam. BYOB, and bring your younger brother along to lug the beer from the car while you're partying with your friends.

Is drinking on the dam dangerous at night? Yes. Is it dumb? Absolutely. Everyone's gone there to catch free shows at Betty's for years. It's practically a Condor Lake tradition, and the cops only bust it up at the end of the month when they need to make their quotas.

"Fennec," Mama said, "I think you need to explain about this girl. Is it true?"

I tried to make my voice sound calm. "The dam is dark at night. She fell over the railing and went in the water. I think she hit her head on the rocks—she floated down toward the lake, and no one was helping her."

"The band was loud," Eddie clarified unhelpfully. "We didn't hear her."

Weren't paying attention was more like it. My brother never paid attention to anyone but himself. "Anyway, I dove in and swam. I found her."

"She wasn't breathing," Eddie added.

She died. I think she died. For a minute. A few seconds. I think she was dead.

There was no breath.

No life.

"What?" Mama said, eyes widening.

I just wish Eddie would have kept that between us. He was the one who nearly had a breakdown back on the beach and begged me not to tell our mom. Now he was yapping like this? I didn't know if it was because he was drunk or just not bright upstairs.

Either way, now I had to explain the rest of it to Mama. "It wasn't a big deal," I told her in the most casual voice I could muster. "I found her in the water and pulled her in to shore. She wasn't moving, so I did CPR on her. It didn't take much. She coughed up water after a couple compressions."

Push hard, push fast. She wasn't a CPR dummy. She was a dying human, so small, and I didn't know how hard to press. What if I broke her? What if I screwed it up?

It was the scariest thing I'd ever done in my life.

"Mother of God," Mama whispered, clutching her chest. "I

told your father those CPR classes were important. Thank you, Saint Gregory!"

Here come the saints. Gotta wind this up and *fast*. "Anyway, her head was bleeding—"

So much blood. I thought she was dead.

"—and she was out of it. Someone called an ambulance."

"By then, the band stopped because people across the lake had noticed what was happening," Eddie added.

"The ambulance came and took her away, just to monitor for concussion, or whatever. They said she'd be okay," I assured Mama. They said she might have memory loss.

She might not remember that I pulled her out of the dam.

"Hero!" Eddie said, slapping me too hard on the back for the millionth time that night. I slugged him in the arm, and he staggered. "Ow, dude. That hurt, you freak."

"Calm down," I told him. "You'll wake the twins." If our brother and sister woke up, then Dad would be next. I couldn't handle him right now.

Mama shook her head slowly, holding her mouth as if she couldn't believe it. "Who, my baby? Who was the girl?"

I gave Eddie a quick but dirty look: *Don't blow this.* Then I told Mama, "No idea. Just some summer girl, here for the festival." Summer people: what we called the out-of-towners who flew, drove, and carpooled to turn two thousand of us into two hundred thousand by late July.

"You don't know her name?" she asked, dark hair frizzing wildly around her temples.

And here's where the *real* lying began. I knew exactly who she was. And I knew why she was at the dam: she was one of Eddie's devotees who treated him like he was some kind of Pope.

I didn't get it. He farted in his sleep, told dumb jokes, and had the worst taste in music. Yet, he could do no wrong. And it wasn't just girls. His teachers adored him too. The only reason he even graduated from high school was because he charmed his way through makeup tests. I'd bet everything in my wallet that he couldn't name the current US president; he thought Switzerland and Sweden were the same country.

And yet, one smile was all it took, and he had a passing grade. My dad was one of the most important people in town, but you wouldn't know it. Eddie Sarafian was the real star.

"Who is this girl, Eduard?" Mama asked. "Was she with you?"

For once, Eddie had enough sense not to elaborate and incriminate himself. He just shook his head. A little too much, maybe, but he didn't say anything. Like we'd rehearsed in the car. Like he'd begged me. *I asked her to come to the dam. People are going to say this is my fault because that's how people are. Cover for me, bro,* he'd said, crying a little. I hadn't seen him cry since we were kids. I wasn't sure if it was the beer, or if he was scared of getting caught, or if he was upset about the girl because he genuinely liked her. Maybe all three, but it was still weird.

My mom's brown eyes glinted in the moonlight as she stared at him, then me. My pulse sped. I didn't think she was buying it. Why should she? Everyone knew Eddie, and Eddie knew everyone. He even knew the girl who almost drowned. He shouldn't. She was my age—too young for Eddie. But I saw them talking earlier that night. Then I saw her crying.

That was a few minutes before she fell in the water.

Look. I'm not saying he was to blame. I didn't even know what the two of them did. Eddie damn sure wouldn't tell me. But I *did* know if Mama found out he was hitting on a sophomore, she'd be pissed. And she would explode in white-hot fury if she knew who the girl was.

Jane Marlow, the chauffeur's daughter—Mad Dog Larsen's chauffeur.

Oh, yes, *that* Mad Dog. The famous rock producer. Owner of Rabid Records.

Forget his Grammys. Forget the fact that he'd produced some of the biggest albums of the last couple decades. The problem was that Mad Dog only spent the summers here at Condor Lake because my dad sold him the dream of this town like he sold it to everyone, a fairy tale in the Sierra Nevada. My father was the last of the great music promotors. Serj Sarafian.

My dad created one of the biggest indie music festivals in California.

But he'd have lost the amphitheater and festival grounds that hosted it if he didn't have a cash infusion from a major player. His nightmare was being forced to sell the whole thing off for half of what it was worth to a national events promoter.

Unless someone with a lot of money was willing to invest. Someone like Mad Dog.

And he came. He brought his family and his name to a multimillion-dollar summer house on the other side of the lake. And he started working with us, little by little. But the contract for the amphitheater was coming due in two years.

Mad Dog was extremely private about his family: four daughters by three different wives. But the rumor going around the lake was that the girl I pulled out of the water tonight *could* be his illegitimate daughter by one of the housekeepers who died years ago—and that the chauffeur might be raising her as his own kid. Who knew if that was even true, but if it was? If my mom found out that Eddie was messing around with Mad Dog's youngest daughter while she fell off the watchtower and almost died— *please, please, please don't let her die tonight*—and if Mad Dog found out Eddie had anything to do with her being out there?

My family could lose everything.

So I was lying for their sake—for my mom and the twins. Erasing Jane Marlow for them. Not for Eddie, who I resented tonight with a heavy blackness that sat in the pit of my stomach like a rock.

But it didn't stop me from thinking about Jane's face when I closed my eyes.

A light flicked to life in the arched doorway past the stairs. Ms. Makruhi, our nosy housekeeper. And was that the sound of twin feet above us? *Please, no!* I was on the verge of having a breakdown. I just wanted to get upstairs and go fall apart in the privacy of my own room without waking my father.

Was that too much to ask?

"My baby? My shining star?" my mom said, holding my face. "Fen-jan?"

"I'm okay, Mama."

She nodded. "You're a good boy. So honorable. Always thinking of others."

That gutted me. Made me sick inside. I *hated* lying to her. My dad could fall in the dam for all I cared, but I did not enjoy lying to her. All I wanted to do was tell her that this was the worst night of my life, and that nothing was going to be okay again. But I said nothing.

"The family can always count on you," Eddie said to me behind her back. The tone in his voice held something I couldn't quite understand.

For a moment, I wondered if my brother wasn't as dumb as I thought he was.

Condor Festival Freaks Private Messages

Eddie Sarafian:

What up remember me hozws it been girll

Jane Marlow:

Eddie?

Eddie Sarafian:

Ya haha its me, official checkmark and all wuzup

I saw yr name pop up on that thread in the app about band lighting

Thot id hit ya up. Howz LA? Been a few weeeks

Jane Marlow:

Wow. So surprising to hear from you. But good!

LA is the same. How's Condor Lake? Hate that I missed the festival

Eddie Sarafian:

All good all good.

You recovered from the dam?

Heard u had speech therarpy??

Jane Marlow:

Small brain issues from being underwater so long. Not back in school yet

Eddie Sarafian:

Ugh. But no school? Sounds sweet hahaaha enjoy!

Jane Marlow:

Not really. It sucks

But my doctors say I should be OK in a few months

Eddie Sarafian:

Shit I feel awful.. Cannot tell you how sorry god

Jane Marlow:

Not your fault that I'm clumsy

Eddie Sarafian:

Glad you say that..

Bc if you could keep itt on downlow abt us kicking it

I dotn want the big dog hating me if you havnt told him

Jane Marlow:

Why would I?

???

Eddie Sarafian:

Cool you are the sweetest best best best

Hey I might be drivin down to LA in the fall

Musikbiz stuff

Wanna meet up? Just you and me . . .

11

Jane

Now

All I'd wanted was for them to like each other. Leo Marlow and Eddie Sarafian, aka Dad and Boyfriend. The two most important men in my life. But after a disastrous introduction, my father now stood at the side of the private airport's tarmac, brooding like the Hulk near our employer's 1965 Fintail Mercedes. Dad was *not* impressed by my S.O. "Like" was out the window. We weren't even at ambivalence. Oh no: this was contempt with a side of I-dream-of-your-death.

Dad held Frida's leash for me, and she was whining, trying to break free.

My father. The dog. Me. Eddie. No one on this airstrip was happy.

I gave Dad a signal: *Just a little longer.* Eddie was about to fly overseas with a couple of entertainment lawyers, and this catastrophic meeting was affecting more than my heart. It was affecting my brain. Literally.

"Hey, I've got to take this call. Yoo-hoo," Eddie said to me, whistling as wind blew across the tarmac. "Ground control to space cadet. Baby?" He gave me a pitying look.

"Take the call," I insisted as he held up his phone. Honestly, it was a relief to have him walk away for a second. I needed a break to catch up. Words unraveled at the tails of his sentences, and I was having trouble concentrating on what he was telling me. The part of my brain that was injured in the accident was agitated about all this stress.

The doctors called my condition "aphasia." In a nutshell, it was a communication disorder caused by my fall into the dam. I wasn't dumb or damaged or slow. I just had problems with a few words now and then. Like, when people got chatty (long speeches, yawn), my brain blocked out pieces of it—which is why it was better if you sent me directions on my phone rather than tried to tell me where to go. And when I was under a ton of pressure, I sometimes reached for certain words, but they disappeared before they could make it out of my mouth. Poof! Gone.

And that was the worst part. The rest of it, I could cover up. But people tended to notice when you forgot simple words.

Sometimes it felt like a demonic word-eating pixie was living inside my brain.

I hated that fucking word-pixie.

Thing was, I hadn't had problems for weeks, so it was beyond frustrating that my word-pixie was rearing her ugly head right now at the start of summer vacation. Right when I was ready to burst out of my cocoon.

Dad and I were on our way to spend the summer at Condor

Lake in the Sierras. We'd just driven over three hours from Mad Dog's Bel Air house in Los Angeles. The rest of Mad Dog's domestic staff already arrived yesterday to get the lodge ready, and Mad Dog and "the Family," as we called them, had flown in by private plane earlier today. One that was sitting on the tarmac now.

Dad and I were the last to arrive at the lake because I'd attended my high school graduation this morning. (No big deal.) And I was the caretaker for Frida Kahlo—that was the excited, pointy-eared Mexican hairless miniature trying to lurch away from my father. She belonged to Mad Dog's daughter Velvet, and this pooch did *not* like to fly. So she'd ridden up here in the car with me instead.

The Condor Lake private airport was a few miles outside of the lake proper, so we'd stopped on our way in, but it had delayed Dad's military-tight schedule. On top of that, afternoon sun was hot on my neck, because I'd gone and cut off all my dark hair in a wild whim last night. *Whoosh!* Cropped pixie cut to match my pixie body. After the hairstylist was finished, he said it was a *Rosemary's Baby* haircut, which didn't bother me until we arrived here a few minutes ago and Eddie told me it made me look "way younger."

Now I was paranoid.

Dad's sharp, unhappy eyes followed Eddie across the private airport tarmac. Eddie had one hand pressed to his ear, trying to talk on the phone as wind whipped through his white T-shirt and long shorts. He was minutes away from boarding a plane headed to the Philippines for a couple of weeks. I hadn't seen him since spring break. These precious few moments we had in person were going down the tube. Eddie didn't seem to care. Everything rolled off him.

Frida gave me a plaintive bark, not understanding that Eddie was allergic to dogs.

I was just trying to hold it together.

"What's that thing when an old male lion sees a young male lion, and he gets paranoid that his pride is in danger for no good reason?" I asked the tall Black man in the expensive suit who approached on the airport tarmac.

"Law of the jungle?" he guessed, moving his carry-on bag from one shoulder to the other. Gordon Goodman was Mad Dog's top entertainment lawyer. He lived in L.A. and was always at the Bel Air house. He came up here early with Mad Dog.

"The old male only has one cub, and she's not in danger," I added unhelpfully. The word was right there. . . .

"He's being a good king," Gordon said.

"No, that's not it either. It's overprotective pissing . . . something."

"Territorial?"

I clapped my hands. "That's it! Territorial pissing."

"Leo is your father, Jane. Territorial pissing is his duty. He does it for Mad Dog all day long—weeds out the threats. It's second nature."

"Eddie's not a threat," I insisted.

"Hey. Don't know the boy," Gordon said matter-of-factly as

he headed toward the open door of the plane, holding on to his hat. "But I'm about to spend some time with him. The flight to Manila alone is well over fourteen hours, and then we have to travel by car, ferry, and helicopter to get to this remote island. So I guess I'll be forming an opinion, won't I?" He didn't sound thrilled. "See you later this month, Miss Marlow."

Gordon was flying to some beautiful private island in the Philippines with Eddie and the Sarafians' lawyer to sign a leasing contract that would affect the future of the Condor Music Festival. I didn't quite understand the ins and outs of it, except that they had to get it signed by the end of June or next month's festival was in jeopardy. Like, cancelled. Millions upon millions of dollars were on the line. Tickets were already sold, band visas were procured, advertising was running, hotel rooms booked.

But Eddie was going to make sure everything went smoothly. He was heir to the Sarafian empire, and his father, Serj, legendary music promoter, was teaching him the ropes. In the few months that Eddie and I had been dating—online, mostly—I'd learned a completely different side of the music business from him than I had from living in the domestic quarters of Mad Dog Larsen my entire life. Maybe more.

Eddie wanted to teach me the biz and introduce me to musicians.

Mad Dog wanted me to take care of his pets and fetch him lemonade.

Eddie pocketed his phone and smiled at me, brown eyes squinting in the afternoon sun. Wow. He really was goddamn stunning. Everyone said he could model. He'd clipped his hair short and lightened it, so he truly looked golden from head to foot. "Gotta run, babe," he said, rubbing his nose. "We've gotta make a flight at LAX. This crop duster only goes so far."

Crop duster? Please. I couldn't fathom how much it cost to fly them to L.A. by private jet. This one was Mad Dog's regular charter home. I'd never stepped foot on it. The only domestic in our house who had was Mad Dog's personal bodyguard.

"You've got to leave now?" I complained. "But I've barely seen you."

"Well . . . when you said you were meeting me here, I didn't know you meant you were bringing Daddy along," he said, laughing a little stiltedly as he flicked his gaze toward my father. When I protested, he amended, "He'll warm up to me. Everyone does."

True. He had a way of charming people into doing things. One minute, you were trying to decipher his nonsensical texts, the next, you'd lost your best bra in the backseat of an Italian racing car.

"You'll be back at the . . ." I couldn't find a word—big blue thing with water in it . . . ? I panicked a little and tried to rescue myself before he noticed. "In a couple weeks?"

He gave me another sad face that told me he was feeling sorry for me and my brain struggles. "Should be. This mogul dude's house is remote, so service is weird. I'll try to call, but if you don't hear from me for a few days, I'll send word by slow turtle from China."

"Okay?" I said, squinting.

He smiled. "It's a joke. Get it? Slow boat from China? But I'll be in the Philippines, so they'll have turtles instead of boats."

Right . . . No use pointing out the obvious to Eddie. I used to think it was my word-pixie stopping me from realizing his potential as avant-garde humorist, but no: he just wasn't all that bright. But he was very pretty. And sweet. I'd been gaga over him since I was in pigtails. The first time he'd ever noticed me was that night he invited me to come to the dam. The second time was when we reconnected online after the accident. That's when I found out that he was the one who ended up pulling me out of the dam and saving my life.

His one saving grace in my father's eyes today. I think. My father's hard to read.

Anyway, funny that such a horrible thing could bring two people together who had nothing in common. Silver linings, I supposed.

My phone buzzed. Norma. Mad Dog's head housekeeper, asking where we were. And another text, asking us to pick up ice, because the freezer in the lodge's prep kitchen wasn't making ice fast enough. Ugh.

"You're blowing up," Eddie said.

"Work," I mumbled.

"The big dog? You're on vacation, bae. He needs to chill and leave you be. You're my girl, not his."

No, I was not on vacation. I was being paid to do a job, and as long as I lived under Mad Dog's roof, with my room and board provided, I wasn't just on the clock, I was one with the clock. Besides, I wasn't sure how in tune Mad Dog was to my affairs. We saw each other in passing every day and had a conversation now and then, but when I asked Dad if Mad Dog knew that Eddie and I were seeing each other, he just grunted and said, "He's aware there's something going on."

Whatever *that* meant.

"Hey, make sure they put my blue bag on there," Eddie called to the Sarafians' family lawyer, who was boarding the plane. "I'm right behind you!"

Crap. This was it. He checked his phone again. Time to go.

"So when you come back, we'll spend time together at the lake?" I knew I sounded clingy. I *felt* clingy. I hated that. But Eddie made me feel that way, because he was never there, and I could never pin him down to anything. Would he answer my texts? Would he call when he said he would? Would he fly into town this weekend? I never knew, and everything was "our little secret." It was exciting but exhausting. I knew he was busy helping his dad. And yet.

He was always promising me tomorrow.

Tomorrow, tomorrow, tomorrow.

I didn't want to cry, but I felt tears prickling the backs of my eyelids. How dumb was that? This whole day was just too much. Graduation. Returning to the lake. Eddie and my dad.

"Hey! *Hey*," he said, eyes flicking back and forth over mine. "None of that, now."

"I'm okay," I told him, reeling in my emotions. "I just wish we had more time."

"Listen. When I get back, let's look for an apartment at the lake. Like we talked about. You and me. If we find one, maybe you don't go back to L.A. after the summer's over . . . maybe? You're not in school anymore. You could go to college here if you wanted, or maybe work for my dad. Or just chill. All kinds of possibilities. Whatcha think? Would you be down for that?"

"Eddie," I said in the lowest voice I could manage over the sound of the jet's engine in the distance, afraid to look back at my father. "Are you serious?"

He put his hands around my neck. "No cap. Just think about where you'd want to live at the lake. I'll have a word with my old man. Nothing can happen without his approval, so I'd need to finesse it with him first. No promises. But it *should* be fine? Let's keep it between us for now. We'll talk more when I get back, okay?"

He was talking a mile a second, and I couldn't answer. My heart was filled with too much joy. He'd said that, right? I hadn't gotten it wrong? This wasn't a word-pixie brain mix-up?

"The two of us living together? Our own place?" I asked.

"Hey," he said instead of answering me, "remember to tell Velvet to vote for Tell & Show at Battle of the Bands. That's *super* important. You're her assistant now, so make sure she gets that right, because it's what my dad wants. It's this weekend—don't forget, okay? Promise?"

I didn't care about Battle of the Bands. I cared about moving in together. "Wait! The apartment—"

"Wish me luck!" he said, pulling away and putting a finger to his lips. Our little secret. "See you in a couple weeks! We'll talk more then."

He skipped away backward, flashing me a princely smile, and then jogged onto the plane. Just like that, he was gone. I wished he'd kissed me goodbye, but maybe he was worried about my father watching. And maybe it didn't matter. Who needed a kiss when I had a promise about moving in together?

Jane

Dad and I drove away from the airport in uncomfortable silence after Eddie's plane took off. It was hard to be happy while he was so miserable, but I was trying my best to block out his bad vibes as sun winked on the corner of a road sign. I shielded my eyes and smiled as I read it:

CONDOR LAKE, 2 MILES

GAS—FOOD—LODGING

Finally! This was all exactly as I left it two summers ago. The mountains. The giant sequoias. The rocky landscape before we got to town. Nothing had changed. But I had. Goodbye Klutzy Jane, chauffeur's daughter who fell into the dam. Hello Jane, future fiancée to the heir of a Californian concert empire. Okay. Maybe not *fiancée*. But moving in with Eddie—our own place? I could barely think about it without feeling giddy.

No amount of moping my father was doing in the driver's seat was going to get me down.

"So . . . that was the famous Eddie Sarafian," he said, one big hand slung over the wheel as we cruised down the freeway, approaching our turnoff.

I sighed heavily. "Spit it out, Dad. I know you've got something to say."

He stewed quietly for one pine tree, two pine trees, three. . . . Then he could hold it in no longer. "He's full of himself, cub. And too old for you," he complained, tilting a golden mane of messy curls my way to peep at me over dark driving glasses.

"He's twenty. I'm eighteen."

"*And* he was surprised Mad Dog would let me drive the Mercedes across the state?"

I groaned as lingering embarrassment rose like an unkillable zombie in a horror flick. "A joke. His sense of humor isn't great."

"Damn right it isn't. I fucking rebuilt this car with my bare hands, and I've been with Mad Dog for twenty-one years—before what's-his-name was born."

"Eddie."

He gestured wildly, not taking his eyes off the road. "*And* he's not polite. Why did he call me 'the chauffeur'? He should call me Mr. Marlow. What's wrong with kids these days? Privileged pricks with no manners . . ."

He wasn't letting that go. Part aging surf punk—the old-school Agent Orange playing over the car's stereo was his music choice—and part Gulf War vet, my dad lifted weights, was very protective, and liked it when people were on time. He had a faded pinup tattoo of my mom with angel wings on his forearm and my name scrolling delicately on the inside of his wrist.

"Eddie's casual with everyone, not just you. I think he was nervous because we caught him off guard. It's a big deal, what he's doing in the Philippines. It's the first big thing his father has trusted him to do alone for the business, and the farthest he's traveled from . . . from . . ." Ugh.

Dad glanced at me. "Home."

"Home," I repeated, frustrated, petting Frida.

He turned down the music. I quietly sang along with the chorus until I felt calmer. Music had a way of hypnotizing the word-pixie. The rhythm was the thing. My brain craved it.

"Cub?" Dad said in a gentle voice. "I don't have to like him. You just graduated, and you're eighteen—that makes you an adult. It's your life. Your choice. If you need me to step in, or you want advice or help—or a ride home—you tell me. Okay?"

I nodded. "Okay." You could always count on a ride home. That was Leo Marlow's policy. No matter what you'd done, what trouble you were in, call him. He'd come get you and take you home, no questions asked. "Thank you."

"I will do my best to keep my opinions to myself. But I will not tolerate anyone hurting my kid. That's where I draw the line. Deal?"

"No one's hurting anyone. He wouldn't even kiss me in front of you. Be happy."

My father didn't seem happy. Probably best that I didn't bring up the whole shacking-up possibility. Let him get to know Eddie after he came back. In the meantime, I had plenty to keep me busy at the lake. And that included the sleek brown bundle in my lap. I double-kissed Frida behind one pointy ear as she stretched tiny front legs to watch the moving view out the window.

"Here we go," Dad said, exiting the freeway by the big gas station. "Ready?"

Was I? I blew out a long breath and held on to Frida as I watched the familiar landmarks, feeling a mix of excitement and apprehension as afternoon sun dappled the mural painted on the gas station, a collection of the music royalty that had played the Condor Music Festival since it debuted in the 1990s—everyone from Prince, who owned his own record label, to Nirvana, who played the festival back in their Sub Pop days, and headlined later, right before their tragic end.

Anyway, the festival was known for breaking the Next Big Thing. Not just during the festival, but all year, all over town. You could always count on live music at the lake. Music biz people owned homes or vacationed here so they could catch up-and-coming acts who played clubs and bars along the town's historic main drag, known as "the Strip." It gained a reputation for being the music lovers' paradise in the Sierras.

But it wasn't always a music haven. This tiny hamlet tucked in the middle of Nowhere, California, used to be a gold rush town, back in the 1800s. You could still see it in the buildings and street names as Dad and I drove through the rugged outskirts— Mother Lode Antiques, Eureka Lane.

And with the gold rush country came wild land. As in mountains and forests. Part of the lake butts up to a state park filled with some of the largest trees in the world, giant sequoias.

Dad and I drove past one now, one of the last of California's kitschy "tunnel trees." A sequoia that was hit by lightning a hundred years ago, in the 1920s, and instead of cutting it down, the locals turned it into a tourist draw and carved a tunnel through it that a single car could drive through. These days, they don't let cars go through, but you can pull over and walk through it on foot.

"We need to take our yearly photo," Dad noted. We always have our picture taken together under the tunnel tree. Dad prints them out and adds them to a frame with photos of us that go back to when I was six. It's our thing. We missed last year's photo.

But I didn't have time to worry about that too much, because when we passed the tunnel tree, Dad turned onto the Strip. Between tall pines, the town opened its arms.

Condor Lake.

Teal-blue water ringed by snowcapped mountains. Rows of brick old-west buildings lined the packed downtown, a mix of live music venues (bars, quirky clubs) and family-friendly lake tourism (canoe rental, a million ice cream parlors, the California Condor Flight ride). The streets were too narrow, and parking was a mess. Tourists rode the Bonanza, a streetcar that went up and down the Strip, clanging a bell. But I didn't care about any of that at the moment. My eyes sought out the arrowed sign pointing away from town that made my heart pinwheel:

CONDOR PARK AND AMPHITHEATER

HOME TO THE WORLD-FAMOUS CONDOR MUSIC FESTIVAL

A SARAFIAN EVENTS PRODUCTION

Yep, there it was. Dad and I were huge music nerds. You didn't grow up like I had and hate music—not possible. And I loved festivals. Coachella was down near L.A., and there was Burning Man above us, but that was something else entirely. Condor, however, was in the forest by the lake for a weekend, with tents and lights, and there were unsigned bands playing all the tiny venues on the Strip, and the bigger outdoor shows in the day.

Condor was magic.

Anyway, all anyone was talking about this year on the festival boards was something so new, it didn't have a label yet. People just called it the Sound. West Coast indie, *post*-post punk. It just exploded over the scene, and suddenly there were, like, ten bands, then a dozen. Then who knows. But I was really into it, just watching clips online. Dreaming of getting back to the lake.

So, yeah, I'd made a mental list of bands I wanted to see this summer. Maybe even meet some of the band members. You know, through Eddie. Sometimes I met bands at Mad Dog's studio in Bel Air, but I had a feeling it would be different meeting them as Eddie's girlfriend rather than the Help. How could it not?

Driving past the festival grounds today, Dad and I couldn't see much from the road, but we could see something I wished we could avoid. Blue Snake River. Betty's on the Pier.

And the Condor Dam. My nemesis.

Dad gestured as we took the auto bridge that crossed the river behind the dam, and said unceremoniously, "There it is."

Whoomp. I craned my neck to look behind the seat as the Mercedes bumped along the bridge. "They put up a gate?" He came up here last summer when I stayed back home in L.A.

Dad cleared his throat. "They lock it up after dark. It's a good thing, baby. No one else can fall in now. Positive change. That railing is dangerous at night."

My throat tightened. Now I was the girl who made the town lock up the dam at night? The kids here must hate me. Jane, the Summer Girl who ruined the party—forever. Ugh.

My father never wanted to know the details about that night. He didn't ask. I didn't tell. I hid behind the excuse that I couldn't remember much after my fall, and Dad hid behind his fear. Why had I been at a party at the dam? How had I gotten a ride out there? Who was I was with? How did I fall in? Who pulled me out? Those questions weren't as important to him as *Will my daughter ever be able to speak again?* That was his priority at the beginning. When I started talking, then he focused on my speech therapy. When Eddie and I started talking online—and meeting up in L.A. on occasion—we kept it on the down-low. Until today.

Eddie wanted to keep us a secret. Drama-free, just us. That was fine back in L.A., but I couldn't do that over the summer here at the lake. I hoped he wasn't mad at me for showing up with my dad and popping our little bubble of privacy.

It's just that it was going to be hard enough for me, returning to the lake for the first time since my fall. I needed him as part of my present. Someone who'd changed and grown up. Not a secret. Not a murky memory from a terrible night that was haunting my nightmares.

I wanted to let go of that. I was *trying*.

"Hey," Dad warned me gently as we drove away from the

dam. "Don't let seeing the dam get you down. We're Marlows. What do we do?"

"We get back up on the board again," I recited, even though I actually couldn't get up on a surfboard if you paid me. He'd tried to teach me. The sporting life and I weren't compatible.

"That's right," he told me. "When you had trouble talking in the hospital, the doctors said it might be permanent. I said nope. She just needs time. We get back up again. And look at you now? Graduated. Back at the lake. And Velvet's personal assistant."

He was right. Though, the last one wasn't all that impressive. Yes, I was going to be a rich music daughter's personal assistant this summer. But here in the Larsen house, "PA" meant shopping, returning calls, booking appointments, and picking up their pre-scriptions. Like, my dad was sort of Mad Dog's PA. But Mad Dog had an actual professional assistant who handled music biz stuff back in his Bel Air studio—Denise, a fiftysomething ex–record executive who didn't "do" Northern California. She got paid the real money. My father didn't make much more than me, and I was a minimum-wage peon. Mad Dog was cheap.

"Hey, PA is better than dog walker on your resume. . . . *Shit*," Dad mumbled, glancing at his phone screen. "That's Mad Dog now, asking where we are."

Dad sped up. So much for a leisurely drive through town. We were still ten minutes or so from the lodge. And by lodge, I'm talking a sprawling 1920s luxury estate on the northern side of the lake, away from the Strip and the festival grounds. Away from everything, no neighbors for miles. It was built by some rich railroad tycoon from San Francisco who kept live tigers and prostitutes in different bungalows. It had its own dock, a pool, and a multicar garage in a separate building called the carriage house—where us domestics stayed. And as we pulled around its horseshoe-shaped driveway and stopped in front of the entrance, it loomed in front of us, larger than life. For a moment, I forgot all about the dam—and Eddie.

"Why aren't we parking in the carriage house and going through the kitchen?" I asked. We always went through the back. Never through the main house entrance. Ever.

"Mad Dog's coming down. He wants me to drive him into town."

"Now?" I complained. "The backseat is filled with luggage and ice."

"Hustle, cub. Get Frida inside with Velvet and see if she needs your help. I'll dump everything here. Get Kamal and Norma to help move it after we're gone. Just don't forget to tell them that there's forty pounds of melting ice out here, okay?"

Welp. Thirty seconds at the lodge, and we're already back to work. Hooking the dog leash, I gathered my purse and cross-body bag. Then Frida tugged me across the driveway toward the people arguing in the main house's open doorway, which sat between two giant California condor sculptures, perched on pillars.

"I may not have my first kitchen delivery," an unhappy voice was saying. When I crossed the threshold, I spied a familiar figure wearing a cross-back linen apron and a yellow scarf tied around her head. "How can you expect me to throw together a party?"

"Not a *party*-party," someone a couple of years older than me answered. "Just cocktails and a low-key dinner. Small plates. It's just four extra people. And Daddy. And Rosa. And me. And I guess Starla and Leo because I should include the assistants. And—look, my very own assistant is here! Whoa. You cut your hair for graduation? I likey."

She did? If Velvet Larsen liked it, that made me feel better about cutting it.

"Jane will be attending—casual summer dress. Something sleeveless with sandals will look good with your new hair. I may have a tiny thing you can borrow," Velvet told me, smiling. She stood in bare bronze feet on the tile of the entrance hall, wearing a billowing maxi dress. When she reached toward Frida, dozens of gold bangles tinkled on her wrist. "Come, *mija*!"

Frida pranced her way to Velvet and stood up on her hind legs to greet her. "Oh, doggie kisses, muah, muah, muah!" Both parties quickly lost interest. For Frida, there were too many other smells to sniff, like the elaborate floral arrangement that was taller than me. Frida gave it a bark, just to be sure it wasn't an enemy in disguise.

I stood under a massive mission-style chandelier that hung between two joining staircases. A window overlooked the pool out back. "What's this about a cocktail party?"

"It's not happening," Exie said. "*That's* what it is."

"Too bad. I already invited them," Velvet said, undeterred. "No shrimp, by the way."

"Who?" I asked.

"Just a little romantic icebreaker." She winked at me

confusingly. I never knew what her winks meant. They were confusing. Especially because I didn't know she was seeing anyone. Were others up from L.A. already? Condor Lake was all locals during the off-season. That didn't mean there weren't plenty of interesting singles that might be in Velvet Larsen's orbit, but she dated a lot of UCLA art school dropouts, sons of Hollywood actors, the young nephew of a wealthy Latin American *narcotraficante*—you know, everyday people.

"So now it's ten people?" Exie said, annoyed. "Tomorrow night? Does Mad Dog know?"

"He knows . . . that there will be some people here." That sounded vague. She elaborated. "When I asked, he said, 'Make it so, number one,'" Velvet said in a comic voice that was somewhere between her father's deep Danish accent and Patrick Stewart.

Exie swore filthily under her breath. Mad Dog was a big, tattooed metal Viking, but he had a soft spot for old-school Star Trek and sci-fi shows. That definitely sounded like him.

"Look, this is a nice thing I'm doing," Velvet argued, gesturing broadly. "You'll see. It's a surprise that everyone will like."

Velvet was the youngest of Mad Dog's brood, his only daughter with his current wife, Rosa Garcia, a former poet laureate, and Velvet was the only Larsen kid at the lodge this summer. She was high energy and generally fun, but she was a princess; her mother's family in Mexico City was rich too. She sometimes had unrealistic expectations, which caused headaches for the domestics.

Like now. Parties were easy to plan but hard to execute at the drop of a gold bangle.

But we did it. The main party-executer here was Exie. She was a thirty-eight-year-old Black chef from Baldwin Hills who joined Mad Dog's crew a couple years before Dad and I did. I wouldn't say she was a motherly figure because she would hate to be called that, but when I hit puberty, she did more birds-and-bees duty than Dad. She was unofficially second-in-charge on the domestic staff—officially third, after head of security.

I didn't like when there was tension between them. Definitely didn't need it today.

"What can . . . I do?" I asked Exie, fumbling words while trying to control Frida. "Help? Ugh." I raised my hand and signaled to let her know I was struggling.

The thing about having a brain injury is that everyone treats you differently. Dad was overprotective. Eddie got impatient—I could tell. Exie just kept on treating me exactly the same. She didn't help me when I was lost for words. She ignored it and kept going.

Her laugh was dry. "Don't know how you can help, baby. You're not mine to command anymore. Norma's neither. Ask your new boss here. You're attending the party too, remember."

Velvet smiled. "Exactly! But first, I think I forgot my special shampoo, so you might have to make a trip somewhere to find me a bottle before Thursday night, Jane. I doubt they'd have it here. Maybe Fresno. Or somewhere in the Bay Area?"

"Velvet Larsen," Exie complained loudly in a voice that echoed through the hall. "No one is driving hours for a bottle of shampoo. Your split ends will survive if they don't get the exact shit they sell in Bel Air. Jane is your PA, not your baby sister to boss around. Hear me?"

Velvet made a pouty duck face. "Fine. But those small plates better be good Thursday night. I want sunshine on a plate, or I'm walking."

"Oh. You're walking, all right." Exie swatted the air with a kitchen towel as Velvet laughed, racing up the stairs away from her. Just like that, the two of them were on good terms again. My shoulders relaxed, and I felt lighter. Crisis averted.

"Come hither, assistant," Velvet said playfully, hanging over the upstairs railing. "Let's get me unpacked and enjoy this glorious day. Daddy's going into town. The lake is ours."

All at once, it came back to me in a rush, the heady joy of this place. Here, I could be somebody different. Maybe even a princess like Velvet . . .

After I hauled in forty pounds of melting ice.

CONDOR LODGE SUMMER DOMESTIC STAFF

Carriage House Room Assignments

Room 1: Norma Dewberry, head housekeeper

Room 2: Exie Johnson, chef

Room 3: Kamal Reddy, Mad Dog's bodyguard/head of security

Room 4: Starla Pham, Rosa's masseuse and PA

Room 5: Marie Keyes, junior housekeeper and server

Room 6: Leo Marlow, chauffeur and Mad Dog's PA

Room 7: Jane Marlow, pet caretaker and Velvet's PA

Jane

Dad was still stewing about Eddie the next morning. I could tell. So when Velvet sent me into town on my first personal assistant mission to buy shampoo at the lake's one true salon—Mandy's Hair Caboose and Big T's Barber didn't count—I had a pit stop in mind for a gift that could turn his mood around.

When my father isn't happy, no one is. *I* definitely wasn't. And I needed him on my side right now. I wanted to be basking in the glow of future plans with Eddie, not avoiding my father's scowl. I was going to fix it with the one thing he loved more than old cars. Music.

Specifically, old records.

"This town is a fried-chicken-bucket of charm," Starla said, whipping the hybrid car into a packed parking lot off the Strip to let me out. "Everyone is so nice. I came into town yesterday with Norma, and in five minutes, I'd booked a job with a man who needs hip work. A sweet man, not a creep who thinks just because I'm a massage therapist, I give happy endings."

"Rosa isn't going to want you doing work outside the lodge," I warned her. "Same as when we're back in the Bel Air house. You have to get it approved in advance."

"Everyone needs a side hustle," Starla said, giving me a playful smile as she tossed a mermaid-dyed ponytail over one shoulder. "Besides, Rosa doesn't control what I do during Starla Time. She doesn't own me. Right, Frida-pup?" she cooed.

Frida panted at her from my lap and tried to lick her nose. Starla Pham was a few years older than me—twenty-one—and had been working as PA and masseuse to Mad Dog's wife since the fall. She was in the process of getting acupuncture points tattooed all over her arms and legs. I wish I could've been as laid-back as she was about the house rules.

But I'd lived with the Larsens for too long. I'd seen a lot of domestics fired. Mad Dog treated his staff fairly, but he left the day-to-day management to the head housekeeper, Norma, aka Mother Superior. Norma didn't suffer fools or rule breakers. So far, Starla had escaped her wrath, but it was easy to screw up at the lake. I should know.

I thought for sure Dad and I would be fired two summers ago after the dam incident. After all, I caused a public scene, and Mad Dog didn't like publicity. He was very private, a man of few words—not someone who threw wild drug-fueled parties and trashed hotel rooms. He liked the lake because he could retreat here and stay out of the press. I definitely disrupted that. The local paper and TV station were all abuzz about the dam and Betty's when I fell into the water that summer—unwanted attention for Mad Dog. But I guess he felt too sorry for me to kick us to the curb. Or maybe he just loved my dad too much. When you're at Mad Dog's level, it's hard to trust people, and Dad is as loyal as they come.

"Well," Starla said, "I say what Norma doesn't know won't hurt her. If I can fit in a few extra massage clients this summer, I'm going to make that cash. Transportation is the issue. Why is the lodge so far away from town? If I were Mad Dog, I would have picked a better spot."

Since Starla and I were both PAs, we'd be sharing this car this summer . . . along with Exie and the junior housekeeper. We had to sign it out when we left the house. She wasn't wrong. The limited vehicle situation and no public transportation other than the Bonanza streetcar meant a lot of juggling rides back and forth to the lodge.

As for gas, that went on the company card. I just got mine this morning. I had to log every purchase and save every receipt. I couldn't just buy myself lunch. If any expense were unexplained, it would come out of my pocket *and* I'd be fired. Which meant I'd also lose my home.

Everything.

One day I wouldn't have to worry about this kind of stuff. Maybe one day soon. Eddie needed to hurry up and get back from the Philippines so we could talk about our own place.

"Thanks for the lift," I told Starla.

"Leo's picking you up, yeah?"

I nodded. On his way down from the mountains. He'd taken Mad Dog and Rosa up to some guru for sunrise meditation this morning, so I had about an hour in town.

"All righty. Don't do anything I'd do," Starla said with a grin. "See you back at the lodge."

I jumped out of the car and headed down the Strip with Frida. It was too early in the season for a lot of tourists, but the weather was nice, and a family in shorts and sunglasses were renting kayaks. I skirted around them and spied what I was looking for half a block down—a sign above a windowed storefront in bright gold retro lettering:

VICTORY VINYL

NEW AND USED RECORDS SINCE 1980

An institution at the lake, and one that was connected with Eddie's family. Not the Sarafians, though. The record shop was owned by Eddie's other grandfather—on his mother's side, Grandfather Kasabian. When he first bought it, Victory Vinyl was just a hole-in-the-wall. Now it was run by Eddie's aunt—Eddie's mother's older sister, it all stayed in the Kasabian family—and was where some of the festival bands occasionally did signings and surprise promo events. Tugging Frida's leash, I strode toward the shop's entrance, where a motley collection of peeling decals was plastered on a mirrored front door—Zildjian cymbals, 2Pac, Dead Kennedys, the Armenian flag.

On the wall nearby was a collection of framed regional honors. National ones too: the shop had been listed on a bunch of national Best Of lists. Next to that was an article in the *San Francisco Chronicle*, "Two Immigrant Families Bond Over Music."

"Hey," I warned Frida. "I need you to be on your best behavior. Don't embarrass me, and after it's over, I'll let you gnaw on Captain Pickles, okay?" We shared a silent agreement, and I quickly set an alarm on my phone to remind me to get the shampoo—a trick I'd learned from my father, Mr. Military. Never be late when you're working for the rich and famous.

Jangly guitars and soft, snared beats pulsed through speakers as I stepped inside the rustic shop. Wooden bins of LPs lined narrow aisles. Old linocut concert posters. High walls. A dark balcony sat above the ceiling rafters, where autographed guitars hung. Everything smelled pleasantly of musty cardboard and old plastic. That scent overwhelmed me with good feelings.

The shop wasn't busy, but space was limited, so me and my size-five sneakers had to turn sideways to step around a couple customers intently flipping through records. I was also keeping an eye on the pup, who could decide to have a meltdown any moment and either start barking or pee on someone's shoe.

Mainly, though, I was keeping an eye out for Pari Kasabian, Eddie's aunt and his mother's sister. There might be another aunt across town, not sure. He didn't talk about his mother's family much. Anyway, I didn't think she'd recognize me, not with my new hair, but if she was working today, I didn't want to be caught by surprise.

The shop's checkout area was at the back, under the guitar-filled balcony. To the left, a willowy woman leaned on a counter near the register below a sign that said BUY, chatting with a customer—was that Eddie's aunt? I wasn't sure. On the right was a smaller glass display case marked SELL. No one attending that. Good. That was the place I needed to check out—where they kept the good stuff.

Dad had a massive rare-record collection, an obsession he

shared with Mad Dog—a love for old vinyl. There was one rare album my dad had been hunting for a while, his Holy Grail. Rare alternate pressing of iconic L.A. punk band Black Flag's *My War*. It had been my father's favorite band since he was my age; he had signed copies of Henry Rollins's poetry books and framed photos of them together. You've never seen a grown man turn into mush like my father did around Henry Rollins. He'd chauffeured a thousand stars with nary a twitch of his muscular arms, but Henry? Full-on fanboy swooning.

I was always on the lookout for his Holy Grail when I was in a record store.

As I perused the rows of album covers in Plexiglas holders, a shop attendant approached from the other side of the display case. My heart hammered for a moment, but it wasn't Eddie's aunt.

Not Eddie, either. Of course it wasn't. He was on a flight to the Philippines.

But it *was* a boy. A striking boy, about my age.

He had a head of messy, voluminous rich brown hair and intense vibes. A couple of badges were pinned to a wrinkled black button-down layered over a T-shirt: a tiny enamel piano and a record-shaped name tag that said WRONG.

He was definitely appealing in one of those tortured and stormy ways. I mean, not that I was looking; next to Eddie, no one stood a chance. Besides, that wasn't it. There was something underneath the surface that was hidden from me, just there but unreachable. Like a word on the tip of my tongue I couldn't quite grasp. And that hidden thing was flipping on all the lights inside my head, which was worrisome—not in a stranger-danger kind of way. More because I didn't want my word-pixie waking up.

He had hawklike eyes that I avoided. When I did, I found myself looking down at his hands. I'd never noticed anyone's hands before, but his didn't match the rest of him—long, elegant fingers that moved in an uncannily malleable way when he stretched them out, templing them against each other.

I was staring, and he'd noticed. Our gazes connected and stuck. For several moments too long. I was a fish who'd bitten a hook, panic firing through. I was caught.

Embarrassment finally gave me the strength to look away.

Words. I needed them. Come on.

"Sorry," I mumbled while Frida pawed at the counter.

"What's that?" He took a step closer until we were across from each other, separated by the narrow glass of the counter.

"I was looking for a certain record," I explained. "Uh . . . I don't see it. Never mind. It's super rare, so . . . It was a long shot. Sorry. Thanks. Sorry. I mean . . . sorry."

Good God. How many times could a person apologize? At least I hadn't slipped up with any words. Time to abandon the quest for my father's Holy Grail and get the heck out of here before I made a bigger fool out of myself.

But as I turned to leave, the boy spoke to me again.

"Holy fuck. It's *you*," he said in a deep, dark voice. "You're . . . alive."

Fen

Of course she was alive. I knew that. She was standing in front of me, one, and two, I'd seen her posting in the Festival Freaks discussion community. Not like I stalked her. It's just, you know. When you see someone's limp body being carted away in an ambulance at midnight, and your knees are about to buckle because you're scared out of your goddamn mind that you broke her rib doing the CPR wrong—*and* your asshole brother is leaning on you to cover it all up and stop asking questions about her . . . ?

It tends to make you curious.

At least for a while. Then life happened, and I put her in the back of my mind.

Just a little shift from the front to the back. But she was always there, my Ophelia, unconscious in the water, her face all bloody and strangled with hair when I pulled her up to the surface.

I hadn't fucking forgotten her. I would never. Even with more flesh on her bones and all the hair gone. She looked better now. I liked her petite–Snow White vibe, a little forest fairy, and her leopard-print shoes—a little trashy and loud. But she still had that scared-bird look in her eyes like she did when she used to follow Eddie around years ago.

"Do I . . . we, why . . ." She squished up her face and started over, speaking hesitantly. "Do you know me?"

"Jane. Jane Marlow? Over at the Larsens' place."

She nodded, confused as to why I knew her name.

"You really don't remember me," I said, stunned.

"Should I?" Her dog was pawing at the case. She gave it a command and it stopped, but not before she stole a glance at the BUY counter. She seemed more interested in what my aunt was saying to Mr. Applegate than our conversation.

I ignored the pang of frustration in my chest. "Guess when we last saw each other, you were a little out of it."

Whoa. The scared bird disappeared. Now Snow White was miffed. "I don't think so."

"Pretty sure."

"You have me confused," she said, signaling for her dog to sit. "I haven't been around the lake for a couple years."

Shit. She really didn't remember me. "You *are* Jane, though?"

"Yes, but you are still wrong, apparently," she said, nodding at my name tag, a little edge to her voice. "Or is that Mr. Wrong?"

I chuckled to myself, but it came out sounding mean. Guess I was angry that she didn't remember me. I was angry about a lot of things these days. "Let's try this again," I said carefully, propping my palms on the edge of the counter. "What can I do for you, Miss Marlow?"

She frowned. "If you think that you're . . . look. You don't scare me. You saw my name on the thing—with the talking reporters. Program. Weather, traffic, and . . ."

What was wrong with her? Was she on drugs? She *looked* sober.

"The news?" I guessed.

"News," she enunciated as if she wanted to cut off my head and throw it into the lake. Forget scared bird. She was now angry as hell. And I felt embarrassed that I'd pissed her off without realizing it.

"I don't need your pity," she said.

"Okay?" Was there something wrong with her speech? Maybe it wasn't a sober thing after all. Now I felt doubly embarrassed. And confused.

"I just need your help."

The way she said this, I heard it as, *Don't treat me differently.* So I didn't.

I leaned over the counter on one elbow. Super casual. "If it's a signed Taylor Swift album, you're shit out of luck. I can get you one, but we can't keep them in stock." I paused. "Just saying, you've got the look of a Swiftie about you."

Her nose wrinkled. "I'm going to ignore that."

"Nothing wrong with it."

"Didn't say there was. She's a brilliant songwriter."

"Didn't say she wasn't. I own all her shit. It's just that I'm the rare records buyer for this store, and that includes any signed stuff, so I know what we have and what we don't."

"Why don't you let me tell you what I want before you decide it for me?" she said, tiny brows lowering to make a tiny V.

I crossed my arms and waited. "Go."

"I'm looking for a particularly hard-to-find piece of vinyl."

"If it exists, I can find it," I informed her. *I will find anything for you. . . .*

She tapped her middle finger on the glass. *Tap, tap, tap.* As if she were matching time with a slow metronome in her head. Something was definitely different about Jane.

Just when I thought she might not respond at all, she said, "Only twenty-five existed in 1984. One is in a jukebox in a Highland Park bar on Figueroa. One is owned by their former lead singer, Henry Rollins. One went up for sale last year online, but I got way outbid at the last minute. A few are supposed to be floating around the state with private collectors, and nobody knows where the rest are."

Huh. Okay. I ignored the tapping and the odd way she was matching the cadence of her voice to the rhythm of those taps. I even tried to temporarily forget about the fact that she was my long-lost Ophelia. My Jane.

Just the girl who'd haunted my thoughts for the last couple of years.

No big deal.

But I did my best to pack all that baggage up and try to look at her now as a stranger. Which she was—when it came down to it. And when I thought of her that way, as someone I didn't know anymore, I was simply standing in front of a girl who wanted to talk vinyl. A pretty girl my age, not some cracked dude older than my dad who smelled like weed and cheap aftershave.

This was exciting. It didn't happen every day.

"You're talking about Black Flag," I said. "The Double Deuce pressing of *My War*."

"Correct," she said, speeding up her tapping a bit. "First pressing was screwed up and had 'Side 2' printed on both sides of the first twenty-five copies."

I leaned closer to her. "Some say the Double Deuce doesn't really exist."

"It does, though. Trust me. My dad is a Black Flag fiend. They were a little before his time, but he saw Rollins Band play on the first Lollapalooza tour in 1991, when he got home from the Gulf War. It was a huge awakening for him."

My hands were starting to sweat. It was strange to be this close to her again after living with her inside my head for so long. I tried to pretend that she was another Jane. A random Jane. "Can't go wrong with Henry Rollins."

"You know, a lot of people assume Henry Rollins is this super intense, scary dude."

"Right. Because he's Henry fucking Rollins."

"But he's really a decent guy, if you haven't met him."

"Oddly enough, I have not."

She stopped tapping, and her eyes met mine. "You obviously know who I work for."

I nodded.

"Once, he made the kitchen give us ice cream sundaes and sat down and ate with me." She smiled and shrugged lightly with one shoulder. "I was an eleven-year-old kid and was having a bad day. He was just . . . kind. That's all."

"Sure, sure," I said as the funny-faced, hairless dog whined near her feet. "Relatable. I think most folk can say that Henry Rollins magically appears like a fairy godmother to conjure ice cream sundaes."

She laughed once, softly; a really nice laugh that instantly made me feel warm inside. Like it was used to you. That was my Jane. The Jane I used to know.

How could she not remember me? Had I changed that much in two years?

"You into old L.A. punk yourself?" I asked.

She shrugged, pulling out a dog toy from her bag—something that looked like a green dildo. When I gave it a long look, she held it up so that I could see it had a face and was wearing a pirate hat. "This is Captain Pickles. Her favorite toy."

I cleared my throat. "It most certainly is."

"Really." The shells of her ears turned pink as she bent down to offer the toy to the dog, who instantly went bonkers for it and stopped whining. Then she stood back up and said, "Um, so, old-school L.A. punk . . . ? Not so much. I like a little X. The medley at the end of *Golden Shower of Hits* is fun—the covers of the singles?"

"The Circle Jerks?"

"My dad and I sing along to that. I like some of the nineties punk revival that he listens to, like Bad Religion. But a lot of that early hardcore stuff is way too problematic. Have you seen *The Decline of Western Civilization*? About the L.A. punk scene in the 1980s?"

Holy shit. I didn't know anyone who'd seen that. "Sure."

"A time of much aggro." *Tap, tap, tap.* It was back again, her finger metronome. "I think it's funny when bands play so hard, they can't wear shirts, yet they insist on wearing leather pants in Southern California. So weird."

"Now I've got the punk version of 'Afternoon Delight' stuck in my head. Thanks for the earworm."

"That's a definite mood." Her cheeks lifted as she smiled, and I felt it in my chest.

"Anywho, all I'm trying to say is that my dad's been searching for the Black Flag—"

"The rare Double Deuce pressing."

"Yeah, that. He's been wanting it for years. We call it his Holy Grail of records, and nothing would make him happier."

Which dad was she talking about? Mad Dog or his driver? The driver, right? A part of me was curious, mostly so I could connect a picture to the man she was talking about in my mind. But it wasn't my business, so I didn't ask. "I'd love to be able to make your dad's day," I said, "but I can tell you right now we don't have it in stock."

"But can you find it?"

"Wrong question."

A little dent appeared in the middle of her forehead. "What's the right question?"

"*Why* should I find it? You don't even remember who I am."

The tapping stopped. She squinted at my face. "I . . . should know you. We've met before."

"Mm. Tried to talk to you the last summer you were at the lake, but I was covered in acne two years ago and was just a lanky skeleton who walked while looking down at the ground. Ring any bells?"

The dog panted at her feet while her gaze raced across my face, back and forth, as if she were attempting to build a map. It sent a little chill down my arm, which felt nice. Until Bob Hayworth, our UPS driver, breezed behind the counter. "Mr. Sarafian," he said cheerfully. "Where's your aunt? Picking up, and I've got two overnights for ya. One needs her signature."

I pointed him in the right direction, but he'd already given me up.

Jane stared at me. "Wait. Sarafian?" she said in a small voice.

I nodded. *Think, Jane. Not that hard. How many Sarafians do you know?*

She drew in a quick breath. "You're *him*."

"Am I? Who would that be?"

She blinked rapidly. "You're the brother. You're Fen."

"The brother," I scoffed. Always measured against Eddie.

"You're supposed to be . . . You left the family."

I held up a finger. "My father told me to leave the house over 'creative differences.' I moved in with my aunt, and everyone's happy. One big, happy dysfunctional family."

She glanced back at the other counter, at Aunt Pari. "That's your mom's sister."

"Gee, you've really kept up with us after all these years. The crush on Eddie lingered, huh? We aren't the Kardashians, you know. Find another Armenian family with more money. Oddly enough, we are only getting by because of your employer. Mad Dog's money infusion really helped Sarafian Events. So I should probably bow to you, or something."

Confusion. Then her eyes darkened. "Eddie warned me about you."

"I'll bet—" Wait. Hold on. What?

"If I knew you worked here, I wouldn't have come in," she snapped. "And just . . . just so you know, I think it's terrible how you've treated your brother."

A giant fireball exploded inside my head. "Me? What the hell are you talking about? And since when have you talked to Eddie?"

"Since yesterday morning. When he was leaving on a plane."

I stared at her. "Bullshit!"

"What's your problem? He's my boyfriend, and he's flying halfway around the world, so I wanted to see him. It's what people do—not that it's any of your . . . your . . . Whatever!"

Shock made me feel momentarily light-headed. "*Boyfriend?* Boyfriend? Boy-friend?"

She didn't answer. Maybe because I was acting like a malfunctioning robot. Customers were staring. I just couldn't wrap my head around it.

I cleared my throat and lowered my voice. "Since when?"

"For a while. Months. I . . . we . . . Stop it, Frida!" She untangled the dog, who was running around her legs with the green pirate pickle. "I don't know! We've been talking online since my accident. You probably don't remember what happened that night because you were too drunk, but he was my . . . my . . ."

What the hell? Was I in upside-down world? *Eddie* was the drunk one that night—not me. And she'd been seeing him for months? Since I'd moved out of my parents' house.

That piece of rotten garbage shitstain racoon-fucking . . .

I silently screamed.

"He was my . . . that thing in armor," she said weakly. "Shiny. On the horse."

It took me *way* too long to realize what she meant.

"Knight?" I gritted my teeth. "Are you fucking kidding me? Eddie, a knight?"

"You're an agent of chaos. That's what Eddie told me. Ruiner."

I pressed a hand to my heart. "Me? Ruiner?"

"You got him kicked out of college."

"As payback for what he did to me!" I said, nearly shouting again. "He's a liar, a manipulator, and a con man. He's Machiavelli with dimples."

"Um . . . no," she said with a bitter chuckle. "Eddie's many things, but he's no evil genius."

"Wanna make a bet? He's got everybody fooled, even you. The real Eddie isn't good. The real Eddie stole my girl and got me kicked out of my family home."

My aunt whistled and gave me peeved look that told me to tone it down. I got that look from her a lot lately, so I just raised my hand to signal that her message was received. I was scaring our customers away.

No one likes an angry sales assistant.

Jane didn't like it, either. She squared her shoulders as if I'd insulted her. "Well, I don't see why you expect me to just . . . believe you."

"Why?" I was taken aback. Not sure why. It was just so insulting that she would question things I knew to be fact.

"I'm sorry. I know Eddie. I trust him."

"Oh, do you? Do you really?"

"Yes!" she said loudly. "We're serious, actually."

"Ha, doubt that. Maybe you are, but he isn't. Trust me."

She was furious now too, and now my aunt was coming over to break this up.

"When Eddie comes back from the Philippines," Jane said, picking up her tiny dog and stowing it under one arm, "he told me we're going to find our own place at the lake this summer."

"*What?*"

"So when he moves out, you're welcome to make up with your father and move back in. Life is short. Stop being so angry."

"Not a chance," I said, feeling hot all over and more alive than I'd been in months. Were my eyes welling up with angry tears? I didn't care. Let her see me cry. "He's made a wreck of my life, and I will lay waste to anything that brings him joy. You tell him that."

"I'm sorry for what's happened to you, Fen," she said in a small voice.

"And I'm glad you're not dead, Jane Marlow. But if you're with Eddie, then you're my enemy now. You've haunted me for far too long, but I will not allow any of this shit to defeat me anymore!"

Any pity she may have been feeling was now erased by confusion. It was all over her face and in the rigid lines of her body. I had that effect on people.

"What do you mean by I'm your enemy now?" she asked.

"I mean in a metaphoric, poetic sense."

"I don't know you," she said, just as upset as I was. "What kind of person says this stuff to a stranger?"

"You aren't a stranger. But maybe you should ask yourself what kind of person *you* are to not know that the person you're dating might be lying to you?"

That struck a nerve. I'd gone too far and immediately regretted it, but I was afraid to admit it. She was riled up, fuming. She backed away from the display case, protecting the barking dog from me. "You are unbelievably screwed up, you know that?"

"Hell yes, I am," I agreed. "No one's more dangerous than the person who thinks he's pure of heart."

"Now you're quoting James Baldwin to me?"

"I . . ." She wasn't supposed to know that. It threw me off that she did, but I shut it out and refocused. "I'm saying I *know* I'm not, Jane. My heart is impure, and my mind is screwed up. But I think if you search your memories, you'll remember why. Because you may have forgotten me, but I've never forgotten you."

She bumped into a man behind her. And before Aunt Pari could make it over to us and play referee, Jane jogged through the shop and out the door.

Not exactly the reunion I'd pictured in my mind.

Jane

Early-summer sun warmed my face as I exited the beauty salon with Velvet's shampoo, delicately nested in tissue at the bottom of a bag that dangled from one arm. My head was a tangle of credit card receipts—so Norma didn't chew me out back at the lodge—and worry over trying to meet up with my dad on time, and why Frida was being whiny, and—

FEN FUCKING SARAFIAN.

I remembered him. Of course I did. Now that I could put together the image of the wild-haired hothead in the record shop with the memory I had of him from past summers at the lake. The geeky boy who was all sandy-brown arms and legs and a beak-like nose that was a little too big for his face.

Fen hung back when Eddie stepped forward. Was quiet when Eddie spoke up. He was my age. The last time I spent any time with him, when I was fifteen, we talked about music.

He said he was at the dam that night.

My horror night.

I couldn't remember his face there. Then again, I couldn't

remember much of anything at all from the dam. If I tried, I could still feel myself falling off the railing. The terror. And a moment where I gave in to it because I knew I couldn't do anything about it. Yes, I remembered that. Then nothing. Not until the next day, when I was in the hospital, long gone from the lake.

But that wasn't entirely true. There *was* the tiniest, tiniest image tumbling around in my head of that night. Fractions of images that I couldn't piece together.

Maybe my brain didn't want me to.

Regardless, it didn't matter now. I was getting upset over nothing. So I'd seen Fen. So what? Eddie had warned me that his little brother was an ass. I wished I could tell Eddie that I'd met Fen. In fact, I'd started to text Eddie several times in the hair salon but stopped myself. He'd landed in the Philippines already, but he said he'd be "off the map" for a couple days while he traveled to a remote island. So I didn't want to bombard him with texts about his black-sheep brother that would be waiting for him for days.

Ugh. Why did I have to walk into the record shop today? I was fine until Fen lured me in with his companionable music banter—*oh, la-la-la, I'm the music buyer. Look at me and my elegant alien hands, I know all about the Double Deuce.* What was he? Some kind of siren? Eddie didn't even know what punk was—how was his horrible brother better musically educated?

At that moment I felt as if I'd saved up money to buy tickets for a once-in-a-lifetime concert and another band came out onstage and played. This was not what I expected, and nothing could make it better. This boy, with all his wild, dark hair and his laser beam eyes, and all the shouting—my God! If I acted like that at work, I'd be out on my ass.

Then again, I guess there was a reason Fen wasn't living at home anymore. Bad seed. More than bad. Rotten.

But. Then, at the end of our argument, there were the unshed tears in Fen's eyes. He was upset. Wounded. And I didn't understand that at all. The men in the Larsen house didn't show emotions. My dad barely did. Anger, I understood, but not tears.

All I'd wanted was to daydream about finding an apartment with Eddie. Now I couldn't even do that without seeing Fen's face.

I shouldn't be letting him get to me like this.

Dad was exactly where he said he'd be, sitting in the perfectly polished blacker-than-black Fintail with the driver's side window rolled down. But my mind was looping around Fen, so I couldn't comprehend that he was waving me into the backseat instead of next to him in the front—my usual seat when I caught a lift in this car. It didn't compute, not until the door to the backseat popped open, and Mad Dog's face stared back at me.

Shit. The last thing I needed right now.

Squinting at me through a pair of thick-rimmed glasses, Mad Dog tugged a graying ginger beard that covered the tattoos peeking from a blousy white meditation shirt, snarling mythic beasts and Viking wolves woven in Scandinavian patterns with runes.

The backseat of the Mercedes cowered beneath his colossal frame.

"Hop in, *kattekat*," he said in a low voice tinged with a Danish accent.

Nothing to do but enter the vermillion-red leather interior of the Mercedes. Like sitting in the mouth of a whale. "H-hey, Mad Dog. Didn't expect a rideshare with you, sir."

"I can walk, if you want the car to yourself," he joked. "Now that you've got that big high school diploma, I guess it's gone to your head. Congratulations, by the way."

I laughed nervously. "Thanks. And I guess we *are* heading to the same place. Might as well carpool," I replied, hoping I sounded as breezy as he did. "Hey, Dad."

"Hey, cub. How's day number one of being Velvet's assistant? Got what she sent you out for?"

"Success," I said, shutting the door. It wasn't the first time I'd ridden in the car with Mad Dog, but I didn't do it every week or anything. He took up so much room, physically and spiritually, and it felt weird to be sitting back here. Where I didn't belong.

Frida didn't mind. She leapt over Velvet's shampoo bag to greet him, all wags.

"Hello, little one. How's my other daughter?" he teased.

My dad glanced at him in the rearview mirror. A look so brief. But I caught it.

"The hairless wonder," Mad Dog clarified.

Of course he meant *Frida*. But the fact that he had to explain spoke volumes.

I mean, it wasn't as if I hadn't heard what people said about me. My mother was a junior housekeeper. She and Dad fell hard for each other. One thing led to another, and she got pregnant. Nine months later, I was born . . . and when I was five, she died.

That should be the end of the story. Only, it wasn't, because some-one in the house—one of the dozens of housekeepers or garden-ers or *whoever*s in service over the years—started a rumor.

The rumor went like this:

My mother was hooking up with Mad Dog at the same time as Dad. Or right before Dad. Or there was a wild night with the three of them. Pick one. It all amounted to the same outcome.

I could be Mad Dog's kid.

First time I heard about this, it was from Velvet's former nanny who sometimes took care of me right after my mom died, and I didn't understand. In one ear, out the other. The second time, I was ten, and it was at school. My dad had to sit me down and assure me that the rumor wasn't true. And that if it could ever be even the *slightest* bit fractionally possible, he would never agree to a paternity test, because he didn't want to know. That he was my father, and I was his kid, and that was the end of it.

Period.

We didn't discuss it. That was the Marlow way: if you didn't talk about something, it went away. But I did think about it sometimes. Because I don't look like my blond lion of a father. I don't look like ginger-headed Mad Dog, either, though. I look like my mom. And that's all I knew. So I tried not to worry about it too much.

"Where's Rosa?" I asked. His wife—Velvet's mom—was a good buffer. Plus, she was nice and was always offering to let me borrow books from her library.

"At the lodge," he said. "Leo and I dropped her off earlier

because she had a little back pain. She walked too much today. Needs to rest plenty before Velvet's party."

Party. It was almost noon, and I wasn't sure what Velvet still needed me to do to help her get ready for that besides fetch shampoo. Guess it was my job to know. Maybe if Eddie's family would stop accosting me in record shops.

"How's your noggin?" Mad Dog asked as the car turned off the Strip.

Bad. Messy. In a tizzy. And it was all Fen Sarafian's fault. I know he saw me tapping my finger on the counter. I had to do something, or I wouldn't have been able to speak full sentences. It's easier when there's a rhythm; my word-pixie falls asleep and leaves me alone.

But talking about the current state of My Brain was another uncomfortable subject when it came to Mad Dog. Because our health insurance didn't cover the doctors I saw after my accident. And months later, when some enormous hospital bill came, my dad almost had a couple nervous breakdowns—first when he thought he owed it, then when he owed nothing.

Now *I* felt like I owed Mad Dog. Some honesty. Not all, but a little. So I answered, "Been struggling a little since yesterday. Might be stress. Returning here after being gone."

He nodded. "You need to settle in. The lake is a pure place. You bled in its waters, so now you need to make peace with it. Forgive each other," he said in a very Zen-like manner.

"Uh . . ."

"Go to the dam and see where you fell."

Dad coughed in the front seat. "I don't know about that, M.D. Not right away."

"I didn't say today." Mad Dog shrugged. "But soon. Make peace with the lake so your brain can finish healing. Then you can enjoy the festival in a few weeks with your cheesecake boy, if that makes you happy for the summer."

Cheesecake boy? What the hell . . . ?

Mad Dog flicked me a look. "Don't act surprised. I know about you and Serj's kid."

Okay, so this conversation was happening. Anxious, I shifted in my seat to stop my restless leg from bouncing while the unspoken piece hung between us: domestic girl dating semi-famous business associate's son was crossing class lines. But as I told my father when I first broke the news about Eddie, it wasn't as if Dad and I were working for some 1950s old-money billionaire. Mad Dog *was* rock and roll, rule-breaking and whatnot.

Modern times: get with them.

"Serj Sarafian and I go way back," Mad Dog said, watching the scenery out his window. "We're partners. I have opinions about our business . . . business in which your cheesecake is unfortunately at the center. It clouds my feeling about him. I wanted Serj to go to the Philippines, but he was too busy with the festival."

"Oh?" I hadn't heard this part from Eddie. Then again, after everything Fen said in the record shop, it made me wonder what else Eddie wasn't telling me.

"If Serj's kid doesn't fuck up the amphitheater lease renewal in the Philippines, then Leo and I will bless the two of you like the Pope and welcome him into the Family with open arms," Mad Dog said. "Right, Leo?"

"With all due respect, speak for yourself, boss," Dad muttered from the front seat.

Mad Dog laughed. "Hey. I tried, *kattekat*."

"Yes, sir." I feigned a chuckle, pretending that none of this talk was affecting me. But it was. It felt as if Mad Dog was saying that he was attaching performance-based conditions to my dating Eddie. If Eddie did good, then Mad Dog would . . . what? What did his approval entail? I didn't know, and I didn't like him involved in my personal life. But I felt too small to tell him that, and my head was too full of Fen Sarafian's accusations.

No one believed in Eddie. Not Fen. Not my dad. Not Mad Dog. All of this negativity was creating doubt in my head, and I needed to sort it out. Figure out what was real and true.

"For the time being," Mad Dog suggested, "let's just all try to put on a good face for Velvet's surprise party."

"I don't think it's a surprise for anyone at this point," I told him. "Exie's got it in hand."

"When Velvet's planning a party, there's *always* a surprise," he said enigmatically, scratching Frida behind the ear. "Right, little one?"

Frida rolled over on the seat between us. I wondered if Dad and I were rolling over too.

We just hadn't realized it.

NORMA'S COMMANDMENTS

BE PROFESSIONAL

- Wear your uniform from 8AM until 8PM.
- Knock/ask permission before entering private spaces.
- Never touch the Family's private belongings unless you have permission.

BE RESPECTFUL

- Absolutely no gossiping about the Family, their business, or their private lives.
- Remain quiet at all times in the house; phone ringers must be on silent.
- Use "sir," "ma'am," "please," and "thank you" when speaking with the Family.

BE RESPONSIVE

- If anyone in the Family makes a request, we get it done, zero questions asked.
- "No" is not part of your vocabulary; figure out a way.
- Do it now; if someone has to ask you about the status of a task, you've waited too long.

BE A TEAM PLAYER

- No arguing with your supervisor or other domestic staff, even in domestic spaces.
- Outside visitors require prior approval; no overnight visitors in quarters.
- No unmade beds, dirty quarters, or leaving messes in the shared domestic spaces.

Fen

It took me exactly two minutes and forty-eight seconds to move after Jane left the store. That's the running time of "September Gurls" by Big Star, which played over the speakers while I stared over the record stacks, cataloging all the things she'd told me.

All the things I'd said wrong. I could tell by the way my aunt was giving me her disappointed face that I'd screwed up. And once I replayed everything in my head, by the way Jane reacted to me.

Everything goes from a *tranquil two* to a *tense ten* for me these days.

Regret gnawed at me from the inside.

When the song ended, Haley came in to work a closing shift on register. And I took full advantage of the fact that I could now leave the sales floor. My mind wasn't on work anymore. It was on Jane's face. And how I'd made her so unhappy in such a short amount of time.

How Eddie could ruin my beshitted life when he wasn't even here.

Aunt Pari was chatting with a regular customer, so as soon as

Haley clocked in, I dipped out, heading past an EMPLOYEES ONLY sign and ascending steps to the dark timbered balcony above the sales floor. When I got to the top, I threw open the door and was momentarily blinded.

Squinting away midday sun, I ducked into a light-filled office that perched over the back of the shop. It was chaotic: piles of packing slips and stacks of books on a sad couch that looked like it died in 1985. Don't think the desk had been cleaned in twenty years. I was supposed to be helping Aunt Pari reorganize up here, but we'd only managed to make our way through about a third of the hundreds of records filed in cubbies lining the walls—stuff for our mail-order business and rarities that we didn't put on the sales floor. A few scratched-up LPs.

But none of that mattered. What mattered was the office window.

What mattered up here was the perfect view.

Half of the far wall was glass, and it looked out over the lake. All you can see is blue water. Sky. Mountains. The edges of the town hugging the lake. The waterfall. You can see everything.

Everything.

You feel like you're king of the whole damn town in here. It helps when you're feeling like I felt at that moment. Filled with regret and bewildered.

But also—

Keyed up. Overwrought.

Beside myself.

I was a nervous wreck.

Because Jane had just walked back into my life. She was at the lake for the summer. I would see her. The girl who'd been haunting my dreams for years.

The girl who was dating Eddie.

"Fuck my life," I groaned, spinning around in the desk chair as I held my face in my hands.

"No complaining in the office," Aunt Pari said as she waltzed into the room, tossing me a look through wire-rimmed glasses. "Scream your head off down there, and you'll cost us customers. Scream your head off up here, and it will eventually break your heart. I don't know what was happening down there today, but don't bring it up here. The office isn't for negativity."

"Sorry," I said. "I'll keep it bottled up inside until I explode."

"That's what we did back in my day. I turned out all right."

My mother had two sisters—the three Kasabian girls. Since my father kicked me out of the house, I spent most of my time with the Kasabian side of the family. I think their weird ways were starting to rub off on me.

"When your grandfather saw this view, he knew he had to have this location," Aunt Pari said, telling me a story I'd heard a bajillion times. "Not Brady's shop, two blocks down. That was the cheaper choice, but Papa wanted this view."

"Because it was the best."

"The best. So he paid out of the nose, and now he's in Glendale, enjoying retirement, while we enjoy this view," she says, looking back at me with a soft smile. "This is special. It's a good view. Don't take out your aggression on the lake."

"I wouldn't dream of it."

"And I won't ask you why you were shouting at that girl," she said, handing me the green, dildo-looking dog toy. "She left this, by the way."

Oh. Huh. Probably because she got distracted when I was shouting at her. Like an angry troll. I mean . . . what was wrong with me?

Aunt Pari searched through a stack of papers on the long desk that stretched below the great window. A tiny gold cross swung free from her neck and glinted in the sunlight as she pressed a button on a phone. "Haley? Where is that list of bands for the festival? The ones with in-store events?"

"In your email," I murmured. "Just open it and read it on the screen."

"I need a print copy," Aunt Pari said, gesturing. "I have to hold it in my hands. You kids don't understand. When all of this technology breaks down, I'll have the printed copy."

Aunt Pari was always concerned about techno-failure. For someone who insisted on positivity in the office, she was seriously hung up on the doom of the internet.

After a moment, Haley's voice came through the speaker: "If you can't find it, you can print another copy from your email. But remember that the last print job got cancelled when the labels got stuck in the printer, and you need to clear it first. Do you want me to show you how again?"

"No," Aunt Pari replied, eyeing a giant printer on the desk as if it were a predator before her gaze shifted to me. "Can you hard clear a something-something job from a print spool whatchamadiggy?"

Sadly, I knew what she meant. And though it took her about three lifetimes to find the right email to print, once she did, I fixed the printer issues and gave her the printed piece of paper she desired. It was five minutes that I wasn't thinking about Jane. And as I soon as they were up, the universe threw me back into my own misery.

"Okay, fine. I take it from all the shouting downstairs that she is Eddie's girlfriend? The girl with the green dog toy," Aunt Pari said, gesturing to the rubber pickle sitting on the desk near my elbow.

"Apparently so," I said, trying to force my stomach not to knot up.

"Didn't know he was seeing anyone."

"Knew he was seeing lots of someones. Just not one in particular," I corrected.

Not *that* one. Not Jane. My Jane. Not that she was ever truly mine. But I spent a lot of time when I was younger wishing she'd just look my way for five seconds. Then Eddie started blocking the view.

"Well," Aunt Pari said, shrugging. "Not as if I run into your brother much these days. Wouldn't really know what's going on with his personal life. But I'm surprised that your mother didn't say anything to me. She tends to share gossip."

My mother shared what she wanted to. She definitely knew what Jane meant to me. If Eddie was dating Jane, I'm not sure my mother would tell me. She might be afraid I'd react . . . like I did today.

"Didn't Eddie leave for the Philippines?" Aunt Pari said.

He did. Which meant Eddie wasn't here.

I stared at the green dog toy.

"Aunt Pari?" I asked. "Do you believe in second chances?"

"I believe in anything that involves hope," she said, smiling.

I believed in anything that involved retribution, holding a grudge, and long-term plans for revenge. But maybe I could make room for a little hope. Just to switch things up.

I'd been in the dark for so long. Maybe it was time to crawl out of my cave and act like a human being. I could start by apologizing to Jane for acting like a monster.

Maybe we weren't enemies after all.

Maybe we could be friends. Friendly? Not shouting?

I just knew one thing. I could not exist in the same town with Jane and stay silent.

That I could not do.

Jane

The remainder of the drive back to the lodge lasted forever and a day. Dad dropped Mad Dog off at the main house's front door, and we parked the Fintail safely in the garage without discussing anything Mad Dog brought up about making peace with the lake. Dad was bothered by it, though. I could tell. So I whispered "I'm not going near the dam" against his back as he locked the car. He reached back and patted me, nodding once, but didn't reply.

Maybe that helped. Sometimes it was hard to read him when feelings were involved.

When I stepped into the carriage house and let Frida Kahlo off her leash, she made a wild dash through a narrow entry hall for her water bowl in the connecting prep kitchen—and nearly caused a pedestrian collision in the process. Curses were discharged in her direction. Guess all the domestics were getting ready for Velvet's shindig. Including our boss, the head housekeeper.

I tried to sneak away but wasn't fast enough.

"I've been looking all over for you," Norma Dewberry said, one hand on her hip, the other fanning her face. Exie thought she might be going through menopause; Norma was always talking about being hot when no one else was, and she was constantly tetchy for no good reason.

"Wow, it's a circus back here. I'll just grab some chow for lunch and get out of your hair," I said.

"Chow" was code for staff food, which was different than the food that Exie made for the Family. Different meals for different people. Different ingredients kept in different refrigerators, and all of it tallied to a strict budget.

Norma frowned at me from behind bobbed gray hair. She was wearing the required domestic uniform of the Larsen domestics: khaki pants and a black polo shirt with Mad Dog's personal emblem stitched on the breast. "Did you use your company card? Where's the receipt?"

"You said to log it and turn it in . . . " Never mind. No sense in arguing with her. Frida was running around underfoot while I struggled to fish the receipt from my purse. "Here."

She glanced at it briefly. She didn't want it now. Just proof that I'd saved it. "Why aren't you on a walkie? Not that I can understand you half the time anyway."

Exie was walking behind her with a pan of water and gave Norma a middle finger behind her back. *Thank you,* I told the chef with my eyes as quickly as I could. Norma notices too much.

All the domestics were supposed to carry walkie-talkies from morning until 8 p.m. But it was mostly for Norma to bark orders to the rest of the staff, and it could be challenging to listen to chatter about toilet cleaning and kitchen supply emergencies for hours on end. My word-pixie didn't like it. So I conveniently forgot to carry it, or I turned my earpiece off.

"And why are you in street clothes?" Norma asked. "Where's your polo shirt?"

"Do you need me to help Exie with the dinner prep?" I asked brightly. A smile, but not too big. "Because Velvet also needs me to help her with assistant stuff before the party. Which I'm supposed to be attending. I need to bring her this shampoo . . . stat."

See what I did there? Deflection and reminder, which is key when you're dealing with a Negative Vibe Merchant like Mother Superior.

"Oh, right." Norma lifted a hand to adjust her earpiece, and light shone on a scar that crossed her cheek. Before Dad and I came to Mad Dog's house, Norma fought off burglars who were trying to rob the Bel Air studio. In the tussle, Mad Dog was stabbed in the leg, and Norma ended up with ten stitches on her cheek. The burglars, however, lost an eye and broke a leg trying to escape through the window, and both ended up serving a lot of time in the state prison.

Norma was negative. Mean. Tough. A bully. But she would literally take a knife in the face for Mad Dog, and she ran this house as if it were a duty bequeathed by a higher power. She was not going anywhere.

If I didn't want to spend eternity bowing to Mother Superior, I had to get out of domestic service.

"Velvet's with Rosa at the pool," a voice called across the kitchen. Kamal Reddy. The thirtysomething Indian American bodyguard had been in charge of Mad Dog's security for about five years or so, having taken over from his father, who was back at the Bel Air house. Though he was mostly a nerdy tech guy— cameras, computers—he was trained and always armed to the teeth. Ever since the stabbing incident, Mad Dog had been paranoid. "I'm headed out there. I'll take that to her if you'd like," he said, nodding at the shampoo bag. "I just dropped off something in your room that she had me bring over from the main house. A dress for tonight. Might want to check on it . . . stat," he said playfully.

Kamal could be nice. I mean, I had hoped Velvet would have forgotten about lending me clothes. That made me feel uncomfortable. But at least it got me away from Norma, so I gave him the shampoo, and he gave me a look that told me he was on my side.

"I don't like that. I'm going to have a talk with Velvet. You don't see me borrowing Rosa's clothes," Norma complained. "And why in God's name is the dog whining like that? Where's her toy? Get her settled upstairs before I have Exie put her on the dinner menu."

Before Norma could change her mind, I grabbed a sandwich and drink from the staff fridge, then whistled to Frida, and the two of us jogged away from the chaos, up a short set of stairs that led to a second story over the carriage house's garage.

Staff quarters. Quiet, at least for a few moments.

Nothing that interesting up there, just a shared rec room with a TV and couple of couches, and in the corner, Frida's fenced playpen area—a dog bed and a graveyard of rejected stuffed toy carcasses. I suspected she was using the furry carcass pile to escape, climbing the bodies *Walking Dead*–style, so I spread them out strategically when I sat her in the pen. Then I headed down a narrow hall lined with bedroom doors.

Well. "Bedroom" was being generous. Other domestics have called them prison cells, considering the gray paint on the walls and the matching gray tile on the floors. I made a quick turn inside the room I'd been assigned that summer, but it was just like everyone else's: nightstand and single bed pushed against one wall with a tiny window overlooking a gravel road that led into the garage below. The tile floor was easy to sweep but a little cold on bare feet, especially first thing in the morning when I had to run into the rec room to pee, because that's where the shared bathroom and showers were.

But still. I had my own room. And before Fen ruined my day (summer, life), I could dream about getting out of this room and into my own apartment with Eddie. I checked my phone for any messages from him, but nope. I thought about texting a couple friends back in L.A. about my current straits, but they wouldn't understand. We were friendly, but not "listen to my weird boy problems" close. It was hard enough trying to maintain friendships, living under Mad Dog's roof. Dealing with the speech therapy, missing half the school year . . . I lost bonds with people.

The dress Kamal had dropped off was here. I ignored it and ate my sandwich. I barely had time to finish and slip into work clothes before Norma was calling me back downstairs. Once she got her hooks in me, I was done. It was one thing after another, menial tasks that added up. Because the lodge grounds were expansive, running from the carriage house to the main took time, back and forth through the covered walkway that connected them. Never mind all the stairs.

Somehow, I also managed to help Velvet sort out clothes and helped set her hair. I didn't realize I was signing up for hair duty. Or for being in the background of her video calls with her friends. But a half hour before the guests were due to arrive, I realized I wasn't dressed or showered and that Frida hadn't been fed or walked, and I'd never been so happy that I cut my hair this short, because it pretty much dried in a minute and styled itself.

Still. I was late. I raced from the carriage house to the main house, slipping a walkie into the dress's side pocket and attaching the clear earpiece so that I could radio the kitchen if Velvet needed anything quickly during dinner—the only task I knew an assistant did during parties like this. Starla had filled me in on that much. Still, I wasn't moving fast enough because my phone—juggled in my other dress pocket—buzzed with a text from Velvet:

Where are you sis??

Crap. Laughter and music floated up from the pool as I hurried through a living room filled with modern bookcases. The big glass doors were open to the courtyard patio, where a kidney-shaped pool curved around natural stone, and the sky above it was that soft ombré of orange and purple—almost dark, but not quite.

Candlelit tables dotted the patio, and behind them, an Indian sitar player was plucking out hypnotic melodies that reverberated around the pool. For a moment, I wondered if he was the "surprise" of Velvet's party. Then I took stock of the guests.

Dad hovered to the side, near some shrubbery. Mad Dog lounged at a nearby table alongside Rosa in her wheelchair. She had scoliosis and a lot of back pain that came with it. Hence, Starla and her healing hands. Speaking of, Starla cheerfully chatted with someone I didn't know—a forgettable white guy in his thirties—and some people I vaguely did: a middle-aged Black couple, the Taylors, who owned a winery in Sonoma County. They were friends with Mad Dog and dined at the lodge every summer—he knew them through ex-wife number two.

Then I spotted Velvet and her party companions a few yards in front of me. A graying dark-haired couple in their forties. The woman was taller than the man, with a big head of wild curls and heels that made their height difference even more pronounced, and if you'd told me I was standing in front of Frank Zappa with a horseshoe mustache and a wide soul patch, I would have believed it.

I realized with a shock who they were.

The Sarafians. As in, Serj and Jasmine.

Eddie and Fen's parents. Their *very important* music-industry parents. Who I'd never met. And Eddie wasn't here to introduce us.

"Surprise," I whispered.

Jane

"There she is!" Velvet announced in a peppy tone.

She blinked at the dress she'd picked out for me, which was baggy up top and just the tiniest bit see-through, making my already underwhelming bosom resemble two frightened kittens hiding in a pillowcase. With my clipped hair and sandals, and the walkie and my phone in my pockets dragging everything down like the weight of the goddamn world, I might've been mistaken for a lost waif in need of a bowl of porridge.

Had I known I was going to be meeting the Sarafians, I would have summoned up a magical army of singing birds and bugs to help me stitch my own gown from the curtains in my room.

"Serj and Jasmine, this is our Jane Marlow," Velvet said, smiling it all away. Under her breath to me she murmured cheerfully, "Who didn't have to wear a walkie, haha."

Yeah, regretting that now. Norma's voice barking commands to the staff in my ear only made this worse.

"She's practically a baby sister," Velvet said. "We shared a nanny and everything." Uh, yeah, but *no*. Where was my dad? I hated when she said stuff like that. . . . "And now she's Eddie's girl.

Those sneaky kids have been dating behind all our backs—can you believe it?"

Oh God. No, I cannot believe . . . that you just said that.

Want to kill Velvet. Want to kill her so hard.

"Jane," Serj said, mouth turning up beneath his mustache. Friendly. Kind and casual enough, but there was a little formalness to the way he greeted me in his black suit coat and jeans. And as he reached back to grab a glass of wine from the table, his gaze quickly surveyed me, head to foot, and I swear I saw him make a face. The kind of face you make when you want to laugh at something, but you know it's not the time or place to do so.

He was confused by me. Or didn't approve. I felt as if something was wrong with me—was it the dress? My boyish cropped hair? A slow and heavy humiliation crept over me. I gave him the best smile I could and canted my head politely as his wife stepped toward me.

"You are Eddie's girl?" Jasmine said. "I can't believe he kept this from me. I'm so happy to meet you. Let me see you, Jane. That's not short for anything, right? How old are you, dear?"

Whoa, a lot of questions. My response got eaten by my word-pixie. I stood mute and nervous, dying a little inside, as Jasmine's arms emerged from the glittery black shawl draped over her bare shoulders. Her hands were soft and warm as they gripped mine.

"Just Jane," Velvet offered quickly, seeing that I was struggling. "Freshly graduated from high school back home in L.A. Eighteen."

"Fennec's age," she murmured, steadily holding my hands in

hers. She smelled faintly of sweet flowers. Brown eyes ringed with heavy makeup searched mine as if, like her husband, there was something she couldn't figure out. But there wasn't judgement from her. Just curiosity. "How long has this been going on with Eddie? I'm just trying to figure out how . . . logistically. You aren't in the same cities."

"Oh, we started talking after my accident at the dam." I struggled for the words. "After. The festival app. We . . . just talked." Privately. He hadn't told his mother that I existed, apparently, which was freaking me out a little. But how could I judge? I didn't tell my dad about Eddie until I was introducing them at the airport.

"Online?"

I nodded.

She made an amused noise, as if she couldn't believe it. "Eddie is no wordsmith."

That made me laugh a little. I relaxed. "No, ma'am. But he's nice."

Jasmine smiled softly. "He *is* nice, isn't he? Sometimes. He tries very hard in whatever he does. He wants to be the best, like Serj."

"No such thing as second place," Serj said from over her shoulder, raising his wineglass to the Taylors. "Isn't that right?"

"Competition is for the young. I had a stroke. I just make wine now," Mr. Taylor said.

Mad Dog lifted his glass. "And good wine it is. I'm the same. Just want to make good music and get paid." He pointed at Serj.

"And the longer I don't hear from my lawyer on this little seven seas trip your kid took, the longer I'm nervous about that last part."

"He'll call, big dog, just relax. Meditate or whatever you do," Serj said, laughing.

Yikes.

Jasmine didn't seem bothered by their talk about Eddie. She lifted my hands to her face and inhaled. "Onion."

My ears burned. "I . . . helped prep dinner in the kitchen."

Velvet looked as embarrassed as I felt. "It's an all-hands-on-deck situation at the lake, Jas. Sometimes I even help."

Well. She sometimes ate breakfast in the kitchen and chatted with Exie while she was prepping food. I guess that counted.

"Don't be ashamed," Jasmine told me. "Onions remind me of cooking with my mother when I was your age. We would cut up a dozen red onions for her to pickle, and our hands would smell like that all day." She laughed. "I still like to cook with Ms. Makruhi, my housekeeper."

"You do?" I felt a little spellbound by her. Maybe it was the tiers of teardrop diamond pendants that spilled down her throat in a neat little row, each lower than the one above. Maybe it was her bountiful hair, all ringlet curls. It reminded me of Fen's. But on her, it was so glamorous.

"I think you'll be good for Eddie." She squeezed my hands and let go, smiling genuinely. "I'm very happy to get to know you. We will be good friends. Come, tell me about yourself."

Could you fall in love with someone's mother? I was pretty

sure I was in mother-love with Jasmine. She had some kind of weird magnetism, and I wanted to follow her around like a puppy and tell her everything. I didn't care about my word-pixie tripping me up. I didn't care about the droopy dress, or that Velvet had left us alone. She asked me just the right questions. My brain unlocked, and I could answer. Before I realized how much I was talking, I'd told her about Frida and graduation, and I'd taken her over to Dad and introduced them.

"We've met before at a fundraiser that Mad Dog attended a few years ago," she said. "You kindly drove me and my son to the ER. He'd hurt his leg, and I couldn't find Serj."

I forgot about that. . . .

"I remember," Dad said. "You sang to him in the car. Was that opera? You have a beautiful voice."

"I sing in my church choir; it's nothing. And my son got a few stitches that day. Kids . . ."

Kids? She was talking about *Fen*. He's the one who rode in my dad's car and got stitches. I remembered that now. I think I was fifteen, and I'd talked to Fen that day before he hurt his leg.

"You've raised a fine daughter," she told my father. "I'm sure it hasn't been easy."

"No, ma'am," he said. "But she's worth it. Would do anything for her."

She nodded slowly. "Yes. The things we do for our children . . ."

But that wasn't exactly true, was it? Because they'd kicked Fen out of the house.

As they chatted lightly, Norma's voice crackled in my earpiece.

This time, it was much louder and insistent. "Norma for Jane, repeat—Norma for Jane!"

Shit. I turned my head to the side and pressed the talk function on my earpiece cord. "Pool patio," I informed her in a low voice, reporting my location.

"You have a visitor at the front door of the main house," she hissed unhappily.

"Go again?" I said, not comprehending how this could be true.

"Unauthorized visitor, front door. Make it fast."

I didn't know anyone here, and I didn't want to be torn away from Jasmine. But it was getting really dark now, and they were bringing out all the small plates that Velvet wanted circulating. If I was going to slip away, now was a good time. So I excused myself, leaving Jasmine with my father—who had heard Norma's message over the walkie and was giving me the eyebrow arch of the century. I just shook my head, confused, and swiftly headed back through the main house, into the foyer, past the giant floral arrangement.

Making myself small, I peeped through the sidelight at the entrance to see if I could tell who was there.

A dark figure stood on the porch, back turned to the big front doors.

I took a deep breath.

The figure turned around when I cracked open the left door, and the porch light shone down on his face.

Fen.

"Having a fancy party, are we?" he said, hands clasped behind his back and rocking forward on scuffed black low-tops. He was standing at a funny angle, as if he was hiding something. "Must be, if Mad Dog's got some Ravi Shankar wannabe cranking out tunes. What the shit is going on in there? Are people dropping acid? And why are you dressed like a member of Charles Manson's cult? This isn't very metal."

A storm of confused emotions gathered inside my chest and threw bolts of lightning around my body. I'd just spent the last fifteen minutes talking to his mother. Now *he* appears?

Had I angered some god?

He shouldn't be here.

"W-what are you . . . ?" I started.

"Doing here?" he finished, squinting as he pushed hair out of his eyes that was an utter disaster. He nodded toward the cars parked in the gravel driveway: two luxury sedans up front, and past them, a white Jeep with no doors, just a skeletal frame—every flat surface covered in band decals, muddy tires. "Funny, because that's what I said to myself when I drove up and spotted my parents' BMW. Did someone forget my invite, or maybe it got lost in the mail?"

"Your parents are guests of Mad Dog." I was tempted to leave it at that and shut the door in his dumb face, but he was wearing a T-shirt (big block print on the front, PSYCHO KILLER, and in a talk bubble, QU'EST-CE QUE C'EST) with the sleeves cut off, which was infuriating, because it was as if he was trying to show off his arms. Like, *Look at me, I'm skinny and muscular—it's not even hot outside, but I'm going walk around with nude arms, like a swaggery guttersnipe.* Ugh! He just set every cell in my body on fire with *fury.*

"You're trespassing," I told him dumbly.

"On the front steps? I rang the doorbell . . . a mean woman sneered at me and then went to fetch you. That's not trespassing. A delivery person trespasses far more than me."

"Why are you here?"

"You asked that already," he said, pulling out a paper bag stamped with VICTORY VINYL from behind his back. It was crinkled around a long object, and from the shape and the pirate hat sticking out of the top, I could guess what. "Left your phallic toy at my place of business."

"It's Captain Pickles. Don't say it like it's dirty."

"Please. First, dogs love me. Second, there are dildos at the sex shop down the street from us that are less raunchy. Maybe your little guy is trying to tell you something. Is he neutered?"

"*She* is spayed. Her name is Frida Kahlo. Put some respect on it when you say it."

"Damn, okay," he said. "Didn't know she was the reincarnation of a famous painter."

I tried to take the toy from him, but he held it just out of reach, and I nearly bumped into him trying to snatch it. "She's not my dog. I watch her for Velvet. It's my job. I'm her PA."

"Are you now?"

I crossed my arms over my baggy dress. "What do you want from me, Fen?"

"Nothing, really. Might be nice to continue our conversation."

"Were we having one? I thought you were yelling at me."

He held up a finger. "I was, and for that, I apologize. I let my emotions get out of control, and no good can come of that. I'm truly sorry for the shouting. Can we try again?"

"Try what again? The part where you tell me that I'm your enemy because I'm dating Eddie?"

His jaw clicked to one side, as if the sound of Eddie's name had some kind of power over him.

"And again," I reminded him, "Eddie told me to steer clear of you."

"Why would he do that?" Fen asked. "Little strange, don't you think?"

I did, actually. "I thought we'd already established that you're the black sheep of the family. Kicked out of the family house. All that. Seems reason enough to me."

Fen paused. "Do you know why I got kicked out?"

"Not my business why you don't get along with your father."

"It's true. I don't." But he could tell by my face that I didn't know why. And after a short silence stretched between us, Fen offered an explanation. "My brother and I have always been . . . competitive. It's how my dad raised us. There can only be one winner. Who loves Daddy more? Eddie does, so he gets a trip to Los Cabos. Fen loses, so he gets no dinner. So Eddie started making sure he'd *always* get the trip, understand?"

"Um, okay?"

"Things escalated over the last couple of years. Eddie saw that I was happy with someone about a year ago, a girl whose father worked in marketing at Sarafian Events, so Eddie asked our father to have him fired. He made up some shit about catching her father stealing something from the festival offices."

A small noise escaped my mouth. "Eddie wouldn't do that."

"Oh, he would. He does. And he did. The girl's family ended up moving across the country. She didn't want anything to do with me after that. And that was the final straw for me. That's when I went after my father and Eddie."

"I don't—"

"I filed a formal complaint with Eddie's university and said that my father had paid the school thousands of dollars to get Eddie pushed past the admissions board. I threatened to take it to the FBI. They quietly kicked him out rather than get the press involved. Which is when my father told me to get the hell out of the family house. Now I'm in exile."

"I . . . don't believe you."

He shrugged. "It's the truth. Ask Eddie if you trust his word over mine. It's just that I can't figure out how you got to that."

"To what?"

"Trusting his word over mine."

I stared at him, dumbfounded. "I barely know you."

"And that bothers me. Because I've thought of you every day since you fell in the dam."

Was he mentally unwell? Or was my word-pixie acting up and I just hadn't realized it? Had I mixed something up? Should I be concerned?

"We shared something that night," he said in a low voice. As if he were trying to remind me of a drunken hookup. But I'd definitely remember that. And no. Not with Fen. Definitely not that night at the dam. Events around my fall were a touch foggy in my head, due to my injury, but I'd remember *that*.

I glanced over my shoulder into the dark, open doorway, unable to see past the foyer, then whispered, "People might hear you. And what the hell are you talking about? I never talked to you that night before I fell."

"Not talking about before. Talking about *after*. You really don't remember? My mouth, your lungs," he said in a seductive voice. "The gift of life."

I stared at him. My hands started shaking.

Our eyes met, and a long moment hung between us as frogs sang in the darkening trees by the lake. He was serious now. This wasn't a joke, and he wasn't teasing.

"Coming back to you now, huh?" he said softly.

Was it? I remembered him at the dam. . . . I remembered someone's face in front of mine when I was choking up water. I remembered someone shouting for help. But I could not see who rescued me. I'd never been able to see that face. Not in the two years since the accident.

I tried to deny it. "You didn't . . . did not. You weren't the one who got me out of the water. Who rescued me?"

It was Eddie. Had to be. When I introduced Eddie to my father, I said, "This is the guy who saved me." It was Eddie's only redeeming feature in my father's eyes.

"I pulled you out of the water," Fen insisted quietly. "You have to believe me, Jane."

I believed him. I couldn't say why, but we both knew it. Some things you can lie about. But the way I was feeling, like my chest was bursting with dam water and the world was spinning around us, like there was nothing but the weight of what we shared . . . that was real.

We both stood together, staring off at the lake, then at each other.

"Why?" I asked in a small voice.

"Because." He shook his head, and there was that emotion in his eyes again. He was upset. Over me? "I don't know why. You fell in the water. I jumped in after you. It was just instinct. I've been over it a thousand times. Why me? Why didn't someone else do it?"

I gripped one elbow against my side to stop the trembling. "You were . . . just there."

"Maybe," he said, shrugging with one shoulder and shaking his head. "For a long time, I've been dismissing it as just a random part of my life that just happened for no reason. Then here you are again. Now I don't think it's random anymore. I was right the first time. We're connected, Jane Marlow."

He tilted his body inward to show me why he'd been standing at an angle. It wasn't the bag he'd been hiding, but a tattoo on his far shoulder. A tattoo that looked like a pre-Raphaelite painting of a beautiful, drowned girl in a river, surrounded by flowers.

Ophelia, from *Hamlet*.

"Got that a year ago," he said.

"Sweet holy night," I murmured, brain sputtering. "That's . . . a dead girl? I'm . . ."

"I know. I was embarrassed to show you, but there it is," he said, covering it up with his hand. "It's weird. I'm weird. I'm screwed up. That's not fair to you. You've been haunting me. And I don't know what to do about it." He paced away from me and turned around. "I probably shouldn't be here, huh?"

"What do you want from me?"

He shook his head. Shrugged again. If he was trying to play casual, it wasn't working. His eyes betrayed him. There was nothing casual about the way he was looking at me. I didn't know much, but I knew the longing there. I wasn't sure how because I didn't remember Eddie ever looking at me quite like that. Didn't remember *anyone* looking at me like that.

I glanced away, flustered. "I'm with your brother."

"Do you love him?"

"What kind of question is that?"

"What kind of *answer* is that?" he said, confidence rebounding. "Do you love him, yes or no? Simple question, really."

I loved the way Eddie looked. I loved the way his arms felt around me. I loved the way people looked at me when I was with him. But none of those were the right answers. And I was taking too long to get to *any* answer because all I could think about was how Eddie had lied to me about rescuing me from the dam.

My silence said more than I'd intended.

And I could tell by how the corners of Fen's mouth slowly curled, it said something to him, too.

Heels clicked, and a sweet floral scent wafted behind me. "Fen-jan? My shining star? What in the name of the saints are you doing out here?" Jasmine reached for Fen and pulled him toward her, staining both his cheeks faintly with her lipstick. "What's going on? Are you upset?"

"Mama," he protested, sniffling briskly. "I was, uh, returning a dog toy that was left in the record shop." He awkwardly handed me Captain Pickles with those long fingers of his. "I didn't know you'd be here."

She gave a cursory glance at the crumpled bag in my hand as I tried to compose myself and hide my wild emotions. She was quick, though. And sharp.

"Small world," she said in a gentle voice, turning toward her son. "It's been a whole week, my love. You've lost another pound. I'm coming over to your aunt Zabel's tomorrow to feed you. Tell me how you two know each other?"

"We just met," I said.

"Again," he added.

She started to say something, tilted her head, and then thought better of it, biting her lip.

How close were Jasmine and Fen? Closer than I'd realized. He was on the outs with his father and Eddie, but there was a bond between these two. She'd obviously seen his tattoo—I mean, there it was. Did she know about him pulling me out of the dam?

"Jane was actually telling me all about her and Eddie," Fen said to his mother in a falsely bright voice. "Like how they are going to be shacking up when he gets back to the lake."

I blinked at him. A sickly feeling gathered in my stomach.

"What?" Jasmine murmured. "Is this true, Jane?"

Captain Pickles was heavy in my hand. If ever a rubber dog toy could maim a person, I wished that time could be now. Why would he say this? After the last few minutes?

"We . . . that is, uh, Eddie mentioned that . . ." Oh God. I was sweating now. "He said he wanted to find . . . a place at the lake for us. Not a house. Smaller." Damn you, word-pixie!

"An apartment?" she said, not noticing that I was struggling. "Move out of the house? Oh my. This is more serious than I thought."

"He said he would have to . . ." I tried to remember Eddie's exact words. "Run it by Serj first. That he might help out with a place. When Eddie gets back from overseas. That I should think of where I want to live. But Serj would be the final say."

One hand flew to her heart. "Of course Serj will help. Serj is never the final say."

"Classic rookie mistake," Fen said. "Could've told you that."

Jasmine hissed and made a closing gesture with her fingers at Fen, then relented and smiled. "Eddie is like his father. He thinks they are the center of the world. People who think that are fools. But we love fools, because you cannot help the heart, can you?"

"The heart is a big, dumb muscle, Mama," Fen said.

She smiled softly at him, then at me. "Well, this all very interesting and unexpected."

"Isn't it just?" Fen said.

"Well. I won't say that I don't have reservations. Moving in with someone is a big deal. At least, it was when I was your age. Maybe it's different now. Tell me, Jane, is this what you want?"

Jasmine said to me. "You want an apartment with my son?"

Uh . . . What kind of question was that? I didn't know how to answer. It felt like she was asking, *Do you want to sleep with my son?* So I said, "If that's what Eddie wants?"

Fen made a distressed grunting sound.

Jasmine shook her head. "No, no. What do *you* want, my dear? You." When I didn't answer, she held both hands together and said, "Let me rephrase. Would you like to move out of Mad Dog's very big house and into your own very small apartment?"

I answered. "Yes."

Fen said something wicked and filthy under his breath. I slid him a glance, but his eyes were so dark and narrow, I couldn't tell what he was thinking. But I knew what *I* was thinking, and I tried to project it to him with the power of my mind: *You're the one who brought this up, asshole. You! Your fault!*

"Very well," Jasmine said with a curt nod. "We will go apartment hunting."

"What?" A clammy terror snaked through my limbs.

Fen laughed, but it was the kind of humorless reflex laugh people sometimes make when they've just been informed that a person they love has died.

Inside, my head was filled with white, hot panic.

"Next week. Give me a few days to arrange it," she said. "My sister has an ex who's a realtor. They can find something nice for a young couple. Let's go inside and tell your father."

No, no, no! I absolutely wasn't ready to drop this on my dad.

Fen gave me dark look that I couldn't identify—but one that

set off a few more crackles of lightning in my chest—and then his mother interrupted what was between us, cradling his face with both hands. "Scram, my Fennec. And you'd better hope *your* father doesn't catch you here, or there will be hell to pay. I love you forever and ever, until the sun burns out."

"I love you so much it feels like the sun already died," he responded darkly.

Who *were* these people?

They were nothing like Eddie. Nothing at all. Eddie was all Serj's boy, apparently.

And I wasn't sure where that left me.

Jane Marlow:

Eddie, when you get this, can you please text back?

I'm pretty sure you're in Manila right now

Jane Marlow:

They have Wi-Fi and beautiful hotels in Manila

I know for sure Gordon is staying at a five star

Jane Marlow:

Just text me when you wake up, okay?

Jane Marlow:

I talked to Fen

Jane Marlow:

Eddie?

Fen

My body was buzzing. I was a hive of bees that had just been kicked, and all this pent-up energy was pinging around inside my rib cage. I needed to fly. Sting. Swarm something.

Instead, I just peeled out of the Larsens' driveway a little too fast for Ye Old Skeleton King, my 1997 stripped Jeep, whose wheels kicked up a shit-ton of gravel while the engine protested. Nearly spun out. That's all I needed, a rollover. I couldn't die in a fiery crash in front of Mad Dog's house, where my father already waited with a glass in hand to celebrate. Too easy.

"Breathe," I told myself, gripping the wheel as soft green light glowed from my dash. All I could see was Jane's face. The shock in her eyes when I dropped the bomb about her and Eddie wanting to find an apartment . . . Why did I open my big mouth? If I could've erased everything that happened after Mama came outside and continued from that point, who knows what would have happened.

Maybe it still could?

Jane had come back into my life. Eddie was trying to *destroy* my life. And because I had no self-control, I was now trying to help him get the job done faster, apparently.

"Brought this on yourself," I told the rearview mirror. "How're you gonna fix it?"

I couldn't tell my mother to call off the apartment hunt. It was too late for that; I could see it in her eyes when she had her mind made up about something. But if I did nothing, I was going to lose any chance I had to have any further normal conversation with Jane. And that's all I wanted right now.

Well . . .

I tried not to think too hard about *everything* I wanted, or I really would roll the Skeleton King over on one of these rocky curves, and then we'd all end up back in a watery grave. The lake giveth, the lake taketh away.

If I was going to talk to Jane again without making the conversation go all finger-pointy and shouty, I'd need to figure out how to stop sabotaging myself. Get control of my emotions. Be a normal, polite person.

Let's face it, I needed help. Advice. To get these fucking bees out of my body.

The woods around this side of the lake were dark and deep, and the wind sent chills under my shirt. I put on some nice, dark electropop and let my mind wander with the curve of the road. Halfway into town, I realized where I was going.

"Friend-o, we're going to Moonbeam's," I told the Jeep.

I needed to make a pit stop first to find something he'd want. That took longer than I wanted. It was almost ten by the time I made it around the lake.

Moonbeam wouldn't care. Up all night, sleep all day.

I texted him to let him know I was coming and parked the Jeep outside his lake house, which sat on the northeast side of Condor, just past where the Strip petered out into warehouses and rental cabins. Not ideal lakeside property. If there were a low rent side of town, this would be it, but there wasn't, so it was just quiet and away from everything else.

Which Moonbeam liked because he was agoraphobic.

He needed to be as far away from the festival grounds as possible. Not just because of the crowds. He had his reasons.

His house was just a basic two-story, zero frills. I headed up the back steps that led to an enclosed deck overlooking the lake. Ivy covered a chain-link gate that was locked at all times, and there was a camera and a buzzer. He got his groceries delivered—everything, really.

I rang the buzzer and showed him what I had in my hand. "It's me, man. Let's trade."

"Is that imported Curtis Mayfield?" a rough voice said. "*Sweet Exorcist* Buddha label?"

"Also got a German 1970 import of his first solo album," I said, showing a peek at the second album I hid behind as a tease. Moonbeam had a soft spot for 1970s soul. "I need to look through that eighties punk crate you showed me a few weeks ago, and I want to see whatever new stuff you've picked up since I was here last time. Not the usual crap. No reissues."

"Chasing rare wax, huh? Come in, my friend. Let's trade," an excited voice said through the speaker. He buzzed me in. I knew he would. Moonbeam was a longtime friend of my aunt Pari's cousin. He'd done business with Victory Vinyl for decades—trade only. My grandpa Kasabian used to bring him weed from some guy in Humboldt County back in the early 2000s.

I pulled the door shut behind me and stopped to pet his two longhair cats, Peaches and Herb, who immediately rubbed their loose fur all over my jeans. The back part of his deck was covered and extended to his living room through a pair of doors that stayed open. His elaborate vintage stereo equipment was inside—he was all about hearing the authentic warmth of the wax—and hooked up to speakers out on the deck. Half his shabby living room furniture was out here too. My parents had a fancy open-air room at their villa with an outdoor kitchen near their lake dock, but this was *not* that.

"Let me see those," he said, emerging from the house with two stacked record crates, flip-flops smacking against his heels. The big man was dressed in his usual poncho-and-shorts combo, and his long silver hair was tied behind his neck . . . longer silver beard covering his chest.

"What are you listening to?" I asked as I sat on a couch that looked out toward the twinkling lights of town. "Boz Skaggs? Turn this shit off."

He set the crates down and groaned as he plopped across from me on a worn recliner. "Learn to love the Boz. I thought I taught you better than that. How's Pari?"

"Busy," I said, handing him the Curtis Mayfield records. "And before you ask, she doesn't care that I've borrowed these. Officially I'm the store's buyer now. They aren't stolen."

He was too enamored to care. "Damn. These are beautiful, Fen. No wear. You must want something important if you're bringing me this," he said, one brow shooting up. "And what's up with you tonight?"

"Nothing." Everything.

"Got a look about you. Did Zabel kick you out of her place? You can't live here. I don't need a roommate."

"Jeez, no faith," I complained, wedging one of the record crates between my knees to flip through the sleeves. "No one kicked anyone out. I've had . . . a major spiritual awakening."

"Sounds serious. Does it involve drugs or a girl?"

"Not *a* girl. The girl. Ophelia," I said, nudging my shoulder in his direction to remind him.

"The girl in the water? Mad Dog's secret bastard?"

"That's just a rumor, man. Anyway, she's back in town. Staying at the lodge. Working for Velvet as her PA. Came into the store. Did not know me."

"No shit?" He was truly surprised and understood the gravity of all this. I knew he would. I'd told him . . . too much about my problems. But he'd told me a lot about his, too. It was strange what you shared when it was past midnight and the lake was quiet. Besides, Moonbeam was easier to talk to than half the wet noodles I hung around back at school, who just wanted me to get them free festival passes and backstage access so they could make fools out of themselves.

"But it's not all good. There's a problem," I told him. "It involves Eddie."

"Always does," he said, resigned to hear my pitiful story.

But once he had, he put the Mayfield records down.

"Go on," I said, miserable. I'd lost my place in the record stack, getting riled up over Eddie again. "Tell me I screwed up."

"Why are you asking me for advice about matters of the heart?"

"Because you understand how horrible love is," I said.

That hit him, but he didn't dwell on it. "Hey, I'm not trying to harsh your buzz, but, dude . . . you don't know this girl. You barely even talked to her before she fell in the water—you've told me that before. Only person you know is the fantasy you've created in your head."

"I'm not dumb. I can separate fantasy from reality. But I also know my own feelings. I've spent a lifetime with them. I'm telling you, an explosive thing happened between us when we met. Like, yes, I ranted at her, and there was shouting—she shouted back at me, okay? But after all that, on some kind of inner level, we had a connection."

"Okay?"

"It was like . . . my gut knew something that my conscious brain didn't understand. And now my head feels like it's waking up for the first time, and I'm just . . . ugh. My nerves. They're like bees in my chest."

"Is that like ants in your pants?"

"I hate you. Truly. Fuck off."

"Well, you're making *me* nervous, so dial it back a notch."

I blew out a long breath. "I just want to find out if my feelings match her feelings. You know? I want to get to know her."

"Just realize that she may not want to get to know you."

"Definite possibility," I said, flipping through the record stack as I thought about how red her ears got when I mentioned Eddie and the apartment in front of Mama. A nice shade of hateful. "Why don't you organize your records by artist like a normal person?"

He shook his head, pitying me. "How long before Eddie comes back?"

"Days. A week or two? Fuck, man, I don't know. It's that contract for the lease on the festival grounds. Dad won't give up the lease and sell Condor to Live Nation or AEG. Serj Sarafian will go to his grave as the last independent concert promoter in California."

He stared across the lake at the line of white lights moving down the Strip. "Festival used to be half the size. Whether your dad runs it or a conglomerate, it's not getting smaller. And your family still makes money."

"Not according to my dad. He loses millions."

"His corporation loses millions. How much money does he need? You're living in a barn and driving a Jeep with two hundred thousand miles on it. Aren't you happy?"

"I'm fucking miserable, and you know it."

"Does it have to do with money?"

I shook my head. "I just want Eddie to suffer. I don't want to hurt my mom or the twins."

"Look, kid," he said. "You 'just want' a lot of things. Make a decision and stick with it. But stop scaring this girl away, popping off with your rants. You're too dark, too. . . ." He gestured at me with his hand. "Whatever this new thing is. Lighten up. That's why Eddie has a million girlfriends. You're going to give me that evil eye of yours, but you could take notes from him."

I'd rather chisel my own gravestone.

"You want some nice mint tea?" he said, pushing up from his chair. "I'm making tea. Soothes the soul. And whatever it is you've got going on here. Some kind of twisted brother-revenge, Stockholm syndrome, rescuer's lust."

"Shut the fuck up, man." I sighed heavily. "But yeah, give me your hippie mint tea. Lots of sugar. I want my teeth to rot out while my soul is chilling."

This was getting me nowhere, talking to Moonbeam. Maybe it was dumb to come out here. I forgot sometimes that he was too Middle Path with his advice. Take it easy, Fen. Don't do anything dramatic, Fen. Cutting the brakes on Eddie's car is a bad idea, Fen.

"Hey," I called into the house. "You ever run across anyone who has problems remembering words? Something's wrong with Jane. She understands what you say, but every once in a while, she's kind of like Miss Sara, out at the gas station?"

"She has dementia?" he called back.

"No, she's all there. It's just that she's trying really hard to find a word and will describe it instead of saying the actual word. You think she could have brain damage from when she hit her head during the fall into the dam?"

He flip-flopped around the kitchen counter as the kettle boiled. "I've read about near-drowning victims having speech problems. I think it's the oxygen deprivation that damages a part of their brain that controls communication."

"Shit," I mumbled. "Is it permanent?"

"Don't know. Why don't you ask her?"

Hello. Trying my best! Which was more than I could say for his 1980s punk collection. No Black Flag to be found. But there was a rare twelve-inch by a Bay Area band that had some crappy artwork of a little boy trying to stand on his tiptoes to reach an old-fashioned pay phone on a street corner.

That's when the bees in my body gave me a honey of an idea.

It was almost eleven. Probably too late, but I had to try. I took out my phone and called my mom. It rang too many times. I expected it to go to voicemail, when she picked up.

"Baby?" she said in a hushed voice. "Why are you calling so late? Is something wrong? Are you hurt? Where are you?"

"Mama, I'm fine. Are you back from Mad Dog's? Need to ask you something."

After a silence, her voice returned. "I'm listening. Be quick. Your father is in a foul mood."

"What else is new? Can you get in touch with Mr. Zahn in the Philippines?"

Another hesitation. "Yes. I believe so."

"Tell him that Live Nation would pay a higher lease for the festival grounds."

"Fen . . ."

"Get him to call that guy from Live Nation out to his island in the Philippines to throw his hat in the ring along with Eddie."

"Muddy a done deal? Why would I do that?"

"Because you're sick of the business; you told Dad to sell the rights to the festival, and he wouldn't—he went behind your back and got Mad Dog to invest money instead. And he's sent Eddie there to sign a contract for show. Make Eddie do some actual negotiating. Is he just there to smile? Can't contracts be signed on an app?"

"I will not sabotage your father's work."

"I'm calling in my marker, then."

"Baby—"

"*You said* if I moved out, I could ask for one favor, no questions asked. I moved out and kept the peace. I did my part."

"Is this about the girl?"

I hesitated. Moonbeam's electric teakettle was beeping.

"Fen," Mama warned. "You are being reckless. She isn't a pawn."

"I know that. Will you make the call?"

"Over a girl you don't know? She may despise you."

"But she might not."

"And it could ruin the festival."

"But it might not," I said, hoping it would. "Eddie could come through and negotiate a better contract. The lawyers are both there. They won't let him do anything . . . too dumb. Mostly it will just keep him busy. And distracted. Why should it be easy for him?"

She made a noise. "Ah, you *are* trying to buy more time with the girl before Eddie comes back. You are ruthless and wicked."

"I learned it from watching you."

"I will go to church and pray for you this weekend. Eddie hasn't made it to the island yet. They've just arrived in Manila and won't travel until tomorrow. He isn't scheduled to come back for three weeks."

Three weeks? That was a long time. Blood pumped faster into my blackened heart.

Mama made a *tsk*ing noise into the phone. "You could have asked me that, you know, but your problem is that you always use a nuclear weapon when a simple knife to the back would suffice."

"I like to make sure my adversary is dead."

"Eddie is your flesh and blood, and you aren't at war. However, if I *were* to do what you've asked—and I have not agreed— keep in mind that I would have to tell your father."

"No!"

"And fair warning—it will not stop me from showing Miss Jane an apartment."

"What? *Where?*" I asked, heart hammering. "Mama?"

"Mm, maybe we'll see you. It's a small town."

AHHH. I held the phone away from my face and briefly considered pitching it into the lake but stopped myself. I'd already sacrificed two other phones to rage under my current wireless contract. I couldn't afford a new one again. "Mama—"

"Good night, my love. Don't call again so late unless you are dead."

Kind of felt like I already was. Mama wasn't going to do anything about Eddie. I'd asked too much, too impulsively. Which meant he'd be back in three weeks. Or . . . he could be texting Jane right now and telling her to stay away from me, and maybe Jane really did like him, and I was reading all her signals wrong, and this was all pointless.

But the way she'd looked at me tonight . . . ? I had to think there was a chance. I needed to see her again. If she told me to fuck off, then I'd leave her alone and be miserable forever.

"Tea's ready," Moonbeam said from inside the house. "Did you fix your problem?"

"No, I fucking did not."

"Well, you tried."

Did he know me at all?

If I only had Jane's number! I couldn't just keep showing up at Mad Dog's. Sooner or later, that would get his security after me, because Mad Dog was on Team Serj. And no way in hell she was going to just show up at the record shop. I didn't know where else to find her.

Hold up. Jane said she was working for Velvet. I knew *exactly* where to find Velvet on Friday afternoon. Same place everyone who was anyone in town would be. Not only that, but Velvet was making an official appearance as one of the judges.

If I could find Velvet, then there was an infinitesimal chance I'd run into Jane, too.

I'd risked more for less.

I texted Aunt Pari: Remember how I said I'd rather burn off

all my own skin with a cigarette lighter than go to Battle of the Bands this year? Oops, jk. Looks like I'm gonna need that free pass after all. And the day off.

PS I stole two Curtis Mayfield records.

Jane

"Who is this 'J.H.' person?" Velvet teasingly asked my dad from the backseat of one of the Larsens' SUVs as we took another steep switchback turn up the mountain. "They're texting you like the world's falling apart, Leo. Might be an emergency."

Dad grunted from the driver's seat. "Just a friend."

"Someone from here?" she asked.

"Santa Monica, right, Dad?" I sat in the passenger's seat next to him, brushing dog hair off my jeans. Frida wasn't with us physically this afternoon—Exie was watching her back at the lodge—but her spirit lingered.

"Yeah. Helicopter pilot for a famous actor. Won't say who, so don't ask me," Dad said, eyes tightening in that funny way they do when he's getting anxious. I knew why.

Pretty sure Dad was using an online dating app. He was very private about his love life—if he really even had one. Maybe this magical J.H. person truly was a *just a friend*. He wasn't saying.

Honestly, he wasn't saying much to me at all, not since the pool party and Mrs. Sarafian spilling the beans about me staying at the lake at the end of the summer and moving in with her son.

Let's just say he was blindsided, and we were still speaking, but not warmly.

Relationships were complicated. And the funny thing was, I honestly couldn't tell you what the status of mine was with Eddie right now, so thanks for all the doubt, Fen Sarafian. Doubt had pretty much been at the forefront of my mind the last couple of days. That and the tattoo of a dead girl on Fen's arm. He said *he* was haunted? Well, now I was.

Fen's dark eyes burning a hole in my brain.

Dad asked Velvet, "When can I expect a call to pick you ladies up from this event?"

"Depends on who's there," she said, fixing her lipstick in the mirror, and then remembered I was involved. "Oh, yeah, the whole shebang will be done by early evening. That's when my part's over and Jane can go back home. She'll call you. I may play it by ear, though—might catch a ride with someone else. Don't worry about me, Leo. I'm resourceful."

"Text me if you need me," he told her seriously as he pulled into a packed parking lot at the top of the mountain. "Even if it's six in the morning. I'll come. Always."

"We'll be fine." To me, Velvet said, "Let's judge some bands and eat some *barbacoa*!"

We jumped out of the car to join crowds of people meandering through the lot toward Mission Bluff: a beautiful park built high in the foothills, a few miles above town. Spanish missionaries started building a church here in the 1800s, but an earthquake leveled most of it before it could be finished. Now it was just an open-air plaza surrounded by bristlecone pines with sweeping views of the lake.

And a space for outdoor events like the Battle of the Bands.

Woodsmoke and spice filled the air as we approached the gate. Tickets were expensive—money went to the Mission Bluff fund—but Velvet was on the guest list. Even if she weren't, they knew who she was. That was the advantage of traveling with the Family: doors opened for them, and I followed behind.

"Welcome," the woman at the gates said, giving us both badges. "Greenroom for the judges is to the left of the stage—see the judges' stand? That door. Ask for Cindy," she told me, looking a little anxious. Sometimes people acted that way around the Larsens. "Velvet needs to check in with Cindy to go over, uh, some preshow prep? She radioed me to look out for her."

I gave her a thumbs-up that I understood. And I had a job now. *Greenroom . . . Cindy.* I kept repeating that as we stepped into the plaza, with its white Spanish-facade buildings. The stage was set up in front of the gorgeous view of the sunny sky, and the place was already packed with people roaming, some eating plates of carne asada, some signing up for local political causes at tables. Some waving at Velvet, who was reunion-hugging half the people here.

I'd never been to one of these, only read about it on the Festival Freaks blog. Basically, two regional unsigned bands play, three judges make comments—like a TV musical contest—the crowds cheer or jeer, then the judges decide which band opens the second stage at the festival this year. There's ringing of the mission bell involved, and it's all a big Condor tradition.

Last year, Eddie was a judge. He still hadn't answered my texts. I'd sent eighteen over two days. A cringeworthy amount. Maybe he truly couldn't answer. When I saw his mother, if I still hadn't heard back from him, I'd ask her about it. For now, I wasn't going to think about him. Just wish I could say the same about his brother.

"There's the judges' stand," I told Velvet. "We're supposed to go check in there."

"Food first, *manita*."

"You have some preshow stuff to do," I reminded her, wondering if there was a time frame on that. "Maybe we can check in first, and I'll bring you food?"

"Perfect," she said, slinging an arm around my neck. "Best assistant ever. Oh my God—Erika Jones! What's up, party girl?"

Just like that, she was off to the next reunion. How many friends did she have at the lake? More than I realized. I tried to be patient, but others were joining her hug-a-thon. When I touched Velvet's arm to remind her, she groaned. "Okay, okay. Look, why don't you go check in for me. It's that door, right? I'm right behind you. Be there in five minutes, max. Just delay them for me, okay? Thank yo-o-ou!" She turned back to her group. "That's just Jane. She's doing assistant work for me. I know, right? Now, one of you hags has to help me out. . . ."

Frustrated, I headed to the greenroom and showed my badge to a young volunteer. It was disappointing inside, just a small church rec room lined with long tables. Nothing was green. Not sure why they call it that. In fact, for something that was supposed to be a VIP space, there was nothing special about it at all. Just some bottled water and a woman who looked like Norma—not physically but in the way that she was stressed. Cindy.

"Excuse me," I said to her. "I'm Velvet Larsen's assistant. She's outside."

Cindy wasn't happy. "She's late. We told her what time to be here, no exceptions. She's supposed to go live in fifteen. I have a script to go over with her and the other judges, who have been waiting." She gestured to the other two. Frowns all around.

Shit. "She said she'd be here in five. I'll . . . go get . . . ?" I suggested, unable to finish.

"Now," she said sternly. "Immediately, please."

Texting emergency messages to Velvet, I jogged out of the greenroom and headed back into the crowds, toward the last place I'd seen her. But she was no longer there. Or anywhere. Not answering my panicked texts, either. When I swung around, I ran smack into someone's chest. Pain jolted through my eye socket. I covered my cheek with my hand.

"Fuck! You okay?" a concerned voice said. Warm hands steadied my upper arms.

I lifted my head to see the chest that had slammed into my nose. A black T-shirt that said MOFI in white script. My gaze flicked upward. Adam's apple. Tawny skin. And Fen Sarafian's hawk eyes staring down at me, crackling with electricity.

"No!" I said as if I could turn back time and prevent running into him.

He laughed with dark delight. My face might be fractured,

and he was giddy about it? "Thank you, Saint Gregory!" he said to the sky.

Who? I didn't care. "Not now, Fen," I told him, pushing his hands away. I didn't have time for this. Or him. *Focus, Jane, focus.*

"What a fucking icy glare. Is that an eye injury, or do you really hate me that much?"

"Both! And I have to find Velvet right now," I said. "They need her . . . the room that's a color. Grass. Shamrocks. She's late. Judge. They need her onstage ASAP."

He blinked at me. "Greenroom."

"Yes!" I said, then cradled my cheek. "Ow, my eye."

"Damn. Really am sorry. Listen, you need me to help you look? I've been to this shitty thing a bunch of times. They always set it up the same. Where is she?"

"If I knew that—"

"Okay, dumb question!" he said, smiling a little. "She's somewhere out here?"

I explained as quickly as I could and pointed out the greenroom. He understood and was already craning his head to search for her. "Easier if we split up. Can cover more ground. Give me your number so we can communicate."

"Sounds like a ploy to get my number," I said, looking around.

He snorted lightly and handed me his phone. "Trust me, I've been scheming all kinds of ploys to get your number—this was destiny or angels or something. Type it in, Jane, and let's find your lost princess."

A few seconds later, he took off, dark head of curls disappearing in the crowd, and a text appeared on my phone that just said: It's me, your savior. Add me to your contacts.

I rolled my eyes, too panicked to be truly mad, and went in the opposite direction.

How hard could it be to find one rock socialite? As I dialed her number and listened to it ring without end, I looked for small cliques of people and her telltale armful of bangles, listening out for her infectious laugh, but she was nowhere. She'd said she was hungry, so I tried the food trucks. Not in line there. Not eating at the tables.

Most of the crowd had made its way down to the front of the stage, and the crew was done with their equipment testing. That couldn't be good. I checked the time. Fourteen minutes had passed. A cold sweat washed over me. She was going to blame me for this. I couldn't wrangle her. This was my job, and I'd failed.

My phone buzzed with a text: Got her.

SWEET MOTHER EARTH.

He didn't say where he was, so I ran back to the greenroom, threading my way through the crowd as they filed toward the stage. By the time I made it there, I was drenched in sweat and close to having a heart attack. But I saw him holding the greenroom door for her as she laughed. Her eyes were open super wide, her lashes like a painted doll's, and she was bizarrely energetic.

"Velvet!" I called.

She didn't even hear me. "Let's get this show on the road!" she was saying in a superbly cheerful voice. "Battle, baby! Let's ring that bell!"

As the door shut behind her, the young volunteer who was guarding it had a mildly horrified look on her face.

"Where was she?" I asked Fen.

He crossed his arms over his chest. "Doing a mountain of coke in the bathroom with Erika Jones."

"Wh-a-a-a," I whispered, completely freaked out.

"It's practically snowing up here," he informed me oh-so-casually. "Can't walk two steps without tripping over someone offering me to do a bump with them."

I didn't know what to say to any of that. This was beyond my pay grade. "I need to make sure she's . . ." Not making a fool of herself. I started to tell him goodbye, then I changed my mind. Not sure why. Maybe because he'd already been helping. "Can you wait for me?"

The hard lines around his eyes softened. "I'll be right here."

I spent several stressful minutes inside the greenroom, waiting for Velvet while Carol held her and the other judges' attention, but when the crowd outside roared, it was too late. I followed like a puppy as Velvet bounced out a different door to the judges' platform.

"Are you okay?" I whispered.

"Never better!" she assured me, exiting the room. "Let's battle some bands, people!"

Then she was gone. I didn't know what to do. They wouldn't let me follow her out the door—that headed straight up some stairs to the judges' stand. All I could do was drink my body weight in bottled water. So I left.

Fen was still waiting for me outside the greenroom. Something leapt inside my chest when I saw him leaning against the building, maybe because I expected him to have gotten bored and bolted.

It's what Eddie would have done; they really *were* different, weren't they?

We both started to say something but paused to listen to Velvet talking enthusiastically over the sound system: "Hello, Cleveland!"

"Mother of Mary," I mumbled.

Fen just laughed. "Cocaine . . . it's a hell of a drug."

"Not funny," I said.

"Oh, it's definitely funny. She's fine. But she needs to stay away from certain people up here, or she's going to develop a nasty habit. One reason my dad wanted Eddie to take a nice, long trip out of the country."

He was implying what I *thought* he was implying—right? Inside, I was freaking out, but all I could do was stare at him. If I asked about Eddie, I sounded like I didn't know anything about my own boyfriend. If I *didn't* ask, then I'd be in the dark.

Fen calmly stuck his hands in the pockets of his jeans. "You wanna get lunch? All these grilled meat smells are making me hungry. Wonder if they have fish? Besides, Tell & Show is about to go onstage, and I know they're darlings of the new scene—the Sound, or whatever everyone's calling it. But they sound like a cavity removal by a dentist in a clown costume."

Crap. "Tell & Show? I forgot to tell Velvet to vote for that band. Eddie made me promise to tell her. He said your dad wants them to win or something?"

Fen made a retching noise. "Of *course* my dad's trying to rig the contest. What a complete bastard. Do what you'd like, but that's cheating. And Eddie's only following orders, so you'd be following his orders. Why would you do that?"

"Why would I do what *you* ask?"

"I'm not asking you to do anything. I'm just challenging you to think for yourself. You don't work for me; you don't date me. We barely know each other. You don't owe me shit."

"Right, just my life—savior."

"Oh, *that*. Pfft. Anyone could have done it. I'm no hero."

I think he was teasing. Or maybe being a little self-effacing. His smile was barely there, but fireworks erupted behind his eyes.

"For real, do you want to have lunch, though?" he asked. "It's Mr. Hernandez's food trucks. He makes the best tacos in town and his fries are craveable."

"I actually am starving," I admitted. Starving and at my wit's end. "Really thirsty."

"Then fuck all this noise and come with me." He motioned with his head and upper torso, urging me away from the green-room.

This was probably the Mistake of All Mistakes. But I joined him.

Track [12] "What If"/Frankie Cosmos

Jane

We snaked through the crowd as Tell & Show's twangy dual guitars began playing—soon joined by a peppy vocalist who was trying too hard—and stood in a short line at one of the food trucks. We walked away with a big plate of fries covered in cheese and carne asada, a couple of pineapple aguas frescas . . . and a packet of Tylenol Fen had talked his way into from one of the cooks when I complained that my eye was hurting where I had run into him earlier.

Velvet was still on the judges' stand. She'd be up there for both sets, Fen informed me as we walked our food behind one of the mission buildings to a private break area for workers that was away from the music. Not totally quiet, but it had a peekaboo view of the lake between a break in some trees. We sat next to each other at a picnic table looking out at it.

I downed half the pineapple water with the packet of Tylenol.

"Shit," he mumbled. "You okay?"

"Heat. And stress."

"Ah." He handed me a plastic fork and got quiet as he ate, picking around the carne asada, but I didn't ask him why. The longer we sat together in silence, the more my brain raced through jumbled thoughts—about Velvet, and Fen's latest bombshell about Eddie. How maybe he was only telling me bad stuff about Eddie because he was trying to tear Eddie down.

"The stress affects your injury?" he said out of the blue. When I looked at him from out of the sides of my eyes, he added, "I've been trying to figure it out since that first day you came in the shop. So I've been trying to research it. My friend Moonbeam said it could be a brain injury."

He's been talking to his friends about me? Good lord. "It's aphasia."

"That's what I thought. Should've just told me. You need a T-shirt or a sign or something to tell people when you can't remember words."

I unzipped the bag that was slung across my chest and dug out a business-size card. I watched his face as he read it:

> I have aphasia as a result of a head injury. That
> means I occasionally have difficulty expressing
> myself, and I sometimes may not remember
> certain words when I'm under pressure. You
> can help by speaking clearly, taking things
> slowly, and giving me extra time.

"Damn. Bet you hate giving this out," he said.

I held up a single finger. "One time. That was it. The look on the guy's face . . ." I shook my head. "Nothing but pity. I couldn't do it again. The humiliation . . . easier to suffer through it."

"Understandable," he said, gazing at me from the corners of his eyes. "I'd choose pride over pity any day."

That I believed. Fen was definitely proud. It was etched into every line of his face. "It wasn't pride, exactly. I'm not strong. I'm a coward."

"Seem plenty strong to me. The cowards I've known always pretend they're not afraid."

I didn't know how to answer that. "Anyway, the cards were from my speech therapist, and I don't really need them anymore. It's mostly okay these days. At the beginning, I had to relearn how to talk. They said I should be recovered by now, but you know . . . it lingers on."

"Like a ghost."

"Guess we're both haunted," I said with a tight smile.

He stuck his fork in the goopy pile of fries and left it standing up. "I need to know something. Was it an accident, you falling in the dam? Or were you sad about Eddie? Did he do something to you? Reject you? Did you . . . fall on purpose?"

I blinked at him. "It was an accident."

"I want to believe you," he said in a low voice, dark eyes locking on mine.

My throat tightened. I had to push out my words. "Really don't need you to. It's my past, not yours. Just because you happened to jump in the water on instinct doesn't mean I owe you answers. You don't bond with the ER surgeon who saved your life. He's not showing up at your door, telling you that stitching you up really messed him up, and that's your fault for walking into the ER that day."

He flinched as if I'd physically wounded him, and the air between us changed. I could feel him withdrawing, him and his intense energy. And I didn't know what to do about it.

Okay, so, maybe I *was* being a little unfair. Enough that I felt pretty awful.

They didn't go over this in my therapy. There wasn't a handout for How to Interact with the Boy Who Saved Your Life at my doctor's office. But first, I thought I had already been interacting with that boy—Eddie. He was easy and cool, and he never wanted to talk about that night at the dam or my injury. So we just ignored it. Fine by me.

Now here came Fen. My actual rescuer—because my boyfriend had been lying to me for *whyyy*? Yet Fen wanted to do nothing *but* talk about it. I was mad that Fen needed something from me. And mad that I didn't know what that was. I felt like he was one of those giant mega-size cups you get at fast-food restaurants, and I didn't know how to fill him up.

He started to get up from the table, but I put my hand on his arm to stop him, then immediately took my hand away. It felt weird to touch him, too intimate.

But he sat back down.

I turned to face him, careful to keep a little distance between us. "I'm really sorry I said that. I didn't mean it. I just don't . . . This is new to me? I'm confused."

"No, you're right. It's not your responsibility to fix me.

Besides, what do I have to complain about? I've always caused all my own problems, as my father likes to remind me."

That sounded sad, but I didn't know what to say. "Your dad surprised me. When I met him at Mad Dog's? I guess because Eddie talks about your dad like he's a god, and because he's Serj Sarafian. A legend. I don't know. I just expected him to be super excellent. Like your mom."

"He's a salesman and a shark. If you're in the market for what he's selling, he's all charm. If not, you're the sidewalk below his feet. He just walks right over you."

"People are never what you expect."

His gaze flicked over my face. "No, they are not," he said softly.

"Fen?"

"Uh-huh?"

"What did you mean about your dad sending Eddie to the Philippines when we were talking about Velvet and the drugs?"

He laughed without humor. "Always comes back to Eddie."

"You brought it to my attention! Practically dared me to ask. You were . . . provoking me."

"Trust me"—his gaze hooked to mine—"if I'm provoking you, you'll know it."

A little warmth spread up my neck. I quickly covered it with my hand before it reached my ears. "I obviously didn't know what you were talking about, so if that was the win you were looking for, then you got it, okay? Zing. I had no idea he partied. None. Zero. Please elaborate so I don't go home and stay up all night worrying."

"Wasn't trying to zing or one-up you, for the record. All I meant by it was that Eddie occasionally lets the partying get out of control. This Christmas was a particularly bad incident. Just ask him if you don't believe me." He gestured with his hand. "Go on. Text him."

"I can't, okay? I'm maxed out. I sent him . . ." I couldn't remember how to say the number. "An excessive amount already, and he's not answering."

"Oh," Fen said, his mouth a round circle as the syllable hung in the air.

"Don't, okay? My life has been one long nightmare since the accident—is that what you want to hear?"

"Jane—"

"People treat me differently," I told him. "The few friends I had wanted to go out and be with their girlfriends and boyfriends. Life went on without me. And school? A disaster, okay? I went to a charter school filled with supersmart overachievers, while I got really behind with my schoolwork. Forget college, at least next year. My dad can't afford it, so I need better grades, and honestly, it took everything I had to even . . ." I waved my hands, exasperated. "The diploma."

"Graduate."

I nodded. "Eddie has been the only bright thing in my life this past year. And now you're telling me that was a sham? So please, at least spare me my dignity and tell me about this incident that I know nothing about. Because I'm tired of being coddled and babied and pitied—and yes, even *rescued*, Fen Sarafian."

His throat bobbed, and then he nodded. "I get it, I think. And I'm sorry. Let's truce this out and just be civil, okay? I don't want to fight with you. It's way too emotional, and I like you too much."

That hit me in the chest like a soft blow. Not a painful one, but it had some heft behind it, and I felt it. "Just tell me."

"Isn't much to tell. There's a place outside town, near the private hospital. If you drove in on the freeway, you saw the signs for it. Condor Wings Clinic?"

"That place? I thought it was for injured birds."

He gave me a soft smile and shook his head. "People call it Wings for short. Eddie's best friend is Tim Albertson. Tim's parents sent him there for two weeks in January, and probably Eddie should've gone too. It was after Tim and Eddie showed up drunk at my parents' house at Christmas, made my baby sister cry, and then the two of them disappeared for three days on a bender right before New Year's Eve."

"What kind of . . . bender?" I asked, wanting to know yet wishing I didn't.

He squinted. "Coke and booze, mostly. MDMA. My dad found them when one of the ski resorts called him to say that Eddie and Tim had caused thousands of dollars of damage to their best chalet with a baseball bat, and someone was running around naked in the resort's lobby at three in the morning. They were about to call the cops until they realized who Eddie was."

Heat rose in my chest. It's not like I'd never been around drugs, though not from Mad Dog, who only smoked weed now and then and fell asleep after a glass of wine. But now I was wondering if Eddie was ever high around me and I hadn't noticed.

"I don't think Eddie's an addict, in case you were wondering," Fen added. "I don't know. Maybe? I definitely think he spends too much time with the wrong people on occasion and makes bad decisions. Did you want to know who was naked in the ski resort lobby, or . . . ?"

I held up a hand to stop him.

He relented with a shrug.

"Maybe he's been under pressure," I said, more to myself than Fen. "Maybe he was too embarrassed to tell me. People make mistakes. If he's sober now and trying to make good with your father by succeeding with this deal for the festival, then doesn't he get credit for that?"

"Sure, okay. Why not," Fen said, sounding mentally exhausted. "Eddie gets credit for most everything he does, no matter how badly he screws up or who he hurts."

"It's hard for me to respond to that. He hasn't hurt me like he's hurt you." Just lied to me, apparently. Again and again . . .

Fen gave me a pointed look, like there was something he wanted to say but thought better of it. Then he got distracted. "Listen—hear that?" It was the sound of mission bells. "The horrible dental clown music is over. Time for band number two. Which means Velvet will be heading to the bathroom between sets."

"Are you serious? Not again," I said, panicking as I pushed away from the picnic table. "I didn't sign up for this! What if she overdoses?"

"I think that mostly happens when you're addicted?"

"But isn't it ridiculously addictive?"

"Oh my God, yeah," he admitted, standing with me. "I'm not trying to say it's no big deal. Cocaine is risky and dumb as hell."

"Mad Dog will kill me if anything happens to her." And I was worried about her too, but I didn't want to say that.

Hesitantly he touched the back of my hand with the tips of his fingers. The touch was both an assurance and a question, and it felt incredibly bold.

Strangely, I didn't mind.

Not at all.

"Hey," he said, looking down at me, "if you want some help checking in on Velvet, I'm off work. I know you don't need rescuing, or anything. But my Jeep is parked up here. I can drive you guys back."

I wavered. "Why are you being so nice to me?"

"Easier when I'm not?"

"Sort of, yeah," I said, smiling a little.

He smiled back and scratched the back of his neck. "I *could* be a dick and ruin both our afternoons if that would help. Just let me know. I can be Monster Fen."

"Or you could be like this a little longer and maybe we could figure out how to help each other out. You know. With exorcising our shared ghosts, and whatnot."

"Earworm, 'If You Have Ghosts' by Roky Erickson."

"Perfect song is perfect," I said appreciatively.

He held out his hand as a peace offering. "Fellow ghost hunters? And maybe friends?"

I accepted his hand, and long fingers clasped mine, warm and gentle. We shook slowly, not taking our eyes off each other, for far too long. I forgot about the bands and the mission bell and Velvet. For a moment, I forgot about everything but the delicate electricity we were generating in that handshake.

It felt as if I was agreeing to much more than friendship.

Maybe to something I hadn't intended.

Or to something I secretly wanted but couldn't admit.

Fen Sarafian:

Checking to make sure you and Velvet survived Mad Dog

This is Fen, in case you didn't save me in your contacts

Jane Marlow:

We did, and I did. Thanks for offering to drive, btw

Fen Sarafian:

It was probably best that you didn't ride in the Jeep

V was kind of sloppy

Jane Marlow:

BTW, when you took off . . .

Didn't want you to think I was avoiding you meeting my dad

Let's just say he's not fond of Eddie

Fen Sarafian:

Smart man. Liking him already

Jane Marlow:

No comment : 😛

Anyway, sorry V was such a headache

Fen Sarafian:

Q: I've got a vinyl collection appraisal Sunday afternoon

Would you be interested in a ride along?

Local vinyl collector. Might have some 80s punk

Jane Marlow:

My dad's Holy Grail? The Double Deuce??

Fen Sarafian:

Never know until you look

And people's private music collections can be fascinating

To me, at least. Maybe to you? If you aren't working

Jane Marlow:

Sort of working, but if ride-along is dog-friendly, then yes

Frida revenge peed all over the lodge yesterday

She doesn't like to be left alone

Fen Sarafian:

Respect, pup, kindred soul. I know the feeling

Fen

"I thought you'd be alone," the silver-haired widow told me as Jane and I entered her ranch home. It was one of those places outside of the city limits, way out on the other side of the freeway near the private airport, all flat scrubland and rocks. Mrs. Tybalt's late husband was a rancher, and they'd once had money. He died a few months back, and the house was going up for sale, along with his record collection.

Any other day I'd be one-hundred-percent focused on this collection.

Any other day, I *would* be alone.

Right now, though, I was more interested in the peculiar little way Jane's hair swooped to one side over her left brow. It was the exact shape of meringue on pie.

I couldn't look at her the entire way here in the Jeep—not *really* look—and now I'd somehow used up my oxygen supply trying not to trip over my own feet walking from the driveway to the front door.

"Mr. Sarafian?" the widow asked testily.

"Right, you see . . . Jane is an expert on certain musical

genres," I ad-libbed, enjoying the way her eyes widened when I said it. "It doesn't hurt to have a second opinion when Victory Vinyl is putting a price tag on a collection like yours. Remember, you can take our assessment to your insurance company, or use it for leverage when you're ready to sell."

My aunt should pay me more. I'm a goddamn genius.

"Can I sell everything to the record shop?" she asked. "I just want to get rid of it before my son tries to hang on to the records for sentimental reasons. I know it's worth *something*."

They always say that. It almost never is. "Let me see what you've got first, then we can talk. If we can't buy it, I may be able to arrange a sale for you."

Mrs. Tybalt looked frustrated. She eyed Frida, who was tucked under Jane's arm and making a tiny growling noise while showing even tinier teeth, which was kind of adorable. I mean, the dog was the size of a rat. "She's very well trained," Jane assured the widow.

I laughed. I couldn't help it.

Jane gave me a dirty look, and that sent a dark thrill through me.

Good God. I probably shouldn't be in a public place with her. I was going to embarrass myself. It was only a matter of time.

"Keep the mutt off the furniture," the woman warned before showing us into a marigold-colored den with big glass windows that faced the lake in the distance, if you squinted. Could probably see the lights from town at night. The walls were covered in spindly shelves that had been neatly filled with records. "Here it

JENN BENNETT

is. About two thousand albums, and most of them from the fifties to the seventies. My son spent several weekends organizing these by genre."

Of *course* he did. That was the first blow. More important was that it was painfully clear now that there was no Holy Grail for Jane in this sad marigold room. We both knew it, and that meant I'd dragged her out here for no reason. Little ripples of panic fluttered against my ribs.

When the widow left us alone, closing a set of French doors behind her, I slipped a backpack off my shoulder and got out a spiral notebook and pencil, trying to pretend I wasn't thinking about her Holy Grail, and how we definitely weren't finding that here today. "Just so you know, there's only one way to organize vinyl, and that's by artist. Not by genre, not by year, and not by color of the goddamn spine. All the vinyl shelfie people can burn in hell."

"Boo," Jane said, giving me a thumbs-down sign. "I like a good shelfie. Not everyone thinks by artist. Sometimes you remember a record by the color of the cover. Otherwise Weezer wouldn't have a 'Blue Album' and the Beatles wouldn't have a 'White Album.' Those were self-titled, but people call them that because color and memory are tied together. *Your* brain doesn't speak for *all* brains."

"Okay, I get that, but . . ." I gestured around the room. "Two thousand records. All but twenty of them are going to be worth less than a dollar. If they were organized by artist, I could whip through them and look for anything important. Now I've got to go through them all."

"So this is just an inconvenience for you, really," she said, setting Frida on the floor.

I stuck the pencil behind my ear. "Pretty much, yes."

"Admitting you have a problem is the first step," she joked, smiling a little before she glanced around. "Okay, so I'm not feeling super great about finding the Double Deuce here. . . ."

And there it was. My heart shriveled.

"Look, I've got a ton of resources at work," I bargained, "so I've got feelers out online and alerts set up, and I've got a beat on a serious big-time collector with a summer home in Condor. Like, she's got a massive collection and she's super wealthy. DJs in San Francisco tell wild stories about her." She looked nervous, and was she staring at my hands? Why? That was making *me* nervous. "But I guess this is a waste of your day if you're supposed to be helping Velvet, or whatever. If you want, I can take you back to her before I start?"

She shook her head and made a dismissive noise. "Velvet? She's asleep."

"At two in the afternoon?"

"She stayed out late last night, and I'm still mad at her for Battle of the Bands. I left her a note. I'm supposed to get Sundays off, anyway. And every day after eight p.m."

"Why do you have Frida if it's your day off? Shouldn't she be sleeping in with Velvet if it's her dog?"

"Ha, no. Frida sleeps in my bed. And the only time I don't watch her is when I leave her with Exie, our chef, or one of the other domestics."

"Sounds like Frida is your dog."

"Nah, we're just buds. I take her to her vet appointments and the groomer. I tried to take her to training lessons, but she failed spectacularly—the fool." She laughed a little, watching Frida's tail wagging. "Anyway, her fancy dog papers say she belongs to Velvet. Who takes care of your pets? I mean, back at your family home. I know the Sarafians have domestics too."

"Just one, a housekeeper who is kind of like an aunt, Ms. Makruhi. She cooks, cleans, and was our nanny. No one else is live-in. They just hire people to landscape or whatever. If my mom has a bunch of people over for dinner, she has it catered."

"Huh. That surprises me."

"My parents drive their own cars too."

"Mad Dog is legally blind," she said, a little defensive.

"I get that.

"Your dad has his own PA, I'm sure."

"At the office, for work. Not at home. And my parents don't have pets, which I assume you already know." Don't mention Eddie's name. *Please.*

But she didn't. She just nodded. "So, like I was saying, since there's no L.A. punk section here, maybe you can tell me how I can help you make this go faster—I can write stuff down or help organize. Whatever you need. I'm yours for the afternoon."

Damn. I mean, I knew she wasn't flirting. But still. Most importantly, she *was* staying. Which meant, I supposed, that she didn't hate my company.

It was a start.

She blinked at me and asked, "So, um, what are you looking

for? I know a little about vinyl, but I'm a quick learner. Two hands are better than one. Wait . . . four? Ha."

"And four paws." I pointed at the dog. "Wouldn't have happened to bring the green toy?"

"Oh—Frida, no! Stop!" Jane scolded. "No chewing on the mean woman's rug!"

Once she got the dog under control, Jane let her off the leash with the pickle toy. I didn't want to take any chances that she'd change her mind and call her dad to pick her up, so I plunged into all things music as we started digging into the record collection, explaining what I was looking for. I went over basics, like record size and RPM. Picture sleeves and inserts. Acetates versus vinyl. Record condition and grading systems. Warp. Wear.

My God, she smelled good. I tried not to breathe in too deep. Or to look at her too much when she was close. I kept getting lost and forgetting what I was saying.

"It's amazing how big the covers are. Art was important. It's so tiny on our screens. I never even think about it when I'm streaming music, but look at these that you open up like a book and there's artwork inside—what are these called again?"

"Gatefolds," I told her. "Bob Dylan's *Blonde on Blonde* was one of the first gatefold sleeves to have two albums inside."

"Cool." I liked that she respected the vinyl and touched it with care, even when it was shitty Christmas records that weren't worth anything. "Hey, I bet they played this with their kids every year," she said. "Look how scratched it is. And the cover is sticky. Peppermint. Wow."

"Not wow. Worthless. The same messy kid probably grew up and rearranged these records all wrong."

"I've always loved the idea of a big family having a nice Christmas."

"Just because your family's big doesn't mean it's always nice." I regretted saying this. I didn't want to think about my mom telling me that my sister cried last year. And how I wouldn't be there this year. But mostly I didn't want Jane to think about my brother, not when our talk had been blissfully Eddie-free today.

But she just nodded and put the record back. "Still, I value this holiday section here at a very high price. That's my expert opinion. Anything that conjures sparkly lights, family, food, and happy memories is valuable." She pulled out a Townes Van Zandt album from the shelf above it. "This has the sad song 'Waiting Around to Die,' and therefore I value it at one cent."

"Oddly enough, that depressing shit is worth a little cash if the vinyl is in decent shape. I've got a system for flagging the good stuff. Here. Let me show you. . . ."

Surprisingly, she was interested in both my method and sorting through this man's collection. We sat on the floor together, pulling out small stacks, with Frida excitedly wagging her tail and jumping from lap to lap. The record collection was crap. I'm talking completely worthless. But Jane and I talked nonstop about music. The bands she'd heard recording in Mad Dog's studio. The sound checks I'd watched from backstage at the festival. The stars who sounded terrible in person, and the ones who had real talent.

We were talking so much that I was surprised to see we'd

made our way through a third of the collection. More surprised when the doors to the den flew open.

"Get out!" Mrs. Tybalt shouted in a panic. "Both of you, now. My son's coming."

"We're not done with—" I started to say.

She didn't give a damn. "Come back later. If Chet catches you here, he'll be furious."

We scrambled to get out, collecting my notes and Frida on her leash, rushing through a cloud of Mrs. Tybalt's cigarette smoke on our way out. "We're still going to bill you for this," I told her as we strode down the driveway.

"Fine," she called back. "I'll call the shop when it's safe for you to return. What about all those Elvis Presley albums? How much were they worth?"

Shit. There was Elvis? Would have known that if the collection were organized correctly. "Whatever you do, don't let your son take those, Mrs. Tybalt. Call the shop. I'll come back." I backed up the Jeep in a haze of dust and pulled out of the driveway, then booked it toward the freeway on-ramp.

"Is it always like this?" Jane asked, checking the rearview mirror to see if the car behind us was slowing down to pull into the Tybalts' house. "Damn, I think that's Chet."

"Collectors are always a little weird, no matter what they collect," I told her. "But I've never been rushed out of someone's house like a lover in the middle of the night."

"She wasn't a collector."

"Huh?"

"She just wants the cash," Jane said. "Her husband was the music lover. And maybe her son is right to try to hang on to the records instead of selling them. What's more important, making a quick buck or love of music?"

"He's probably just sentimental because it was his father's stuff," I pointed out, getting on the freeway.

She shrugged. "So? The gods of music have a soft spot for sentimentalists and the downtrodden."

"What?" Something was wrong with the Jeep's steering. Weird.

"That's what my dad says. Maybe their son will be a music lover one day. Or already is."

Damn. She was making sense. I loved everything she was saying, and I wanted to keep talking about it, but all of my focus was on what was going wrong with this vehicle. Because something was. Wrong.

"Fen?" she asked.

"It's never done this before—what?"

"What's going on? What did you do?"

"I didn't do anything!"

The Jeep cut out. Engine died. No power steering, brakes were stiff.

I managed to coast to a stop and pull it over to the side of the freeway. Once I got it there, though, I was clueless.

"Any idea what's gone wrong?" Jane asked.

"No idea," I said, quietly panicking. "It's never happened before. I've been driving it a couple years with no problems."

I tried to restart it. Cranked but wouldn't turn over.

"You have gas?" she asked.

I gestured toward the half-full fuel gage. No, this was serious. I popped the hood, but I didn't really know what I was looking for. Everything checkable looked okay to me. Nothing was on fire or corroded. I had oil. No belts were missing.

The Jeep was dead, dead, dead.

"I think I need to call a tow," I told Jane as she jumped out with Frida, careful of the cars flying past. "I'm really sorry. This has never happened."

She shielded her eyes from the sun with a hand. "It's an old car. It always happens."

But now, of all times? My bank account, which I quickly checked through the app . . . contained enough for a couple of cheap meals. Not a tow. Spiraling downward. "Shit. I've got to make a call." I tried Aunt Pari. The store was closed on Sundays, and she wasn't answering. I tried Aunt Zabel. Nothing. Were they together?

No way was I calling Mama. Not when I already had asked her for a favor. Plus, she'd murder me if she knew I was hanging with Jane. "I'm going to try my cousin. He owes me some money anyway. Hold on."

"You need it for the tow?"

"No way am I borrowing money from you," I told her.

"No, I mean, let's call my dad. He's a mechanic. Old cars are his thing."

I crossed my arms. "Uh, you sure about that? I mean, what with . . . Eddie." Welp. Board reset to zero. We went all of how many hours without mentioning his ass? Fuck my beshitted life. And this Jeep. If I could flip it over into the ravine and set it on fire right now, I would.

She hesitated, blinking rapidly, as if she was unsure. Then she shook her head and smiled, brushing away sweat from her brow. "I'm just helping my boyfriend's brother, for the love of Pete. There's nothing wrong with that. We're, uh . . . What's that thing when it's okay to be hanging around each other because we're practically related, and we're not doing anything wrong?" She put her hands on her hips and blew out a long breath.

"But we're *not*. Doing anything wrong." I stilled. "Unless you want to? Because my afternoon just opened right the hell up."

She chuckled.

I wasn't really joking, but I pretended like I was. Look at me, goofing around. I'm *so-o-o* lighthearted, and not the least bit tragic and ready to pledge my undying love for you in the middle of this open road with blood rituals and a ring of fire.

"I know we aren't doing anything wrong," she said, "but no one will *think* that, because we're that thing—Frida, baby, stay away from the freeway, unless you want to be roadkill!" she said, tugging the leash and snapping her fingers. "How has she stayed alive without me? Anyway, no one will suspect anything, because—not that there's anything to suspect."

"Because . . . we aren't doing anything wrong?" I repeated, on the verge of passing out.

"Exactly," she said, laughing nervously and tap-tap-tapping her finger against her leg.

My heart raced. Holy shit, *she thought we were doing something wrong*. And if she thought we were, then we most definitely were. We were both on the same wrong page.

Dear God. My knees felt weak.

"In-laws," I told her. "That's the word you were looking for, right?"

She brightened. "That's it! Brother-in-law."

Oh, yes. That *definitely* sounded wrong. Like some kind of porn category.

"Let's call my dad," she suggested. "He'll fix your Jeep. He's a genius."

"Call him up." That's right. Let's get your dear ol' father's blessing. What did I care? Couldn't be as bad as my dad. I was gambling everything today and suddenly filled with a strange kind of joy that the Skeleton King had broken down.

Her ears turned a little pink as she waited for her father to pick up. "Just . . . whatever you do, don't called him 'the chauffeur,' okay?"

Jane

"You need new crankshaft position sensor wiring," Dad said, ducking out of the hood of Fen's Jeep. "Maybe a new sensor. Wires are corroded and shorting out. I don't have those with me, but we can run by an auto parts store and pick them up. The wiring and harness set is maybe fifty? You'd be talking a hundred for the sensor, though."

Fen blew out a hard breath. "Don't have it right now. My aunt does payroll on Tuesday. I can probably borrow it and work it off with my other aunt, but it may take a day or two. . . ." He shook his head. "Sorry, I didn't mean to drag you out for no reason, Mr. Marlow. Even if I have to leave it out here, it's good to know what's wrong when I get it towed into a shop."

Cars whipped past us on the freeway. "Not a problem. It's my off day." He squinted at Fen. "Just surprised, is all."

"That I'm broke, and my family's loaded? Guess Jane forgot to tell you that story."

Dad leaned against the front of the Jeep and looked at me, then Fen. "I know a little of that story, but it didn't come from Jane."

"Dad," I pleaded. He'd been doing so well. No scene. No

weird vibe. This was the opposite of Eddie at the airport. Every-thing had been fine so far. Fen hadn't called Dad "the chauffeur" or made any off-color jokes about domestic life, and Dad hadn't freaked when I told him about being stranded on the side of the road.

"Look," Fen said. "Whatever you've heard about me is prob-ably true. Eddie and I don't get along, and Jane knows that. Honestly, if fratricide were legal, I'd be hunting him in the streets like it was the Purge."

Dad raised a brow.

Frida barked and stood on her back legs, pawing at Fen's shin. He scratched her head. "It's not murder if they deserve it, right, little pup?"

"He's joking," I explained to my father. "Dark sense of humor."

Dad wiped his hands on his jeans. "I get satire, Jane. I just don't get why the two of you are stranded on the side of the road together."

"Told you, this lady has a record collection—" I started.

"There's nothing going on," Fen told my father. "If that's what you're worried about."

I froze, mouth still open. Why would he say that?

But he didn't stop. He just kept on talking. "We reconnected in the record shop. I was surprised to see her, since it had been a couple of years . . . you know, since the dam incident. And we have common interests. Music. Eddie. Or my family, at least—my mom."

"I like your mother," Dad said. "Very nice lady."

JENN BENNETT

"She's pretty amazing," Fen agreed. "We rode with you once in your car a few years ago. I'd hurt my leg at a fundraiser downtown. You probably don't remember."

"Wrong about that. I remember everything," Dad said, squinting one eye closed at him.

Ugh. This was going off the rails. Bad feeling in stomach.

I panicked and blurted out, "Fen's helping to look for your Holy Grail for us."

One of my dad's brows shot up. "Oh, really?"

"Double Deuce," Fen confirmed. "Can't promise anything, but I have some connections online. I'm trying to track one down. Not an easy thing to find. Henry Rollins fans typically don't want to part with their stuff. But I guess you know that already."

Boom. My dad was a goner now. The two of them talked shop for a minute. Two. Ten. Long enough for me to pull out a bottle of water and a tiny plastic cup I carried around in my pack for Frida—jeez, she was super thirsty. Long enough for me to watch Fen in secret from where I crouched on the ground near a pine tree, as if I were a bird watcher stalking a rare bird . . . observing him in the wild.

His hair was in disaster mode, which I knew made him look like some kind of hoodlum in my father's eyes. It seemed as if all his clothes were black to match his dark moods. Probably another strike against him.

But.

I liked the way he was serious about what he was saying, making definitive gestures with those sexy, elegant hands of his. He

144

knew what he was talking about, and when he didn't, he wasn't afraid to admit it. He did a lot of listening. His eyes were sharp and wary. He crossed his arms over his chest a lot. But he didn't talk down to my dad. I was thankful for that.

Fen was a lot. Dramatic. Dark. Not easy or golden. He required special instructions.

So did I.

My observation was interrupted when Frida decided she had to poop, so I walked her through the shrubland, away from the road, behind some manzanita bushes. By the time we came back, Fen was in the cab of the Jeep and Dad was under the hood yelling, "Try it now."

Fen turned the key, and the Jeep started up.

"Oh shit!" Fen called out. "You did it!"

"Told you he was a genius," I said.

Dad slammed down the hood. "Yeah, well, it won't hold forever. That wiring has got to be replaced. It could go out again in five minutes, or it may hold for a month. No telling. So why don't Jane and I follow you home, just to make sure you make it? Then when you get enough cash for the wiring, let me know. I'll come into town and replace it. Won't take long."

"Yeah," Fen said. "That sounds good. I really appreciate it, Mr. Marlow."

"Call me Leo. And you're welcome."

I gave Fen a thumbs-up, and he held up his hand. See? Just two people who definitely were only hanging out, bonding about music and our mutual connections. Like I told Dad.

Everything was fine.

But when I hopped in the SUV that Dad had driven from the lodge, and we pulled out onto the freeway behind Fen, I could tell that my father had something on his mind.

"Oh my God," I told him, sinking behind the seat belt with Frida in my lap. "What now? Did he say something to offend your gentle sensibilities? Did he besmirch the Marlow name—or worse, did he say something about Henry Rollins or the L.A. punk scene?"

Dad shook his head slowly. "He knows his shit. Smart kid. About music, at least."

"But . . . ?"

"No buts."

Okay. That was weird.

"He know about your aphasia?" Dad asked, watching the Jeep ahead of us.

"Yeah," I said. "He actually figured it out himself. But I told him."

I didn't want to let Dad know that Fen was the one who pulled me out of the water. I wasn't sure why. Maybe because he'd read too much into it. Or maybe because I liked that it was our secret for now. Besides, Dad and I stayed out of each other's business.

It was the Marlow way.

"He's not a bad person," I told Dad, stroking Frida's sleek body. "Serj kicked him out of the house because of personal stuff. Just drama with him and Eddie. Fen and his mother are still close."

"The same mother who wants to help you find an apartment for you and her *other* son?"

I sank a little farther down in the seat, feeling guilty for no reason. Why should I? We were just looking at records. We didn't even shake hands this time. No touching whatsoever.

"I know how it sounds. It's just . . . complicated," I told Dad.

"It always is," he murmured, brow creasing with lines. "Always is."

Fen Sarafian:

Hey, was wondering if your dad's offer still stood?

I got the $$$ for the auto part.

Jane Marlow:

That was fast! One day. Did you do some stripping for cash

tips?

Fen Sarafian:

Sold some of my personal vinyl. So, pretty much?

Respect for sex workers, but this was pure desperation

Me=hurt

Jane Marlow:

GASP. You=Mrs. Tybalt

Fen Sarafian:

Gonna start smoking Marlboros and yelling at kids to get off

my ranch!

Jane Marlow:

HOW MUCH WILL YOU GIVE ME FOR THESE TOENAIL

CLIPPINGS?

EVERYTHING IS FOR SALE, INCLUDING MY SOUL

Fen Sarafian:

I'm a little scared to go back, honestly, but: the right Elvis wax?

Would sell my soul too.

Jane Marlow:

Soul sellouts! If she wants to sell candy-crusted holiday records,

let me know

Dad's in bed early with headache, so I'll ask in morn about Jeep

But I know he'll say yes. He was cool with you

Fen Sarafian:

A father that doesn't hate me! Miracle of miracles . . .

Jane

I didn't know Dad and Fen had exchanged numbers until Dad called from town the next afternoon to inform me that he was on his way to the record shop to fix the Jeep. That was where we'd left Fen after following him into town, in the parking lot next to the brick building that housed Victory Vinyl, just off the Strip. Fen said he had some work to do in the shop, and that his aunt would pick him up—that if he had to get the Jeep towed, it was closer to repair shops.

But I guess I assumed Fen would contact me and not Dad to arrange the rest of it. Now I felt weird. Like maybe they'd talk about something while I wasn't there. Not that my dad was a big gossiper. Or any kind of gossiper at all. Still. It made me feel strange.

Nothing I could do now. Velvet was out with some friends and had left me with the important task of rearranging her closet. But Exie stopped me in the kitchen to ask me and Starla if we wouldn't mind helping her cart some food to a small outbuilding where Mad Dog was setting up a temporary studio for mixing an album. I pulled a small red wagon loaded down with drinks while Starla and Exie schlepped bags.

Birds chirped as we made our way down a tree-lined winding path dappled in sunlight. There was a fallen pine tree with big fungi growing all over it that Frida loved to inspect every time we came this way on walks. Two mornings ago, we saw a herd of blue butterflies—or whatever a congregation of butterflies are called. But the most magical thing in this area was definitely the place where Mad Dog was setting up shop: the Grotto Cabin.

It was very rustic and small, just a bedroom and an ancient bathroom, and an open floor plan for the rest of it, sparsely furnished—and most of that furniture had been moved aside to make room for Mad Dog's mixing equipment and various musical instruments that he used for recording backing tracks when he was tinkering with alternate mixes. Out back there was a patio that opened to a craggy rise of shoreline rock, and tucked beneath a vine-covered overhang, you could follow a curving path into a shallow grotto. Lights had been installed into a narrow ledge in the rock, on which there was just enough room for a few people to sit and enjoy drinks or lounge in the water. And if you got tired of that, you could just paddle out of the hidden cavern and swim right into the lake from there.

"Let's get everything staged here," Exie said, gesturing toward the cabin's kitchen island after we'd hauled it inside, all of us a little winded. "I have a list to check off, and Norma will be out here soon to get the linens done and the place dusted. The walkies are hit-or-miss this far out, you know, so I want to be done before she shows up with no warning."

Amen to that. "This is a hella bunch of food," I observed,

unhooking Frida from her leash to let her explore. "Is Mad Dog moving in here for the rest of the summer, or what?"

"You know how he gets when he's working," Exie said, unpacking meals that had been portioned into individual containers, along with bags of fruit and cut-up vegetables. "He'll be in here until three in the morning. Sometimes he'll sleep here. . . ."

"Sometimes he'll wander down here at five a.m. in his kimono and get attacked by a grizzly bear?" I joked, lifting bottled water onto the counter.

Starla laughed, running fingers through her mermaid-dyed ponytail. "Rosa said he can have this cabin all to himself because grottos are gross."

"Don't blame her," Exie said. "After what went down at the Playboy grotto?"

"What went down at the Playboy grotto?" I asked as Frida sniffed her way around the kitchen.

Exie sighed. "You're way too young. Playboy Mansion. Hugh Hefner? He had a famous grotto in his basement. Before Hefner died, like two hundred guests at a party got sick. They thought it was the flu, but the L.A. Department of Health investigated and discovered it was Legionnaires' disease—they'd caught it from bacteria in the dirty grotto."

"Ewww!" Starla and I both made faces.

"Thanks for ruining this cabin for me," I complained. "I thought it was cozy. You think it's safe to let Frida sniff around?"

"It's fine," Exie said, waving her hand as she watched the little dog jump on the couch.

"Was Mad Dog ever at the Playboy Mansion?" Starla asked.

"Are you kidding?" Exie said. "Mad Dog at a party?"

We all chuckled. He never went to large public gatherings if he could avoid them.

"I wonder how many sex parties have happened in this grotto?" Starla mused. "Bet if we hunted around here, we could find hilarious nudie pics from the fifties. Kamal told me that a few summers ago he found a condom with no expiration date taped under his bedside table. He searched for the brand online, and they stopped manufacturing it forty years ago."

Exie unloaded the last of the bags. "If there were sex parties years ago, it was probably because folks were just bored."

"Right?" Starla agreed. "Rosa says no there's no Wi-Fi in this cabin."

"You just know that Mad Dog's going to be calling Norma from that old landline over there, all day long, like, 'Mother Superior, will you bring me my favorite wool blanket? It's c-c-cold down here.'"

We all laughed. Better Norma than me. This cabin was a long walk from the main house. No way did I want to haul stuff all the way here for him on the regular. Was bad enough to fetch stuff for Velvet from the carriage house.

"So, Jane . . ." Exie said, counting up her food bins and checking them off on a list. "What's all this about Leo fixing one of the Sarafian boys' cars, hmm? You're getting awfully chummy with that entire family."

"And I thought you were dating the older brother," Starla

said. "Wasn't this the boy who was kicked out of the family house for doing massive amounts of drugs, or something?"

"Drugs?" I said, offended.

She shrugged. "It's always drugs."

"Fen isn't doing drugs, and he's not bad."

"Fen is not a bad boy," Starla repeated, making a face at me. "Did you hear that, Exie?"

"I heard. Stop teasing the girl."

"And if we're pointing fingers about partying," I said, "those accusatory fingers should be pointed a little closer to home," I mumbled. "Like, right up at the main house."

The two of them stopped and looked at me. Then Exie said, "You got something you need to tell us?"

I shook my head. I'd said too much, and regret was seeping into my clothes and making me feel uncomfortable. But no one could pry out a secret like Exie could. She put her hand over mine on the counter and looked into my eyes. "Go on, then. You'll feel better when you've unloaded it."

"We won't tell," Starla said. "What's told in the grotto stays in the grotto."

I groaned and finished stacking the bottled water. "First of all, I just want to say that I thought cocaine was a myth, like, something that only happened in movies from the eighties."

"Oh, Jane," Starla said. "I told you that charter school education wouldn't prepare you for the real world. Wait . . . who are we talking about? Not Rosa. Mad Dog? No way. He can't even finish a glass of wine."

Exie made an exasperated sound. *"Velvet."*

"Yes." I covered my face. "What am I supposed to do?"

"Is it bad?" Exie asked. "Like, how much are we talking?"

"I don't know," I admitted. "I never saw her doing it back home. But Fen warned me that it's all over the lake, and he said she shouldn't be hanging out with certain people. Pretty sure she's with one of them right now." I gave them a little rundown about Battle of the Bands and some of Velvet's recent video call activity that made me suspicious.

Exie shook her head. "Mad Dog is going to go ballistic."

"So mad," Starla said. "He can't find out."

"No, you have to tell him," Exie said. "What if something happened to her? You'd be responsible."

Ugh. Too much stress. "You *cannot* say anything. I'm not even supposed to know. Fen is the one who found her doing . . . the credit card thing on the mirror . . . ?"

"Lines?" Starla said.

I nodded. "What do I do?"

"Proceed carefully," Starla advised. "We're not supposed to stick our noses into the Family's business. Remember Norma's rules."

"You think Mad Dog cares about rules when it comes to the safety of his children?" Exie said. "You haven't been in this household long enough. He'd want to know."

"What if it was just a one-time party thing?" I asked. "What if she doesn't do it again?"

Exie mumbled to herself unhappily while the cabin was

silent. Then her eyes narrowed, and she asked, "This Fen boy who helped you with Velvet—that's where your daddy is right now? Fixing this boy's car while his brother is out of the country?"

"Oh-ho!" Starla laughed. "When you put it that way, it sounds a little fucked up."

How did this get turned back around on me? "No—not fucked up. My dad was just helping out. And we aren't doing anything wrong. I've tried to talk to Eddie about all this, but he won't text me back! He's lied about a bunch of stuff, which is probably why he won't text me back. But I know he's on the island already, unless he's shipwrecked in some storm and drifting on the back of a slow turtle."

"What?" Exie frowned at me. "Slow down. You aren't making sense."

"Check her nose, Exie," Starla said, laughing.

"Never mind," I said. "And Fen and I are just friends! We aren't doing anything. Okay, we shook hands. There. Are you happy? We shook hands, and we shouted at each other, and it's been a little emotional. But no one understands what we've been through."

They both stared at me, but I wasn't going to explain.

"We're practically brother and sister," I said, still unable to recall that dumb word. "You know, if Eddie and I ever did get serious, then Fen and I would be . . ."

"Having the affair of a lifetime?" Exie said.

I held up a finger. "We just talk about music. That's all." Frida barked near my feet, as if to confirm my story. "See? She can back me up."

"That sounded like an accusation to me," Starla said, laughing.

"No," I said. "Frida is there the entire time. To supervise. What could happen?"

Exie made an amused noise.

"Damn, girl," Starla murmured, completely titillated. "This is almost Playboy Mansion–level drama. Next thing we know, you'll be bringing the brothers to the grotto."

They were teasing me. Good-natured. Fun. But underneath it all, my stomach was knotting. I needed to try to text Eddie again. If I could just get in touch with him, all of this would be better. I could let him know that I'd been hanging out with Fen, so I could stop feeling so guilty. And Eddie could tell me his side of the story.

But would I really want to hear it?

Track [16] "Story of My Life"/Social Distortion

Fen

I didn't think this through. When I texted Jane's dad to ask him about fixing the Skeleton King, I should have probably tried to move the Jeep out to Aunt Zabel's place. Quiet out there. But here, in the tiny record store parking lot off the Strip, it was anything *but.*

Road traffic. Foot traffic. And the worst traffic of all: Aunt Pari traffic. Because Mr. Marlow had only been here forty minutes, and my lovable but extremely busybody aunt had already ambled out to the parking lot a couple thousand times, first with water, then an old blanket—"In case you need to get under the Jeep. You won't get dirty."

He told her he didn't need it. She didn't care. That's one thing that she has in common with my mom. All three Kasabian sisters, really. If they think you need something? You will fucking get that thing. Argument is futile.

"How long have you been doing this?" my aunt asked Mr. Marlow, peering into the engine over his shoulder. "Fixing cars, I mean."

"All my life, really. Since high school," he told her. "I've always been good at tinkering."

"Mad Dog must have a lot of cars to keep you on full-time," she said.

"Auntie," I warned, feeling mildly panicky. "It's none of our business."

Maybe I was too self-conscious about the stuff Jane had told me—that her father hated Eddie. And I was no Eddie, thank the saints, but I was still cut from the Sarafian cloth. Mr. Marlow could decide that he didn't like the looks of me and tell Jane not to hang around that horrible Fen Sarafian anymore.

Basically, I didn't want to piss the big guy off.

And I didn't have a great track record when it came to fathers.

Thankfully, Mr. Marlow wasn't offended by my aunt's curious poking around into his life. "I take care of all the vehicles for the family and staff too," he said. "But yeah. I do all the maintenance, and I've rebuilt a few old cars for Mad Dog too. And he's legally blind, so I drive him."

"That's right," she mumbled. "One summer, about four or five years ago, my brother-in-law, Serj, had a driver. For the life of me, I can't remember what happened to that guy. . . ."

"Dad kicked him out of the car in the middle of the Strip because he wouldn't follow directions," I reminded her. "He sat in front of the Bait Shop for two hours, waiting for a ride back home to Fresno."

"Ugh," Aunt Pari said, gritting her teeth and looking embarrassed. "Forgot about that. My brother-in-law is a demanding man, Mr. Marlow. I'm sure you've heard."

Jane's father lifted his blond head from the dark of the hood.

"I try not to listen to gossip, but eventually there's no avoiding it."

"You can't walk through a mud puddle and come out clean," I agreed.

"Our family can be quite the mud puddle," Aunt Pari said with a soft smile, then she handed me a printout from an online order. "Can you fix this in the system? The status is stuck as 'shipped,' but I never mailed it. It's the one with the damaged sleeve—remember?"

Was she trying to get rid of me? Oh, yes. Distinct whiff of *Adults only* look in her eye. Why couldn't she just let the man fix my car and go?

I gave her a look that said, *You will have to cleave me in half with an axe forged from the souls of the damned before I move from this spot.*

But she was immune to my dark powers. "Thanks, babe."

Frowning, I snatched up the printout and strode toward the shop's back door. As I made my way around a delivery van, I heard Jane's father say, "Speaking of mud puddles, I am curious about why Fen isn't living at home anymore."

Ah, shit.

I stood in place, hiding behind the van, and listened to my aunt's response.

"That's complicated," she said. "But in a nutshell, it comes down to Serj driving his two oldest boys into a competitive frenzy. I don't have kids myself, but most parents I know go out of their way to make sure everything is equal for their kids. Same presents, same privileges. Right? You treat them the same."

"Only got the one, but sure."

"Not Serj. He had a different parenting philosophy, and no matter how much Jasmine disagreed, he raised those two boys to compete for everything—if there was a band they both wanted to meet, then Serj would only let the boy with the highest test score backstage. He gave Eddie an Alfa Romeo that's worth more than the record store, but only after Eddie 'proved himself' at the festival grounds in some scheme Serj devised to see which of the boys could sell more T-shirts."

"Huh," Mr. Marlow grunted.

But that was only half the story! She wasn't telling him what Eddie did, that he cheated on the test to get that backstage band meeting, and that he locked me in a festival outbuilding for two hours until a janitor found me—just so he could win our dad's ridiculous T-shirt selling game.

"Serj raised them to be competitors, not brothers," she was telling Mr. Marlow. "No surprise that the boys would be out for blood, really. It just escalated. Eddie got more competitive—and craved more of Serj's attention. And before you know it, the boys were always bickering, accusing each other of treachery. It was high school. How much treachery could there be?"

She'd be surprised.

"Honestly, I'd rather be redeployed in a war zone than have to go back to high school," Jane's father said.

Thank you.

"Well, it basically amounted to terrible shouting matches," my aunt said, "and to keep the peace, Fen moved into my sister

161

Zabel's place. He was already hanging out here after school, so I put him on payroll."

"What about his mother? How does she feel about all of this?"

"She wants a happy home, so she's trying to keep everyone calm, always playing referee. But she's miserable about what's happened with those boys. She wants Fen at home. But she sent him to us to keep him safe."

"Is Serj, uh, physical? I mean, is he violent?"

Does shouting in your face count?

"No, nothing like that. It's just the constant arguing. It's mentally exhausting. She's got the twins, too—her youngest? She didn't want them seeing the boys fighting all the time. It wasn't healthy."

"I see."

"But Fen getting kicked out of the house? That was never as bad as all the talk around town said it was. So if you hear that Fen did this or that, it probably isn't true. He's a good kid. Little dramatic, but that's better than boring."

Well, thanks, Auntie.

"I won't listen to gossip," he assured her.

Thank you, Mr. Marlow. Jane was lucky to have him. I was a little jealous, to be honest.

"You've only got one kid?" my aunt asked. "You get along?"

"We do," Mr. Marlow said. "I would do anything for her. That's why all this is bizarre to me. I can't imagine my world without Jane."

Yeah, well, I could definitely relate to that. Her face popped into my head, and a corresponding happy ache tugged at my chest. If I didn't watch myself, I might do something dumb-diddly-dumb-dumb like declare my very messy feelings about Jane right here in front of Mr. Marlow, my aunt, and the group of loud tourists dripping ice cream across the parking lot.

Better to tell Jane in private.

Bees in my chest....

Screw all this. I started to turn and jog into the shop, when I heard my aunt's voice again.

"Heard some mud about your Jane, too," she said.

"Is that so?" Mr. Marlow replied.

"That Mad Dog keeps her as close as he would a daughter."

Silence.

Awful. Fucking. Silence.

Dammit, Aunt Pari! Why did she ask that? He was clearly uncomfortable. I debated rushing around the van and making up some excuse to interrupt. But then he finally spoke up.

"Jane's my girl. I was there the night she was born, and I was there a few years later when her mother died. I changed her diapers, rocked her to sleep, and helped her with her homework. And since I won't be paying attention to gossip about Fen or Eddie or even Serj, then maybe you shouldn't pay attention to gossip about Jane. As long as no one's getting hurt, let 'em be."

Hell yeah! Ten points for the Henry Rollins fan.

Just let us be.

No one was getting hurt. How could you get hurt when you weren't doing anything wrong?

Fen Sarafian:

Hello

                                              Jane Marlow:

                                              Hello yourself

Fen Sarafian:

So . . . What are you doing tonight?

                                              Jane Marlow:

                      Watching TV in the domestics' rec room. You?

Fen Sarafian:

Sitting in a barn, wondering what you're doing

                                              Jane Marlow:

                                            Barn???

Fen Sarafian:

Long story. Do you ever leave the lodge at night?

Or is that forbidden?

                                              Jane Marlow:

                Don't know. Never had access to a car until this summer

Fen Sarafian:

Some of us have newly repaired vehicles, thanks to cool dads

What if I picked you up? There's a music collector I'd like you to meet

No Double Deuce, but you'll like him, I think

Jane

I'd been to my fair share of sketchy back door club entrances with Dad, tagging along when he picked up Mad Dog from some meeting with a band, or sitting backstage with Velvet while we watched a musician rehearse for a live album that her dad was recording.

But none of them made me feel like I was about to be shipped out on a boat to Russia in the dead of night. Or maybe I was just nervous to be out with Fen after dark. I wished I'd told someone where I'd gone. Not because I was actually worried about being out with Fen. But if I'd told someone, then I wouldn't feel guilty.

I could text someone now. Not my dad. Maybe Starla?

"You okay?" Fen asked. "You're checking your phone. . . ."

I shoved it in my pocket. "Nope, all good. What's with all the security cameras? This isn't a human trafficking ring, right? FYI, I'm worth nothing as a kidnapping victim."

"Another thing we have in common. My dad would probably pay kidnappers to take me away." He hit a buzzer on the back gate at the top of the deck's stairs. "Yo! It's us, man," he said into a speaker. "Let us in."

"Where's my near-mint?" a low voice replied. "You promised me a rose garden, Fennec."

"Let us in, and it's yours."

"You better hold the dog until we see how Peaches and Herb take to it," he warned.

Didn't like the sound of that. Frida stayed tucked under my arm as we entered the gate. I spotted Peaches and Herb—two longhair cats who quickly jumped to higher ground when Frida barked—and their owner, a biracial old hippie who looked a little like the man who ran the Sierra Mono Indian Museum near the giant sequoia tunnel tree where dad and I take our photo every summer.

"Moonbeam Bowland, this is Jane Marlow," Fen said, walking us into an outdoor living room.

"Heard a lot about you," the man said, giving me a reserved but kind smile.

A *lot*? That made me nervous. I glanced at Fen. He glanced at the lake. Frida barked at the cats, who were perched atop a bamboo shelf filled with plants. "Quiet!" I scolded. "It's ten o'clock at night. You'll wake the neighbors."

"No neighbors to wake," Moonbeam assured me.

"Welcome to hermit life, Jane," Fen said, sitting on one of the couches. "Moonbeam is a vegan vampire who watches the lake all night," he said, gesturing toward a telescope that sat near the deck's railing, pointed toward the other side of the lake. "So if you need to know if anyone's dumping bodies, he's your man."

"Condor's been body-free for a decade," Moonbeam assured

me, gesturing for me to have a seat. "All clear since Mrs. Abrams dumped her husband."

I was pretty sure they were joking, but not *totally* sure. "Should I ask . . . ?" I sat next to Fen, letting Frida explore around our feet, but keeping her leash wrapped around my wrist.

"Abrams didn't kill him. She was just cheap," Fen explained. "No money for the funeral."

I grimaced. "This town is so strange."

"That's what's great about it," Moonbeam said, sitting across from us in a recliner. He squinted at me, and it was a little awkward. Warm light spilled over his shoulders from his house, and I tried not to look inside, but there were shelves filled with records, and something was playing on his stereo that I didn't recognize.

"Penguin Cafe Orchestra," Fen volunteered. "Moonbeam doesn't listen to anything past 1985. He's a walking, talking time capsule."

The man ignored that. Maybe he didn't care because he was too busy staring at me, which was a little uncomfortable. Then he clapped his hands. "*Breathless*! Jean-Luc Godard. What was her name? Jean Seberg. That's who you remind me of, with your hair."

I touched the nape of my neck, fidgeting, before I realized what I was doing. "Oh? I haven't seen that. I've heard of it. It's important, or something? French."

"French New Wave," Moonbeam said, nodding. "Groundbreaking and shocking, about two lovers—an ugly young criminal who thinks he's tougher than he is, and the girl he's in love with, beautiful and bubbly on the surface, but actually might be as nihilistic as he is."

I shook my head, unable to tell if he was paying me a compliment. "You're not selling it to me."

"Jane's not big on nihilism. She likes fluff and Christmas lights," Fen explained.

"What a coincidence, all your favorite things," Moonbeam teased.

Fen flipped him off and leaned his head close to mine, pretending to talk conspiratorially but speaking loud enough for the man to hear: "Honestly, he's like this all the time, so don't expect his manners to get better. But he does subscribe to your no-selling-out philosophy. Moonbeam loves music and hates money."

"Wrong. I don't hate money," Moonbeam said. "It pays for what I need, no more, no less. Beyond that, it's useless. Why do I need gobs of it? I don't leave here."

"Ever?" I asked.

He shook his head. "Fen didn't tell you about me?"

"What's to tell, Moonbeam?" Fen said, patting his lap to invite Frida. She happily jumped up and stood on his chest to lick his face. "Whoa! Too much, pup."

"Calm, Frida," I told her, accidently touching Fen's hand as I settled her down.

He didn't seem to mind. His eyes were sharp tonight, watching me. Observing. Never leaving me, even when I was talking to Moonbeam. I could feel his gaze on my face, and it sent a little wave of warm chills down my arms.

"There you go," Fen said in a low voice, scratching her behind her ear as he spoke to Moonbeam. "She knows you stay up all night, and that you're clearly a hippie, living out on your deck, who watches too many old movies. Eventually I guess you'll decide if she's cool enough to browse your vinyl. I already told her that Victory Vinyl's been trading with you since before the festival existed, back in the nineties. Now he stays as far away from the festival grounds as possible."

"Fen's being purposely vague," the old man said in a strained voice, causing me to look up at him. "I was Condor Festival's first lawsuit, settled out of court."

Huh. Something shifted in a dusty corner of my brain. I'd heard about a settlement, back in the early days of the festival. I only vaguely remembered why. But I felt uncomfortable admitting this, so I just said, "No one's told me about this." Which was the truth.

"Figured as much. See, I got married the second year of the festival," he explained, "and my wife fell off some elevated seating they'd rigged up out in the big field. The crowd surged, rammed into it, and knocked her off. Lung collapsed. Couldn't save her in time. They tried to blame it on drug overdose, but she had asthma."

"Oh God. That's . . ." I shook my head, unable to get the picture of a stampede out of my mind. "I'm so sorry."

He nodded. "I know you've experienced your own tragedy at the dam."

"I was fortunate," I said in a low voice. I flicked my eyes toward Fen's face to find him looking back at me.

"You were," Moonbeam murmured. "Tina wasn't,

unfortunately, and I still miss her. But we bonded over music, and she wanted to be at the festival. So in a way, she died doing something she loved, as strange as that sounds."

It did. It was terrible and heartbreaking, and I was so sad for him. But I couldn't say that. So I just said, "I'm very sorry, Moonbeam."

"It's okay," he replied. "I didn't tell you to make you sad. It's good to share, though."

Maybe it helped him a little to talk about it. Surely he couldn't have a ton of people to talk to, living like this. "How long were you married?" I asked.

"Two weeks. She lived in Fresno but would come to the lake every summer to hike. She liked birds and swimming. Outdoorsy type. She also loved seeing shows outside, and that's how we met. I worked at a bar on the Strip called the Anchor, and she came in to see local bands play."

I knew that one. Not personally, but it was close to Betty's on the Pier, my nemesis. A few of the bars by the lake had stages that were either out on the docks or on patios that faced the lake.

"Yeah, for me, Tina was *the one*," Moonbeam said. "Looking back now, I knew it for a year before I ever asked her out, but I wanted my freedom. That's my biggest regret. Not even the festival. Just waiting so long. We could've had more time."

"My mom died of an aneurysm when I was five," I said. "I don't remember much about her. Just small things, like her reading a book to me, and the chair she sat in—it had a pillow with roses on it. Mostly know her face from looking at pictures." I shook my head. "Anyway, it was thirteen years ago, and my dad still misses her. He says that a lot too—that he wishes they had more time."

He nodded and squinted. "Yeah, it's funny how it lingers on. You get better, but it lingers. That's why I stay here. I don't go to the festival. Don't like crowds. Don't like a lot of people, honestly."

"Especially not my father," Fen said. "We have a lot in common."

"True," Moonbeam said with a small smile. Then he looked up at his ginger cat. "I think they're going to stay up there, so you can probably let your little one roam free. The doors are all closed, so there's no place to get loose besides what you see here. I keep things tight. You like mint tea?"

"Uh . . . ?"

"It's good if you add sugar," Fen told me, gently knocking his shoulder against mine before offering to help me off the couch, eyeing his friend all the while, who was watching us. "Come on, Moonbeam, I brought the record you wanted in my backpack. Can I show her your Beatles?"

"Slow down, man. You're always in a such a hurry. . . ."

It was easy to see how Moonbeam could feel that way out here, so isolated, with nothing but two cats for company. As we drank tea, he opened up about the fact that he hadn't left the house for more than a short walk in years—how he didn't need to, because everything came to him, and the settlement he'd received from Sarafian Events would provide for him until he died. And there was something pleasant about his little refuge. I could see why Fen liked the man, and why he spent a lot of time out here, clearing his head.

"Music and conversation," Fen told me as we looked through Moonbeam's record collection, all neatly tucked into plastic sleeves to protect them from the elements. "And the stars."

But also the sadness. Because there was some of that here too. An abiding, soft sadness that clung to all the records and furniture like a hug that went on too long. The lake wasn't healing this man. He was sitting here, nursing his pain, standing guard over the spirit of his dead wife. He wasn't letting go.

And that's when I knew that maybe there was some kind of twisted logic in what Mad Dog had told me. "Get back on the board," I whispered.

"Huh?" Fen said, giving me a strange look.

I shook my head. "Just something my dad says. But . . . if I asked you to take me somewhere tonight, would you? You're not going to like it."

For a moment, he didn't say anything. Then, "I'll take you wherever you want to go."

After cleaning up our teacups, we thanked Moonbeam and took off around the lake. I checked my phone to make sure I didn't have any texts—I was a little paranoid to be out. Not sure why. No one seemed to notice I was gone. And why would they? It wasn't quite eleven, not terribly late, especially for a warm summer night, and there was still a little traffic on the Strip when we headed back through town. I spotted the place where Moonbeam used to work, Anchor, and could hear live music from another tiny pub down the block.

Not too much else was open: a diner until midnight, the gas station out by the freeway, and a couple of restaurants. But when I gave Fen directions where I wanted him to go, and we turned off the Strip, chugging up a dark road that ran up Blue Snake River, away from the lights of town, the one thing that wasn't open came into view up ahead.

The Condor Dam.

"Can you pull over and park?" I asked.

"Are you serious?"

I nodded. "I just want to see it."

"It's closed to the public," he said, slowing down. "You can walk around in the park next to the dam, but you can't walk across it until morning."

"Dad told me. But maybe we could just sit on one of the benches in the park? I need to. Please, Fen. You said you wanted to ghost hunt with me. Well . . . ?"

He idled, making up his mind, and then drove farther up the road and pulled the Jeep into a parking space in a small empty lot that visitors used during the day. There wasn't so much a park on this side of the dam, more of a small green space with some trees and grass for walking your dog or getting out and stretching your legs to look at the dam and take photos. Couple benches and a trash can. If you crossed over the dam, then you'd be on a wooded point of land between the river and the lake—affectionately nicknamed Neverland—with flowers, a place to fish, and a meandering walking path that led to the Condor Visitors Center.

But crossing the dam to the Neverland area meant using the wooden walkway.

The one that was now gated.

The one from which I'd fallen.

Fen cut the engine. I held on to Frida, who wanted to bound out of the Jeep. We stared at the back of the dam, which was connected to a quaint Arts and Crafts–style control building with a roof, ten square windows across. Just a hundred feet or so—very picturesque and sweet, not some big Hoover Dam, or anything. Tourists loved to take photos of it, and there was a permanent stone chessboard and two stone bench chairs that sat near the railing here, where locals could come listen to the calm, flowing water and play a game.

Now it was dark and silent.

"Have you been back here?" I asked, trying to ignore Frida's soft whimpers to be let down and explore.

"So, *so* many times," Fen said in a low voice. He sighed deeply. "Come on. There's a place near the railing. I'll show you."

We were alone. Traffic sped in the distance over the auto bridge that crossed the river a quarter mile or so up. In the opposite direction, toward the lake, if I listened hard, I could hear music across the water from the Strip. No band at Betty's tonight, just music from some of the smaller bars. But I didn't really want to hear any of it, so I just concentrated on the soothing sound of the dam.

Fen and I walked together across dewy shorn grass, Frida sniffing in the dark as I looped the handle of her leash on my wrist. He stopped by the railing that looked down over the water that flowed softly from one of the dozen small floodgates that sat under the wooden walkway. The dam could raise or lower the lake by ten feet, depending on how many gates were open. The town gave free tours of how it worked, and Dad took me on one when I was a kid.

"Is it what you remembered?" Fen asked.

Yes and no.

The last time I was here, my chest didn't feel as if it were being held by a vise. But it looked prettier than it did in my mind. A peaceful spot to rest. An in-between place. Liminal.

It was not supposed to be a place for drunk parties and rude kids to run around like wild things, screaming for the bands that they could hear across the water while their friends snuck off across the walkway to the dark of Neverland and had sex in the woods, leaving empty beer cans and used condoms for the park service people to clean up the next day.

"I was there," I said, pointing at the end of the dam's walkway. "Sitting on the railing. That's where I fell. That's it, huh?" It wasn't very far.

"Ten feet," he said. "You hit those rocks there, and you floated out toward the lake."

"Where did you dive in?"

He scrubbed his face with his hand. "There, in the middle of the walkway. I swam . . . to about somewhere down there." He pointed farther down from where we were. "I couldn't find you at first. I was worried you'd floated out into the lake. It was dark and confusing, and one of the floodgates was open, so there was a little flow? Not much. But you got stuck on the rocks."

Stuck on the rocks. Because I was unconscious.

"How did you get me out of the water?" I asked.

"Carried you . . . tried to keep your head above the surface, and pulled you up those rocks there, onto the island. It was the only place that didn't have a railing."

"You knew CPR?"

He nodded. "Mama made us take classes when my dad bought a new boat."

Traffic lights flickered across the auto bridge in the distance. The vise on my chest crushed harder, and I knew I couldn't make peace with water. Not until I gave up a secret that was clawing at the back of my throat, trying to get out.

"I wasn't clumsy," I confessed.

Fen's arm stiffened next to mine on the railing. He didn't respond or look at me. I didn't want him to, or I couldn't tell him the rest of it.

"I wanted to know how it felt to fall," I continued in a small voice. "I didn't want to die. Eddie and I had just been across the walkway, in the woods. . . . Nothing really happened. He was too drunk. And then he just left me there, in the dark. He wanted to be with his friends."

Fen made a noise, but he didn't say anything.

I looked down at Frida and brushed away streaming tears I

could no longer control. "I never told anyone because it was so dumb. Just a lapse of reason for a single moment, and it completely changed my life. I was only trying to get his attention. What kind of idiot am I?"

His head lolled as he processed what I was saying. But it was too late to take it back. And I guess I was glad to finally be relieved of the burden. The secret had an unexpected weight that had been holding me down for so long.

I wanted to thank him for listening to me. For not judging. He turned from the railing and stared at me, face contorted with feral emotions that I couldn't identify.

Was he . . . mad at me?

"I've never told anyone else this," I said. "Are you angry that I told you?"

"I'm something."

"What does that mean?"

"It means just that. Something."

"Fen—"

"Yes, I'm upset, okay? If you think what you just told me is no big deal, then you wouldn't have kept it a secret."

True. I couldn't argue with that.

"You asked me why I rescued you?" he said in voice that sounded like thunder. "Remember? You couldn't figure out why I of all people would jump in the water after you."

"Yes. I did wonder that."

"It was because I was head over heels for you, okay?"

His words jolted through me. It couldn't be true. We'd never even hung out before this summer. Barely even spoken. Not for years. "How?" I said, blinking. "Since when?"

"Since forever. Since we were kids, and I tore up my leg at a fundraiser for local musicians downtown. You were there with Velvet and Mad Dog, remember?"

God. I did remember. We were fifteen, and though we'd run into each other before, that was the first time we spent more than a few minutes in each other's presence. "We talked about K-pop. . . . You cut your leg on a rusty nail—that's . . . when my dad drove you and your mother."

He didn't have to answer. I knew I was right.

I thought about how he reacted when I first saw him at Victory Vinyl. How weirdly intense it had been between us. His Ophelia tattoo. Why I couldn't stop thinking about him when I should have been thinking about my own boyfriend.

"Why didn't you tell me?" I whispered.

"How do you tell someone that they're your entire world when they're staring at the person next to you?"

"How could I be your entire world when you didn't know me?"

"How could you get so sad about a boy you didn't even really know that you'd fall in the water because of him?"

The vise on my chest squeezed until it cracked me.

Fen stormed away, walking the length of the railing toward the dam until I could only see his dark silhouette in the gray shadows. His tall shape bent over the railing, and he shouted obscenely into the water.

Frida whimpered at my feet. I crouched down and held her to tell her it was okay. To make me feel better. Then I felt Fen's hands pulling me up to my feet.

He gripped my shoulders and stared down at me with dark eyes, not saying anything. That was unbearable. His silence.

I wanted to tell him that I was sorry.

For not seeing him before. For screwing up his life. Then for walking back into town and not even recognizing him.

But part of me was angry, too. And *not* sorry. Because I didn't ask for any of this.

I didn't ask him to rescue me.

He shook his head over and over, still not saying anything.

His hands dropped to his sides, and I shut my eyes. He was going to tell me this was over—the two of us. No more ghost hunting, no more records. We were not friends. We weren't even . . . that word I could never remember. We weren't doing anything wrong.

We just *weren't*.

Then, abruptly, he slipped one arm around me and pulled my body against his chest. He was hugging me? It was so strange and unexpected; I didn't know what to do. Hug him back?

Before I could decide how to react, he said in a low voice, "This is how I held you in the water."

I collapsed against him and fell apart.

I wept.

He wept.

And when I couldn't stand anymore, we crumpled onto

the dark grass, clinging to each other. I held on to him until his T-shirt was a damp mess of makeup and tears. He held on to me until it got so chilly, he put his hands inside the back of my shirt to keep them warm. We held on to each other until Frida's leash got so tangled around our limbs that she gave up trying to get loose and went to sleep next to me.

But we didn't do anything wrong.

Not that night.

Unknown number:

Miss Jane, this is Jasmine Sarafian. Miss Norma gave me your number.

I found a nice apartment for us to view.

Pick you up Wednesday at 2PM in front of the lodge?

Jane Marlow:

Oh! Okay, yes. Thank you

I'll need to check w/ Velvet if I can leave during a workday

You know, for personal business, since I watch her dog/am her PA

But that should be fine?

Jasmine Sarafian:

Tell Velvet Larsen if she has a problem, she can come see me.

Bring the dog.

Jane

Jasmine paused at the door to the second-floor apartment, key in the lock. "Tell me again what he said exactly."

I wasn't very good at "exactly," especially when it came to words. But I tried to remember what Eddie had told me about getting the apartment. "I *think* he said that nothing could happen without your husband's approval, and that he'd need to smooth things over with him. Or sweet-talk him? That he couldn't promise me anything, but he'd figure something out? And that it was our little secret."

Jasmine made a low sound in the back of her throat.

"Have you heard from him?" I asked, sweating a little. "I was hoping maybe you had, since he doesn't seem to be getting my texts."

The noise in the back of her throat became a growl.

This wasn't going well. I'd been walking around in a daze since my night visit to the dam with Fen, unable to process simple commands from Norma. Unable get the scent of him out of my nostrils. I'd memorized the way he felt and how I fit against him. And now my already weird brain had rewired itself to accommodate all of this . . . newness.

And I was overwhelmed with it. With him. With us. What we were or could be.

How could I go back to this apartment hunting? Eddie had been gone over a week. No reply to my texts, but then again, I stopped trying.

Honestly, I wished I could just think about Eddie the way I used to, before Fen had gunked up my spotless image of him in my mind. The old Eddie was golden and imperfectly perfect—a little dumb, yes, and impossible to pin down, sure. But he had a perfect smile that always cheered me up, and he knew just the right thing to say.

Now I couldn't conjure that Eddie inside my brain. I kept seeing Eddie the Coke Addict or Eddie the Liar. I didn't know those Eddies. If I could just have one five-minute phone call with him, maybe I could clear up some of this stuff.

Maybe?

Regardless, I didn't want to pass up a chance to find out what was going on with him in the Philippines if his mother had some news about him. Mood: torn.

Jasmine was being very patient and kind, and it was hypnotic to be around her—something about her voice or the fresh, floral way she smelled, or her classy pencil skirt. How she smiled at me. It was completely different than my closed-up brick wall of a father or all the busy go-go-go of domestic life at the lodge, with Exie and Starla teasing me. She had all the time in the world, and that was enticing.

Too enticing. I didn't quite trust it. Maybe because I wasn't sure I wanted to move in with Eddie anymore. Not after all his lies. And then there was what I did with Fen. Which wasn't anything, really. But it wasn't nothing, either. I didn't know! I just didn't.

Was I a bad person for lying in the grass with Fen? For crying with him?

Holding him.

My boyfriend's brother.

We didn't kiss. We didn't even talk. But we stayed there until well after midnight, and we couldn't look at each other when he dropped me off. He just texted me later—like, four-in-the-morning later—and it said: Thank you.

What did that mean?!

And, *ohmygod*, Frida was driving me up the wall, pawing on the tile outside the door, begging to be let inside, which wasn't making this any easier.

"Maybe we should just wait until he gets back," I suggested again, wiping more sweat from my brow. "At least until he texts me back when he gets settled in the Philippines? He might be a touch, uh, cranky with me that I didn't keep it between us."

She left the key in the door and leaned against it, holding up her finger. "Never let a man talk you into keeping a secret between the two of you that benefits him only. That is no secret. That is a lie."

"But—"

"No." Her head shook as she waved the finger. "I do not care that it's my son. I would not care if it's my husband. Sisters keep secrets. Lovers keep secrets. But secrets should be equally shared. They aren't lopsided. They aren't a burden to one and a benefit to the other."

"How is this a benefit—"

"Just consider my advice. It will come to you eventually. Eddie learned from his father to wheel and deal. But I learned some things too." She unlocked the door. "Let's look at your new apartment, my darling."

Might as well be entering a Halloween spook house, the way my pulse pounded.

It didn't seem like the kind of place where people dressed like ghouls jumped out from behind doors. Big open space, white walls, fresh paint. Wood floors that creaked with each step, but in a homey sort of way. It reminded me of a loft apartment with a small, modern kitchen on one side and a painted white fireplace on the other. Exposed brick on the outer wall that held two big windows that overlooked the lake.

"What do you think?" Jasmine said as Frida's nails lightly clicked across the floor. "So spacious for a one-bedroom, right? It's almost two. There's a tiny room over here that could be an office or study—do you play an instrument or paint?"

"Uh, no. I wish I did," I said. "I like to read."

"Me too. Fen is named after a fennec fox in my favorite book, *The Little Prince*. Serj named all our children but Fen. He was my little fox."

Huh. I didn't know that.

"Anyway, plenty of wall space for bookshelves," she said,

walking toward the big windows. "Pretty view of the lake. Wouldn't a piano look nice right here? A baby grand."

That jostled something in my memory, but I couldn't remember *what*, exactly.

"I suppose so?" I said.

"Do you like classical music?"

"I like all kinds of music," I said, unsure why she was asking me this. It felt like bait, as if she were looking for a certain answer. That made me more nervous than I already was. And why was she trying to push this apartment on me? The girlfriend that Eddie apparently forgot to mention to his parents. She was hinting around that she knew Eddie kept secrets, and yet she wanted to reward him with a beautiful apartment?

I was confused. Maybe it was because my dad and I didn't operate this way.

She abandoned her questions about my interests and just stared out the window, saying, "You'd be close to everything on the Strip. The streetcar stops outside, so if you worked anywhere downtown, there's your transportation. Groceries at the corner store, a block away."

Sounded wonderful. There had to be a catch. "Where's your house from here?" I asked, just to make conversation. I knew vaguely that they lived in a multimillion-dollar home on the other side of the lake—everyone knew. Just like everyone knew that Mad Dog summered in the lodge. It was common knowledge around Condor. Sometimes you'd see their living room in the background of photos that Eddie posted online. I'd just never been there in person.

She squinted and pointed. "You can't really see it, but we're ri-i-ight across the lake. It's a villa on the southern side. Below the Mission Bluff."

Right. Mission Bluff, where they held Battle of the Bands. That made me think of Fen and how he helped me find Velvet that disastrous afternoon. Unfortunately, I was nearly positive Velvet was hanging out with that same cocaine girl from Mission Bluff tonight. Yet another problem I didn't know how to fix.

"What are your plans?" Jasmine asked. "I know that your accident has put a crimp in your future. I can't imagine it's been easy, going through speech therapy."

This caught me off guard. "You know about, uh, my apha-sia?"

She nodded and pushed dark hair over one shoulder. "From Fen, not from Eddie. He didn't tell me anything about you, I'm afraid. Eddie and Serj keep a few secrets from me."

I didn't like that. "Why?"

"I don't know, but I suspect it has to do with Mad Dog." Her eyes narrowed. "I don't like to circle around matters, so I'll ask you this, woman to woman, and you can answer if you like. Are you Mad Dog's daughter?"

Heat rushed through my neck and ears. "No. That's a . . ." Word. What's the word? "People talk. But it's not true. My dad says wild horses couldn't stop him from being my father."

She relaxed and let her head loll back to laugh quietly at the ceiling for a moment, but not in a mean way. "I'm glad to know the truth, because I admire Mad Dog, but I quite like your father.

You can just tell sometimes what people are made of inside—if you really pay attention. And I'd like to think I'm pretty good at it."

"My father likes you too," I said.

She glanced at my hand. "I noticed you tap your fingers in a rhythm. Is that to help your memory, or your speech?"

"Both. It's connected," I said, stilling my hand against my leg. "It's a little trick I taught myself. Music helps when I'm stressed, and sometimes I can sing the sentence I'm trying to say—inside my head? And I'll remember the word I'm missing."

"Fascinating. Someone in my Ladies Guild at church was telling us about a friend in San Francisco who's studying music for therapeutical applications. I believe she's doing it so that she can work with the elderly, in hospice. Music can be very healing." She cocked her head to the side. "Our church choir is always looking for younger members. . . . Do you happen to sing?"

I shook my hand. "Not where anyone can hear me, no ma'am."

"Understood," she said, smiling. "Tell me, Miss Jane, what did you mean when you said earlier that Eddie had not texted you back?"

I hesitated. "He hasn't answered my texts since he left last week. I was hoping you could tell me if he was okay."

"I see. . . ." Her brows knitted together. "Actually, he isn't responding to me, either. Serj says he's heard from our lawyer, and that they've arrived on the private island—that they had some small complications with customs, but that things are going all right now."

"Oh?"

"I think perhaps I will try to get in touch with Mr. Gordon to see if I can get some info."

"Mad Dog's lawyer? He'll give you the lowdown." I'd actually considered asking Norma if she could text Gordon for me, but then I'd owe Norma a huge favor. Not a good place to be.

"Indeed," Jasmine agreed. "Don't worry about Eddie any longer, and I will let you know if I hear anything, yes?"

"Thank you."

She gestured with her head. "Now, let's look at the bedroom while you tell me about your college plans. Got any? Or are you a student of life?"

We strolled through the apartment, and I told her in all honesty that I wasn't sure what I wanted to do. I told her about my high school in L.A., and how hard it was to finish. How I used to love school.

"I just don't want to be a domestic for the rest of my life," I said. "That's all I know for sure right now. I love music, but I'm not a musician, and I'm not sure I'm all that interested in what Mad Dog does. He's stressed out most of the time and worried about money. Eddie said he was going to teach me about the events business, but I don't know."

Jasmine made a noise. "Eddie needs to be taught about the events business before he can teach anyone else. He's eager, but he's still learning the ropes and doesn't know where he'll land yet. We employ almost a hundred people. Marketers. Booking agents. PR. Accountants. Graphic artists. Salespeople. Human resources. It's an enormous operation."

"I'm sure."

We walked through the empty bedroom. "Maybe you need to take some general college courses until you find your niche."

"Maybe," I said, feeling insecure about where this was going. Was it rejection? From his mother? I couldn't tell.

"Not everyone knows their calling when they're eighteen. Serj pushed Fen and Eddie. Eddie responded. Fen resisted—explosively. You cannot force blood from a stone. But you can give that stone a push down a hill. Now my little stone is rolling around on his own."

"Fen?"

She nodded. "One day he'll be a great boulder, but for the moment it's important for him to roll freely. I'm so very proud of him. I'm proud of Eddie, too, but they are very different. I feel as if I've failed to guide him. It's really up to both of them now. I need to concentrate on the twins. They'll be driving soon, then I'll lose them. . . ." She sighed. "Being a parent isn't easy."

"Yes, ma'am."

Her gaze flicked to my face. "I can see that I've confused you, and that wasn't my intention. You are always welcome to work at the festival offices, of course. We can find something for you, if that's what you want. All you have to do is come to me and ask. I didn't mean to rule that out."

"Uh . . . thank you? I wasn't intending, I mean—"

"It's down the line. Let's not worry about it now." She smiled. "One thing at a time."

I let out a shaky breath. "Okay."

She gestured loosely toward the walls. "This is a nice corner bedroom. One window toward the lake, and one toward the building next door—which is not as good, but you can put up window treatments, yes? Come. Let's look."

We walked across the empty bedroom, and Frida immediately jumped up on the built-in window seat to peer out. Jasmine was right. There was only a small space between the two buildings, and this was nearly level with the window across the way. Talk about privacy issues. What was in that building? I wasn't quite sure where we were on the Strip. Jasmine had driven us here, and I was too nervous to pay attention to where we'd parked. But the room inside the window across from us looked to be some kind of office.

An office filled with shelves of records.

A funny feeling crept over me.

As I continued staring into that office, Jasmine pulled out her phone and made a call, whispering to me, "Pardon me, please."

Someone jogged into the office and picked up the phone. A tall, dark-headed male.

"Hello, darling," Jasmine said into the phone. "Having a good day at work? Yes? Why are you not ironing your shirts? Doesn't Zabel have an ironing board in her house? I know Pari keeps one of those tiny travel models in the record store. I think it is in that little closet behind you."

Oh my God.

The person on the phone in the office turned around, paranoid, and glanced out the window. It looked as if his face was melting. Or maybe that was just shock.

Jasmine waved.

I just stared in horror.

Frida stuck her nose against the glass.

"Okay, well, I am showing Miss Jane an apartment that she might share with Eddie," Jasmine said. "We are in the bedroom. Anyway, have a good day. I love you, Fen-jan."

Frida barked at the window. It was probably at her reflection, but it sounded like "help."

Same, Frida. Same.

My phone chimed in my pocket. Once. Twice. And again.

"Oh my. Please answer it," Jasmine encouraged. "Must be important."

Answering it was the last thing I wanted, but it chimed again and again—and when I slipped it out of my pocket, a series of texts from Fen flashed up my screen.

Tell her I'm calling back my marker

New marker request

No. Tell her I'm not speaking to her

She's dead to me

Tell her that!

No. Wait. Don't tell her that

I take it back

But I don't forgive her right now

Jasmine craned her neck to peer at my phone, then stood back quickly. A slow smile spread over her face. "Ah, that's all I wanted to know."

"Ma'am?" I said nervously.

"Nothing at all. Would you like to come to lunch at my house? I would very much like you to meet the twins. One day when Serj is at work, perhaps. Yes?"

"Um . . . okay?"

"Perfect. I'll text you." She turned away from the window and raised her arms, turning in a circle, while my phone kept chiming. "So, tell me . . . how do you like this sweet, little apartment? Ideal for a young couple who is trying to find their way in the world, yes?"

Dear lord. This woman was an evil mastermind. I blinked at her, unable to speak, and then stared through the window at Fen. He put his hand on the glass and stared back. So close, yet unreachable. "Yes," I mumbled, my breath fogging the window. "Ideal."

"I thought so," Jasmine said behind me. "Mothers have instincts about these things."

I wouldn't know.

Fen

I checked my phone again, waited for her to respond. It had been six minutes since they left the room. What were they doing, signing a lease? That apartment was occupied last week. I know because I saw movers taking furniture away a couple of days ago, and then the blinds disappeared.

It wasn't the first time I'd seen inside it. I'd voyeuristically peered into that apartment for months when the couple who used to live there opened their blinds. Not like that. It was just their day-to-day living. Watering plants, a cat that slept on the window seat. Nothing sexy.

I told Mama I wanted to live in that apartment building because it was close to the shop. And looked so peaceful. Like freedom. I could picture myself living there and breaking away from my family. It once represented a future of independence to me.

Now it looked like betrayal.

"Stop pacing," Aunt Pari said, squinting over her glasses at the computer screen as she ticked boxes on a bill of lading. "You're going to wear out the office carpeting."

"It's already worn."

The office chair squeaked as my aunt swiveled and stuck out her leg to stop me. "You're driving me strawberries, kid. We're past bananas and onto strawberries. I love you, but you've got to calm down. Go to lunch. That's where you're supposed to be anyway. Tom can't run the register all afternoon. Forget about the apartment and stop pining over this girl."

"Easy for you to say. You don't have Jasmine for a mother!"

She laughed and pushed her glasses on top of short, dark curls that matched mine. "No, just an older sister, what do I know? Why do you think I ended up with your uncle? She's a meddler and a matchmaker. Whatever she's trying to do, ignore it."

"You love Uncle Charlie."

"Sadly, I do. And I blame her. Go to lunch." She kicked at my ankle to shoo me out, and when I was almost out the door, she called, "By the way, that Tybalt widow wants you to come back tomorrow to work on her record collection. Alone. Now there's a match for you. Lonely old white lady on the prowl—bet you could make some extra cash servicing more than her collection. Pay me back for those Curtis Mayfield records."

"You are my least favorite aunt."

She threw me some folded-up cash. "You are my second favorite nephew. Bring me back some iced tea and I'll move you up to number one."

I jogged down the stairs that led onto the sales floor, where I ignored the customers milling around and the fact that Tom was overwhelmed at the front counter. I had to get to the apartment and stop whatever it was Mama thought she was doing. But when I rushed out the front door into the sun and pulled on a pair of dark sunglasses, I stepped onto the sidewalk and came face-to-face with one pixie and a hairless dog.

"Hey," Jane said, wide-eyed and breathless. Red cheeks. "I was . . . trying to catch you."

"Caught me." I glanced behind her. "Where is she?"

Jane looked over her shoulder briefly. "Your mom? I waited until she drove away." She chuckled nervously. "Seems silly now. I don't know why it matters. . . . Uh, she was going to drive me back to the lodge, but I told her my dad would pick me up. That while I was in town, I had, um, that thing, when you have stuff to do. A list of chores . . . ?"

"Errands."

Her face brightened as she smiled. "That's it."

God, I wanted to touch her again. Just her hair. Hold her hand. The tip of my finger on the back of her hand. Anything.

"Fen? I don't know what just happened," she said, looking up in the direction of the apartment. "But that wasn't my idea. She texted me—I didn't know it would be here."

I nodded. Licked dry lips.

"I didn't know," she whispered.

God, she was really shaken up. As much as I was, maybe. That made me feel less anxious. At least we were in the same place. "Welcome to the Sarafian family," I said. "This is very much a Jasmine move."

"It was, I don't know . . . like she was trying to test me?"

"No, she did it to rile me up. It's okay. I can take it."

She shook her head. "No, I think she knows." She leaned closer. "About us."

Us.

Did you hear that, world? There's an us!

Jane was not in the mood to share my excitement.

A customer was walking toward the shop, so I moved out of the entrance to let them get inside. "Hey, want to walk with me?" I asked Jane. "Where we can talk alone?"

She nodded. No hesitation. That was good.

I definitely didn't want to hang out here where Aunt Pari could see us.

"How long before you need to get back to the lodge?" I bent down to scratch Frida's head as we walked.

"Soon," she said. "But I'm okay for a little while. Can we get something to drink? It's so hot today. Why is it so hot?"

I glanced around the block. "Mother nature is getting revenge—probably against my kooky family for bringing thousands of people into the woods for a festival every year. Come on, this way."

Without speaking, we walked in tandem toward the corner, and I steered her toward a stucco storefront there that was painted an electric shade of blue. A sign above the door read:

THE BAIT SHOP

IF WE DON'T HAVE IT, YOU DON'T NEED IT.

NOMADS WELCOME.

Condor's corner shop. Maybe more of a general store.

The original owners were hippies from San Francisco. Flower power and acid trips, free love, all that. They opened the Bait Shop in 1969, and it was one of those places that are sort of stuck in time. You either loved or loathed it, but it was an iconic part of the lake.

I pushed my sunglasses up on my head as we stepped inside. A few unhurried customers browsed narrow aisles between rainbow shelves bursting with a strange assortment of granola snacks, knickknacks, flip-flops, and health food. Beach towels and bright umbrellas hung from the ceiling next to an old-fashioned machine that roasted almonds. There was even a rotating display of random hardware—just in case you needed to buy one loose nail or screw, and who didn't? And then there was the obligatory homemade kombucha and yogurt for sale next to a closed dispensary window with a giant marijuana leaf.

"I love this place," Jane murmured. "Mostly because Frida gets distracted by the smells on the floor, so she doesn't bark at people or try to take anything off the shelves. So I can spend a lot of time browsing."

"They probably haven't mopped in thirty years," I told her. "Are you hungry or just thirsty? I'll get it."

"Just thirsty, thank you," she said. "I need to give Frida some water too. Maybe we can sit outside? Do they still have those little café tables out back? They remind me of Paris. Not that I've been. Paris in my mind. Just with more pine trees, ha." She wiped her forehead. "There's never anyone out there this time of year. At least, there didn't used to be. Maybe that's changed. Everything has around the lake since I was here last. Are you hot?"

She was talking a mile a minute, completely flustered and anxious. Fucking adorable. I was going to die from her adorableness. At a small deli counter next to the register, I bought one giant limeade and a bottled water from Condor's resident Jimmy Hendrix look-alike. Then I held the back door open while Jane ducked under my arm, and we walked out of the shop onto a sprawling lake patio.

Alone at last. Us.

"Yes, excellent. This is the best view on the Strip," she said, sounding a little calmer as she took out a little cup from her bag and filled it with bottled water on the patio for Frida.

She wasn't wrong about the view. The wooden patio was half on shore, half over the lake, where a few sailboats glided in the distance. It was a perfect June day, not a cloud in the sky. The mountains beyond the water looked like something out of a storybook, capped in snow.

My mind was spinning a million miles an hour. About the apartment and my mother. About Jane sitting next to me now. I was trying to process how I felt and what I wanted to say, but nothing was coming out. Jane put up the dog's water cup and drank half the limeade through a striped straw. I drank after her while her eyes stayed on mine, and it felt ridiculously intimate to put my mouth where hers had been.

Behind us, the door creaked open, and a couple emerged from the shop. They sat down on a bench by the patio wall, under a sign that said RIPPLE. As in, Grateful Dead. Still water. Pebbles.

All that. I wasn't a Dead fan, but that was their best song. So peaceful and beautiful . . .

And I wanted to murder the Ripple couple for interrupting my moment alone with Jane.

She held on to her elbow and gave the couple a tight smile.

"We can take those deck stairs down," I suggested, pointing to the far side of the patio. There was a walking path that snaked around the lake. All of the shops along the way had two entrances—the main doors from the Strip, and the lakeside entrances around back. No one used the path but locals this time of year. Sometimes you'd see runners here early in the morning, but right now, it was shady from trees and the shadows of the buildings.

Blissfully deserted.

I loosely carried the limeade cup by the rim in the tips of my fingers while watching her from the corners of my eyes. Her black polo shirt had Mad Dog's logo stitched on it, as if she were his property, or something. That pissed me off, which was dumb, I guess; especially when I looked down at the name tag on my own shirt: property of the record shop.

"Does she know?" Jane asked.

"Know what?"

She stopped and looked at the water over a waist-high stone barrier that ran along the path. The lake was yards away. Rocks and trees and small outbuildings marred our view. Frida wagged her tail at a beetle crawling between blades of grass.

"Your feelings," she said. "Your mother, I mean."

"About?" I wanted her to say it.

Her eyes flicked to mine. "I'm just trying to figure out what is going on. My father doesn't do stuff like this."

"Oh, like . . . rent an apartment that your son specifically mentioned wanting just to throw it in his face because the girl chose his brother instead of him?"

She was offended. "I didn't *choose*. There wasn't a bachelor contest. No one gave me a rose and said, 'Here, offer this to the one you want.' I'm not a spoiled debutante who gets invitations to galas."

"No?"

Should've not said that. She was riled. Not much. Riled enough to roll her eyes and look away without answering. A huff of her shoulder, arms crossed. Honestly, still adorable.

"Hey, how am I supposed to know what you do with Eddie? Maybe he takes you out to balls and fancy parties. The ballet at Royce Hall."

She frowned at me. "How do you know about Royce Hall?"

My heart hammered. "Get to know me and find out."

"I do know you," she said.

"You know some of me."

"You know some of me," she argued.

"I think I've been paying more attention than you have." I dared to reach for her hand, just to brush her knuckles with backs of my fingers. Barely, barely, *barely*.

She shivered lightly and sucked in a breath.

But she didn't pull away.

So I stepped closer and inhaled near that little swoop of hair above her eye that looked like meringue. Sun peeped through the pine branches above, and it was so hot. I wanted to taste the salt on her brow.

If I just kept my eyes there, not on her face, maybe it would be okay.

I was losing it. Boundaries melting. I should care more.

Cool wind blew off the lake, rustling through the pines.

Her voice was almost a whisper. "I feel like you've been there the whole time, and I couldn't see you. But I can now." Her index finger hooked around my thumb. A thousand warm chills ran up my arm as her face turned upward.

It was a mistake to look at her eyes.

I dropped the limeade cup. Cold droplets splatted across my ankles when it hit the ground, but neither of us made a move to pick it up.

My head bent. Lower. Our faces were too close now for this to be chaste and decent. She could move away, though, right? I should tell her to go.

"Jane?" I managed, voice cracking like I was thirteen. I swallowed hard and repeated, "Jane." Not a question this time, but a warning.

Her face was turned up to mine, and it was so small. I was aware of how her lips parted and the shallowness of her breath . . . how it matched mine, an expectant rhythm.

I felt it in my body like a call. Something sent from her that pulled inside my chest. A low noise dislodged from me. She murmured a question back, indecipherable. I just wanted . . . everything. I wanted all of her. Wanted her to want me. I was trembling with it and terrified that she was going to duck away. Come to her senses. Leave.

So I slipped my hands around her face and closed my eyes, savoring all of it—the intoxication of being this close, the *almost* of it all.

But my mouth found hers. Barely, barely, *barely*. Touching, breathing. I gave her a soft and small kiss. A little awkward, like trying to get bearings in unfamiliar territory.

Then it was no longer *almost*.

It was happening.

A real kiss—she kissed me back. One kiss, and then another.

Intoxicating kisses, deep and miraculous and so fast.

It felt like we were trying to outrun something, or maybe catch up with it. Not what I'd fantasized about all these years, but that was all gone now. There was only this, and it was *everything*. My world shifted to accommodate the newness.

Her arms wrapped around me, pulling me closer. Like she held me when we lay together in the grass at the dam. I nearly died. Nearly wept. Nearly begged her to lie down with me again right here and now. I was on fire, and I wanted her.

Somewhere on another planet, I heard children's voices. Tiny ones, laughing. And a dog barking. In a daze, Jane and I disentangled ourselves from each other—an action that felt wrong, wrong, *wrong*—to find a woman leading a clustered group of toddlers in yellow shorts and matching camp shirts down the walking path. The kids were trying to pet Frida, who was dragging her leash behind her.

"Oh, Frida, s-shit," Jane slurred, shaking her head. She tried to take a step and stumbled.

I caught her around her waist. "Upright is good."

Her cheeks were rosy. "Knees not working."

"Yeah?"

"Yeah."

Mmm. I was going to need a second to recover, myself. "Who the fuck let Madeline and her boarding school friends out?" I complained. "My mother probably sent them to thwart us."

"Oh God," she mumbled as worry lines formed on her forehead.

Shit. Wheels were turning. She was starting to realize what we'd done—starting to think about consequences. "Don't think about the future," I begged. "Please."

This is the best day of my life, I thought, miserable. I wanted her to feel the same way I felt. I wanted her to be happy too.

She let out a quick, labored breath, and the worry lines on her forehead softened. She nodded twice, short little nods, and held my hand. "I'm not thinking."

Thank the saints.

Wish I could say the same.

Jane

It was only a kiss. It wasn't as if I'd shot Franz Ferdinand and caused a world war. But when I got back to the lodge and Exie asked me to help her with dinner prep, it sure felt as if I'd done something cataclysmic, or at least irreversible.

What if I couldn't go back to the way things were? What if I didn't want to?

I didn't even mean for it to happen. But when I left the apartment and saw Fen, all of my good sense disappeared. He was starting to have that effect on me. When I was around him, all I was thinking about was the way his mouth always looked like it was hiding a smile, even when he was being dark and acerbic. I'd never known an almost-smile could say so much more than a big smile.

A lot of things I hadn't known before I ran into Fen Sarafian. He made me question everything.

But one thing I didn't question was that kiss. It was good. Really good.

How could I see him again and not think about that kiss?

Exie gave me a look and waved a hand in front of me.

"What's happening? What is all *this*? You look like a zombie, the way you're standing around, lost in your own world. Daydreaming in the kitchen can't be good."

"I'm not daydreaming in the kitchen," I mumbled, a little defensive. "I'm just waiting for Velvet. That's my job, you know. I'm a PA now."

"Oh?" One brow lifted. "Is there a buy-one-get-one-free couture sale that you're missing right now? Don't let me hold you up from your important PA duties."

Nothing gets by Exie. "She'll text me when she needs me," I said. "I think I'm done for the day, anyway."

Exie ducked into the pantry to pull out a new bottle of olive oil. "Anything else you need to get off your chest?"

"No, nothing," I said quickly.

She emerged from the pantry to give me a long look but then blinked and gave up. "Fine, then. While you're not daydreaming or waiting on Velvet, you can help. Carrots—washed, peeled, diced," she said, adjusting her apron. "Please and thank you."

Popping in earbuds, I accepted the task with relief. I needed to cool off and get some perspective, I knew that much. Listen to something healing, like Jasmine had talked about. I put on Sigur Rós's *Ágætis Byrjun*, but instead of concentrating on work, all I could think about was Fen.

It was just so surprising—that the kissing happened at all. The kiss itself . . . I couldn't compare it to another kiss because it was something completely different. It was as if everything else before it was just training and this was the real thing.

Which was terrifying, honestly. The world should prepare you for this kind of stuff. Why isn't there a class for this? Who cares about calculus and volleyball? Tell me how shocking a real kiss can be. That's what matters.

As I peeled ribbons of orange from the carrots, I couldn't stop thinking about his hands. Which was ridiculous. But I'd been thinking about them on my bare back since that night at the dam. Okay, yes, I suppose I'd been thinking about them a lot longer. I loved the way his fingers felt against my skin. Like they were discovering me.

I loved the way he said my name. It made me ache. Something hot and needy unwound inside me from my chest to the pit of my stomach. I felt bewitched.

And I shouldn't. I was in no position to have any witchery cast on me. If Eddie would just answer his texts, then—what? I didn't know. I ran through several scenarios in my mind, and then quickly shut them all down. The problem was, I knew in my heart that just because he wasn't texting me back, that didn't give me the right to go around kissing whoever I wanted.

Definitely not Eddie's brother. Someone he hated.

I may not have been doing anything wrong before, but I was now. And I knew it.

I wasn't built for this.

What was I going to do?

Norma stormed through the kitchen and gestured wildly at Exie, interrupting my thoughts. I turned down the music in my earbuds to make sure Norma wasn't complaining about my not answering the walkie.

". . . coming in at seven in the morning after being out all night. Kamal reviews a daily security file that contains the times we punch in our alarm codes, you know."

"Maybe she's walking the dog," Exie argued.

Norma snorted. "Velvet's never walked the dog in her life. She barely pets it."

Uh-oh.

"What do you want me to do about it?" Exie said. "She's a grown woman. And I'm not her keeper."

Norma turned to look at me. "Next time she's out partying with her trashy lake friends, you better tell your father or Kamal to come get her."

"Me?" I said.

"Or the local police, your choice," Norma said, shrugging. "But if she makes a scene in the press, Mad Dog will be furious."

Norma left the kitchen without an answer from me. She just had an expectation that her wishes would be carried out. And honestly, they usually were. I just didn't know how to handle this.

"Maybe things will calm down for the time being," Exie said. "Velvet asked me for a heating pad a couple hours ago."

Velvet had terrible periods—she didn't leave the house for a couple of days. I felt bad for her, but at the same time, I was a little relieved. Maybe I could have a talk with her. And ask her nicely . . . not to make my life difficult? Ugh, no. This wasn't about my convenience. It was about Velvet's safety. But at the same time, I wasn't sure what Norma really expected me to do, ride around behind Velvet with binoculars? I didn't get invited to these parties. Maybe I should mention something to Fen, since he knew about these people more than I did.

Or maybe I was just looking for another excuse to see him again. Best to resist.

Later that night, I didn't have to. He un-resisted me.

Fen Sarafian:

Hey, you probably aren't up, but I thought I'd check

Jane Marlow:

I'm up. Can't sleep

Fen Sarafian:

In a bad way? Or a good way?

Jane Marlow:

In a "this is all new to me" way?

Fen Sarafian:

This is all new to me, too

Not sure if that helps

Jane Marlow:

It does. Because I have so much in my glitchy head

Fen Sarafian:

I like your glitchy head

And all the rest of you too

Jane Marlow:

I wish I could hear your voice

Fen Sarafian:

SAME

Can you talk? I'm absolutely alone

> **Jane Marlow:**
> I'm in domestic quarters
> Walls are paper thin

Fen Sarafian:

Outside? Don't you need to walk the dog?

I think you should

> **Jane Marlow:**
> Give me five minutes to get Frida's harness on
> I'll call you

Fen Sarafian:

Call sooner. I'm dying

Velvet was still feeling bad the next afternoon, and Fen was working away from the store, so he suggested picking me up so that we could spend the last part of the day together on a mysterious outing that involved "sun and fresh air."

It didn't take much convincing. I was a nervous wreck, wanting to see him again after our late-night phone call . . . knowing it was wrong. Those feelings created a sharp anxiety in the center of my solar plexus. I knew it wasn't rational, but I had to be near him soon, or it felt as if that sharpness was going to break me apart.

Fen sounded much less frazzled than I felt. Cool and breezy behind dark shades that covered his hawk eyes, so it was hard to read his emotions. Or maybe mine were so dangerously fragile that I was having trouble focusing on anything else. But he didn't act like he'd spent the last twenty-four hours replaying our kiss in his mind until life had no meaning.

Not that I'd done that.

He was out of the record store for the day because he'd been finishing up the Tybalt collection assessment. It was worth a cool $2,700, thanks to a couple of Elvis records and one or two other rarities, but the widow wasn't happy. She'd been hoping for much more.

"There was shouting," he told me from the driver's seat of the Jeep as we sped away from the lodge. He glanced in the rearview mirror as if someone might catch us. Honestly, I was afraid of that too. I reminded him about the lodge security cameras, but he pointed out that to anyone watching, we were still just "in-laws" hanging out.

That old chestnut.

Still, neither of us had come closer to each other than where we sat right now, with the parking brake between us. No touching, no nothing. I think we were both afraid to look each other in the eye. I was definitely afraid to look at his hand on the gearshift. Nay! Here there be dragons!

"Where are we going?" I asked.

"A toddler-free zone."

No interruptions. Flutters went through me. I wasn't sure if I trusted myself. Or us. But I also wasn't telling him to turn the Jeep around, either. And when Eddie's face popped up in my head, I brushed it aside along with the guilt I was accumulating.

I'd deal with that later.

When we got into town, we crossed over the river behind the dam, and for the first time, I didn't want to curl up inside myself. Fen gave me a look and nodded, as if he understood. Then he turned right and drove a couple blocks away from the Strip.

This was familiar territory, especially when we passed a massive field full of ruts used for parking, and across from it, a smaller paved lot near a large park gate—one that's built to look like the entrance to a medieval town. The sign near the gate read CONDOR PARK AND AMPHITHEATER.

"Um . . . ? I thought you were excommunicated from the festival biz. Why are we coming here?"

"I am," he assured me. "We're cutting through. Be prepared to see firearms."

"What?"

"Kidding," he said, driving through the paved parking lot. "Mostly."

Parts of the park were open to the public, except during paid events, so there were park visitors walking through a turnstile area guarded by park rangers, and plenty of others at minivans with strollers and sun hats, heading to a puppet show at a children's stage in the woods. But Fen was driving past all that. Past the performing arts center and the shiny office building, where his father worked, to a locked gate in front of one of the main festival fields: Avalon.

Not open to public.

Fen jumped out and ran to the gate in long black shorts and a faded black T-shirt with Mozart's portrait and name in a heavy metal font. He punched a code into the gate lock. The bar lifted, and he jogged back to the Jeep just in time to drive through before it closed again. He laughed to himself. "Whoo! You can lock me out, but you can't lock out my mother, asshats!"

"That was . . . ?"

"My mother's code. They'll change it next week, but she'll just give it to me again. It's fine, don't worry. Hold on to the pup. This gets bumpy."

He drove at a slow speed through a field I'd been in many times as a guest—once backstage with Mad Dog and Velvet—but never before the festival started. Never this early. Condor had several festival fields with stages, but Avalon was for camping. Half of it was pitch-your-own tent—the jokes abounded—but right here was Merry Village, where you could rent a tiny medieval-style tent, complete with cots and Wi-Fi, and walking distance to pop-up "shops," which were run out of trucks and stalls.

It was so strange to see it being erected. All the little gray tents, flat on the grass, waiting to be put up. Some already had their red flags waving on top. Several workers were hammering in stakes as we drove past, and they looked up at us but didn't seem bothered when Fen lifted his hand and waved.

"I always wanted to stay in one of those," I said. "They're so expensive. Who can afford two or three thousand dollars for one weekend? I don't understand how they fill these things."

"And yet they sell out in minutes every year," Fen said. "Nearly all profit at this point. The tents were a couple hundred each, custom made, and the cots were cheap in bulk. It's just the labor of getting them put up and paying minimum-wage employees to check in the tenters during the festival. Half a million net in my dad's pocket." He snapped his fingers. "And that's not including all the shit Festival Freaks buy over the weekend."

I was shocked. Eddie would brag about the tents, but he never explained it to me like that.

"I should write a festival exposé," Fen said, mouth upturned. "Piss my father off."

I laughed. "Haven't you already pissed your father off?"

"Rage momentum," he said. "You have to keep upping the stakes, otherwise, what's even the point?"

He was teasing, but for the first time, I heard sadness behind the bitterness. And as we drove away from the tents, I was bothered by it, because I didn't want him to hide things like a hurt dog, limping on a hurt paw and pretending everything was okay because weakness equals death.

But I put it out of my mind. I grew up around limping dogs; I knew how to hide too.

At the end of the field, he turned down a dirt service road that looped around the back of the field, and then took another that headed into the woods, once he'd skirted around a KEEP OUT sign on a chain, which was easy enough to get past in his Jeep. Now I thought I understood why the tires were always muddy.

After a few minutes, the trees got taller. Much taller. I spotted a state park sign—one for rangers, not for the public. There was a place on the shoulder to park near a trail, and Fen pulled the Jeep over.

"Have you ever been down here?" he asked.

Into the heart of the park? "Not sure exactly where 'here' is."

"The giant sequoia grove. Just a short walk. Come on." He lifted his chin toward a hilly path into the woods, beckoning. Frida jerked forward on the leash, sniffing the air, unfamiliar with the territory but forever willing to be a volunteer guide into the unknown. The courage of small animals is a marvel.

The three of us set out in companionable silence past a ranger log cabin outbuilding that was closed. A little farther into the trees, we passed someone, a serious cyclist—wearing all the specialist racing gear and pumping the pedals of a hard-core mountain bike.

After that, it was just us and the woods. It was lush and quiet here, and it smelled earthier, less of sunlight and more of damp ground and moss and fungi. That made me feel more relaxed, like the world was slowing down here, peacefully decomposing, so I didn't need to rush either: *breathe deep, take your time*. We walked among sugar pines companionably not saying anything. Not about the kiss. Or about our midnight phone conversation, which rambled for well over two hours last night. I couldn't even remember half the stuff we talked about now. New groups we'd found on Bandcamp. His high school. Mine. A ranking of fruit juices by thirst-quenchability. (Orange juice, high; grape juice, all-time low.)

Nothing at all really.

Funny how all the nothing conversations I had with Eddie never made me smile like that, though. I honestly couldn't think of one that lasted more than five minutes. Eddie didn't do phone calls. I didn't used to. Guess everything was a surprise lately.

There was no one around, and Frida was tiring out, fairly calm. So I let her off the leash. She didn't even notice it was off, silly dog. She just trotted at the same distance, veering off occasionally, but easily called back with a clap and a whistle. It was a relief to let her loose and know that she wasn't going to bolt off and not come back.

"Of course she'll come back. Who would feed her?" Fen asked. "She's no dummy."

"She eats her own vomit."

"That's just practical," he said with an almost-smile, pushing sunglasses on top of his head to nest in his windblown curls. "Oh, here we are. Just up here. You ready?"

"For what?"

We rounded a sharp downhill curve on the wooded path, and there it was—the *for what*.

The tallest tree I'd ever seen in my life.

"One of the largest giant sequoia trees in the world," he said. "It's not the Red Knight. That's closer to the main hiking trail on the other side of the grove, and it's the eighth-largest sequoia. This is only number twenty-seven, so tourists don't come out here. But I think she's spectacular. Her name is Lady of Hope."

"Wow," I said, awestruck as I hiked down to the base of the tree alongside Fen and Frida. We had to crane our necks backward to glimpse the green branches that met the blue sky above.

"She's something, yeah?" Fen said.

Marvelous. Big fans of ferns surrounded the tree's backside, but the front of it was mostly cleared ground. The roots were twisted and gnarled in the most beautiful way, and the deep lines in the bark were deep enough to fit my arms. My legs. I was used to feeling smaller than most people, but she made me feel more than small. Humbled.

"I've never been in this grove," I told him. "All the summers I've spent at the lake."

"Never?"

"Never seen the Red Knight, either. Just the tunnel tree when you come into town."

He scoffed. "That's definitely for tourists."

"My dad and I take our photo there every year," I argued, feeling a little embarrassed.

I felt his gaze on my face. "As far as kitsch goes, it's pretty cool kitsch, I guess."

"Well," I admitted, smiling and gesturing. "It's not this."

"Our Lady."

"Lady," I repeated in an upper-class accent, teasing him.

He took it good-naturedly, folding his arms over his chest. "I come out here a lot to look at her. There's a little spot around the back in the ferns where I like to sit and think. . . ." He gestured with his head. "She keeps me from losing my shit."

"Yeah? I've never seen anything like her," I said, walking with him around the roots. "She makes me feel like an ant. These trees have been here forever, right?"

"Around two thousand years."

"Wow."

"Right? She was here before Columbus even shat the bed. When the Vikings were still invading England. When the Miwok tribes were living up in the foothills. She's lived through every war, slavery, holocaust, school shooting, and forest fire."

"Human beings can be awful, huh?"

"Pretty wretched," he agreed.

"She's seen all the bad things we've done. . . ." A voice in my head whispered that I had much to feel guilty about.

Fen lightly bumped my shoulder with his arm—our first touch of the day, and it surprised me. I looked up at his face to find his eyes searching mine. "She's seen good things, too," he argued in a softer voice. "Peace treaties. Refugees finding shelter. The Emancipation Proclamation. When the Wright brothers flew the first plane. People falling in love . . ."

Oh. I definitely couldn't look at him now. Why did he have to go and say that? I didn't know how to respond, so I scrambled for something that would shift us into a safer conversational space while I physically moved myself away from him.

"Yep, she was here when Brian Wilson wrote *Pet Sounds*." There. Music. That was the place we didn't get into trouble. Where we were just friendly, and we weren't doing anything wrong.

And yet my heart raced madly.

Frida's tail disappeared under a fern and her head appeared on the other side. I reached down to scratch her ear as Fen walked behind us.

"Back up a second," he said, "I was listing momentous occasions in history. Are you putting forth *Pet Sounds* as your nomination for greatest album of all time?"

"Maybe not *the* greatest. I'm just saying that no one in their right mind could argue that it's not technically an incredibly innovative album. 'Wouldn't It Be Nice' is a masterpiece of bittersweet, and I can't even listen to 'God Only Knows' without breaking down." Frida sniffed dirt while I continued yammering. "But Mike Love is an asshole, and then of course a couple decades after *Pet Sounds*, 'Kokomo' pretty much ruined the Beach Boys' legacy. What a hack."

"Hard agree."

Fen's voice was closer than I expected. I turned my head to glance at him over my shoulder. His gaze trailed over my neck and met my eyes briefly before I looked away again.

I stretched my arm away from my side and let my fingers brush over the fern fronds. "What would *you* throw in as your greatest of all time?"

"Shit, I don't know. Too hard. But somewhere at the top would be *The Velvet Underground & Nico*. That's chased away a lot of storms for me. Then maybe Carole King's *Tapestry*."

"Huh. I've never listened to that." I mean, I knew who Carole King was, obviously.

"Reminds me of family road trips when I was a kid. My grandma's favorite album."

"High praise," I teased.

"Say that to her face. You think my mom's intimidating? You haven't met Mina Kasabian, terror of Glendale."

I stopped walking. "Glendale? Like, L.A. suburbs Glendale?"

"Hey, it's no Bel Air," he said, dismissive. "But yeah. I pilgrimage down to Southern California once or twice a year to see my grandparents on holidays or birthdays, that kind of thing. Half the Kasabian side of my family is down there."

Of *course* Eddie never once told me that he had grandparents nearby when he came down to L.A. At this point I was starting to wonder what he *had* told me. Anything? Maybe he was just a mirage and I'd never really been with him at all. Eddie who?

"All this time we've been closer than you realized," he said. "Not just during the summers."

"Guess we really have. . . ." That's how he knew about the concert hall at UCLA, but—

"Jane?"

"Yes?" I turned around to look at him and did a double take when he wasn't right behind me anymore. His warm hand wrapped around my ankle, pulling my attention down. He sat on the ground in a small clearing between the tree's roots, an arm slung around one bent knee.

"Sit. Please?"

"Here?" Guess this was his thinking spot.

"Afraid of me now?"

I chuckled nervously. "Um . . . no." I sat down next to him and all the air left my lungs. "Not much, anyway."

"Funny, because I'm terrified of you."

"Stop."

"I'm serious. You scare the shit out of me. Look." He moved, huddling closer, and gently picked up my hands to open them so that my palms faced upward. "See this? Here's where I am, right here. You have all the power. You can fucking crush me," he said in a low voice. His face was near mine, bent low. "All you have to say is that you're done with this. I'm the side piece. Second choice."

"Don't say that," I whispered. "It's not true."

His breath hitched as he started to say something, then changed his mind. Started over in a rough voice. "I have *nothing*. Nothing to give you, and no power. No right to ask for anything from you. But I'm asking anyway."

"Fen . . ."

"What makes you get out of bed in the morning?"

"Huh?"

"The things that make all the shit you endure worth it. You, Cinderella, toiling away in the palace . . . for what?"

I didn't have an answer. It wasn't a word-pixie thing. I just didn't know, really.

"You have to have reasons. Day after day we sat through the nothingness of school," he said, "and we didn't learn anything, because half the time we knew more than the teachers anyway. Do you know how many times I had to correct my history teacher? It was supposed to be an AP course, and he didn't know anything about the Cold War."

"Um . . . ?"

He exhaled. "Sorry, off track. What I'm trying to say . . . There are only a few things that make my life worth living. Music.

My family—not including my father or brother, who I hope both burn in a fairy-tale witch's oven until their eyeballs pop out—"

"Good God," I whispered.

"But the rest of my family, yes. I care about music, them, and this tree."

"This tree," I repeated.

"I *love this tree*," he said deliberately. "I have a deep spiritual attachment to this tree. I brought you here because I wanted to share it with you."

"I'm glad you did."

"But, Jane, I just want you to know that if you told me the only way I could be with you was if this tree was dead, I would take a rusty axe to this two-thousand-year-old beloved tree and chop it the fuck down for you."

He wasn't joking. I mean, I knew he was aware that he was driving Exaggeration Train off Hyperbole Cliff. But the sentiment behind it was all too serious. "Um, please don't?"

"I'd do it for you. Because now I have another reason to wake up in the morning. Told you—all the power."

"*Fen*. When you talk like this, it sort of scares me."

"It scares me to feel this way."

"It's not fair of you to say this to me when you know I'm with Eddie."

Slow blinks. "I know it's not fair. I wish it were—fair. For you. I wish we just met each other, and there were no strings or baggage. Are you sorry you got involved with me?"

It felt as if we were on a great fault line that was about to give way, and that I *did* have power. I could walk away right now and prevent all kinds of tragedy. Save lives. Homes. Entire towns.

But I could not.

"Not one bit sorry," I confessed.

He made a low noise.

His eyes were dark and hooded. He lowered his head to my hands and kissed each of my palms. "I swear to all the saints, if you don't touch me again, I'm going to fall to pieces."

"What if I'm just a walking disaster?" I said, feeling wild and out of control. On the verge of tears. On the verge of stripping off all my clothes in front of him. "I tried to make a spectacle of myself in the dam two years ago, and that was a flop, so I'm doing my best to take you with me now. I'm not Cinderella. I'm probably, I don't know—your witch with the oven."

He shook his head. "You can't out-disaster me. Told you, I've already got ghosts. Let's go down together, Bonnie and Clyde style. Rob some banks. Run through the night. Build some cottages with ovens and be witches. You and me."

And Eddie. Where did Eddie fit into this?

Eddie wouldn't promise me bank robbery and cottage witchery. Eddie was golden and good, quick with the big smile, always positive.

Only he *wasn't*, was he? Golden Eddie was just someone I invented in my head. The real Eddie was hiding a drug addiction and disappeared off the map the first chance he got to party on a beautiful island. The real Eddie clearly didn't care that I'd met his brother.

The real Eddie lied about rescuing me from the dam.

As I settled my forehead against Fen's, he closed his eyes.

"If you'll have me," he said, "I'm yours. And if you want me to stop talking to you because of Eddie, I'll do that, too. Tell me what you want, Jane."

I didn't answer him. I just pressed my mouth to his. I'd never done anything like that—ever. But he made me feel reckless and bold. And when he kissed me back and his hands cupped the back of my head to hold me, I sank against his chest, propped on my hands, and my body melted into a pool of lava. His tongue moved against mine, and I moaned.

He touched me, and I was wax beneath his hands.

This time, our kissing wasn't frantic. We weren't in any rush. Not at first. But it was so much more serious.

And it was different because we definitely weren't strangers anymore. So what if we bumped teeth or my tongue went this way when it should've gone that way?

We just chuckled—my God, the sound of his dark, low laugh!—and then tried again.

Plus, it didn't matter, because everything felt good—his soft lips, and the way his open mouth brushed over my jaw on a path to my ear. The way his flexible fingers molded in the curve of my back beneath my shirt. The way he whispered and groaned when my hand reached down to touch what I could feel between us. . . .

"Jane?"

"Huh?"

"We have to take a break," he said, out of breath, "or I can't."

He was right to stop things. I felt too out of control, and we weren't thinking. Or prepared. I didn't know where Frida was, and we needed to go find her before she got too far away. But as we forced ourselves to separate, still holding hands, all I could think was how happy I was.

Everything felt good.

So how could it be wrong?

I didn't think it was. I was done with Golden. I knew that now. Maybe I'd known it all along. It was just so shiny and bright that I'd been momentarily distracted. Like a cat wearing itself out chasing a pinpoint of laser light until it realizes it's pawing at nothing.

Keep your laser lights.

Give me the boy with the axe.

Jane

When Jasmine texted me an invitation to lunch at their house three days later, I must have stared at it for a solid minute like a dummy, because that's how long the screen shutoff function on my phone was set for. It's just that I'd been so busy, sneaking off with Fen every chance I got, I guess I forgot all about her asking me about lunch. Or about her.

Or about the fact that she just might not appreciate that I was putting my hands all over the wrong son. And if things didn't slow down, it was going to be more than hands.

Not that it mattered. It was wrong any way you looked at it. I knew from the escalating feelings of guilt. The more we saw each other, the more I imagined Eddie finding out and how it would hurt him. And that was the last thing I wanted.

If we could just talk on the phone or text, it would change so much. That's how I felt, anyway. Either he'd explain all the stuff Fen had told me, and the feelings I used to have for him would come back—or they wouldn't. But I couldn't have that conversation with dead air.

Some part of my brain was still reminding me that Eddie had

ghosted me plenty of times before. Like . . . lots. He'd disappear for a couple of weeks and then be super friendly. But I guess if Jasmine had heard anything from him, she would have told me. And it didn't excuse the fact that Eddie had not texted me back. He knew I was coming to the lake for the summer. He had to know I'd run into Fen sooner or later—he specifically told me to avoid him, so of course he knew. In a way, shouldn't he have prepared me for this?

Or I was just grasping at any excuse to make myself feel less guilty about what I was doing with Fen.

Maybe at Jasmine's lunch we could just avoid the subject of Eddie. I could talk around him, like I talk around things with Norma. Deflect and distract. I was good at that.

And who was going to be attending this thing, just me and her and the twins? She did make a point of saying that it would be when Serj wasn't at home. I guess that was better, since there wouldn't be any awkward questions from him about the apartment.

Ugh. Was I kidding myself? Was this too much?

I thought about trying to back out of it. I even asked Fen what to do. He just texted back: You don't turn down Jasmine Sarafian. Not if you want to keep all your teeth and toes. Looks like you're stuck hanging out with my kooky family.

I *so* wanted Jasmine to like me. I wanted to go back to when I was in mom-love with her and she made me feel like everything was going to be okay. Could it be like that?

I guessed I was going. It was only lunch, after all. Maybe it would be okay. And if it was painful, how long could lunch last with one kooky family?

Bring on the kook.

Velvet was feeling better—tons less crampy—so she was going back out with her friends. Which was more bad news for me. But when I told her where I was going for lunch, she let me borrow a striped top, one that didn't resemble a baggy sack—huzzah—and it matched pretty decently with a full skirt and black ballet flats I'd packed.

There. Perfectly acceptable. I almost looked collegiate—Exie said so, in fact, and lent me a pretty red bracelet to complete my ensemble when I passed off Frida to Starla after she agreed to watch the pup for a couple of hours. Dad was running an errand for Mad Dog, so I was relieved I didn't have to bear his silent judgmental gaze. But I did have to bear Norma's when she caught me on my way out and motioned for me, saying, "Hey, come here."

I thought I might be in trouble for doing something personal in the middle of the day, but she handed me a bottle of wine. Not just any bottle: a really expensive one from Mad Dog's ex-wife's vineyard. "Do you need me to take this to Rosa?" I asked.

"No, you should take something for the boy's mother. It's polite. Don't tell Mad Dog I gave this to you." She turned to the room and pointed. "Not a word out of any of you, hear me?"

Norma was breaking the rules? WHAT WAS HAPPENING?

"I can't accept this," I told her, feeling awkward. For one, I couldn't stand owing Norma any favors. And secondly, everyone thought I was going to this lunch because of Eddie. And I was . . . technically. Only, it was a lot more confusing because of all the time I'd been spending with Fen.

"Hush," she said, pushing the bottle into my hand. "And don't make us look bad."

Exie gave me a wide-eyed look behind Norma's back: *Hell hath frozen over.*

This was getting too weird, and I didn't want to be late. After Starla confirmed that we wouldn't need our shared car, I pulled out of the garage and texted Jasmine to let her know I was on the road. Then I felt weird asking where she lived because I felt like I should know. So I texted Fen instead. I felt bad about that, too, but he seemed okay about it: **If you apologize one more time, I will punish you by forcing you to listen to Steely Dan on repeat. Wait, that was me all morning in the record shop, thx to my aunt. FML.**

He gave me the address, which I plugged into the GPS. Other side of the lake, where she'd pointed it out from the apartment window. The exclusive neighborhood below Mission Bluff. The GPS advised me not to take the normal road into town but to instead head through the property and exit that way, taking some weird back road into no-man's-land.

It was another lovely day at the lake, and the trees that weren't evergreens were lush and full. Everywhere I looked in the cozy woods along the private road, branches glinted with sunlight that filtered in through the canopy. The road meandered around some of the lodge's outbuildings, like the caretaker's cottage and a little place called the Poker Shack. I turned at the junction for the Grotto Cabin, and instead of going one way toward the lake, I drove the other way—where I'd never gone, to the back of the property. Where it ended.

There was a tiny public road that joined up to the lane back here: Bluff Road. No exit gate from the lodge's property, I just drove right onto it. No wonder Kamal was all tied up in knots about all the potential "security holes" around the lodge. Anybody could just waltz right in.

Or waltz right out . . .

I drove without seeing any other cars for a couple of minutes, then the sun broke through the trees to my right, and the lake came into view. Weird to see it from this side. It was only a few yards away from me, and the road ran parallel with the water for a long, lazy stretch. I passed by an old state ranger building and, on my left, a quirky mailbox painted with black-and-white dalmatian dog spots next to a long driveway—I could spy a red house at the end of it, set farther back into the woods up a hill.

Immediately on my right, I spotted the Sarafians' stone villa behind a fancy gated drive.

It was no lodge, not by miles. But it was stunning in its own way, so much closer to the water and more of a classic lake house, a couple of stories high, nestled in pines, with almost *too* much flagstone in the landscaping and greener-than-green grass.

Instagram-pretty, especially in the bright midday sun.

The gate automatically opened when I drove up. I pulled into the driveway near a white catering van and let out a long breath.

"You can do this," I mumbled, steadying myself as I slipped my phone into my side skirt pocket, grabbed the wine, and exited the car.

Like a lot of the bigger places on the lake, this house had a lot of stone-covered terraces all around it, to maximize the outdoor living space—more time spent looking at the lake and the mountains. The entrance was tucked under one, two doors behind decorative ironwork gates, and when I rang the bell, one of the gates opened. An older Armenian lady with dyed reddish-brown hair and a small, tight mouth stared at me over a pair of black eyeglasses for several moments.

"Yes?" she said, a little impatient.

"Uh, hello? I'm Jane Marlow. Mrs. Sarafian invited me to lunch," I told her. "Are you Ms. Makruhi?" Fen had told me that was the name of his family's housekeeper. I thought that was right.

She looked surprised. "Yes, come in. This way."

Ugh. Should I not have said that? Norma wouldn't like people knowing her name, so maybe I just made a faux pas. Never piss off the head housekeeper or the cook.

She led me into a tall foyer with Italian tile and a sweeping banister. An enormous glass chandelier that looked out of style with the rest of the house, like some kind of sea monster.

"That's our Chihuly," a voice said from the stairs.

I looked up to see Jasmine descending in jeans, high heels, and an off-shoulder top.

"If you hate it, don't blame me," she continued. "Once upon a time it was Serj's had-to-have purchase, but now we are all tired of looking at an exploding octopus when we come downstairs every morning." She smiled and reached for my hand. "How are you, Miss Jane? I'm so glad to see you again."

Her fingers were warm as they squeezed mine. "I'm good. Thank you so much for having me . . . uh, under your exploding octopus."

She laughed. "Delighted. Oh, for me?" she said as I handed her the bottle of wine.

"It's from the house. I didn't nab it or anything. Norma wanted you to have it."

"Norma," she said, knocking my shoulder with hers like Fen does. "She's a softy underneath all that grit, don't you think?"

I wasn't too sure about that. But I was sure about one thing. Something smelled really nice, lemon and mint, garlicky. Before I could ask about it, a dark figure moved in a shadow behind the stairs.

"Ani-jan, come here, my little assassin," Jasmine coaxed. "I want you to meet Miss Jane."

A slender girl stepped into the foyer holding her hands in front of her. Younger than me by a few years. Hair as dark as mine but super straight and long. The biggest brown eyes I'd ever seen looked at me like an animal caught in headlights. She was twitchy, and that revved up my nerves too.

"Hi," I said. "Ani? You're one of the twins."

I didn't know much about them except that they were fifteen and Eddie referred to them as "the brats." She didn't *look* bratty.

The girl said, "It's not an octopus." Her voice was small, and she kept her face partially hidden within the waterfall of her dark hair. "It has one hundred and five legs. An octopus has eight."

I looked up. "Oh? Good point."

Jasmine slung her arm around her daughter's shoulders. "Ani likes numbers."

"I like precision," the girl corrected.

"She likes driving me wild, my little weirdo," Jasmine said, kissing her cheek affectionately until the girl smiled, a little embarrassed, and pulled away. "Come, Miss Jane. We're dining alfresco out back. No sense wasting it inside."

I followed them through the foyer toward an airy living room with a towering wall of windows that looked out over the lake. So marvelous to have the water right outside your back door. I mean, there was just a patio, some green-green sloping grass, and then a set of docks. Really close. And unlike the lodge, this house just felt homey. I expected glamor—signed photos of rap stars, maybe. But there was something so much better. Family photos lining the wall. Pictures of Saints Perpetua and Felicity hanging under an ornate gilded cross. A flat-screen television that was actually turned on, playing anime with no sound. A coat tossed over a chair. A soccer ball stuck in the corner.

Signs of life.

Back in the lodge, us domestics cleared all that away.

"Move, Ari," a deep voice said from a dark hallway nearby.

Ari . . . That would be Ani's twin brother.

The boy grunted and stumbled torso-first into the living room, complaining, "Hey! Fucker!"

"Language!" Jasmine cautioned.

My pulse ratcheted up as Ari turned around to face the person behind him in the hallway. For a moment, it was just a tangle of skinny boy arms. Friendly wrestling, I was pretty sure. Most of it was happening behind a big monstera plant that was taller than me, so I couldn't make out much, only that Ari had pretty much the same slender build as his twin, and the same dark, straight hair that flowed down to the middle of his back. Very metal.

In one last push, Ari got shoved back inside the living room, complaining, "Oww! Cut it out, dickhead—you win. Mama! Make him stop."

Wait. Make *who* stop?

"Stop it, boys. Don't be boring while we're entertaining a guest," Jasmine instructed the breathless twin boy and the person swaggering victorious into the living room behind him.

Fen. Wild hair completely disheveled by the wrestling. A pair of folded sunglasses hung askew at the neck of a short-sleeve black button-down that was untucked from soft gray chino shorts.

"That's my brother," Ani told me.

"Uh-huh, yes, nice to meet you," I said to Ari. But I was staring at Fen, feeling dizzy in places I shouldn't feel dizzy. My head. Feet. Ribs. Oh, I wanted to be mad at him for not telling me he was going to be here. I really did. But my body was so delighted to see his body—*hello, friend*—that I couldn't pull myself out of the hypnotic spell he was weaving.

Who had a witchy oven? Not me. He was the dark sorcerer. If

he'd raised his hand and commanded me to fall to my knees right then and there, I might have.

"Fennec," Jasmine commanded in a voice that sounded faraway.

"You don't have to introduce them, Mama," Ani said matter-of-factly.

I blinked and glanced at the girl in a panic—she definitely knew something was going on between me and Fen. Then I glanced at Ari, who was confused, which was a relief. And lastly, I glanced at Jasmine, who had a look on her face that only could be described as *smug*. Why, I did not know. Jasmine was on a different playing field than the rest of us mortals. But she was brewing up something, and it sparked guilty feelings to twist inside my gut.

Sweat broke across my forehead.

This was going to be the longest lunch in the history of lunches.

We headed outside, onto their main back terrace. It had an outdoor kitchen with a bar and a long cedar dining table. The green grass rolled down beyond it toward a pier, where a black speedboat was moored, and four chaise longues waited for sun worshippers.

"How have you been?" Fen said, feigning formality as we hung back from the pack. They could still hear us, along with the two caterers who were prepping food at the grill. We had no privacy whatsoever. But when no one was watching, his fingers brushed down the middle of my palm.

I inhaled sharply and snatched my hand away. "So good, I've been. Um, hello."

He chuckled, a dark little laugh. Barely there, but I heard it. I slapped the air, missing his arm, but eventually got it. He cleared his throat and cut his eyes at me. There was humor there, and it sent a little thrill through me.

S-u-uch a long lunch.

"I didn't think you lived here," I finally managed. "In this . . ." Dammit. Word missing. "Line?" I whispered, feeling a little frantic.

"House?" he guessed, and when I pointed at him in confirmation, he continued, "The house's owner is out of town, and whenever that happens, I get to sneak back in, like a poor beggar child."

"Our dad's a dick," Ari explained, leaning on a chair.

Jasmine pointed at him. "No. Your father is doing the best he can. We love and respect him. He is a good man."

Ani lifted her hands. "He is an important man. Let's choose more precise words, Mama."

"Important," Jasmine said, smiling. "Agreed."

"Hard disagree," Fen mumbled.

"Yeah, I'm sticking with 'dick,'" Ari said.

"Word of advice?" Fen said, clapping a hand on his brother's shoulder. "Don't use 'stick' and 'dick' in the same sentence."

Ari laughed and shoved Fen away.

Jasmine's head dropped. "Saint Gregory, please help me tame these wicked children."

"Can we eat before we call down the wrath of the saints?" Ani asked. "I'm starving."

"Yes, my sweet girl," Jasmine said before waving me to the cedar dining table.

I pulled out a seat with my back to the house, the lake in front of me, and was all too aware that Fen moved around his brother to grab the seat next to mine. Not Jasmine, though. She sat across from us. All the better to watch us, I realized with dawning terror.

Was she testing me and Fen because she suspected we were together? Or was she pushing Fen's buttons because she knew he used to have feelings for me when we were younger? Team Eddie or Fen? I didn't understand her endgame, and that was beyond frustrating.

But it wasn't just her watchful, sharp gaze. Everything was stressful. The twins were curious, and the caterers were bringing out big plates of food, family style. It was beautiful and smelled amazing, but I didn't know what any of it was. Falafel? Were these salads? I wasn't sure, and I didn't care about that so much as how incredibly odd it was to *be served*.

I was usually the one who did the serving.

I would sit in the wings, catching glimpses of the beautiful view, wishing I were the one at the table who was enjoying it instead. I shouldn't be here, should I? Not sitting next to Fen. I was having an affair, that's what I was doing. I was a fraud. A cheat.

A cheater.

But even as I wiped my sweaty brow, close to a minor breakdown, no one noticed. Not even Fen. He was . . . extraordinarily happy. Maybe even radiant. His bare leg pressed against mine

237

under the table, and I nearly jumped out of my own skin. He noticed that. Without looking at me, he put a firm hand on my knee, not in a sexy way, but in a calming way. I blew out a long, slow breath and shut my eyes for a moment.

I could do this.

He gently squeezed my knee, and I put my hand atop his. Then we glanced at each other under our eyelashes and broke apart. I looked across the table. Had Jasmine seen us? I couldn't tell.

"It smells wonderful," I said.

Fen shook his head. "No need to pretend. We'll show you. Have you never had Lebanese food back in L.A.?"

I spotted familiar bright pink pickles on the table. "Wait, like Zankou Chicken?"

He gave me a thumbs-up as his mother cheered. "Armenian! There you go, Miss Jane."

"My dad's addicted to their garlic sauce," I admitted, and they pointed it out to me, along with a lot of other dishes, including hummus, tabbouleh, and a meatless tartar made from bulgur.

"Don't touch the fattoush unless you like soggy bread," Ani advised when the caterers were out of earshot.

But when they brought kebabs of chicken and shrimp that smelled of lemon and woodfire, everyone dug in.

"Shrimp!" Fen said, cheerful.

"I'm going to weep," Ari agreed, filling up his plate with skewers of charred shrimp.

"Calm yourself," Jasmine said. "My goodness, you act like I don't feed you."

Fen explained, "My father hates shrimp and throws a fit if it shows up in the house—you know, screaming at a caterer in the middle of a party, blood pressure danger, that kind of thing."

Jasmine sighed. "We all have our foibles. Let us not spoil this beautiful afternoon. Just eat your shrimp and be well. And if any of you speak of this to him, I will deny it and forget I ever knew your faces."

Ani grinned and quietly took two more skewers before calling out, "We're going to need all the prawns you've got, please," to the caterer at the grill. "What? They aren't actually shrimp, you know."

Things got better after that. Shrimp or prawn, the coveted kebab actually was worth hoarding—like, craveably, mouthwateringly delicious. We all indulged while talking about food . . . and about Serj, to Jasmine's constant exasperation. But that put her on the defense, and as long as she stayed there, it meant I had some breathing room. And most of it was buoyant teasing. Fen never got too angry about his father, and Ari was only casually spiteful, just your average teen with a chip on his shoulder. Nothing serious.

Eventually, though, the conversation turned to the missing Sarafian sibling when Fen called me "one of the fairy folk" because the heels of my feet didn't touch the patio floor in the seats. Ani began reciting a list of everyone's heights—like Fen, she definitely inherited her mother's tall stature.

"Eddie is two and one-quarter inches shorter than me," she reported.

Ugh. Next topic, please. But it was already hanging in the air,

JENN BENNETT

and I could feel Jasmine's eyes boring into my face from across the table. *Please don't ask me about the apartment.*

"By the way," she said in calm, low voice. "I heard back from Gordon."

Mad Dog's lawyer.

"Oh?" I said, thrown off balance. I didn't really want to talk about this in front of everyone. Especially not Fen. It felt as though she were putting me on the spot, forcing me to play the role of the patient and loyal girlfriend, waiting on news about her noble beau, continents away.

She nodded. "They were involved in a legal snafu with customs. It seems as if Serj's lawyer is getting it all straightened out, though."

Uh . . . ? What?

"'Legal snafu'?" Fen repeated. "What the hell does that mean?"

Jasmine raised both hands and shrugged slowly. "It's all I know, my love. Your father is seeing someone about it today in the bay."

Oh boy. That didn't sound good.

"Is Eddie okay?" Ani asked, sounding concerned.

"Of course he is," Jasmine said, smiling. "Your father will take care of everything. Don't worry."

A pall fell over the table. I heard what she was saying, but I *felt* discombobulated. It was as if I'd just been told that a relative I'd thought was long dead had been found alive. Suddenly everyone felt sorry for Eddie, including me.

All those texts I'd sent . . . Maybe he hadn't been ghosting me on purpose after all, huh?

I felt terrible. Awful.

Scum of the earth.

I was the worst girlfriend in the history of girlfriends.

Fen scooted his chair away from the table and stood. "Fuck that. There's more to this story, and I'll bet my entire record collection that this is Eddie's fault."

"Fennec," his mother cautioned. "Do not disparage your brother in front of Jane."

He glared at her, muscles tense, fist on the edge of the table. Nobody said a thing. My chest felt as if it were going to collapse under pressure.

I realized I should say something. But what?

I was trying to balance on one tiptoe above an active volcano, and how was this any better than sitting on the railing of the dam?

It wasn't. I could speak up now and end this. Come clean. Tell Jasmine that I was seeing Fen. She already knew. Didn't she? Maybe? And if she did, then maybe her having me here today was some kind of endorsement of Fen. Fen and me. That thought made me feel slightly less sick, just for a moment—that someone else might know our secret, and they weren't spitting on us, telling us what horrible people we were.

I should just tell her. But I was already an interloper, and everything in this house felt as if it were so fragile. Schisms already existed. I knew that before, but sitting here in their family home, with the twins? It was all too real now. The whole family might be ripped apart. And what could be more priceless than this? I would give anything just to have half of what they had here, the family photos and the bickering and the comfy couches and the mother who was trying to keep them all together.

I couldn't ruin this. What was I going to do?

"Jane?"

I blinked at Fen. He was squinting at me, a worried knot between his brows.

"I just . . ." I looked around the table at staring eyes and felt like a coward.

Fen's hand lightly touched the back of my shoulder. "Hey. Want a tour of the villa?"

I swallowed. Cast a look toward Jasmine.

"That's a fine idea," she said, not sounding enthusiastic. "You can take the boat out."

Fen tapped me and whispered, "Come on."

"I heard there's a bowling alley in Mad Dog's lodge," Ari said. "But we've got a new popcorn machine in our home theater."

"You can leave the popcorn in it and still eat it the next day," Ani said.

Jasmine waved us away, but anyone could see she was troubled. Fen inherited his dark seriousness from her. Because with her arms crossed at the table, it looked as though a storm settled over her in the sunny afternoon light as I followed Fen and the twins around the terrace to a flagstone path down the hill. And I wasn't sure I'd made the right decision by keeping quiet.

But what could I do now?

I wanted to talk to Fen, but we weren't going to get any time alone—I could see that already. By the deep sighs and eye rolls he gave Ari—who had volunteered himself as unofficial tour guide—he was aware of it too.

However, we all stuck together, traipsing around the grounds of their home. They showed me their basketball court. A sauna that only got used on the coldest days of the year. Their father's speedboat. A firepit area near the shore where Ari had once stepped on a nail that went through his foot—he took off his shoe to show me his scar.

Dear lord, these twins didn't stop. I gave Fen a look as we headed back inside, and he smiled so big, it did something to me. He adored them, and he was so happy to be home. "I feel like I should go soon," I said in a low voice while we wiped our feet on a mat by the door. "So you can spend time with your family, or whatever . . ."

His hand wound around my wrist, gentle but firm. "Please stay."

Ms. Makruhi popped her head around the corner. "Dessert shortly. Cake."

"You like cake?" Fen asked.

"In any shape or form," I answered. "Never met a cake I didn't like."

"You will love my cake," Ms. Makruhi assured me. "Mikado. Very special. Fen's favorite."

Fen put his hands together as if praying and raised them to her. "The best. I'm going to eat half of it—prepare to see gluttony in action."

Ms. Makruhi waved a hand, but she looked pleased.

We headed upstairs, and I got tours of both Ari's and Ani's rooms (a disaster and neat as a pin, respectively), and after puttering around a game room, we all headed into Fen's old room.

"I actually need to grab something," he mumbled, heading to a closet. "I'm only here once every few months, so I've got to nab stuff while I can."

I looked around the room while the twins meandered freely. The bedroom was enormous compared to my quarters at the lodge. A double bed and small lounge area with a desk. A gaming chair and computer monitor, but nothing hooked up to it. The walls were covered in band posters and promo flats, probably from the record store. A lot of them were signed, which I guess was unsurprising. It was just strange to see them so casually pinned to the wall like it wasn't a big deal.

A bass guitar sat in the corner by a beanbag along with an empty stand for a keyboard. And near me was a shelf filled with trophies and ribbons. Musical notes. I leaned closer to read the inscriptions. They were from grade school and junior high.

"You were in orchestra?"

He mumbled something from the closet, then stuck his head out to look at me. "Oh? Yeah."

Ani plopped on his bed. "Don't let him fool you. Fennec's a virtuoso."

"Nerd is more like it," Ari teased.

I started to ask Fen what instrument he'd played, and why

he'd quit, but shouting from outside the room captured all our attention.

Fen straightened from the closet. "Fuck."

"Oh no," Ari mumbled.

"Sneak out the side door," Ani said, jumping off the bed. "I'll cover for you."

What was happening? Even as I thought it, I knew, because Fen dropped whatever it was that he was scrounging out of the closet.

Serj.

Fen held out his hand to me. "Come on. I'll take you back home. We've got to go now."

"I drove."

"Fuck. I gotta go." He strode to Ari and kissed his brother on his ear. "Bye, dum-dum."

Ani raced to him and swung her arms around his neck like a monkey. "Be careful. Don't die."

"I'll try," he said, squeezing her tightly. "Don't let him be an assbag to you guys, okay?"

I felt panicky, as if he were leaving me, too. But I also felt the urgency to get him out.

"What can I do?" I asked.

"Distract him," he said. "Talk to him while I escape. Shit. My keys! I'll have to sneak into the living room and race out. Hopefully he got dropped off and hasn't seen the Jeep in the garage."

"I'll take you down," Ani told me, and then to Ari: "You go with Fen and be the lookout."

We filed out of the room and down the stairs, and as we hit the bottom, a loud voice boomed throughout the house.

"FENNEC."

We all spun around to find Serj in the doorway of the living room, coming in from the terrace outside. Jasmine was pulling on his arm.

Serj. Angry as a bull. Heading straight toward Fen.

"Get out of my house!" his father shouted, pointing his finger at his son.

"And hello to you, too," Fen said in a dark voice.

"What the hell do you think you're doing? You aren't allowed here. I should call the cops. I knew I should've filed a restraining order on you."

"Serj!" Jasmine snapped. "I invited him here. Control yourself. Think about your blood pressure and what the doctor said."

"And what is this?" Serj gestured in my direction.

"Did you leave your brain behind in the city?" Jasmine complained. "It's Eddie's girlfriend, Jane. You met her at the lodge."

Serj frowned and grumbled, "I know who Mad Dog's girl is—"

"I'm not—" I tried to protest, but my small voice was lost under the boom of his.

"—I just don't know why she's here." He lifted his head and made a sour face. "And why in the name of heaven does it smell like shrimp in here?"

"We're merely having lunch," Jasmine said, sounding exasperated. "Do *not* embarrass yourself."

"I just want to come home to peace and normalcy," he bellowed.

"Don't worry, Mama, I'm leaving," Fen said, snatching up a ring of keys from a side table. "Mr. Important here can return to untangling his favorite son from whatever snafu he's landed himself in overseas." His voice was slathered in acid.

Serj started to walk away, then turned around. "Just once, could you have some compassion for your brother?"

"Compassion?" Fen snorted.

"Maybe just once you could try for a little class. Try to think of him and not you."

"Oh, I'm *full* of compassion for Eddie. Overflowing with it. In fact, we're all on the edge of our seats, waiting to hear what that charming rascal has gotten himself into now."

"He's locked up in a jail in the Philippines for drug possession," Serj shouted at Fen. "Does that make you happy? Go on, then—gloat."

Fen looked as shocked as I felt, as if someone had slapped both of us in the face.

Jail. Eddie was in jail. In a foreign country.

Everything Fen told me was true. About Eddie.

About Serj being a shouting, angry jerk.

But mostly about Eddie.

Serj shrugged and gestured dramatically, as if he'd used up his allotted anger and was now just very tired. "How do you like that? What a fucking embarrassment," he muttered, running his hand over his head. "Drugs. Of course it was drugs with him. He promised me that he was done with it, but that was a lie."

Oh my God.

"Papa," Jasmine warned, looking at me. At the twins. At Ms. Makruhi, who walked up behind them, holding a platter of cake in her hands and looking as if she might collapse.

But Serj kept talking, more to himself than Fen. "Do you know what they do to Americans who get caught with illegal drugs over there? He's facing twelve years in prison. Minimum!"

"Twelve?" Jasmine said, clutching her chest.

"You don't walk into another country and disrespect their laws," Serj argued. "How many times have we talked about this? It's the first rule of travel!"

Silence fell over the living room.

My head completely emptied. Nothing but white. I was numb. Utterly shocked.

Then a terrible sadness crept in underneath it all. Eddie had a drug problem. One that I didn't know about because I didn't really know him. Even though I should because I was his girl-friend.

His girlfriend who was cheating on him with his brother.

I was an awful person.

Poor Eddie.

My God.

As if we were all connected and feeling the same thing, Serj exhaled a long breath and slumped, shaking his head. "Why?"

"My baby," Jasmine said, swiping at her eyes. "My foolish, beautiful baby."

"I'll fix it, Mama," Serj said in a softer voice. "I talked to the woman in the consulate office and that attorney I told you about. I'm flying over there tonight. I'm meeting up with Joe and Gordon. I'll sign the contract and get Eddie out of this mess."

"Yes, you will," Jasmine said. She was hurt and worried, but also angry now. "He should not be traveling without you. He has already proved that he is not capable of being mature. This is Christmas all over again. I don't care about the contract or the festival—hand the reins to Live Nation for all I care. Our child has lost his way."

Serj shook his head. "I'm not throwing away my life's work because my son can't keep his nose clean. I will go get him, the festival will go on, and that's the end of this conversation."

A rock had taken the place of my stomach. I felt sick and strange, unable to process what was happening. I turned to Fen, but he was no longer there. When I looked through the shadowy hall toward the foyer, the front door was closing.

He was gone.

Jane

I made an excuse and left Jasmine to grieve with her family. I didn't belong there.

A stranger. Interloper.

Cheater.

When I drove away from the Sarafians' villa, I held myself together until I was far enough down Bluff Road that I could pull over. And cry.

I cried for Eddie, because he never felt close enough to me to tell me his problems. And I cried because I felt the same way I'd felt two years ago, sitting on the dam after he'd rejected me in the woods.

Like I wasn't enough for him.

Maybe I never was.

Maybe a different girl could have helped him. Seen signs. Pushed him to open up. Instead, once I found out he'd lied to me, I'd just given up on him and moved on to his brother.

Big lies, though. Not just about the drugs, but about an event that changed my life. That was unforgivable. And what he'd done in the Philippines was beyond dumb. But my heart still hurt for him.

I imagined how scared he must be right now, and it made me sick.

Eddie.

In the middle of sobbing, I looked up and realized I was sitting in front of the spotted dalmatian mailbox I'd passed on my way to the villa, and on the side, a business name was painted in small letters: KASABIAN DOG RESCUE.

That freaked me out enough to pull me out of my spiraling thoughts. I wiped tears from my face and peered up a long, ascending driveway. Sure enough, there was a kennel and a white Jeep parked outside.

Dogs love me.

"Crap," I mumbled, heart racing. This was where Fen lived, his aunt Zabel's place, a mile or so from the villa. It was almost as if the universe kept bringing us together.

Bad timing, universe.

Part of me wanted to go to him, to make sure he was okay. He was really upset, and I knew it had to be doubly bad for him because he'd had a confrontation with his father. I didn't comprehend all the family dynamics in play, but I knew enough about Fen to understand that this was majorly upsetting for him.

But did he want to see *me*? The girl who was in the middle of all this mess? Maybe he didn't want to see my face right now after what just happened.

Maybe I needed some space too.

I put the car in reverse and quickly got out of there, then sped all the way back to the lodge, laying my head on the steering wheel when I got it into the garage. Thankfully Dad wasn't around—I couldn't deal with his stony face right now, judging me about my decisions.

They were bad. All of them. What was I going to do about it?

I stole upstairs to the staff quarters and changed into my uniform. On the way down, I ran into Norma.

"You're back already?" She narrowed her eyes at me. "What's wrong?"

"Nothing."

"Went okay?"

Definitely wasn't going to confide in Norma. Exie, maybe, but I didn't know where she was. So I just replied, "Mrs. Sarafian said to thank you for the wine."

She nodded, glancing over her shoulder as if she'd be caught, then left without saying anything else. After I put on a walkie, I gathered from the hubbub in my earpiece that Norma was still in a tizzy about the dead squirrel floating in the pool and was trying to figure out if she should call a pool professional or animal control to take care of it or scoop it out herself.

Eddie might be sitting in a jail overseas until he was in his thirties, but here in the Larsen household, we were concerned about clean pools.

Finding Frida, I turned off my earpiece and sank into my anxious thoughts about the Sarafians, blessedly alone, until the one person I couldn't ignore strolled into the prep kitchen.

"Quiet. Where is everybody?" Mad Dog said, completely oblivious to the squirrel in the pool. The king didn't always pay attention to the details going on at his castle.

"Out back. Did you need something, sir?"

He sighed. "Makes me feel so old when you call me that."

"Sir?" It took me a second to realize. "Oh, sorry. Um, Mad Dog."

"That's better."

He was dressed in a T-shirt and white linen pants, a chunky pair of professional studio headphones hooked around the back of his neck. He had a red splotch on his arm. At least, I thought it was red. Hard to tell beneath all his tattoo work. But I could definitely tell that the crow's-feet around his eyes were longer.

"You okay?" I asked. "Sleeping out in the Grotto Cabin?"

"Fuck no," he complained. "I'm having a new mattress delivered tomorrow, so if you're the one who answers the door, send the person down there. The current mattress has fleas or something. I'm being eaten alive. Look."

He showed me the splotch on his arm, and I could tell he'd been scratching it.

"We've got cream for that," I told him. "I'll get it."

"Thank you, *kattekat*." As I was rummaging through a drawer with first aid supplies at the far end of the prep kitchen, he said, "You don't look great yourself. Allergies?"

"No."

"Oh. How is your brain? Did you happen to make peace with the lake, like I suggested?"

I stilled over the drawer. Maybe it was because we were alone, and that didn't happen often. Maybe it was that his bug bites made him seem a little less like a giant. Maybe it was because after the confusing afternoon at the Sarafians', I just needed to talk to *someone*.

"I did."

"How did it go?"

"It was hard, but you were right." I pulled the drawer out and peered farther inside.

He made a small noise behind me. "Ah-ha. I'm glad to hear that."

"But I'm not great today. I've been crying," I admitted.

"I see. . . ." Now he sounded uncomfortable. "Uh, I'm sorry. Anything I can help with?"

I turned around. "I just came from the Sarafians'. Serj came back from San Francisco."

"Oh," he said, exhaling. "*That.* He told you about the boy."

"You knew? About Eddie? In jail?"

He shook his head and shrugged. "I just found out. Trust me when I tell you that we all want this matter cleared up as quickly as possible. It's going to take money, but it's going to be fixed."

Could that sound less on the up-and-up? Jeez. "Never mind. Don't tell me any more."

"It's going to be taken care of. We'll get the boy home."

Tears pricked the backs of my eyelids, but I tamped them down, terrified to cry in front of him. I had never. Could never. I shouldn't even be talking to him like this. He was the boss. The man. The king. I was supposed to step back into the shadows.

I know who Mad Dog's girl is.

And then there was *that*, Serj's words, echoing in my head.

I didn't know where my dad was at the moment. But I didn't want him catching me crying on Mad Dog's shoulder. Leo the Lion might be stony, but that only meant he had deeply buried feelings, and he would be beyond upset.

"Hey, *hey*," Mad Dog said, reaching out to touch my face, a strange tenderness in his eyes. *"Min skattepige."* At the last second, he changed his mind and withdrew his hand awkwardly.

I stilled, then I made myself smaller, shrinking away from him.

I didn't know what he'd said, but I'd heard enough of his Danish to know what the first word meant.

Mine.

Mine!

Maybe it meant nothing. Maybe it was just a reflexive sentiment that was hollow and empty. Maybe he literally considered me a possession because I was part of his staff.

All of those things could be true.

And yet . . .

All the strange looks I'd caught, all the weird, competitive energy I'd felt between him and my dad, all the rumors I'd heard. I'd always been able to dismiss all that because Mad Dog never felt like a father. He never treated me special. Never doted on me. Mad Dog had *never* tried to comfort me. Not even when I got hurt at the dam.

But he was comforting me now.

As I stood there with this strange, too-familiar intimacy enveloping us, a bigger realization hit me: whether true or not, Mad Dog thought there was a possibility he *could* be my father.

That's why Serj had referred to me as Mad Dog's "girl." Serj talked to Mad Dog on the regular. They were buds.

So if Mad Dog thought there was a chance he hypothetically *could* be my biological father, then that meant he actually had slept with my mother. A housekeeper.

Someone like me.

A spark of rage flared inside my chest.

"What did you just call me?" I said accusingly.

He shook his head, shoulders lifting. "It's nothing. No translation."

My ass. "You know what Serj called me this afternoon? Your girl. *Yours.*"

"Hey," he said, holding up his hands in front of his chest, as if I were physically attacking him. "I don't know why Serj said that, but I'm sure he meant that you are part of this household."

"That's not what it sounded like he meant."

"Jane—"

"I'm not yours," I told him. "Leo is my father. I don't know what you did with my mother, but I'm not yours."

"You're my responsibility as long as you live under this roof. So you are partly mine."

What did that even mean?

"You grew up in my house, with my kids. I am fond of you. That is all," he said, suddenly very stoic. "And I'm sure that is all Serj meant."

I didn't believe him. But now he was withdrawing, back to his old kingly self.

Putting up a wall. Master and servant.

"As an employee in your staff who is partly yours, I'm not asking for any favors from you," I said, handing him the hydrocortisone cream as I mentally armored myself. "To be clear. I care what happens to Eddie, but that has nothing to do with you."

He squinted at me, confused. "All right? I just thought—"

"May I be excused . . . sir?"

Mad Dog hung his head and muttered dramatically, "You must not kneel to me. I don't deserve it." It sounded as though he were reading lines from a play.

"Sir?"

"Nothing. Thanks," he said, tapping the tube of cream on his palm as he left the kitchen.

When his silhouette disappeared through the doorway, I sagged in relief. I regretted some things I'd said . . . and some things I hadn't.

This house didn't feel like a home anymore. Maybe it never really did for me. All I knew was that I didn't want to feel this way around him from now on—dreading to speak to him. I had to get out of this house, away from him.

Tonight.

Jane Marlow:

I'm going out tonight

I've got Frida

Where are you?

Velvet Larsen:

Love youuuuu

Aaar krj

Oops what lol that was Erika

Jane Marlow:

V, I love you like a sister

But if you don't stop partying

I'm telling Norma

Velvet Larsen:

Um?

Jane Marlow:

I'm talking about all the coke w/ Erika Jones

BTW Eddie is in jail for possession

Sober up before you end up there too

Velvet Larsen:

Shit

Track [23] "I Hear a Symphony"/The Supremes

Jane

Zabel Kasabian's driveway sloped upward into dense trees that opened up to a cleared piece of land with several buildings. A log-cabin style house sat to the left. A big red barn stood in the distance, farther up a grassy hill. And closest to the driveway was a long dog kennel.

A chain-link fence wrapped around the property as far as I could see, and there were extra divisions between it in some places. Fences within fences—dog runs. I didn't see any dogs in them at the moment. Then again, it was almost completely dark, and the only reason I could see anything at all was thanks to several large utility lights posted on tall power-company poles around the yard that cast large pools of bright light.

One of which shone down on Fen's Jeep. He was still parked in front of the dog kennel, so I pulled up next to him and claimed a spot.

But I remembered his mentioning a barn in a text. Hmm . . . "Kennel, barn, or house?" I asked Frida. Anything posed as a question was good to her; she was already scrabbling to get out. Or maybe it was the sound of a lone barker who had now noticed we'd driven up. She answered the call with her own yip. "Keep it down," I told her. "Sheesh."

I was feeling weird about the late hour and not knowing his aunt—would she pull out a shotgun on someone ringing the doorbell after dark? But a flash of movement caught my eye up the hill, where a door opened at the barn.

There, in the doorway, a dark silhouette stood in front of a golden rectangle of light.

My pulse pounded. "Okay, then," I told Frida, pulling her away from the mystery dogs inside the kennel. We found a gate to get into the barn and then walked a long path up the dark hill, where Fen stood in his chino shorts in the open door of the red barn.

Barefooted.

Shirtless.

It was a shockingly nice view. The torso matched the arms I'd already seen. And I'd felt it plenty, but it was another thing to see it all gloriously out in the open. I tried not to stare as I slowed my pace toward the barn, but why do boys get to walk around half naked? I'll never understand it, and yet I was not complaining. Well. Maybe a *wee* complaint about that dead-girl Ophelia tattoo that was so blatant on his shoulder right now.

I just had to keep my eyes other places.

He looked exhausted. His dark curls were a windblown jumble, and his face was a gaunt collection of intersecting planes and shadows, a cubist portrait come to life. But there was a sweet relief behind his eyes when our gazes met, and any worry I had that I was doing the wrong thing was completely erased from my mind.

I pretended as if today hadn't been completely horrible for him and looked around at things that weren't his naked torso. The two-story building had a covered concrete porch and a tin roof, and was less a rural cow barn than a simple utility barn. Next to Fen's open door was what could only be described as a porch couch: like something that you'd see on the side of the road that was put out for trash collection until drunk fraternity pledges hauled it off for their frat house.

"What is this?" I asked, gesturing to the couch, which may or may not have been attacked by a band of wild racoons and was leaning ominously to one side. "Are you taking decorating advice from Moonbeam? Dammit, Frida!" The leash pulled out of my hand as she happily lunged for Fen, tongue lolling.

"Whoa! Hey, goofball," he said, bending down to scoop her up against his chest and let her lick his face. "It's my thinking couch. My aunt was going to toss it."

"You don't say."

"Don't be a snob. What's happening here? Is this a visit? You're visiting me?"

"I believe so, yes."

He brightened a little. "Oh, good. Would you like to come inside?"

"Sure . . ." I glanced down the hill at the house. "Where is your aunt?"

"At her boyfriend's house. I don't see her at night unless I walk down there. We stay out of each other's way. I pay rent and sometimes take care of the dogs, and she lets me live here. Cut and dry. Come on in," he encouraged, unhooking Frida's leash from her harness to hang it up on a hook by the door while letting her loose inside the barn.

I followed them inside, and a pang of worry tightened my stomach when he shut the door behind us. I still had Eddie on my mind, as well as my run-in with Mad Dog. I wasn't entirely sure I should be here.

Then again, it was a barn. That felt wholesome, in some weird way.

To be fair, it was less a barn and more like a big workshop or garage, with tables and metal storage units on the walls, a few pieces of lawn equipment in one corner, and a refrigerator in another.

And a massive piano in the middle.

Baby grand. Black.

Near the piano, utility lights hung from beams where some recording equipment was set up around a threadbare rug. Keyboards. A desk. Sheets of music with penciled-in notes. Boxes of preprinted sheet music. Books. Stereo equipment.

Oh my God.

The awards in his room.

An enamel piano pin on his shirt at work, the day I first came into town.

His Mozart shirt.

"You play piano?" I said dumbly as Frida sniffed around the room.

He nodded slowly, hands stuffed in his pockets.

"Piano hands!" I said, pointing.

His laugh was low. "Yeah. Kids used to make fun of me because they stretch in weird ways. Alien fingers. They're good on the keys."

Then it hit me like a blow to my chest.

Jasmine, standing in the empty apartment.

Wouldn't a piano look nice right here?

"You okay?" he asked, bending his head down to catch my gaze. "I should've told you, huh? I wanted to. It's a definite sore spot for me, because it's been such a big part of my life, and my"—he cleared his throat—"father thinks it's a waste of time. Because it's classical, and why can't I just be like Eddie and be interested in cramming more suckers through the festival gates?"

"Your father is a shit," I said.

"Gasp. How dare you talk about Serj Sarafian," he joked wearily. "He's important."

"I'm sorry," I told him. "For what you have to deal with, you know, father-wise."

He shrugged. "It's fine. I can manage." Dark eyes hesitantly peered at mine under a fan of lashes. "How are you? I'm guessing that hearing the news about Eddie can't have been easy."

Tough question. I wasn't sure how to answer.

"You don't have to lie to me," he said softly. "I'd rather hear the truth from you. Even now. If you came here to tell me that hearing about Eddie made you change your feelings about us, then I'm ready to hear that."

This took me aback. "I didn't come here to say that."

"No?"

I shook my head. "My feelings haven't changed. I just . . . everything is confusing."

"I get that." His Adam's apple bobbed as he swallowed. A tense moment stretched between us.

I exhaled a long breath and admitted, "I mean, I *am* worried about Eddie. It's not that I didn't believe you when you said that Eddie had problems, but I guess *seeing* it . . . ?"

"It's different when you know," he said.

"It's real now," I agreed.

He scratched the back of his neck. "Well, don't worry too much. My father is going to spend every dime he has personally flying all the way around the globe to save his son."

"Mad Dog said the same when I got back to the lodge."

Fen didn't seem surprised that Mad Dog knew about this. "My guess is that they're going to pay off some high-level people to get him out, and it's going to be expensive." Fen shook his head slowly. "At some point, it's so dumb that you just give up. What's the point of caring anymore? My all-powerful father is willing to go to such great lengths to rescue my fuckup of a brother—no offense."

"A little taken," I mumbled.

"Yet that same father can't be bothered to drive a mile and a half down the street to come work things out with me. He'd rather dump me at my aunt's and move on."

My father would *never*.

I couldn't count on much in this world, but I could count on Leo Marlow. I'd kept a lot of secrets from him. It was the Marlow way. We needed a new way.

"I'm sorry," Fen said. "I shouldn't unload on you about Eddie. That's not fair. This is all new to me, you know."

"Oh, really? You don't regularly slink around with your brother's girlfriend?"

"You're my first slink."

"You're mine too," I told Fen. "And I'm not very good at slinking. I drove all the way around the lake in a car that I failed to check out properly on the lodge's automobile checkout sheet."

"Hot wheels? See, I disagree. If you didn't sign it out, then you didn't take it. Smart. Very slinky."

"So basically, I'm the better deviant right now?"

"And to think, you once called *me* the Ruiner."

I snorted a laugh. "Did I really say that?"

"You *shouted* that."

"Pot to kettle," I said, shoving him lightly.

He laughed a little. "You give good shouting. I was just riffing off your energy."

"No, I was raised not to shout. Domestics are quiet. After spending the day with your family, I can tell that you all had to shout over each other to get attention. Ari's got lungs on him."

"Ani's got lungs too, but she chooses to play her cards close to her chest."

"I like the twins. I had fun today. Until . . . you know."

"Tell me more about how you enjoyed today, because that's

making me feel better," he said as we walked to the piano.

"Okay, let's see . . . I liked that you don't have a team of domestics, because it makes a house too sterile and you walk around paranoid that you're going to leave fingerprints on the glass and have to wipe them up before someone sees. People should leave a mark, you know?"

"Never thought about it like that."

"And I liked eating new food."

"Zankou Chicken," he muttered, shaking his head with a smile. "I was dying."

"Hey!" I said, embarrassed all over again.

"It was funny, I'm just teasing. And speaking of food, I'm sorry we missed out on the cake. Ms. Makruhi is very proud of her desserts. They take hours. You would have liked it." He sounded genuinely sad. Maybe it was more for Ms. Makruhi than the sugar.

We stopped in front of the piano. It was a beast, black lacquered, mirror-shiny, with all of its copper strings inside the propped-up lid. "You write your own music?" I asked.

He shrugged with one shoulder. "Mostly fragments. It's hard to concentrate on anything longer than that these days."

"But it's classical?"

"I play other things too. I love all music. But on piano . . . when I play? It's always been classical." He took his hand out of his pocket and touched the keys, tapping out a few staccato low notes.

"Play for me," I asked.

"Mm . . ."

"Please?"

He hesitated, squinting one eye, and then hooked his bare foot around the piano bench leg and pulled it out. When he sat, he patted the tufted black leather cushion next to him. "Watch out for my elbow," he said, but when I made myself small and moved away, he pulled me back closer. Until our thighs touched. "Stay," he commanded.

"Okay. Staying," I said softly, looking at his face.

He was excited. There were those hawk eyes again, peering out from the weariness. "This is a couple of movements from a sonata called 'The Tempest.' It's always been one of my favorites to play. Mostly because it always scared Mrs. Calloway, my music teacher in third grade."

"Oh?"

"I like to improv on it. All right . . ."

It was so strange to sit here with him. Almost as intimidating as the giant sequoia tree: the piano made me feel small. Maybe it was because only the toes of my flats touched the rug beneath us.

Frida brushed by my foot, sniffing out new territory as Fen stretched out his hands over the keys.

He began to play a slow, haunting melody.

One that quickly exploded into rolling, complex, unrelenting passages that caught me off guard. Frida, too. She jumped back from the piano and barked, but Fen ignored it. His body and arms both arched as he moved up and down over the keyboard, locks of curls hanging in his eyes. It sounded like a storm. It felt like one too. Angry and full of grief. Anguish.

Goose bumps rose over my arms.

My legs.

I was afraid to move for several moments.

But I watched. I listened.

His playing was physical, full-bodied. He lurched over the piano like a dark vulture, and I felt every sinewy muscle flexing in his graceful movements, even in his thigh as he pushed the pedal below with his bare foot. And I felt the anguish in the notes he was playing as if I were a sponge, soaking each one up as rapidly as he rolled them out. I carried them inside me, riding out all the feelings they were whipping up until they changed—

The storm subsided into a softer movement. His playing slowed and sobered into something just as dark, but utterly beautiful.

How did he do this? No music in front of him. He'd memorized it. And I didn't know much about classical music, but I knew talent when I heard it.

A sharp jealousy bit. I pushed it away, but it left its teeth marks in me. I was envious of his talent. Overwhelmingly happy for him too. And then a little scared.

Because a light turned on in the back of my head, and I was suddenly aware of how outmatched I was. Maybe we weren't Bonnie and Clyde after all, both screwing up at life.

Fen was so much further above Eddie than I could have dreamed.

Shit, shit, *shit*!

I couldn't stop the tears in time. Squeezing my eyes shut didn't help; they still streaked down my cheeks. *Please don't notice.* I tried to make myself very still, turned my head to the side to swipe under my eyes. But the piano sonata abruptly ended.

"Oh God, I'm sorry," I told him.

He turned his body toward mine and cupped my cheek with his hand. I tried to turn my face into it and hide, but he wouldn't let me. "Whoa, talk to me. You're killing my ego. I thought you'd like it. I know I said it scared my teacher, but I wasn't trying to scare you."

"It's fucking brilliant," I said, growling in frustration as another tear slid free. "You are a . . . thing. That thing. Your sister said you were. A genius. Dammit!"

He didn't offer word help. "I've been playing since I was six, so it's not like I just picked it up overnight or anything. I'm not a genius."

"You're amazing, and that was . . . Please keep playing."

"Um, no."

"I ruined it, I'm sorry. Who's the Ruiner now, huh?"

He gave me a soft smile and wiped under my eye with his thumb. "Nah, it's a ruinous piece. Super emo."

"You're *so good*. Way too good for me."

His eyes narrowed. "Fuck that. No . . . are you serious? Jane, come on. Is that what this is about?"

"I'm a minimum-wage domestic. So is my dad. So was my mom. I'm the Help."

"Who cares?"

"I do. Because I realized tonight that Mad Dog did sleep with my mom, okay?"

He blinked at me.

I exhaled a hard breath. "I'm not even that upset about it. In the end, it doesn't change anything. My dad is my dad. He raised me and loves me. Mad Dog is . . ." I searched for the right word.

"A chiller version of *my* dad?"

"They're the same," I agreed. "Your dad didn't just kick you out, did he? You wanted to leave."

"I couldn't stay in that house a minute longer with him," he said, running his fingertips around my hairline as he studied my face. "If I didn't have my aunts, I don't know where I'd be."

But he did. And that was the difference between us. He had a support system. People who cared about him. A car. A roof over his head. A job. A mother who would do anything for him. And he also had an incredible talent.

"You aren't the bad seed," I told him. "That's what Eddie told me about you, but it was just another lie. You are actually the golden boy."

His fingers stilled at my temple. "Um . . . ?"

"I'm not at your level. You should be dating . . . someone from Juilliard or something."

"You've really lost it. I can't even respond to that."

"Fen—"

A strange look came over him. "Holy shit."

"What?"

He scrunched up eyes, then his shoulders relaxed as he gazed down at me, smiling softly. "You just implied that we're dating."

I sagged. "Oh God."

"Are we?" he asked. "Because if we are . . ."

Well. Were we? For the first time since I'd been back at the lake, I finally knew why Eddie wasn't responding to my texts. In Eddie's head, maybe he'd just had a terrible June, but he could still count on coming home to his faithful girlfriend when this nightmare was all over.

But I'd been waiting on Eddie for a long time. Before all of this. For weeks. Months. Years. Before the fall into the dam, really. The only thing that had changed was that I now realized there were other things to do with my life. I didn't have to wait. I could walk away.

I could be happy.

I found my gaze trailing down Fen's chest. I forced it back up to his face, but that was just as dangerous. Maybe more.

Fen bent his head to mine and kissed my tearstained cheek. Kissed my jaw. My ear. He slung an arm around my back and tugged me closer, until I was straddling his lap on the bench. And the same hands that had played those stormy, cascading notes on the piano were all over me. His skin felt damp and feverish under my hands, and his hair faintly smelled of eucalyptus and mint.

I wanted him. And where our bodies connected, I could feel that he wanted me too.

"Come upstairs with me," he said in a raspy voice. His eyes all lazy and full of sex.

"What's upstairs?"

"My apartment."

I looked up. A loft.

"And condoms," he added. "I think. God, I hope."

My cheeks puffed out a breath. I was rattled. Not thinking straight.

"Frida?" I asked, looking for her pointy ears.

"She can hang upstairs," Fen said, "but I'm not sharing my bed with a dog."

I laughed nervously. My hands were shaky when I slung my arm around Fen's neck. He lifted me off the bench and, upon standing, kicked the seat backward, knocking it over with a thump.

"Upstairs?" he asked, depositing me on the floor.

I took his hand.

Up the stairs, above the rafters to an open door. Frida ran up with us, and when I stepped inside, he shut the door behind us. It was a tiny apartment, barely bigger than my staff room. Kitchenette and living space crammed together. Most of it was covered in books and record shelves. A purple couch was buried in clothes. Fen pushed them to one side, picked up Frida, and deposited her there. Then he led me into the bedroom and shut the door. "One second . . ."

"Ow," I said, tripping over something in the dark.

He flipped on a switch in an adjoining bathroom that cast a slant of light into the room. And as he rummaged frantically inside a medicine cabinet, I perched on the edge of his unmade bed. A laptop sat on his bedside table playing music I didn't recognize.

"Success," he said, chest heaving and hair all disheveled.

He stopped in the slant of light and stared at me. Dark curls hung over one eye. A fine sheen of sweat glistened on his neck and shoulders. From playing the sonata, the kissing after, or the frantic condom search, maybe all of it.

"Seeing you here . . . ," he said in a low voice. "I feel like I'm dreaming. You're not another ghost, are you?"

"I think I'm real." I gave him a soft smile.

His weight made the mattress sink next to me, and for a moment, I lost my nerve. Then he picked up my hand and kissed my palm. "Is this okay?"

"Yes."

"Do you want to be here? If you change your mind, it's okay. I've waited a long time for you. I don't mind waiting longer."

I felt that connection between us click into place, the same one I'd felt the first day I walked into the record shop. He called to something instinctual inside me, and it just felt *right*.

He kissed my throat as I wrapped my arms around him. My body caught on fire, and I couldn't get close enough to him. By the time my flats were slipping off my feet and falling to the floor with two soft thunks, I wasn't nervous at all. I was aching for him to touch me.

"Remember what I told you back at the tree?" he whispered, sliding his hand beneath my clothes. "Nothing has changed. You have all the power. I am yours to destroy."

I couldn't say a word.

All I could do was feel. And touch. And be touched.

All of me. All of him.

And as he whispered my name in the dark, our limbs tangled in the sheets, clinging to each other, it was the sweetest relief not to have to struggle to communicate.

I'd never trusted anyone more.

Maybe he was rescuing me all over again.

I just hoped I was worth the effort.

Jane Marlow:

Eddie, it's over.

Fen

Everything was perfect.

Moonlight shining through the window. Jane in my arms. Her tiny hand on my chest, her body molded against my side. Nothing between us. So close, we could practically share each other's heartbeats. Breaths. Thoughts.

If I could've recorded this moment in time, pressed it like grooves in vinyl, slipped it into a sleeve and shelved it away with the most valuable records in my collection, I would have done it.

I wanted to stay up all night and experience that joy—draw it out as long as I could. But then her body felt lighter on me, like a fern unfurling, and I realized with surprise that she'd fallen asleep. Another joy.

The next thing I knew, it was two in the morning by the bedside clock, and a tiny dog was snuffling my ear. "How the hell did you get in here?" I whispered. Frida obviously understood no human words whatsoever, because she took that to mean "feel free to curl up on the bed with us." At least she was small.

The next, *next* thing I knew, it was morning, and both the dog and Jane were gone.

Not gone. Just up. The toilet flushed in my bathroom, and she'd taken her clothes with her. The reason why broke through my groggy head: Frida was barking at the apartment's front door.

"Shit," I said.

"Literally," Jane said, rushing out of the bathroom. "As in the dog kind. Frida's got to go outside. And I've gotta get back to the lodge before they send out a search party."

"No-o-o-o," I whined.

She stuffed her phone in her pocket and leaned over the bed to kiss me. "Can I come back tonight?"

"You can fucking move in," I told her. "My aunt might make you pay rent. But we'll figure it out."

"Let's not get ahead of ourselves," she said, grinning.

"I'm years ahead. We've got kids already. We travel the world and leave them with Ms. Makruhi. There's cake every weekend. Frida does *not* sleep with us. My ankle is doing that pins-and-needles thing because of her," I complained.

She laughed. "I'll come back tonight. You can show me your record collection. Let's start there, all right?"

It would do.

I was floating on clouds. In space. Cruising fucking galaxies. I forgot all about my father and Eddie. Mostly. Mama was upset, and I called her to make sure she was okay. But she was tough as leather, so she pretended that everything was okay.

Eddie was in my father's hands now. And Mad Dog's. I guess that was as good as God's. And if it wasn't, that was my brother's fault for worshipping false idols.

• • •

Jane and I spent three magnificent nights together, ignoring the rest of the lake. The fourth night, Aunt Zabel invited us down to the house to eat a late dinner with her. Which was fine. Her property. She wanted to meet the girl and the tiny dog who kept showing up here and staying all night. Jane was worried, I think, about anyone finding out about us. But Aunt Zabel was cool— way more chill than Mama. I made sure Jane knew that Aunt Zabel wasn't gossipy and wouldn't run back to Mama with our business.

However, dinner turned into a tour of the dog kennel, and once my aunt got started on the topic of dog rescuing, it tended to go on and on. . . .

No one wants to hear about neuterings gone wrong, especially when they're about to lock the door to their apartment and exchange mind-melting orgasms. Just *no*.

Mostly I was annoyed that the magic border surrounding our paradise had been broken. And once that happened, it was as if the universe decided to open the floodgates and let everything in. Because just when we were finally, *finally* dismissed and heading back to my apartment, Jane got a frantic call from Velvet.

"She's not making sense," Jane said, hanging up. "Something about a fight that just happened, or is about to happen? She's scared. She and Erika Jones are fighting. She's stuck and she doesn't want to call my dad."

"She needs a ride," I said unhappily.

Jane nodded. "I think she's . . ."

"Not sober?"

Jane nodded.

"Fine. Where's she at?" I said, sighing.

"That's the worst part," Jane said, giving me a mirthless look. "She's at Betty's."

I stilled. "Seriously? Inside the bar?"

"Yeah."

"Shit." Well, Betty's wasn't the dam, but it was probably the last place in town Jane wanted to go *other* than the dam.

I didn't really associate Betty's with Jane's drowning any-more. I just hated it because of the kind of people that hung out there. People like Velvet and Erika Jones. Eddie's friend from the ski chalet incident, Tim Albertson. Betty's had become party central.

"We can leave Frida in my apartment," I suggested. The pup was accustomed to it now. I ran her back up there and locked up, then we took the little hybrid car that Jane had driven from the lodge. Unlike my Jeep, it had a roof and sides; if Velvet was going to be a sloppy handful, better for her not to fall out along the side of the road.

It was a warm summer night, and the parking lot was jammed. You could hear the band playing from out here, a group who sounded suspiciously like the clowns that lost Battle of the Bands. "Is this Tell & Show?" I said. "Are we in hell or something? How do they keep getting gigs around here?"

"Don't know, don't care."

"Hey. You good?" I was a little worried that Jane was having some flashbacks from the dam, but she said she was okay. "If you need me to drive or ghostbust anything, I'm here."

"I'm just pissed at Velvet," she said, pulling into a parking space in the gravel lot. "This summer has been one big deterioration for her. It's like she's taking ten steps backward. And she's better than this."

She turned off the engine and texted Velvet, sighing. Then she looked at me and gave me a weary smile.

"Don't get mad," I said, "but you sound more like a sister than her assistant."

"Just someone who's tried to self-destruct and doesn't want to see other people do the same."

I understood that.

We got out of the car. "She's not answering my texts and my phone is about to go dead," Jane said. "How am I supposed to be her ride if she won't get in the car? What do we do? Just wait?"

"Text her my number in case your phone goes dead," I suggested. "That way she'll be able to get in touch with either one of us."

I glanced around the dark lot. People were filing in the main entrance, where a bouncer stood, checking IDs and stamping hands. No sign of Velvet, and we'd never get in through the main entrance, anyway. But I knew how we could. "Follow me," I told Jane, taking her hand. "We're going through the side door where they get their deliveries."

I may have been kicked out of the Sarafian house, but I still had the name. And when we walked up to the door where a guy from the kitchen was smoking a cigarette, all it took was a little smooth-brain small talk.

"Yeah, man. Go on through the kitchen. I didn't see you, though," he said with a laugh.

I held on to Jane, and we strode through the kitchen as though it was nothing. No one even looked up except a guy washing dishes, and when I held up my hand to wave, he acted too tired to bother with me.

Through a swinging door we went. And after a short walk through a hallway with offices and bathrooms, we were in the main bar. It was noisy and raucous, and it smelled like pineapple and beer. Everything was covered in too much pine and multi-colored lights, and the crowd was a mix of rich twentysomething party boys and sad, old drunks who were my dad's age and trying to relive their youth.

Outside on the long pier behind the bar, stage lights shone on Tell & Show, who started up another song. The bass in their amps made the pine floorboards shake in the most obnoxious way possible. More obnoxious was the couple doing coke at the bar, right where everyone and their makers could see them.

"We are *not* splitting up," I shouted over the music to Jane. "Let's just find V and get the hell out."

Jane nodded.

We were roaming around the pine nightmare searching for Velvet when I got a text from an unknown caller: **Where are u?**

"Did you text Velvet my number? I think this is her," I told Jane.

"Finally! My phone still has a little power, so not sure why she texted you instead. Maybe I confused her."

Easy enough to do. I texted Velvet back: **Inside Betty's.** It was all I could do not to add, *Looking for you, dumbass.* It was crowded and hard to see people, so we decided to stick to the bar. Once a stool cleared, we pounced on it, and Jane got on her knees to look around above people's heads while I held on to her hips and gave the trashy-ass wrinkled slosh-bucket next to us the evil eye.

"There!" Jane said. "Restrooms!"

"Fuck." I helped her down, and we shouldered our way back to where we started.

"You can't go in," she said. "Ladies' room."

"I'm not a peeper. This is an emergency." I called out, "Velvet Larsen? We're coming in. Everyone best be decent in there."

A couple of super-drunk college girls were talking next to the sink, and there was Velvet, sweating like an Olympic runner.

"THANK GOD," she yelled, tripping into Jane's arms. "Oh shit, girl, please take me home. Not the lodge. I mean, take me back to L.A. I hate it here. *Please.*"

"Stand up," Jane said. "God, you stink. What have you been drinking?"

"Water? I've been running. There was a man in a bear head trying to kill people, and Erika abandoned me for some rando summer boy. I don't have a ride home."

Holy shitballs, she was high as hell. "How is he trying to kill you?"

One of the girls by the mirror spoke up. "It's the Grizzly Acres craft beer mascot. He's handing out coupons. Erika got bounced after Velvet and her started fighting and left with some tourist. Velvet's been running around, trying to avoid security."

"Shut up, Dana," Velvet said. "No one asked you."

Jane covered her face and made a noise. "Enough. Let's just go, okay?"

Velvet was more than happy to go, and she was definitely sloppy, but no sloppier than half the patrons. So we escorted her out before anyone spotted us, going through the kitchen. Everything was fine, other than Velvet talking a bunch of nonsense that made Jane look as if she didn't blame Erika for abandoning her.

"Hey," I said, interrupting. "It's fine. You texted. We came. Let's go home."

Velvet wiped her face and blinked at me. "What? I didn't text you. Did you call me?"

"You texted me," I said.

She shook her head. "Nope."

Maybe she was just too loaded to remember. That's what I told myself as we approached Jane's hybrid car, and next to it, from a black sedan, a dark figure emerged.

And right then, my gut knew who'd texted.

Because my gut knew that figure coming out of the black sedan.

Tall. Blond-tipped hair. Broad shoulders.

My gut knew before my brain registered the shock of seeing Machiavellian dimples and the most charmed face at Condor Lake.

"Eddie?" Velvet said in dazed voice. "I thought you were in prison."

Jane gasped.

But Eddie didn't even glance at her. I don't think he knew she was there. Or Velvet. He just stared at me with the most horrific look of shock pasted on his face. I'd never seen him look like that. All confidence completely erased. There was nothing there. No pride.

Nothing.

Had being arrested really torn him up like this? What the hell?

"What are you doing here?" I asked as he just stared and stared at me like some kind of soulless alien in a suit. "Why are you dressed like that? Is this an airport car? Did you just get into town? Where's Dad?"

He opened his mouth and nothing came out. Then he swallowed visibly and tried again. "I'm supposed to come get you. Papa's in the hospital. He had a heart attack on the private jet on the flight from Los Angeles to the lake. He's in surgery at the hospital outside of town. They don't know if he's going to make it."

Was this a joke?

"What the fuck is the matter with you?" I ran toward him and shoved him as hard as I could. Knocked him backward into the car. His back hit metal, and he grunted and doubled up in pain. "Are you sick in the head? Why would you say that?"

A sob wrenched out of Eddie—so horrible and guttural, I felt it inside my own chest.

I suddenly felt very cold.

He wasn't joking.

"Oh my God," Jane said behind us.

Eddie crouched at my feet and wept, curling up into a ball. "I fucked up, and he came to help me, and then he collapsed on the plane, and one of the pilots used a defibrillator on him. He almost died. He might still die!"

"Where's Mama?"

"Headed to the hospital with the twins," Eddie said, crying. "She sent me here to get you. I'm a screwup. This is my fault, Fen. I'm *so sorry.*"

I didn't know what to say or feel. There was only numbness and instinct.

I crouched down with Eddie, put my arms around his shoulders, and I wept with him.

Jane

Hospitals are places that force you to embrace change. The kind of change you don't want or need. The kind you can't escape. A couple years ago, that change was speech problems after my fall. But before that, the change was my mother dying.

I remember the hospital more than I remember her: the drinking fountain, the purple bands on the walls, the tiny Christmas tree on the nurse's station. Anchors that helped to weigh me down during the emotional storm of trauma.

After it was over, we retreated to our places in the staff quarters of Mad Dog's house in Bel Air. Dad went back to work, and I was shuffled off to Velvet's nanny. That's when the long, hard work began. The hard work lasted for years. Sometimes I think it's still happening.

Maybe it never ends.

I sat in the half-empty Condor Medical Center lobby with Velvet in the wee hours of the morning, waiting to find out if Serj Sarafian was going to live. No purple bands on the wall at this hospital, but I was sure Fen had found his own anchors while he sat with his family and waited for news. They had their own private family lounge, which wasn't far from us. I just didn't have the courage to go in there and check on Fen.

Not with Eddie around. I couldn't face him right now. Or maybe ever. Every decision I'd made over the last few weeks had ballooned inside my head, and I . . .

Wished that life weren't so messy right now.

My phone buzzed with a text from my dad. He knew I was here with Velvet and was letting me know that Mad Dog and Rosa were up now, and that they'd be on their way soon. The hospital was only a half hour from the lake. I wished they wouldn't come. It made me feel like it was sealing the deal on Serj's life. If Mad Dog stayed at the lake, then Serj's condition was no big deal; if he drove out here, then things weren't looking good.

"Any update?" Velvet said, groggy and hoarse as she huddled inside a coat on the waiting room chair.

"No," I told her. "That was just my dad. He's bringing your parents."

"Shit," she murmured. "Do I look trashed?"

Definitely. She looked awful. But I just said, "They're still an hour away, at least. I'm sure he'll be more concerned with Serj."

She whimpered and curled up inside the coat. "What time is it?"

"Five thirty. Crap, Frida."

"Exie will feed her."

"She's at Fen's place," I murmured, wishing I had his aunt Zabel's phone number. She could unlock Fen's apartment if needed. Or maybe I should just make a quick trip out to Zabel's now, take Frida back to Mad Dog's while we were still waiting.

"Wow. Fen?" Velvet said. "No comment."

"No comment needed," I retorted. "I seem to remember rescuing some people from bar mascots, so . . . you know."

"I don't how many times I can apologize."

"So far that would be zero."

Velvet chuckled huskily. "Oops. Very sorry. No, no—I *mean* that. I truly am sorry. Sitting here is sobering in every sense of the word. I don't want to end up like Eddie. Or Fen—what if Daddy kicked me out of the house like that?"

I watched her for a moment. "He wouldn't."

She gave me a soft smile. "I think you might be right. Daddy is gooey in the center. Serj is stone. That's probably why his heart burst." She stared at the ceiling, thinking about this for a moment, then said, "Can you get me something cold to drink? I need a soda or water or something. Didn't we pass a café down one of these corridors?"

Right. I was still her assistant.

She made a face at me. "I didn't mean it *that* way. It's not a command."

"No worries. I got you."

After peeling myself off the chair, I left Velvet in the waiting room, ambling past blank faces staring at their phone screens. This was an enormous hospital, funded by rich donors who lived around the lake. Signs pointed to surgical wings, elevators, and a snack bar. But when I passed the corridor where the Sarafians were holed up inside their private lounge, I saw a dark figure emerging from the door there. Tall, slender, male. He was heading through a set of glass doors that led outside—into a small meditation garden that sat between two buildings. Fen?

Maybe he needed time alone, I wasn't sure. But I had to find out if he was okay, so I quietly slipped outside, surprised by how cool the predawn air was on my arms. It was nice out here, peaceful. Sculpture and plants, tiny golden lights that lit up the footpath. Two benches. I hesitantly stepped toward the one that was occupied.

"Hey," I said.

"Honestly surprised to see you here," the figure said.

I stilled in place. That wasn't Fen.

Eddie.

How could I have gotten them confused? Panic fired through me, and as I took a step back, Eddie turned his head. The lights from the path shone up on his face. He was haggard—a complete wreck. His suit jacket was gone, and his tie dangled like a noose around his neck.

I had no idea what to say to him. On sheer survival instincts, I tried to conjure up the sweet, smiling boy that I used to know and pasted that image on the body of the boy that slumped on the bench in front of me now. But it didn't help.

He was still a stranger. One who wasn't entirely friendly. Maybe it was just in my mind, all the guilt that had been building up over Fen, but it felt as if he were radiating low waves of animosity in my direction.

"Is there . . . uh, your father?" I said awkwardly, stumbling over words I could quite reach.

"No change," he said.

"Ah, okay. Well, I'll just leave you—"

"What? No hug? It's been a minute." He held out his arm, beckoning.

Hug? Dear sweet lord. I didn't know what to do. Was he testing me? I couldn't tell from his tone, which was strained, yes. But under the circumstances, that wasn't too surprising. I just couldn't read him.

Had he not gotten my texts while he was overseas?

I didn't know.

I damn sure wasn't going to ask.

So what was I supposed to do then? Try to guess what was going on inside his head?

Pretend to be normal?

No doubt he noticed I was dragging my feet, so I quickly bent down to hug him while he sat on the bench. Mistake of mistakes. I'm talking *far* more awkward than I could have imagined.

Eddie wrapped me up like he used to, long arms all the way around me. He hugged me so hard, I nearly lost my balance and fell over into him.

"It's nice of you to be here," he said in a voice that didn't sound like him. "You smell really good."

Oh no. Not good whatsoever. *Make this stop.*

I gently shrugged out of his embrace and tried to think of something to say—to cover up the awkwardness of it all. "How, uh, are you holding up? This must be overwhelming."

He blew out a hard breath and shrugged. "I don't even know.

There's a little boy inside my head walking around in a dark forest. That's how I feel right now. Lost and alone."

"That sounds . . ." Terrible. Awful. My heart hurt for him because I believed that he was being absolutely honest with me. Maybe for the first time since we'd known each other. "I'm really sorry, Eddie."

He leaned back on the bench. "Why are you sorry? You didn't do anything wrong. Oh, wait. . . ." His gaze locked on mine. "You mean about you and *Fen*."

Shit. He knew!

My legs felt a little wobbly all the sudden.

I wasn't prepared to talk about this with him. But here we were.

"Eddie—"

"It's fine," he said, dark circles rimming bloodshot eyes. "I saw your text messages. They let me have my phone in jail. They were actually really cool about things and nice to me over there. I love the Philippines. Weird, huh?"

I didn't know how to respond to that, but emotion caught me by surprise. I blinked back welling tears. "Eddie, please believe me. I didn't plan for Fen. For any of this. When you left for the Philippines, if I had an inkling that we'd end up here—"

"I told you to stay away from him!"

"You didn't tell me *why*," I argued. Upset. A little indignant, too. "You didn't tell me what happened to your family. Why Fen was kicked out of the house. Your role in that. The drug problems—"

"I'm not some kind of junkie, okay? Jesus. A couple of Americans I knew from online met up with me in Manila. We were just going to party on the island, that's all. I just got caught."

"I know about Christmas, too."

He looked genuinely surprised and mumbled, "That was just a bad night."

"You didn't pull me out of the dam," I said, shaking a little. "You *lied*. Why, Eddie? Why would you lie about that?"

Eddie said nothing for several moments. A plane streaked across the dark sky, and in the distance, an ambulance siren heralded an incoming patient. When the sound faded, Eddie scrubbed his face with his hand.

"It was fine when no one knew what happened that night but me and Fen. But someone else saw Fen pull you out, and you know how gossip spreads. Next thing you know, my father is up my ass."

"Why would he care?"

"Papa told me that if Mad Dog found out you fell in the dam because you were upset about . . . if you fell in because of me, that it would ruin the relationship between Sarafian Events and Mad Dog. Papa said I had to clean up my own mess. So if you thought I'd rescued you and that ever got back to Mad Dog, then it would soften the blow."

I blinked at him. "You started seeing me because your father was worried about collateral damage with Mad Dog?"

Because he believed I was Mad Dog's daughter.

"In the beginning," Eddie said. "But I wouldn't have kept it going if I didn't like you. And I did, you know. Like you. That was real."

"I *still* like you, Eddie." Tears slid down my cheek. "Those feelings don't go away. I thought we were close. I was so excited about our future. I thought we'd be moving in together."

He snorted. "I think it would be a little crowded with three."

That stung, but I guess I deserved it. Can't have it both ways, right?

"You know what?" he said in a faux-positive voice. "It's fine. Let's call a truce."

"How?" A part of me wanted to believe that was possible. Another part knew better.

"Maybe it's the misery talking," he said, "but if my father pulls out of this, I just want to focus on being there for him. And my mom, the twins. Maybe even Fen. I think it's time we put our differences aside and concentrate on family. Getting better."

"I'm sure Fen would agree," I said tactfully, though I wasn't sure that was true.

"You don't know what kind of fucking pressure I've been under. No one understands but Fen, actually. And we've been at each other's throats for so long—over what? Petty shit?"

Uh . . . okay. Wouldn't exactly call getting booted out of college petty.

Eddie just gave me a tired, strange smile. "I can't compete with my own family anymore," he explained. "Papa always hammers me about being number one . . . sometimes you just get tired of trying to reach that goal, you know?"

"Not everything is a competition," I agreed.

Eddie surprised me by putting his hand on mine, stroking my fingers a little too intimately. "Exactly. God, I love that about you. I forgot that you always know exactly the right thing to say."

That was not true *at all*. My word-pixie made sure of that.

"If my father makes it out of surgery, I have a lot of work ahead of me to prove myself again. Like, so much. It would be easier for me if Fen were on my side this time instead of being my enemy. Mama would be happier, so she'd be nicer to Papa. He'd be nicer to me. Everything would be better if Fen and I weren't fighting. . . ."

For a moment, a mask slipped from his face, and I saw what Fen had been trying to tell me all along about Eddie—Machiavellian, he'd called Eddie. And maybe Eddie was, because he was sitting here, making decisions about his relationship with his brother based on what would bag him the most gain.

I wasn't sure if that was ruthlessness, though, and maybe that was the difference between how I saw Eddie compared to how Fen did.

Fen saw an evil mastermind.

I saw a boy who needed help and didn't know how to ask for it.

Someone stuck their head outside the door and called for Eddie. When I squinted into the shadows, I realized it was Ms. Makruhi, the Sarafians' housekeeper.

Eddie stood up from the bench, eyes wide.

"Eduard," she said, breathless and excited. "Your papa has woken up. He's going to make it."

Oh, thank God. Relief washed through me as I watched

Eddie's face. He just let his head drop slightly, as if he were saying a little prayer, then he nodded at the housekeeper.

"Tell Mama I'm coming back inside," he said.

The housekeeper disappeared as quickly as she'd shown up, and I was left standing alone with Eddie again. "That's such good news," I told him.

He stiffly stuck his hands in his pockets. "I knew he'd be okay. He had to."

I nodded. There was a different kind of awkwardness between us now. The kind of awkwardness that comes with trying to pretend things are normal in order to navigate small talk. "Uh, Mad Dog is on his way, so he'll be here soon. I guess I'll let you get inside to your family now," I told him, moving a step back to extract myself.

"Thanks."

"I'm so relieved for you."

"Are you?" He squinted at me. A challenge.

"Of course I am."

"Well, I guess there's one positive thing about all this," he said. "Now that my father's okay, I'll be making amends with Fen. And since the two of you are chilling, I guess we'll be seeing a lot more of each other, huh?"

"Will we?" I asked, trying to challenge him like he challenged me, but it didn't come out with the same confidence. I tapped a little nervous rhythm on the side of my leg.

"Sure. You and me?" Eddie said in a dark tone that rumbled somewhere between ominous and threatening. "We're practically in-laws."

Jane

Serj Sarafian's heart attack was major, and his recovery took longer than usual. His doctors kept him in the hospital nearly two weeks: first where he had surgery, then in a cardiac rehabilitation program at the lake.

That's about the time that things got hectic for Fen because everyone who ever knew Serj came into town to visit him in the hospital. In fact, I didn't speak but a few sentences to Fen for several days, and our texting nearly ground to a halt.

Fen was busy and preoccupied, staying back at home in his childhood bedroom at the villa, helping his mother out with the twins.

And.

Catching up with Eddie.

Could only imagine how Fen would handle that conversation with his older brother. . . . *Long time, no see. While you were in prison, I was having sex with your girlfriend.*

Ugh, ugh, ugh!

But really, no. Fen wasn't going to say that. Couldn't. *Wouldn't.* He'd be mature—for the sake of his family. His father almost died, after all. He wasn't going to stir up drama. I was sure everything was different now, and I could imagine that maybe, just maybe, Eddie was right to want to mend fences with Fen. And maybe, just maybe, Fen would agree that it was the right thing to do. And that they absolutely were not talking about me. *Please. No.*

Besides, if something awful had gone down between them, I'd probably have heard about it, right? And all seemed to be eerily placid in the Sarafian house, as best I could gather in my limited contact with Fen. So I tried to put away my fears, and I just figured that mending his relationship with Eddie took a lot of energy, so I gave him his space.

But I'd be lying if I said that there wasn't another reason for me giving Fen his space. Because there was. I was *dreading* facing Eddie after our conversation at the hospital. Deep in my bones. The entire situation between us now was messy and volatile, and I was more than happy to avoid seeing either brother while everyone adjusted to the New Normal of me and Fen.

Early evening on the day before Serj was due to be released from the hospital and come back home, Dad told me if I wanted to talk to Fen, I'd need to be a pest and go over to their house like everyone else. I knew he was right. Time to put on the big-girl pants and go face the mess I'd made.

Starla was using the hybrid, so Dad dropped me off at the Sarafians'. I was extraordinarily nervous to walk down the driveway and ring the doorbell, but when Ms. Makruhi answered and rushed off, leaving me in the foyer, I didn't have time to worry about my own apprehensions. The villa was overrun with family and close friends. From where I could see at the villa's entrance, people chatted in the living room and on the back terrace, everyone drinking and eating.

Were the Sarafians having a party? Maybe I should call my dad and get him to come right back and get me.

"Hey," a voice said from the stairwell above.

I looked up, past the glass octopus sculpture, to see Fen smiling down at me from the second-story railing. He pushed a hand through his dark curls as he bounded down the foyer staircase, turning to the side to make his way around a couple chatting on the bottom of the steps. "What are you doing here? You should have texted me."

"You hadn't responded lately, which is fine. I assumed you were busy," I told him. "But maybe I should've texted, you're right. I didn't know you'd be having people over."

"Pssh," he said, waving his hand. "These aren't real people. This is family. Mostly out-of-towners visiting the big man. I think my mom's going to kick most of these assholes out in a couple hours, but don't worry, you're good. You get a free pass along with my grandparents."

I did? I was *that* important? Grandparent-level important? I felt like a fraud, like I didn't deserve that, after all the cheating we'd done. Maybe I shouldn't even be here, mingling with his family.

Who's the Ruiner now?

But Fen was oblivious to my self-conscious woes. His eyes

darted behind me as if he was checking to make sure the coast was clear, and when the couple on the stairs wasn't looking, he dipped down and kissed me.

Kissed me.

Right there. In the foyer.

Under the exploding octopus.

"Sorry," he whispered, a small smile on his lips as he pulled away.

"Not sorry," I whispered back. "Are you okay?"

He nodded, eyes bright for a moment. "I'm glad you're here. It's hectic, though. Fair warning. I'll introduce you to everyone, come on. . . ."

Crap. People. Family. Why did we do *that* here? I was so happy to see him, achy with it. But I was so nervous and unsure about being here today, which was basically like ringing a dinner bell for my word-pixie. Best thing I could do was try to say as little as possible and hope for the best. Did his mother know about us? I mean, I was pretty sure she had an inkling before, but that was . . . a million years and two lifetimes ago. This was now. Post–heart attack. It was different now.

I didn't want Jasmine to hate me.

I definitely didn't want to talk to Eddie.

Fen took me around the house and introduced me to every Sarafian and Kasabian alive on planet Earth. Three cousins. Serj's half sister. Some great-aunts, and Aunt Pari, who I'd seen but never formally met.

I also briefly met Serj's parents and spent some time with the

Kasabian grandparents, who used to manage Victory Vinyl but now lived in Southern California.

"We're practically neighbors," said Fen's grandmother, Mina Kasabian, a woman almost as tall as Jasmine, only stouter and with short gray hair. "We're almost in Burbank. There's a bakery down the street from our house that makes pastry worth the drive on the 101." She gave me an exhaustive description of what they carried. "You must come see us."

This was the "terror of Glendale"? Could've fooled me. "I heard you like Carole King," I told her.

She gasped. "You heard right. Stereo is right there. Should we play the goddess?"

"Serj hates Carole King," Jasmine informed her mother, collapsing on the couch with Ani. "And she's too sad. Play something cheerful, in honor of Serj coming home tomorrow. Fen, my shining star? You are the DJ."

"Tom Waits it is, then," he deadpanned.

A spirited argument broke out, not too serious, most of it involving people who had no idea who Tom Waits was, some of them confusing him with Tom Jones. But after much fuss, when Ella Fitzgerald ended up on the stereo, no one complained.

Fen and I got separated, and I hung out with Ani and Ari for a bit. Then, maybe it was out of habit, or maybe I was unconsciously trying to avoid both Eddie and any anxiety-triggered aphasia issues, but I ended up in the kitchen helping Ms. Makruhi shuttle food out onto a buffet table. I filled drinks. Picked up garbage. Washed dishes. She was very efficient and a straight shooter, and we worked well together, once I got used to the way she wanted things.

"You are a very bright girl," she finally said after dusk fell, and I hadn't seen Fen for an hour or more because a couple of his friends showed up. "Don't do this."

"Pardon?"

She gestured around the kitchen. "This. Washing dishes."

"You wash dishes."

"I am not young, and I didn't have options. I was alone in a foreign country. The Sarafians took me in. But you don't need to be taken in, so take care of yourself."

"Okay . . . ?"

"Fen tells me things," she said.

I felt the heat wash over my cheeks and neck. My ears were on fire. The way she said this, I had no doubt that Fen had told her too much. That made me nervous. I wasn't going to admit anything about Fen to her, so I just said, "My mother was a housekeeper before she died."

"So?" She shrugged. "If she were alive, she would be telling you to go to college. I think of these kids like my own. Ani is smart like you. There is nothing wrong with washing dishes. I take pride in my work. But if you are smart, do something that fills you with pride. Be strong."

"I'm strong."

"You're weak," she argued. "Go to college. Why has your father not pushed you?"

I didn't know how much she knew about my brain issues. "I've been ill."

"Then go to a special school." She shrugged again.

Good lord, she was frustrating. And outspoken. I didn't want to sit there and explain my life's story to this woman. And there weren't special schools for people with aphasia. If anything, I'd been through so much speech therapy, I could probably teach other people by now. Why was this woman getting into my business?

"Fen needs to go to school too," she said. "I've told Jasmine this. I didn't have the same opportunities you have. If you were my children, I would shove you out the door. No more moping. Life is too short. Just do it."

There was no arguing with her, and she was getting a little emotional. People forget about domestics. I imagined that she was upset about what had happened to Serj too—that she felt as if this family were her own family—but she was expected to keep working. So I just said, "I'll consider it. Thank you for the advice."

"Good," she said, taking something out of the refrigerator. "Now, here is some nutmeg cake I made yesterday. I wrapped it up for you and Fen. Please leave."

I took the plastic-wrapped plate she handed me. "Um . . ."

"Before he gets in a fight with Eddie in front of their grandparents. Take him back to Zabel's apartment, at least for a night. Tomorrow will be hard with Serj coming back home. I'm going to give Jasmine a sleeping pill, and I will watch over the twins. Being a family again takes time."

I was so tired, and I desperately wanted five minutes alone

with Fen, just to make sure he was okay. And maybe one more kiss.

But I wasn't sure I had the willpower to drag him away from the house or if it was even the right thing to do. Fen seemed absorbed with everyone here right now, and maybe that was what he needed, like Jasmine. To be surrounded by people. All these cousins and friends from school. People who cared about him. His very sweet grandparents. And the twins. Even Eddie.

But when I threaded through the villa to let him know that I was going to call my dad and head back to the lodge, I spotted him standing on the terrace between the two friends who'd just shown up—their names I couldn't remember—and he was nodding, pretending to smile a little, but it was clear that he wasn't listening.

He was busy staring across the terrace at Eddie, who was downing a bottle of beer with one of their older cousins.

Just beer. Not cocaine. Either way, Eddie wasn't my responsibility.

Still, it worried me a little, considering everything that had just happened to him. If it were me, and my father had just had a major heart attack after bailing me out of prison in another country for drug possession, I'd probably try to at least pretend I was one hundred percent sober.

I definitely didn't want to talk to Eddie by myself. That would be foolish.

Maybe I could ask Fen privately whether we needed to intervene?

I made sure I was out of Eddie's line of sight and discreetly got Fen's attention. His eyes blinked, and he looked as if he might collapse.

"I'm sorry," I said, interrupting the person next to him. "I need to borrow him."

"She's got you cuffed, bro?" one of them mumbled.

"Kitchen help," the other one murmured.

I felt my ears getting hot, but I was too tired to let it get to me. I just held out my arm to Fen, and he came to me, winding himself around me as we strolled away.

"Thank you, thank you, thank you," he said into my neck. "This is one of the longest days of my life."

"Nice friends."

"They aren't my friends. They're people I used to go to school with. I don't know why they're here. I think Eddie invited them? Fucking prick. I'm *this* close to taking that beer bottle out of his hand and smashing it over his head."

Well, damn. Maybe Ms. Makruhi was right. Housekeepers usually are. I should've realized that, I supposed.

Fen groaned. "Eddie's lucky that I'm exhausted. I can barely stand, Jane. Fen zombie, grrr. Fen need sleep."

"I can help you with that. I've been instructed to drive you back to the barn to get some rest," I told him, showing him the cake. "Or, if you're too tired to leave and would prefer to stay here, I can take you up to your room and call my dad to pick me up—"

"Take me to the barn," he confirmed. "Because Grandpa Sarafian is taking the guest room, my other grandparents are sleeping in my old room anyway. I was going to have to crash on the couch."

"Come on, then," I said, feeling useful. "Let's get you back to your place."

I drove the beast of a Jeep at what Fen claimed was the slowest speed the vehicle had been driven since it rolled off the factory line. But he was happy to feel the night breeze, and when we parked at the dog kennel, the walk to the barn was even slower. We were both running out of battery juice.

"Damn, have I only been away from this place two weeks?" he said when we trudged up the stairs to the barn's loft and he unlocked the tiny apartment. "I came by and picked up some clothes after we came back from the hospital, but it feels like I haven't been here in a century."

"How is it, staying at your family home again?"

"Weird. Good. Confusing." He stared at the floor and then shook his head. "All of those things at once. Mama sat us all down for a family meeting and told us we had to make changes, for my father's sake. No fighting with Eddie, in other words, to save my father's heart. So I'm swallowing my plans for revenge, eating crow like a good little boy. We're going to—get this—family counseling."

He tried to make counseling sound like a chore, but I was pretty sure I heard some hope underneath his disdain.

"Maybe it will help." Inside I worried all that compromising he was enduring with Eddie had to involve me, even just a little. "I know it can't be easy."

"We haven't been yet, so we'll see how it goes. Who knew your entire world could be turned upside down in such a short time," he said, toeing off his shoes. "My father got a new heart. I got welcomed back into a household from which I'd been banished. Eddie decided it's no longer in our best interest to be enemies. . . ."

"He told me," I admitted, putting the cake in the fridge.

The air crackled with energy. "When?"

Ugh. Awkward. "In the hospital. We talked a little when your dad was still coming out of surgery that first night." I didn't want to tell him I'd hugged Eddie. Not that there was anything wrong with a hug. "Speaking of things that happened in the last couple of weeks, I think your milk has gone bad. It's forming a curd."

Fen wasn't buying into my weak attempt at a distraction. "So that's when you talked to him. Interesting . . ."

Uh-oh. *Was* it interesting? I didn't want to talk about it. Maybe now was a good time to discuss Eddie drinking that beer.

"Sometimes," Fen said, "it's hard to tell when Eddie is manipulating information to make things seems worse than they are. Take for instance, he told me something earlier today that I thought was odd."

"Oh? What did he tell you?"

"He said . . . no, he implied . . ." Fen grunted and paused, as if he was hesitant to say.

"What?"

"Eddie said, 'Good luck with that.' And then some other gross stuff that basically implied that you were some prissy girl that was saving yourself for marriage, and that's why he wanted to move in with you, because maybe it would . . . hurry things along?"

"Wow, okay." My chest tightened around a knot of resentment. "For starters, I wouldn't say I was saving myself for marriage, obviously."

"Obviously."

"You weren't my first."

"You weren't mine? It doesn't matter. I just assumed . . . ?" He squinched up his eyes and shook his head. "I shouldn't have brought it up. My mistake was letting Eddie rope me into listening to him. This is not a conversation I ever thought I'd have."

"Me neither."

"It doesn't matter," he said again. "I was just surprised."

"That Eddie and I hadn't had sex."

He pointed at me. "Yep. That."

"We did other things, but—"

"Don't want to know," he said, holding up a hand. "Just like I told him. Don't care, don't want details."

I nodded. A long, awkward moment stretched between us.

"I know it doesn't matter, but it's driving me up a wall that he's trying to shift the blame to me when he literally pushed me away from—"

"I'm begging you, Jane, please don't finish that sentence."

"I'm just saying. . . . He was hot and then cold. I only saw him a few times in person when he came through L.A. Once, we got touchy in his car, and the next time, he wouldn't hug me. He didn't kiss me goodbye when he left for the Philippines, and I hadn't seen him in forever. That was when my dad started hating him."

"I see."

"And maybe some of it was me?" I shook my head. "Maybe he sensed that I never quite forgave him for the dam. Not that it was his fault that I fell in. I did that. But before I fell, when he was drunk and left me in the woods. I wanted him to apologize for that, or to show me that he was a better person."

"But he didn't."

"Eddie is tricky. He's so nice, and he always talks around things. . . . It's hard to tell sometimes if he's just completely clueless. So I gave him a pass. A lot of passes. But part of me held a grudge. I don't think I realized that at the time."

Fen snorted. "He brings out the best in people. And I believe you. I'm sorry I brought any of this up. He shook me up, and I knew better."

"Don't apologize," I said. "It's going to be different now that Eddie's back."

"It's already different," he agreed in a weary voice. He sounded as if he were carrying the weight of the world on his shoulders. In his head. In his soul.

After another long moment of silence he sighed and asked, "Where's Frida?"

"At the lodge."

"I got used to seeing her funny face here. That's another thing that's happened over the past couple of weeks. No Frida in my bed."

"And I had a period."

His brow lifted slowly.

I shrugged. "At least I'm not pregnant. Not that I was really worried, since we've been safe. But still. Whew." I pretended to wipe my brow.

"Here's an idea," he said, a little spark in his eye. "Wanna take a shower together and get in bed?"

I nodded several times. I really would. I wanted to erase everything that had happened the past couple of weeks. Serj's heart attack. Eddie coming back from the Philippines.

I wanted to go back to our happy bubble.

But things were changing. I knew it, and he did too.

Jane

The weeks between the Serj's release from the hospital and the festival were tough. Fen told me countless times that he didn't know how he'd survive reacclimating into his family without me, and I do think I helped—at least, as much as I could. He was on his own journey, and I supported him as best I knew how.

It felt a little like my aphasia, though. If you weren't going through it, there wasn't much you could do to help, unless you were a doctor. I remembered watching the helplessness on my dad's face after the incident at the dam two years ago; back then, I knew Dad wanted to help me and was hurting, but I just couldn't deal with him.

Now *I* was my dad, helpless to do much for Fen, and I saw him looking back at me like I'd looked at my father: appreciative of me, but he didn't have the energy to tell me how to help him.

So when he needed to spend nights at the villa because his father was having a bad time with his cardiac rehabilitation program and Jasmine wanted Fen at home for the twins, I just nodded, even though it hollowed me out inside. Fen was being stretched thin, and we all wanted a piece of him.

Even the press.

Between Serj's hospital release and the festival, they stuck around the lake, snapping photos of the lodge. Of Velvet. Of the Fintail every time Mad Dog rode into town. And of the Sarafians coming and going from their villa. I was used to this back in L.A. But Mad Dog had people who dealt with it—my dad, Kamal and his father, and lawyers if it went too far—and for the most part, it was pretty low-key. Mad Dog wasn't out destroying hotel rooms and dominating the tabloid headlines, so there wasn't much more than "producer caught dropping a box of doughnuts in Sherman Oaks."

Fen wasn't used to it, though, and it was making him cranky. Jasmine hired a security guard for the villa, which was an extra stress. In fact, all of this gathered into one big stress snowball for Eddie and Fen, who seemed to be slowly, slowly reverting to their old ways. Picking on each other. Little digs. Snide comments. Tiny treacheries.

I prayed they weren't about me, but deep inside, I feared they were.

But the weight of an impending standoff lifted for a minute, and strangely enough, it lifted when Eddie and Velvet started hanging out together. I didn't even know they had been friendly until the Fourth of July, when Mad Dog and Rosa invited the Sarafians over to the lodge for a cookout—it was so much food, Exie had to hire two people from town to help her set up grills outside. And when we were all watching fireworks by the dock, Eddie and Velvet were laughing their heads off, telling a story about something they did the night before.

Together. As in, Eddie and Velvet went out together.

"We're just friends," Velvet told me as I tried to calm down Frida, who hated fireworks with the trembling rage that only a small dog could muster.

"I honestly do not care," I said. Much. I mean, it *was* a little weird to think of them together. But whatever. "More concerned about the sober issue for both of you. I saw Eddie drinking when his dad was in the hospital."

"It's a holiday weekend," she told me. "Everyone's drinking. But no one's gone buck wild. And personally, I haven't seen Erika Jones since that night at Betty's, don't worry."

I was afraid this just made things more complicated than they needed to be. I even wondered if Eddie was in a mentally bad place this weekend. A couple hours ago, Jasmine had announced that even though Serj was resting back at the villa—holiday fireworks were too much for his heart—they'd come to a decision about the future of the festival.

And it wasn't exactly great for Eddie.

"Starting next year, we're going to scale back our hands-on production and coproduce the festival with Denis Oglethorpe," Jasmine told us that night by Mad Dog's pool. "He's already running a fifty-person events operation out of Oakland, and they're putting on two festivals in San Francisco without national equity."

"This way, we avoid Live Nation and expand our brand," Mad Dog said at her side. "We'll be branded under S.L.O.: Sarafian, Larsen, and Oglethorpe Events."

Eddie was furious. "Are you fucking joking me? Whose idea was this? Has Papa approved this?"

"Yes, he has. It was a group decision," Jasmine said. "It will cut down on your father's day-to-day stress. We won't have to lay off too many people. Most will be taken under the Oglethorpe branch."

"What about me?" Eddie said. "Where do I fit into the company?"

"Wonder if the new brand hires felons?" Fen murmured, scratching his chin dramatically.

"Welcome to the future, Eddie," Jasmine said, ignoring Fen's remark. "This is how we grow. Would you like to really learn this time? Start at minimum wage, bottom of the ladder, and work your way up."

Eddie was seething. But he held his tongue, maybe for the sake of keeping his family united during his father's recovery, who knows. I wanted to think he was learning and growing.

But later in the night, when he was watching the fireworks, and Velvet was insisting that he'd only had a few celebratory holiday beers, I worried about the darkness behind his eyes.

Maybe I was just projecting something that wasn't there.

Maybe.

Dad and I finally made time to take our yearly sequoia tunnel tree photo. Good thing we got it when we did, too. If we'd waited a couple of days, we would've had to share our annual shot with strangers.

Because the week of the festival, Condor Lake swelled with people.

Thousands upon thousands.

They descended like a plague of locusts, clogging up every street and parking space. The Strip? Forget about it. Bumper-to-bumper traffic all the way to the festival grounds. Which meant all the shops along the Strip were jam-packed.

Most definitely Victory Vinyl. It was one of their busiest times of the year. Fen had to work most of it, so I rode into the festival with Starla, Velvet—and Eddie, of all people.

Nothing like VIP backstage passes.

I just hadn't imagined experiencing them like this.

Starla and I spent most of the first day of the festival together. It was as hot and sweaty as I remembered. Nothing but bodies and booths, an enteral quest for overpriced bottled water, and a longing to chill at those Avalon tents, even though I knew the secret behind them now.

My heart hurt a little thinking about it because I wished I could go back to that day with Fen, riding out into the woods to see his tree. Back when we were in our own little bubble.

The second night of the festival, Fen was able to get away from the record store. Dad ended up driving us to the amphitheater in one of Mad Dog's SUVs with Velvet and Eddie, and there was concern in my father's eyes as he watched us in the rearview mirror. He was seeing something I wasn't, and that made me anxious. Was it Velvet? Was she high? Eddie was a little twitchy, and he kept licking his lips, saying he needed water. But it was hot outside, and maybe I was looking for trouble that wasn't there.

Velvet had promised me several times that she'd been sober around Eddie. Swore. She sounded genuine.

So I tried to put it out of my mind, because even though Fen was tired from working all day, he was trying to get a second wind, holding my hand, and I was grateful to spend time with him. If *he* didn't notice anything wrong, then maybe it really was okay.

All in my mind.

After donning lanyards that pretty much identified us as festival demigods—I would definitely be saving this memento—we entered the amphitheater through the band door around back. I enjoyed it for a while, walking through a dark underground tunnel past dressing rooms and some of the roadies who were friendly to Fen and Eddie. Velvet somehow knew one of the band's managers. One big happy music family, the Sarafians and the Larsens.

And me, the only odd person out.

But I forgot all about that when we stood in the wings, looking out at a crowd of thousands. I was excited all over again. It was music, the thing I loved. A band I loved, and on a warm summer night, all these people made a pilgrimage all the way out to Nowhere to experience this. For them, the fairy tale of Condor Lake was real. You could watch a dozen live clips on YouTube alone in your bedroom anytime you wanted. And that was all good—truly. But you'd never feel what everyone here was feeling right now.

The connection.

The energy.

The joy of being human together.

The roar of the crowd transcended anything that could only be seen on a tiny laptop or heard through a pair of earbuds. Because it wasn't just the band that mattered. It was all the people out there who were listening. Without them, it was just band practice.

Together, it was a shared experience. A give and take.

A conversation.

For someone like me, a conversation was everything. I'd lost all hope of even being able to talk at one point. But I knew I could understand words. I could hear music—this right here. I could always have this. And that brought me more peace when I was in therapy than anything the doctors told me. If I still had music, I had joy, connection, and a conversation.

What magic!

I watched the crowd and the band, and I watched Fen, too. I saw the awe in face, and I was pretty sure he was feeling something close to what I felt. Maybe he was finally appreciating what his father had built, even if he could never bond with the man himself. Maybe there was some peace to be found in the thing Serj created. This festival was more than "scamming" people for luxury tents or trying to pack bodies in front of stages. It wouldn't have lasted this long if that's all it was.

There was some good here.

Velvet was waving Fen over to introduce him to someone semi-famous, a little farther backstage. I squinted into the dark and let him go. I was too enthralled with watching the show and the crowd. Toward the end of the song, someone stepped behind me, and I felt a chin rest on my shoulder.

My head told me it should be Fen, but my instincts said *nope*. Fen didn't smell like beer.

I flinched and looked out of the corner of my eye at the cheek next to mine.

Eddie.

Before I could jerk away, he folded his arms around mine, trapping me, and pressed the length of his body against my back. It was ridiculously intimate. Not a hug between friends.

Eddie had never once made me afraid of him. *Ever.* I wasn't sure if he'd been drinking enough to be drunk, or what was happening. I just knew it didn't feel right. I panicked a little and pushed him off, and when I looked at his face, he was laughing.

A joke? It didn't feel funny to me.

As the song ended, he leaned down and put his mouth against my ear and said loud enough for me to hear over the crowd, "We can hit it on the side, like you and Fen did when we were together. Fen's just using you to get at me, anyway. Let's have some fun."

Then he backed away.

Mother trucker.

I was *all* kinds of panicked now. But Eddie just walked away as if it wasn't any big deal. Was he threatening me? Or joking? Maybe he was high—I honestly couldn't tell.

My eyes searched for Fen's and found them full of fury. *He'd seen.* He was marching toward Eddie, and it looked like he might dismember him.

They were too far away from me backstage, and it was too loud. I couldn't hear them. I could just see the sharp lines on Fen's furious face, and the way he pointed his finger at Eddie.

The way Eddie strolled toward him, unbothered—or pretending to be, at least.

When they met in the middle, Fen pushed Eddie.

Pushed . . . violently shoved.

I tried to shout, to make them stop, but my word-pixie woke, scrambling things up, and the words I *could* speak were lost under the thunder of the concert.

Suddenly, the brothers lunged toward each other in a flash of bodies.

Someone's fist came out. Eddie's, I think. Fen's head rocked backward. Then he was stumbling, and stagehands were rushing toward the boys, breaking them up, blocking my sight.

Everything inside me retracted in pain. This was exactly what I didn't want. *This.*

This nightmare.

Of which I had a leading role. *Ruiner.*

I watched in horror as security held the boys apart until they'd cooled down. Fen was wild-haired, still furious. Eddie was laughing. Both of them had hurt each other—mentally and physically. Utter disaster.

Was this how things were going to be now, with Eddie back? The two brothers were going to be at each other's throats again, and I was the wedge in the middle. I wasn't sure why that was so shocking. Did I truly believe I could float like a bee from one brother to another without any fallout?

Why are love triangles in movies always so fun and frivolous? They aren't in real life. They're tragic and horrible, and if I could have gone back in time and erased everything that happened that night at the dam, I would have saved myself two years of misery.

I damaged my brain. I cost Mad Dog thousands of dollars in medical bills—because God knows my father's crappy insurance didn't cover it. On top of that, Dad worried himself sick over me, and I lost friendships and got so far behind in school.

But it wasn't just the people in my world. It was the Sarafians. I spent *how* long chasing Eddie? Even after he rejected me that night at the dam, I was still starry-eyed over him while I was in speech therapy—while Fen was having a low-key breakdown over the dam incident.

If I contributed to driving a wedge between the two of them, even a little? Just thinking about it made my stomach sick.

If I could have gone back in time and just seen Fen instead of Eddie that night—really seen Fen for who he was—then everything might be different right now. Maybe he wouldn't have spent years being haunted. Maybe he'd be in a music program at school. Getting accolades for his piano playing. Never kicked out of his house.

Who knows, maybe even Serj might have stayed out of the hospital.

Three people can never make it work. Look at what happened

with Mad Dog, my father, and my mother. I didn't want that to happen now. But there was another way that didn't involve two boys I cared about being hurt.

I couldn't change the past, but I could change the future.

A triangle can't exist without the third side.

Dad always said that if I needed a ride, he'd be there, no questions asked. That was the policy. I hesitated, making sure in my head this was the right thing. But as the music continued to play behind me, the band unfazed by the fighting in the wings, I felt it deep in my chest.

I knew this was the right thing, and if I waited too long, I'd talk myself out of it.

So I texted him: I need you to come get me. I want to go home to LA. I want to leave service.

Track [28] "All My Little Words"/The Magnetic Fields

Jane

Dad and I texted back and forth several times. He was frantic.
So was I. The more I thought about it, the more resolute I felt.
This was what I needed to do to save all of us.

It just wasn't easy.

And when Velvet came and took Eddie aside, and security
released Fen, I knew it was about to be the hardest thing I'd ever
done.

"Are you okay?" I asked, walking up to him in the wings,
mouthing my question over the band and the crowd.

Fen threw away a tissue that he'd been holding up to the
corner of his bleeding mouth and dismissively shook his head.
He signaled that he was fine. His eyes searched mine. He was still
upset. Worried. Angry. A jangle of emotions packed into a blood-
ied face. A wave of concern crashed over me, tugging at my heart,
but I had to stay steady.

I pointed at myself and gestured leaving. "I'm taking off. Can
we talk?"

"What?" He shook his head and then put his hand on my
back and urged me farther backstage. We ducked around security

and roadies, descended a set of stairs, and went through a small door that led back into the underground corridor we'd originally come through. It was cool and much quieter down here, though the thump of the music was still ever present. Fen found a place behind some random equipment and leaned against the wall there.

"Are you all right?" I asked.

"Just a busted lip, I think," he said. "Are *you* okay?"

"You saw." Obviously.

He nodded once.

I hesitated. I didn't want to yell at him for trying to rescue me from Eddie. But I didn't want to have to be rescued, and I didn't want to be a toy that got batted around between the two of them. I knew Fen would never do that on purpose, but Eddie?

He was not in his right mind.

"Eddie is messed up," I said. "I think he's upset over your father's heart attack and probably the new direction of Sarafian Events. He needs help. Probably rehab. He's an addict, I think."

Fen blinked at me and scrubbed a hand over his eyes, nodding. "Yeah, you're probably right. I know you are."

"You need to get him help before the two of you end up falling back into butting horns again. I really feel like he's on a path of self-destruction, and he's going to try to take you down with him."

"Shit," Fen muttered. "What did he say to you onstage?"

I shook my head. I wouldn't tell him that. It would only cause more resentment. And I didn't *really* believe that Fen was using me to get revenge on his brother. Eddie was just trying to provoke me. But if Eddie had planted any doubts in my head, I didn't want Fen to see them.

"It doesn't matter," I told Fen. "Just take care of him. He's family, and that's important to you. Remember? You said it was the tree, family, and music. You've got your big tree whenever you need it. And now you've got the support of your family back— your beautiful, strange family."

He squinted at me. Crossed his arms. "Why are you talking like this?"

"Because Eddie is part of your family too. And he's fucked up. You're the strong one, not him. You've got pull with your mom . . . not him. Tell her to do something about him. He doesn't need tough love. That didn't work, clearly. Look at him. He's not well."

He nodded. "Okay, yeah."

"But also? You shouldn't have to worry about him. That's your mom's job." I poked him the chest. "*You* need to be making music. I don't know if it's school or training or what you need to do. Figure it out, though. Because Ani is right. You are a virtuoso. See? My word-pixie didn't eat the word." I smiled.

He reached for my forearm and held it. "I know I need to work on my music. *I know.* Why are you saying it like this? What's going on?"

Tears welled. In one blink, they cascaded down my cheeks. "I'm going home."

"Home?"

"Back to L.A."

His hand started trembling on my arm. "Why?"

I shook my head. "Mad Dog will be packing up the lodge in another week or so, anyway. You know that. He goes back every August. I'm just delaying the inevitable by sticking around. I need to go home. I don't have a place here."

"Of course you do! You can stay with me."

"And do what?"

"I don't know—get a job? Help out at the record store." He blinked rapidly and his eyes went dark and liquidy. "What were you going to do with Eddie? Huh? At the beginning of the summer, you were boasting about moving in with him here."

He was angry. Upset. Hurt.

I couldn't stop stinging tears from falling down my face, and my nose wouldn't stop watering. "I didn't have a plan."

"Then don't have a plan now!"

"Not having a plan was a terrible plan," I tried to explain.

"But it was good enough for Eddie?"

"It *was* good enough for Eddie, because he's just screwing around, doing nothing. But it's not good enough for you, because you're miles above me."

He turned his head to the ceiling and growled. "Stop saying that shit! It's. *Not. True!*"

I put my free hand on his face, which was shaking as much as his trembling hand. "It is true, but it doesn't have to be. I'm gonna go back home, and I'm going to college. I'm not quite sure where or how I'll get the money to pay for it, but I'm about to figure that out. And I'm going to find out who I am, and she's going to be amazing."

"She's already amazing," he said, crying. "I know I haven't been a very good boyfriend lately. I've been too distracted with my father's surgery and everything going on at home. I'm *so sorry*."

"Oh my God, no. Stop. Of course you've been distracted."

"But—"

"This isn't about you. It's about me. I know that sounds like a line, but I actually mean it. You need to concentrate on you, and I have to get out of Mad Dog's house," I told him. "I can't do it any longer. I have to stand on my own feet. I want to be your equal."

He pulled me against him, and I wrapped my arms around him. We both wept into each other like it was a funeral. Maybe it was. Something was dying.

"I'm fucking in love with you," he said. "You know that, right?"

"I'm in love with you, too," I said.

"Not just a little. I can't see a future without you anymore."

"That's why I have to go."

"Now? Today?"

I nodded against his chest. "I think it's better. If I can. I'm going to try to leave now."

"Without saying goodbye to anyone? Ani and Ari? My mom? I don't understand why it has to be now. Please, talk to me."

"Would it be any better if it were a week from now, now that I've told you this?" I said, pulling back to look up at him. "We've been ignoring the fact that I was going to leave at the end of the summer, but here it is, the end. And now that it's between us, we'd both be counting the days, dreading it. It would be like waiting for an execution. We'd be miserable."

"I'll come with you."

"To L.A.? I don't even know where I'll be staying. I told you, I'm not going back to Bel Air. I'm leaving Mad Dog's service."

"But our families are connected. What about Velvet? And Frida?"

"It's not my family, and Frida's not my dog." My throat constricted so hard I couldn't breathe for a moment. I'd forgotten about Frida. If I was doing this, then I'd lose her. And Exie. And Norma. And Starla.

I choked out a sob.

A crew of people walked past us, hurrying down the corridor as they carried cables. For a moment, there was some back-and-forth on walkies similar to the ones we used in the lodge. Fen and I both tried to pull ourselves together, wiping our faces on our clothes. And when we were alone again, he gave me a haunted look.

"Is there anything I can say to change your mind?"

I shook my head.

"We can do a long-distance thing, then."

"That doesn't work very well, trust me."

He paced away from me several steps, screamed into his hands, and then came back. His hair was a nightmare. His eyes were bloodshot from crying. He'd never looked more beautiful.

"I told you that you had the power to crush me, didn't I?" he said.

I sobbed again. "I never wanted that power."

"Too bad."

"I'm so sorry I made you see ghosts."

"I would happily live with ghosts for the rest of my life."

I shook my head emphatically. "Ghost-free. That's the goal. No more hauntings."

"No. The ghosts are what we lived through. They are us, me and you! You don't get rid of ghosts—you befriend them. That's what we've been doing wrong. Please don't try to run away from this."

"I'm not running away."

I don't think he believed me. "When are you coming back? This isn't forever. Let's negotiate."

"Sarafian, through and through," I said, smiling a little through my tears.

"A month."

"I want to go to college."

"We can go together. One of the best private colleges in the state is only a twenty-minute drive from the lake."

"Then why aren't you there?" I asked.

His shoulders fell. He couldn't give me a reason.

"How about next summer?" I said. "If there's still something between us, then we'll meet back here next summer and try again. But you have to promise me that you'll work on your music."

"I promise. And I *will* wait for you. I waited this long, and I will wait for years if I have to. We are not broken up."

"Okay," I said, laughing through another burst of tears. "If you need to break up with me, though, just text me. We know that works."

"Fuck that. The next time I see you, I will still be yours."

"The next time I see you, I hope that dead girl is off your arm."

He wiped at his nose. "Oh. Shit. I will fucking burn it off my shoulder with a blowtorch."

I closed my eyes. For a moment, I didn't think I had enough strength to do this. But every time I worked through the math of me and him here, it didn't add up. Every scenario I could imagine ended up with me stuck. Between him and Eddie. With no way for me to grow. I really knew that I loved him, because it felt like I was trying to separate from myself.

It felt unnatural.

But how could I stay if it was only just to spend time with him? I didn't have that luxury. I wasn't born into wealth. I didn't have a talent like he did. Even if Eddie weren't in the picture, if I was going to be something more, I had to step outside of my comfort zone and push myself.

"Thank you for saving my life," I told him, pulling away until our fingers ran out of room. "See you next summer."

"Next summer."

Jane

I'd been wrong about a lot of things in my life. But there were two things that I was wrong about that actually turned out all right. The first was thinking that my father would never forgive me for asking him to drive me all the way back to L.A. from the lake. He wasn't even mad.

Okay, he wasn't *thrilled* about asking Mad Dog for the time off, or when he had to listen to me tell Mad Dog that I was quitting service with no notice whatsoever.

The point is that Dad wasn't angry. And he forgave me. And he rented a car that night and drove me back to L.A.

The second thing I was wrong about that actually turned out okay was discovering that my dad wasn't just in a seemingly healthy relationship with the mystery person who was always texting him, J.H.; that person was, in fact, a real-life guy named Jay.

Jay the celebrity helicopter pilot was not only real, but he also had a really nice two-bedroom apartment in the Ocean Park neighborhood of Santa Monica, just a couple blocks from the pier, that he let us stay at. It wasn't precisely oceanside, but close enough. It was inside a three-story stucco building with two other garden apartments, and it had an amazing little patio balcony in the back that overlooked a sunny, palm tree–lined alley with a narrow view of the beach, just a half a block away.

A few days after we got back in town, Dad and I sat out there most of the afternoon, watching surfers and beach bums while sipping cherry Kool-Aid in our shorts and no shoes in the dry, hot heat; the Santa Ana winds came early. I forgot how much louder it was in the city, with everyone's car radios thumping and the neighbors fighting late at night. All the smells. Very different than lake life. That's the California I knew. Who needed Condor? Not me.

Anyway, Jay was still in South America, so I hadn't actually met him face-to-face yet. He just loaned us his place to crash while I was sorting out my life. He wouldn't be back for a while, so I basically had this place for about three weeks. After that, I was on my own.

"Oh, here's one, cub," Dad said from the other side of the patio table, squinting into the sun as he browsed want ads. "It's part-time at a pet store. The pay's not bad. Wait, it's way out in Pasadena."

"That's close to Glendale."

"So? What's in Glendale?" His face scrunched up. "Forest Lawn cemetery . . ."

Fen's grandparents.

"Nothing," I said quickly. I couldn't think about that. Not in front of Dad. Had to hold it together. I was the one who dragged us down here. Now I had to make it work.

Dad helped me put together my resume—probably the

shortest resume in history. Dog walker and PA. The end. We had to pad it out with my education. Exie said she'd give a stellar reference for any future employer if I needed one. Surprisingly, Norma said she would too.

"I need full-time work anyway," I told Dad as he continued to scroll through job listings. "Stop looking at part-time stuff. I'll never afford an apartment on part-time pay."

"Keep forgetting about rent," he mumbled as a scooter whizzed down the alley beneath the patio. "Not used to paying for that. Maybe you could get a roommate? One of your old friends from your charter school?"

"They're all living in dorms, Dad. They were achievers, remember? Some are going to college in other states."

"Right. And it's really too late for you to get accepted into any of the nearby schools you wanted to go to? Not UCLA, but Cal State? Even if Mad Dog helped put in a good word?"

"By about six months," I said, thinking of how Fen got Eddie kicked out of school. It made me smile a little . . . until it didn't. Anyway, I didn't want to get into with Dad about how that kind of thing wasn't just frowned on, it was a crime. Dad didn't go to college. This was all foreign to him. "It's okay. Lots of people start in community college. Even famous people." That would make him feel better. "Plus, it's tons cheaper, so financial aid might cover the tuition. Looks like most of them have open registration until the end of August."

"Only decent community colleges I know are in the Valley," he said, gritting his teeth. "So far away . . ."

"It's half an hour."

"On the 101. Maybe there's one closer. What are you going to study?"

"Just going to take some general classes that I know for sure will transfer to any university. Then I'm going to figure it out as I go. Talk to a school advisor or professors—other students. See what floats my boat."

He nodded. "Okay. But how are you going to take classes and work full-time?"

AHH! I held my head in my hands. "I don't know, okay? But I've got a little money in my checking account from what I earned at Mad Dog's, and what does anyone else do?"

I was starting to think I'd made the mistake of the century. There were too many moving pieces to this puzzle, and I still couldn't get my head around the fact that everything in my life was gone.

The Sarafians.

The lake.

Mad Dog.

Velvet.

Exie and Norma . . . the only family I'd ever really known.

Frida.

Funny that losing such a tiny dog could hurt so badly. How did I let myself get attached to her? She wasn't even mine. I had a hard time sleeping without her the first few nights. I still looked around and expected her to be wagging at my ankles . . . still listened for her bark. When we left the lake that night, I kept

Captain Pickles with me out of grief. But then I got worried she would be upset without it, so I overnighted it. When I walked in with it and asked for a box, the woman at the FedEx store looked at me as if it was the strangest request she'd ever had.

As for Fen?

Well.

I couldn't bear to think about him for too long. Especially not during the day. I only allowed myself to completely let my mind fill with Fen-size memories at night when I was listening to music, trying to sleep. That's when I let myself be completely miserable.

In the day, I held myself together and pretended for my dad that I was strong and that everything was a-okay. Daytime was deadtime.

Day and night. A repeating cycle of self-pity and self-punishment. Super healthy. There was probably a better way, and I'd figure it out eventually.

I just hoped Fen was doing better than I was.

A heavy sigh escaped my father as he got up and shuffled to the other side of the balcony, leaning over the railing to watch people heading down to the beach for the afternoon. "Jane, I want you to know that I am behind you. If this is what you want, then we'll make it happen. You realize you haven't lost any words since you asked me to drive you back to L.A.?"

Huh. I guess I hadn't.

Then again, I hadn't been struggling with my word-pixie as much since I'd been seeing Fen. Maybe facing my ghosts cleared out some neural pathways. At the very least, it helped me conquer some stress and gain confidence.

"Your mother never went to school," he said. "I don't think she'd care much about the degree, but she was strong-willed, and she'd like you doing this. But there will always be a part of me that needs to watch out for you, and I think what may be worse is losing you altogether. So can we agree that if you do this, we'll make time to see each other?"

"Dad," I told him. "Seriously. It would be here in the metro area."

"You'd be surprised. Relationships have died on these freeways."

"Good thing I know a professional driver, huh?"

He gave me a soft smile. "Yeah, I suppose so."

It was almost time for his daily Jay call, so I put a pause on the job hunt to give him some private space. Maybe I needed some too. To think.

I hiked down to the beach to stake out a place in the sand and watch the sunset over the ocean. It was warm and windy, and the Pacific was rougher and bigger than Condor Lake. No comparison. But I missed the lake's serene surface and all its tall trees. I missed how quiet and wild it was there. There was room enough for me to breathe. Weird to think that all the Festival Freaks were gone now. I bet the town felt empty without them.

Someone shouted across the beach.

I jerked up my head to see what the commotion was and spotted a dark streak heading across the sand, accompanied by someone giving chase, waving a straw hat. I couldn't tell if something was wrong, so I started to push up from the sand, pulse rocketing, not sure if I should flee or help. My mind processed what was happening right as the dark streak came into focus—

As it leapt at my face.

"Frida!"

"Oh my God!" Velvet shouted from down the beach. "You damn dog!"

Somewhere in the back of my mind, I was shocked to see Velvet, but I was too wrapped up in dog love. Frida was licking my face and wagging her tail so hard, she was falling on me. I scooped her into my arms and kissed her all over her face. "I missed you so much. Oh my goodness, you smell like lavender. You will be breaking out soon, won't you? You are allergic to lavender! Who did that to you? Oh, sweetie!"

"What a tramp," Velvet said, breathless as she trudged through the sand and collapsed next to me in white shorts and a shirt that spilled off one brown shoulder. She set the straw hat on her knee and pushed sunglasses up into her hair. "Catch your breath, dog. It's just Jane, for the love of Pete. Am I going to have to take you to the vet again?"

"Again?" I said, alarmed, stroking Frida's warm back as she wagged like a maniac and made desperate whining noises. She felt so good.

"Do dogs like your voice or something? Or maybe it's because you're so small, like her."

I probably should've been insulted, but I was too happy. "What about the vet?"

"She stopped eating. There's nothing wrong with her. She was probably just depressed that you left. Is she allergic to lavender? How come no one tells me these things? Hello, by the way. Leo said you were down here. Cool little place you've got. I love Santa Monica."

I squinted up at her. "When did you get back into L.A.?"

"Yesterday. Daddy said he was done working, and the Festival Freaks had cleared out, so it was a good time to leave. Plus, I think he was suspicious about the partying."

"Oh," I said. "I never told—"

"It's cool."

"But I didn't say anything. I swear." Only I realized that wasn't entirely true. "I may have said something about the Battle of the Bands to Exie. . . ." I hung my head.

"Ugh."

"I'm sorry, but I was worried about you. That's why I texted you, and then that whole incident at Betty's . . ."

Her shoulders sagged. "That was a low point. But not the lowest. Let's just say that I think I finally realized I don't need to be around certain people right now. I'm at a weird point in my life. I'm kind of drifting, and I don't know what to do."

She had never said anything like that to me.

The gold bangles around her wrist chinked as she gestured. "You don't understand what it's like to live under my parents' shadows. Between the two of them, it's too much talent under one roof. Where does that leave me? Because I did *not* inherit any of these talent genes—how unfair is that? I'm not good at anything."

"That's not true. You're fun to be around and everyone likes you. You plan really good parties."

"I'm good at being social?"

"It's more than that, I think. It's a skill. You've got an eye for planning and you're good at talking to people. Everyone likes you." This wasn't coming out right.

"Not *everyone* likes me. My personal assistant just took off with no warning. . . ."

"I'm sorry. I feel really bad about that." I rubbed Frida's belly as she flipped over in my lap, all four feet in the air, panting. "It's hard to explain, but I'm going through something similar to you, actually. And things got complicated with Fen and Eddie."

Her eyes narrowed. "Yeah, I get that. Eddie's kind of making a fool out of himself around the lake right now, just FYI."

I sighed. "He needs help. I told Fen that before I left."

"Yeah. Fen . . ." She wrinkled her nose.

"What about Fen?" *Breathe. Do not panic. Just pet the dog. Stay calm.*

"I stopped by the record store on our way out of town. He asked about you."

"Oh?"

She shook her head. "He's just really messed up without you. Hurting. That's all."

My heart fell. I was messed up without him. And it killed me to know he was hurting.

"Are you okay?" she asked. "I shouldn't have told you that.

It's not my business why you broke up. Though Eddie says it's because you're not over him."

"Eddie probably needs to believe that," I said.

"He's very wounded. He pretends to be easygoing, but he's definitely struggling."

This surprised me. The entire conversation surprised me.

She turned toward me. "Hey. Come with me to Spain. I'm leaving in two weeks. Just me and my friends Angela and Hayden. Be my personal assistant again. You can take care of Frida and see Barcelona."

"Spain?"

"I'm probably going to stay there for a couple of months, then maybe go to Greece. Who knows. But Angela can't party because of her meds, and Hayden has been sober since her stomach surgery. So, you know. It won't be like the lake. Just good vibes and healing. And you could just take care of all my clothes and the dog. Same as this summer."

I stared at her, a little dumbfounded. "Why would you want me to come?"

"Because . . ." She moved her fingers through the sand. "Like you said, we're going through the same crisis right now. And in a way, we're sort of sisters, aren't we?"

My pulse increased. She always threw variations of that word around lightly—*manita*—but she'd never quite said it like that. "Are we?"

She backed down from that, reconsidering, and said, "Well, spiritual ones, anyway. Come with me to Spain! Look how much

Frida needs you. I can't even handle this dog anymore. She's miserable without you, and she resents me. She actually bit me last night, can you believe it?"

I pulled Frida up to my chest and held her warmth against me. She felt so good, and I'd missed her so much. This was unexpected. A huge opportunity for me to travel the world—if Velvet really meant it. A chance for me to escape my life here in a way I hadn't accounted for. To have a little bit of freedom and maybe find myself in a different way that I couldn't at school.

A choice, but not the right one for me.

Because I imagined myself in Spain, chasing Velvet and her friends around. Even without drugs, I worried it would just be the lake moved to another country.

"I'm sorry," I told Velvet. "I really appreciate you asking me. It's so nice of you to come down here like this—to bring Frida to see me, and to ask me this. But I can't go with you. It's really tempting, and I love Frida more than anything, but I need to do something else right now."

She blinked at me as if surprised and then nodded. "I think I get it. You want to put everything that happed at the lake behind you, right? You want to get past your brain injury and forget all about it. That's why you had to leave? Because Fen reminded you of falling in the dam."

"Not really." I didn't want to forget my brain injury. Or the dam. I absolutely did *not* want to forget Fen. Not sure if I even could.

Holding Frida, I glanced at Velvet, and an idea struck me.

"I sort of have plans for the future. Can I tell you what I want to do?" I asked her. "Then maybe you can figure out a way to make it work. Because I've been trying to talk it out with my dad, and I'm kind of stuck. I need your help. Think of it like a party, but it's my life. Use your magic planning skills."

She leaned back in the sand. "Lay it on me, *manita*. Two heads are better than one."

For the first time since I'd known her, it felt as though we were on the same level.

Maybe not sisters, but friends.

And I could really use one.

Leo Marlow:

Hey. You still at this number?

It's Jane's dad

                                          Fen Sarafian:

                                          Mr. Marlow?

Leo Marlow:

Just wanted to check in on you

Make sure you're doing okay

Jeep good?

                                          Fen Sarafian:

                    Jeep's driving fine, thanks to you

                           I'm alright. Lake's the same.

                                    How's Jane?

Leo Marlow:

In community college out in the Valley

She's trying real hard

I'm proud of her

                                          Fen Sarafian:

                                    That's great

                                    I miss her

                        But I want her to do well

Leo Marlow:

She doesn't know I contacted you

I was just checking in

> **Fen Sarafian:**
> Thank you
> It means so much

Leo Marlow:
No prob

> **Fen Sarafian:**
> Jane's lucky to have you

Jasmine Sarafian:

Miss Jane? This is Fen's mother

Saw that you had that bad wildfire down there

Wanted to make sure you were okay

Jane Marlow:

Hello! So nice to hear from you

All good here. No evacuations where I am

Mad Dog is safe in Bel Air, too

Jasmine Sarafian:

Thank the saints

Jane Marlow:

Is everyone okay up there?

Jasmine Sarafian:

Yes. Everyone is fine

You are missed

Jane Marlow:

I miss everyone too

Jasmine Sarafian:

BTW I'm proud of you for going to school

Norma told me when I called Mad Dog's

Jane Marlow:

Thank you. That means a lot

Fen

October

The last place I wanted to spend my Saturday morning was Condor Wings Clinic. The last person I wanted to spend it with was my father. Only comfort I clung to was that he clearly felt the same way.

Miserable assholes, both of us.

Might as well have stuck us in tuxedoes and asked us to perform a tap dance in front of thousands. That would have been less stressful than weekly family therapy with Eddie the Rehab Patient.

Eddie had been in Wings for a month, and he'd probably be released in a couple of weeks. He was miserable at first. And by miserable, I mean he escaped the first week and went on a joyride with two of our cousins.

But he was better now. He said the food was decent, and he liked his roommate—a thirty-year-old chef from one of the restaurants on the Strip. They got along. They both worshipped their doctor. She was the person who roped us into family therapy, so I didn't like her all that much. But if she was helping Eddie, then great. I was a fan.

"I'll just be waiting out here to take you to the next appointment, sir," the driver told us as my father and I got out of the backseat.

"Fine, Beck," my dad answered. "We'll be back in forty-five minutes."

After the heart attack, my mother hired Beck, the uncle of one of the women in her church, as a family driver. They were converting space in the villa's garage to make an apartment for him, so he could live on the property. Mama believed road rage was just one more thing that could trigger my dad's stress, so she basically took his car keys away.

Oops.

"Let's get this over with," he murmured, rubbing his face as we headed inside the treatment center's auto-opening door.

The scent of lavender potpourri greeted us along with the chipper assistant behind the desk, who checked us in and gave us visitor badges. The lobby of the center was swanky—very white and calm, clearly tons of money floating around here. And mildly busy for a Saturday morning.

Always strange to make eye contact with people here, because it's a mixed bag of Scared, Desperate, Strung Out, and Hopeful. Pretty sure my father hated it because people recognized him, and everyone knew his kid was in rehab. At first, that was the ultimate defeat for Serj Sarafian. He could have fist-fought everyone in the lobby of this place, just out of sheer rage.

Now? He just wanted to get back to the therapy room as fast as possible. In and out, let's get 'er done.

You know, baby steps.

Today's baby steps included a double dose of intimate chatting, because as soon as we were done here, we were headed straight over to Dr. Sanders's for group anger management. Mama and the twins would be there for that one. Just a relaxing, soul-revealing Saturday morning all round.

A smiling staff nurse led us through winding corridors to an empty room, where morning sun streamed over a small group of couches and chairs. "You're a few minutes early," she told us. "Have a seat, and I'll get Eddie and the therapist. Okey dokey?"

"Okey fucking dokey," I said when she closed the door. "Who's excited to get in touch with their feelings, raise their hand."

"That nurse always touches my arm. Is that a therapeutic method?" my father asked.

"Um . . . human contact?" I said, amused. "Pretty sure that's just her way of being friendly."

"Well, I don't like it," he grumbled.

"You should bring it up in session."

His eyes flicked to mine. "Why do you always have to do that?"

"Do what?"

"*That*. Smart-ass little digs." He stabbed the air with an invisible knife several times. "Tiny cuts, over and over. Everything I say, you respond with a smart remark."

I shrugged and crossed my arms over my chest. "You give me good material to riff off of?"

"Hmph." My father shook his head. "You're too sharp, Fennec. If you rerouted some of that jackassery toward something important, it could be a skill for you."

That right there? That was bait, and I wasn't taking it. He was trying to goad me into a fight, which was something I never was able to recognize until recently. But now that I was spending more time in the villa again, I could see it.

I wasn't living back at home full-time—don't think I ever could again. And that was fine by me. Family dinners every weekend and hanging out with the twins was enough. The apartment in the barn did what it had been doing: kept the peace between me and my father. There were a couple things that were different now, though.

All the therapy. That did help. A little.

And my music. That helped a lot.

I was trying to put everything I had into writing new pieces and practicing. I'd even started recording myself and posting videos online. I had a meeting with a dean of a college music department next week: she was going to talk to me and listen to me perform.

I'd promised Jane I would work on my music. That's exactly what I was doing.

If I didn't have music, I would be deep in a pit of despair without her. Right now, I was only clinging to the edge of the pit and trying not to fall inside.

But I don't think it's an exaggeration to say that some days I missed her so much, it felt like I was dying a thousand deaths.

Velvet gave me Jane updates now and then, but they weren't substantial, and Velvet had left for Spain, so I had to rely on Jane's social media for a filtered picture of her life. Which turned out to be a life that moved around the L.A. metro region . . . from Santa Monica to Burbank. Every time she posted a photo, my chest buzzed with bees. But I kept my distance. Left no comments. No follows. No trips down to Southern California to surprise her.

Okay, there was one time when Moonbeam had to physically restrain me from driving after her in the middle of the night. But still. I didn't go, and that's what was important.

I just played my music. And for the first time in my life, it felt as if I had a reason to play. At night, I sat down in front the piano, called forth every ghost I knew, and I had myself a fucking séance.

When I was finished, I prayed to all the saints that Jane was able to commune with her ghosts too.

"Do they have to wake him up and get him dressed?" my father said, one leg anxiously bouncing. "What's taking so long?"

"He'll be here any second," I said, scrolling on my phone to escape conversation.

After a few seconds, he mumbled, "It's the song."

"What?" I asked, glancing up to see him scowling at the built-in speaker in the ceiling.

"The National," he explained. "I tried to book them at the festival a couple of years ago, and their guitarist and I . . . had words."

Huh. He never shared his failure stories. I wondered how

many there were. How many bands had he pissed off over the years? Funny that I'd never really considered it. Maybe because all he did was brag about his achievements.

"Weird you say that . . . ," I told my father. "I did an assessment of Mike Winfrey's record collection last week for the store? It was almost all reissues, and he had everything the National released on vinyl."

My father snorted. "Why doesn't that surprise me? Mike is a sentimental fool."

"Music attracts sentimentalists and the downtrodden," I said, thinking about when Jane told me.

"True," he said quietly. "Anything interesting in Mike's record collection?"

I was surprised he was interested. "Most notable was a Joy Division EP from 1978. Worth a few thousand. And he had a couple early punk singles—got me excited that he might have something I was hunting, but nope."

My father stroked his mustache. "What were you looking for?"

Was I really having this conversation with him? It was weird to go from Outcast to Tolerated Family Member in just a few months.

"I'm looking for a rare 1980s L.A. punk record," I told him. "I've been searching online since the summer, and I nearly had an owner who was willing to part with theirs, but they changed their mind at the last minute."

"Is this for the store? This record? You trying to find it for a store client?"

I shook my head. "It's for Jane. Her father, actually."

His brow shot up.

"Not Mad Dog," I corrected. "Her actual father. Leo. The man who fixed my Jeep. I talked about him in therapy last week."

I talked about *everything* in therapy. Jane. The dam. My thinking tree. Moonbeam. My music. What did I care about holding back anymore? Let him hear everything. Let Eddie hear it too. Every time we had a session, I said my piece, stated the facts, and told how I felt. Nothing more, nothing less. If I cried, I cried.

The private details I kept for me and Jane. Those were ours.

A short silence stretched between us, then my father said, "You know who you need to ask about your record? Miss Tiger."

"Who is Miss Tiger?"

"Lives in the green ski chalet on Old Bone Hill."

I vaguely knew the person he meant, an older trans woman at the far side of the lake.

"They used to call her the disco queen," my father said. "She owned a club in San Francisco in the seventies, then a bar in the eighties. Avid vinyl collector."

"How come I didn't know that? Does Aunt Pari know about her?"

He shrugged. "Miss Tiger keeps to herself, but if you'd like, I can give her a call and ask if she'd be willing to let you come look at her collection."

Head. Exploding.

Serj Sarafian . . . doing me . . . a favor? The son he'd once threatened to legally cut out of his life? I think there was a restraining order mentioned at one point, when I tried to sneak into the villa in the middle of the night to forage some of my stuff out of my old room.

"Yeah, okay," I said, hoping he couldn't tell how overwhelmed I was by his offer.

Hoping that I wasn't falling into some kind of trap or trickery.

But he just said, "All right. I'll make a call."

Some fathers told their children that they loved them. Some showered them with gifts. Some attended every ball game and cheered with pride. Yet, nothing says "I care" like using your influence in the music industry to open doors.

Hey—I'd take it. My father was a giant mountain. You couldn't move him overnight. This was a tiny shift, and that was good enough for me right now.

"If you think it's still worth your time looking for this record," he amended. "For all you know, you'll never see this Jane again. And maybe that's for the best, all things considered. Some relationships are just too messy."

If there was one thing I'd learned in weeks of coming here, spilling my guts, it was that *all* relationships were messy.

And if I could sit in a room with my father and brother without fantasizing about fifty ways to behead the both of them, then I could find my way back to Jane.

Bring on the mess.

Jane

January

Sun glinted off the recycling truck as it trundled down the street, spilling dead pine branches. Nothing sadder than seeing a spent Christmas tree being hauled away in January.

"Guess the holidays in Burbank are truly over," I told Frida wistfully as she panted on the sidewalk in her jingle bell harness. Not that we hadn't milked them for all we could. Even though Dad calls this part of L.A. "the other side of the moon," the San Fernando Valley was less than an hour from Bel Air, and I saw Dad pretty much every week in December. He took us down Candy Cane Lane to see the lights, and Norma invited me to the Bel Air mansion for Christmas Eve dinner, at which I got to see Starla, Exie, and even Velvet, who'd flown into L.A. briefly between her months-long trips to Spain and Greece with tons of stories—and was still sober.

It was a good night.

Mad Dog still wasn't speaking to me much. Ever since our conversation about my mother at the lake, he'd been distant, but my quitting service seemed to hurt him personally. That was just a guess—he'd never outright tell me, I supposed. For Christmas, though, he gave me an envelope containing two things: (1) a printed slip of paper that showed my name added to a list of people who were approved to fly on his private plane, and (2) the credit card I'd turned in to Norma when I left the lake back in July.

He said it was to help with school. If I ever needed it. Just in case.

Funny that something as unemotional as a credit card could say so much. To me, it said that he wasn't willing to dive into the deep end of the pool with me—that was where my dad belonged—but he had invited me to sit in a lounge chair alongside him. And considering how complicated our history might be, that was enough for me.

Anyway, I hadn't used either of his Christmas gifts yet. But I might.

Now that the holidays were over, it was also the last weekend before my community college classes started back up for winter semester. Frida and I were making the trek down to an enclave of shops. They were on a busy road, at an address that was technically no longer Burbank. And I'd become a devotee of the local bakery there.

Levon's Donuts and Desserts of Glendale.

It didn't look like much. Bars on the windows, a sad palm tree surrounded by an iron fence outside. Inside wasn't much better, a long, narrow shop with 1970s glass display counters on one side and diner tables on the other. The walls were filled with children's doughnut artwork; kids have some vivid imaginations about doughnut monsters, let me just say.

Normally there were only a couple people lined up at the counter on a Saturday morning, but today, the narrow shop was packed. I got a little panicky that they'd be out of what I wanted, so I quickly jumped into the back of the line with Frida, who panted after a much bigger dog who was standing with its owner two people ahead.

The bakery smelled of fresh spices and sugar, and they hadn't taken down their Christmas lights. I liked them for that, even though the line moved slowly, and the stack of pink pastry boxes was diminishing as the workers behind the counter filled them, which made me anxious.

I stood on tiptoes, restlessly trying to spy over the line ahead of me. I had to have one of those pastry boxes. Every weekend, I posted a picture of one of those boxes online. It had become like the yearly tree photo with Dad and me—I couldn't *not* take a dessert photo.

Also, I was seriously addicted to the cake. It was my reward for finishing a week. And I needed one, because that's how I had to take things, week by week. School wasn't easy. Living in a new place wasn't easy—alone, outside of Mad Dog's household for the first time in my life. Managing a speech disorder throughout all of it wasn't easy.

I was juggling a lot. I knew that.

"Why is it so crowded today?" I mumbled in frustration, craning my neck to see the cake display as Frida tried to tug me toward something that captured her attention. She was fidgety, but all I wanted was a slice of caramel Mikado cake. Or maybe the nutmeg, which wasn't as good as Ms. Makruhi's, but it was close. "You'd think the world was ending."

"Armenian Orthodox churches hold holiday services tomorrow and Monday for Christmas and Epiphany," someone said behind me, where Frida was tugging, her leash wrapped around my jeans.

"Oh?" I turned around to unwind the leash. The person behind me was crouched and petting Frida. Petting? Well. More like they were all up in each other's business. "Frida," I complained, and started to chide her for being too familiar, especially with someone who was dressed nice. Expensive shoes. Watch. Funny what you can tell about a person in the flick of a gaze. But then the person looked up.

Fen Sarafian.

Sweet holy night, I hardly recognized him. His usually wild hair was a little tamed, dramatic swoops and swirls, not so much a bird's nest but a bird penthouse in a hipster neighborhood.

"You're alive," he said, pushing a backpack farther up on one shoulder as he stood up to his full height, which was still impressive, compared to mine.

"I am." Yes, I was alive. Heart pumping. Every part of me was alert. I felt as if I was either going to collapse from weak knees or bolt out of the bakery in fear.

"And you are, uh, too—alive," I said, recovering. "I've been watching your videos online."

JENN BENNETT

"Oh, yeah. That." He scratched the side of his neck and scrunched one eye closed. "You've seen them?"

"All of them."

Not sure why he was acting modest. He'd accumulated a sizeable following in no time, posting videos of himself playing short but compelling piano pieces that he'd filmed in the barn on his baby grand. The first time I saw one, I thought I was dying. It felt like he was sharing our private space with the world.

Then I realized it was *his* space, not ours. That hurt worse.

"You have a legion of fans online," I said.

"I went viral because of my family name."

"And because you're . . ." Stunning. Beautiful. Dark. Sexy. "Talented."

He gestured to tell me that the line had moved up. I awkwardly stepped sideways to fill the gap, shifting Frida along, who didn't want to leave Fen's brown leather oxfords. Hard to blame her, honestly.

"Why are you here?" I asked.

He blinked and pointed at the counter. "Mikado cake."

"Me too," I said, smiling a little. Then I shook my head. "I meant, what are you doing *here*. In L.A.?"

"Oh. Staying with my grandparents for the holidays," he said. "I'm driving back after the weekend. Grandma Mina talked me into staying for Sunday service tomorrow. Second Christmas dinner is hard to turn down."

"Holiday food."

"You love Christmas."

"You remembered."

"I remember everything," he said in low voice.

My ears warmed, and I was having trouble looking up at his face.

He cleared his throat and asked, "Why are *you* here? At Levon's, I mean."

"Oh," I said, smiling and looking back to check the line. Shuffling up a little. "Um, I actually have an apartment that's not too far. It's Burbank, but that's just, like, I don't know, three blocks away?"

"Sure, sure," he said, gaze wandering over me.

"It's not my apartment. Velvet arranged it. I'm staying in her friend Hayden's studio apartment in Burbank while the two of them are touring Europe. They went to Spain this fall, and now they're in Greece. Anyway, it's only a fifteen-minute drive from my community college in Glendale—funnily enough. Small world, right?"

"Smaller than anyone realizes. What are you studying?"

"Just general courses, some psych." I was a little embarrassed to tell him now. "I actually want to transfer to a four-year university and get a music therapy degree. It's a curriculum that's part music major, part psychology, and you have to get board certified."

"Huh, okay."

"I'd probably be working in a clinical setting and use it to help patients with dementia, children with autism . . . people who have Parkinson's? It can help to improve motor function."

"Maybe people with aphasia?" he said.

I nodded. "Exactly."

"I'm astounded, truly," he said, nodding vigorously. "I knew you were in school, but I didn't know what you were studying. That's kind of genius, Jane. It's perfect."

I felt a little breathless. I didn't need his approval, but it felt good to have. "Your mom was the one who gave me the idea, actually. She didn't have a name for it, but she mentioned that she knew someone at her church who had a relative who was studying it. Turns out there are only three colleges in the state that offer the degree. So that's why I'm starting at community college. Until I can get in next fall."

"Yeah?"

"Yeah."

He didn't smile at me—not quite. But when he nodded, it felt like respect. I looked away for a moment, feeling proud and a little happy, but a little embarrassed, too. When I glanced back up at his dark eyes, he was still watching me.

There it was. That spark. The deep feeling in my gut telling me to pay attention. This one. This guy right here. He's important.

The person behind him accidently bumped into him, and Fen turned around while they apologized, his hand knocking against mine briefly.

A spark. A flame. A bonfire.

"Sorry," he mumbled.

"Mrm," I mumbled back, wishing I could reach out and hold his hand. Oh, they were still the same graceful, oddly long fingers. Piano hands.

I looked away.

We moved up in the line.

"How are things at the lake?" I asked, trying to manage the riot of feelings that was flaring up inside me. *Everything is fine. Nothing to see here.*

He nodded. "Good. Better. My father's adjusting to the restructuring of the festival biz. Mama's helping him. The twins are good. They're all here for the holidays." He glanced at my eyes. "Eddie's not, in case you were wondering. He's with my other grandparents—the Sarafians—at their new house in Vancouver. He spent six weeks at rehab at Wings, then they took him up there to live with them."

"Permanently?"

He shrugged. "Doubt it, but he likes it there for right now. He's doing okay, I think. We're trying to give him some space."

Something shifted inside my chest and relaxed. That honestly made me happy. Eddie had fallen off of social media, and we'd had no contact whatsoever since I left the lake. But I wanted him to get better.

A striking girl with long brown hair and long lashes entered the bakery and walked up to Fen, threading her arm through his elbow. "There you are. I thought you'd abandoned me. Next time tell me where you're going before you just take off, please?"

Oh.

All the feelings that had been rioting inside me suddenly went quiet. He looked at her arm and then his eyes flicked to mine.

"Oh, hello," the girl said. "Did I interrupt something?"

Unexpectedly, tears welled. I tried *very* hard to control them. My throat constricted, and the room felt as if it were spinning around me.

I mumbled something. At least I tried to, then I took Frida and walked as fast as I could, straight through the shop, to the tiny unoccupied ladies' room. And once I'd made it inside, I tried to get control of myself.

I'd waited too long.

Too late.

He'd moved on.

What did I expect? We hadn't seen each other for months. People say they're going to stay together, but feelings change.

A knock on the door made me jump. Frida barked.

"Jane Marlow? I'm coming in," Fen said as he cracked the restroom door open. "Everyone best be decent in there. You too, Frida. Calm down—it's me. Here."

He handed Frida something that she immediately snatched up and took around to the other side of me as I struggled to get up and fell on my ass.

Lovely.

"Ugh," I moaned, trying to stop crying. "Go away. You're not supposed to be in here."

"It's an emergency. I'm not a peeper."

I calmed down a little and wiped my eyes, looking down at Frida. "What did you give her?"

"Cheesy dog biscuit," he said, leaning back against the door. "They give them away at the counter if you ask for them."

I made a face. "I've been coming here every weekend for two months and no one told me."

"How did you know Grandma Mina's favorite bakery?"

His grandmother had told me about it when I met her at the villa, while his father was recovering from surgery. But I didn't want to tell him that. So I just sloppily pushed myself up to my feet, swatting away his hand when he tried to help me, and then busied myself washing my hands in the sink. "I think the girl matters more."

"Frida?"

"The girl! Your new girl," I said, soaping up my hands frantically. "Just go on and tell me who she is so we can get it over with, and I can go back to my life. Because I was fine until you walked in here."

He snorted. "Oh, you were?"

I splashed water from the sink at him, and he moved to the side.

"You were never mean," I said. "I mean, fine—I get it. You've moved on. But you were never *mean*." I turned off the water and pulled too many paper towels from the holder on the wall.

"I can't take it anymore," he shouted, throwing up his hands.

"Me either!" I shouted back. "Just go!"

He got in my face. "That's Emily."

"I don't care. Move."

"My cousin," he enunciated.

I stopped. Looked up at him. And, *oh*, I felt the burn coming. Neck. Ears. Cheeks. The works. "Your cousin?"

"You met each other in the villa the same night you met Grandma Mina, but neither of you seems to remember."

"Your cousin," I repeated, wishing I could erase the last few minutes of my life.

"More like a buffer, in case things went fubar."

I didn't know what he was talking about, but I was so embarrassed, I was afraid to ask.

He tilted his head sideways until he hooked my gaze. "I used her as a buffer because I came here today to find you. I knew from your extravagant dessert photos online that you came here every Saturday morning, but I've been sitting at the coffee shop across the street for the last hour and a half, waiting for you to show up."

I blinked at him.

"If you want me to go, I'll leave," he said. "I just felt like if you didn't want me to know where you were, you wouldn't have posted those photos."

"I didn't know you were following me!"

"You aren't following *me*."

No. I was anonymously stalking him, like a healthy person. But tiny, blissful heart-shaped bubbles were filling up my chest now that I knew he'd been doing the same.

Fen leaned back against the restroom door, studying me. "I absolutely understand why you left the lake now. I didn't before. But I do now. Triangulation."

"Tri . . ."

"It's when one person pits another against a third person. Like an alliance? I learned about it in therapy. It's part of what happened to me, Eddie, and my dad. My father ended up playing the role of a mastermind who tried to manipulate both me and Eddie. But basically, I wanted you to be in my alliance, and Eddie did too. That left you being pulled in two directions. Triangulation."

"Huh." I tapped my finger on my leg. "How do you fix it?"

"We conspire to murder Eddie. Problem solved," he deadpanned.

"Right. Any non-murderous fixes?"

He feigned a heavy sigh. "I suppose we could forgive Eddie for his mistakes, ask him to do the same, and try the messy business of getting along. But that's *so much* harder, when one deadly road trip to Vancouver would solve all our problems—bonus, we'd get that Bonnie-and-Clyde race from the police that we've dreamed about."

I chuckled a little, then wiped at my eyes. "I start school soon. I think an outstanding murder on my record would interfere with my studies. Maybe that other thing you mentioned?"

"I mean, if you can handle that kind of commitment," he said lightly. Teasingly. "Sounds like a lot of work to me."

He was joking, but every move he made was sending wild feelings through me—the way he pushed his curls out of his eye. The way his thumb nervously rubbed against his index finger. Those piano hands . . . why were they my downfall?

"I didn't expect you to be here today," I told him. "I hoped you'd see my posts, but in my reunion fantasy, you just texted or called. This is very overwhelming and unexpected."

"Do you want me to leave?"

I shook my head vigorously.

"I've been in Glendale for a week, and I tried to come here last Saturday, but I chickened out. My grandmother convinced me to give it another shot. And, uh, I had something for you."

"For me?"

He lowered his shoulder and dropped his backpack to unzip it, then dug around inside. He pulled something out and set the backpack on the floor next to Frida. "Here . . ."

I accepted what he was offering with a racing heart. And as I inspected it, I could feel his gaze on my face.

It was a plastic sleeve with a single piece of black vinyl inside. Black Flag. *My War*. Side 2. I flipped it over. Side 2.

It was the legendary Double Deuce.

I couldn't even say anything. I tried. I held up a hand to gesticulate my feelings, but all I could do was wave and point at the record.

"You found . . ." I started. I was going to cry over a record? "You found it."

"I told you I would," he said patiently. Proudly.

"The Holy Grail. I can't believe it. I never thought I'd see it. My dad will bawl like a baby."

"I'm glad." He smiled, satisfied, and then scratched his neck and gestured toward the record. "I looked for it every single night online. I emailed. I texted. I bid. I made so many phone calls to the weirdest people. I even talked to a guy long-distance in France. Funny enough, it was my dad who ended up helping me find it. Someone who lives at the lake made me a trade."

Oh wow. I couldn't process it. Such a plain, simple object. "Weird to think that if I hadn't come inside the record store, we might have never . . ."

"Yeah," he agreed lightly. "Maybe. But I choose to believe we would've found our way to each other."

We stood there together for a moment, watching each other.

"Is it still here?" I asked. "What's between us?"

"Do you think it is?"

"I want it to be," I admitted in a whisper, clutching the record.

We blinked at each other, both holding our breath.

"Let's find out," he whispered, and put his hands on my cheeks. As warm as my skin was, his was warmer. He bent low to capture my mouth with his and kissed me. Softly, trembling. It was unsure and a little desperate, but when I kissed him back, everything inside me lit up and caught fire.

It was warm and good, and *he* was good, and yes.

Oh, yes.

It was still there.

"I'm sorry for leaving you at the lake," I whispered against his lips. "I had to go."

"I understand," he murmured, curling a hand around the back of my neck. "But I still love you, Jane. Just tell me that you still love me."

"I didn't realize how much until right this second," I said. "I don't think I can wait until next summer to be together."

He kissed my head over and over, sweet and divine kisses,

pulling me closer. "Thank the saints. *That* was a fucking terrible idea."

"Can we try to figure out a new plan?"

"I told you I'd wait for you," he said in a low voice. "All you had to do was tell me you were ready by posting photos of bakery desserts, and I'd come runnin'. Let's make a new plan."

"Okay, but I have . . . reading. Studying. Classes." Ugh. Word-pixie!

"School."

"*School,*" I said, relieved to be in possession of the word again. "I'm on a path with school. I've got everything mapped out."

He let his forehead drop against mine as I held the record against his chest. "Understood. Why don't we compare notes for future plans and see if we can't make it work? My grandmother's couch in Glendale is always free on the weekends if that would help."

Suddenly, the world looked a little brighter.

"It's never going to be easy, you know," he said. "Eddie is my brother, and he's always going to be there. We're all connected and share a past, so we have to deal with that."

A bit of fear flashed through me. I knew what he was saying was right, but it was still scary. I remembered how I felt those weeks after Serj's surgery, stuck between the two brothers, and I didn't want to feel like that again. But I knew that wasn't up to me alone.

"I get it," I told him. "And I'm willing to put in the work if you are."

He nodded, and for a moment, jittery excitement stilled my tongue.

"What would you say to some Second Christmas festivities?" he asked. "It's with my obnoxious family, but we're a little more behaved now than we were when you last saw us, thanks to a lot of therapy. My father and I can actually stand to be in the same room as each other for up to two whole hours at a stretch. Besides that, I think you're already used to our brand of kooky."

Yes, I was. Bring on the kook.

"Oh!" he said, moving back from me to shrug off his jacket as Frida pawed at his leg. "I almost forgot. Your request . . ."

After some awkward struggling—and some embarrassment on my part—he managed to unbutton the top few buttons of his shirt and tug down the cotton to show me his bare shoulder.

Ophelia was still there.

But her ink had been touched up.

Her eyes were now wide open.

Fen

June

"Not on the baby grand!" I shouted.

"Fennec," my mother warned. "Why are you angry?"

I took a deep breath as the mover shifted the box from my piano onto the floor. "I am *frustrated*, not angry. That's why I'm using my inside shouting voice, not my outside howl."

"Just checking, my love," she said, pulling the plastic off a newly delivered armchair. "I wish they would've delivered all the furniture at once."

Me too. Everything was in chaos. The movers were supposed to do their thing yesterday, but that got changed, and now they were running into the furniture delivery people, who were coming in two different groups. I just wanted everything perfect, was that so much to ask?

I checked my phone to see if there were any updates from Jane. Nothing yet.

"Where are the blinds?" Mama asked.

"Tomorrow."

"You can't sleep in an apartment without window coverings," she said.

My father made a gruff noise as he emerged from the bedroom. "It's one night. Keep the lights off or put a sheet up with thumbtacks."

"And ruin the window casings?" Mama was horrified.

My father just lifted his hands.

"Tape up newspaper on the windows like they do in old movies," Ani suggested.

"Yeah," Ari said, bouncing on the new armchair as he sat. "Make it look like a criminal kingpin's den up in here. That'll be more fun when I sleep over."

"No sleepovers," I said.

"You can fit a guest bed in that little room back there," Ani said, pointing. "In case you wanted one. You know, for when Eddie comes home from Grandma and Grandpa Sarafian's?"

Hell no. Eddie and I were getting along, but not *that* well. "The tiny room is going to be an office for studying. Everyone stays in their own homes from now on. Can I get an amen?"

My father made another gruff noise.

"Hey, wait a minute . . . ," Ari said, tilting his head as he draped himself over the armchair and peered into the bedroom doorway. "Did you know that you can see into the record store office from your bedroom?"

Yes, I knew all too well. Someone knocked on the apartment's front door, which was cracked open slightly. "Hel-lo? We come bearing tidings of comfort and joy."

A mermaid-dyed head appeared in the door, followed by Starla's body. She smiled as she entered, carrying a box filled with food containers. Exie followed behind her with another box, and suddenly the scent of rosemary and mint filled the apartment.

"What is all this?" Mama said as my father helped Exie with the box, hefting it on the kitchen counter.

"Just some nourishment to keep you going for a few days," Exie said. "Mostly picnic stuff that doesn't need to be heated. Got paper plates and napkins in here too, in case you don't have any yet."

"And homemade cheese crackers so good, they'll make you wanna slap yo mama," Starla said. Then she glanced at my mother's arched brow and amended, "Not literally."

"Thank you," I told Exie. "This is too much."

She gave me a dismissive shrug. "All good. Just didn't want you eating a bunch of junk. Whoa—look at that, Starla. Really is a nice view, huh?"

Starla was already heading to the living room windows to peer outside at the lake, where afternoon sun was glinting off the water. If you squinted hard enough, you could see the villa from here—sort of—and Moonbeam's place. And at night, you could see all the lights on the Strip.

It really was a dream apartment.

The movers from L.A. were finished. I signed off on their paperwork as Starla and Exie chatted with my family, and as the movers were hauling out their dollies, a shadow darkened the doorway.

Mad Dog and his ginger beard stepped inside. He looked lost for a moment, or maybe that was just the dark sunglasses that he refused to take off.

"Hey there," I said. "Sir."

He nodded. "This must be the place. Guess I beat Leo and Jane here."

Jane's father was driving Mad Dog's Mercedes up to the lake from Los Angeles. Jane was following him with Frida in her new car—new to her. It was an old beater that Leo had fixed up as a surprise for her having finished a year of community college. And she'd need it here at the lake, not just this summer, but this fall, when she transferred her credits to the university up the freeway from the lake.

"Hey, big dog," my father called from the living room. "What do you think?"

"Small but serviceable," the producer said. "Planning to film here?"

"My videos? Yeah. There's no one in the apartment below this year. The owners are in Africa, so I don't have to worry about noise, or anything."

"Just a little tight on space," Mad Dog said, surveying with an engineer's gaze.

"Same size as the Grotto Cabin," Exie said.

Mad Dog groaned. "Not staying up there this summer until we fumigate the grotto three or four times in a row. You fumigated this place yet?"

He was talking to *me*? What the hell did I know about

fumigation? Or anything. I just blindly signed off on moving paperwork that may or may not be right. For the love of the saints, I had no idea how to be an adult. I'd thought living in Aunt Zabel's barn had prepared me for a life of easy independence, but maybe I'd been fooling myself.

Right now, I was just flying by the seat of my pants and hoping I did something right.

My parents discussed fumigation with Mad Dog—a conversation that somehow derailed into Velvet, who was on her way back from Europe and coming to the lake for the summer. Meanwhile, I checked my phone again. Nothing. My nerves were starting to jangle, and now I was acutely aware of Mad Dog's complaint about the size of the apartment. With all these people? Yeah, this place was sort of small. It definitely wasn't a party apartment. Or fancy like the lodge. Or homey like the villa. Or big like my barn.

But it did have one thing that all those places didn't have.

And she was walking in the front door now with a tiny dog on a leash.

Jane.

Leopard-print shoes. Tiny swoop of hair like meringue.

The girl of my dreams was now a real live person who had somehow agreed to move in here.

When our eyes met, my gut knew something that my conscious brain didn't understand. My head felt as if it were waking up for the first time, and my chest was full of bees. It was as if my entire body was singing a song that it knew by heart.

"We made it," she said with a smile that I felt in my chest.

"Indeed," I murmured.

Maybe the gods of music had a soft spot for sentimentalists and the downtrodden, sure. But I'd add another group into the mix too.

Survivors.

That's what Jane and I both were. Not rescuer and rescued. Survivors.

We'd survived what happened at the dam, hauntings, and our messy families. We'd survived being apart. And if everything we'd endured over the past few years meant we could be together now, it was worth it.

Don't get me wrong. Love *is* horrible. Excruciating. Confusing. Painful.

But I wouldn't trade my ghosts for anything in the world.

ACKNOWLEDGMENTS

A few years ago, I started taking a medication that had a frustrating side effect: I occasionally forgot a word when I was speaking. Not all words. Not all the time. But now and then, I'd struggle to remember simple words like "car" or "blue." I started using goofy hand signals to communicate when I couldn't reach for the right word. My doctor told me some of their patients forgot pieces of their address or phone numbers. Mental confusion, they said. But what it sounded like to me was something that people with aphasia experience, and that led me down a rabbit hole of research.

I hope that I've portrayed Jane's condition accurately and with care, but if there are any mistakes, it is utterly my fault.

Thank you to everyone who pitched in and helped make the music behind Jane's words, especially my *wonderful* editor Nicole Ellul. Much gratitude also to Laura Eckes and Elanor Laleu; Morgan York; Elizabeth Mims; Erica Stahler; Lauren Carr; Justin Chanda; my agent, Laura Bradford; and my foreign rights agent, Taryn Fagerness.

All the love and thank-yous to my personal support team: Grainma, Papa, Gregg, Heidi, Hank, Charlotte, Patsy, Don, Gee, Shane, and Seph. Extra love to Brian for introducing me to a world of music, clubs, amazing bands, West Coast record selling, and sweaty festivals. We stood mere feet from David Bowie while he played an acoustic guitar, and when we met Elvis Costello, he told you your jacket was cool. Full lives led.

Lastly, if you are struggling with drug addiction of any kind, help is available. Call the SAMHSA National Helpline to speak with someone confidentially for free: 1-800-662-4357.